T0197301

ALWAYS
DOG

ALWAYS DOG

PATTY MCGILL

ALWAYS DOG

Copyright © 2008 Patty McGill.

Author Credits: Patty McGill

All rights reserved. No part of this book may be used or reproduced by any means, graphic, electronic, or mechanical, including photocopying, recording, taping or by any information storage retrieval system without the written permission of the author except in the case of brief quotations embodied in critical articles and reviews.

This is a work of fiction. All of the characters, names, incidents, organizations, and dialogue in this novel are either the products of the author's imagination or are used fictitiously.

iUniverse books may be ordered through booksellers or by contacting:

iUniverse
1663 Liberty Drive
Bloomington, IN 47403
www.iuniverse.com
1-800-Authors (1-800-288-4677)

Because of the dynamic nature of the Internet, any web addresses or links contained in this book may have changed since publication and may no longer be valid. The views expressed in this work are solely those of the author and do not necessarily reflect the views of the publisher, and the publisher hereby disclaims any responsibility for them.

Any people depicted in stock imagery provided by Getty Images are models, and such images are being used for illustrative purposes only.
Certain stock imagery © Getty Images.

ISBN: 978-1-5320-5972-8 (sc)
ISBN: 978-1-5320-5973-5 (e)

Library of Congress Control Number: 2018912232

Print information available on the last page.

iUniverse rev. date: 04/09/2019

CHAPTER ONE

Control …

Must … control … my breathing … or, I'm going to choke on my own blood.

What the hell, I'm going to bleed to death before I make it out of here anyway. Are they gone yet? I can't see, but I think I hear something … "Shit, he's coming back! Didn't these bastards beat me enough?"

Rick heard one of the cops frantically whining … "Roland! He's dead man, let's just get out of here!"

Rick squeezed his eyes shut and willed Roland to listen to his pansy ass partner.

Roland kept walking closer to where Rick lay. He hissed over his shoulder, "Quiet Joe! I thought I saw the scumbag move."

Joe's yelling became louder as he ran closer.

"Roland! Smitty's leaving in his patrol car and I don't want to be here when back up shows! So bring your fucking ass on and leave him! He's dead, I checked!"

Roland still wasn't listening. He was getting closer to where Rick lay paralyzed and drowning on the blood running down the back of his throat from his cracked skull.

Rick tried to move his arms, "If I could only get one shot off, I could at least shoot one of them before they finish me off."

But Rick couldn't move his arms. He couldn't feel his legs.

He heard the footsteps stop in front of his face lying in the mud. Sharp pain stabbed his face as Roland kicked him in his nose. Rick involuntarily moaned.

Roland yelled, "Joe, the scumbag is still alive you asshole!"

Rick felt several sharp stabbing pains in his abdomen. Roland was kicking him, or it felt like kicking; he couldn't see anymore because Joe was stomping his face into the mud. Rick sucked in short quick breaths of blood and swallowed mud as his breath became harder and harder to find.

Rick panicked at the thought of drowning in mud. His mind battled the pain, "Why don't the bastards just shoot me? Of course ... A bullet hole to the brain would be evidence. They want it to look like an accident when they kill me out here in the woods."

Rick barely heard Joe's whining voice. "Alright Roland, if he's not dead by now, he will be soon. We need to run to the car, get to my house and clean the blood off."

Roland breathlessly responded, "Okay Joe, I think you're right. But, just to be sure ..."

Rick heard a tearing sound, like a large object being dug out of the mud. A branch? A rock? A cinderblock?

"This scumbag won't ever fuck with another cop, that's for sure."

With a loud thud, Rick felt heavy, painful weight crushing his eyes out of his head.

"Aaaahhhhhhhhhh!"

Rick jerked his wet body up, dripping with sweat. He rolled out of bed and his wet foot slipped on the cold tile floor. He fell backwards and bumped his head on the dresser. That woke him up.

He cursed, "When will I stop having that fucking dream! It feels so real! I can hear my skull crack open like it was yesterday ..."

He shook his head and mumbled, "Well, maybe that's because I've had a headache ever since; a 13-year migraine."

He gently cupped the sides of his head with his hands and slowed his breathing to quiet the pounding just a little bit. He mumbled, "You think they'd make something that could stop a headache!"

He squeezed his eyes shut and shook his head again. He whispered, "Your skull's cracked, Rick - give it up. You'll never be right."

He gently sat back on the bed and thought about his dreams. They're getting stronger. He could smell 'ole Roland's nasty-ass cigarette breath as he was spitting in his face. And Smitty, he always runs away in the dreams. But he was the one who held Rick down. He was the one who kept kicking Rick in his wounded leg so the blood would keep flowing out of him. He was the one who took his gun and bashed Rick's skull over and over until it cracked.

He nodded slowly and said, "Yeah, I remember Smitty the most, even though it was redneck Roland that dealt the final blow."

Rick put his arm over his face. He couldn't get pansy-ass Joe's whimpering voice out of his head, ever. That's why he's got to be the first to go.

Joe's the reason Rick was back in Virginia after thirteen years. Back in funky town Washington, D.C. To kill a crooked cop named Joe. Then Roland … Then Smitty …

He heard a buzzing sound and followed the it to the table. What? Is that my pager? This time of night, who the hell could that be?

He staggered to the table and picked it up looking at the display … Ah, Deb. She sent me a message. "Call me in the morning."

Rick thought aloud, "Yes! She's found what I need! I'm so ready to do this; I can taste it."

Deb was providing Rick with information. Information he needed to track down and kill three dirty cops. Soon, Rick would have all he needed on 'Ole whiney Joe a/k/a Officer Joseph Ramsey, and his partners in crime, John C. Smith a/k/a Smitty; and asshole Roland B. Hoffman. Deb had proof those three bastards were together on August 20, 1980 in Centreville, Virginia at approximately 10:45 p.m. behind Jorge's Mexican Restaurant waiting for Rick to do his drug deal.

Rick shook his head and mumbled, "It was a no-win-situation."

He was set up! Well, do you really call it being "set up" when

3

you're stupid enough to be doing something that could ruin your life? Like selling drugs. They caught me. I was dead caught. Why did I try to run?

Rick slammed his fist into his hand and yelled, "Stop living that damn scene over and over! Please, get it out of my head!"

He clasped his hands around his head again, trying to quite the pain. The scene played in his sore brain again as he squeezed his eyes closed ...

They were chasing him down Babcock Road; running off the road, crashing, running through the woods, shooting him in the leg, beating him senseless, leaving him for dead. Those three bastards ...

Rick shook his head and said, "They were together. They thought they killed me. They drove my bleeding limp dead body to the Potomac River and pushed it in. They told the Feds I crashed in the river and died. They searched for my body a week and told the family I was a dead criminal. A clean open and shut case."

They had covered all the bases, got rid of all the evidence. One thing they left behind that they didn't count on; A Big Black Joker surviving the beating, the river, and living to avenge my death and kill them all!"

Rick started pacing the floor thinking, "I'm going to get all three addresses. I'm going to find out where they are, and unless they are already dead – I'm going to kill each one of them the way I've envisioned over each and every one of the 13 years since."

Rick pulled out his phone and looked at Deb's message again. She paged him. He knew she had something good! Deb never pages unless she has something good. He couldn't wait to call her; he punched in her number on his phone.

"Hello." Rick heard Deb's sweet sexy voice on the other end of the phone. He rubbed his dick and thought about how he'd like to fuck her, but she's all hung up over the little Mexican Chef in the precinct cafeteria. Rick caught on to Deb and the Chef the first time he met her in the Café at the precinct. She tried to hide it but Rick saw the way she watched tall Chef.

Rick responded, "Hey, this is Rick – you paged me."

Deb's groggy voice responded, "Hey Rick – it's kind of late. Can you call me in the office tomorrow morning, around 9:30?"

Rick could tell she had the Chef with her. That's cool.

"Sure, I was just a bit anxious. Something good?"

Deb became irritated, "Yeah, but we'll talk in the morning. Good night Rick."

Rick heard the receiver 'click', then dial tone.

A smile spread across Rick's face as he thought, "She would fuck me; I know it. I can tell by the way she looks at me. Chicks can't hide it when they interact with a man they would fuck. It's written all over their face."

Rick walked over to the window and looked outside at the cold Virginia landscape. He shook his head and said, "I need to find pansy-ass Joe soon, and get this over with. I'm taking a big chance being back in Virginia. What if someone recognizes me?"

Rick doubted anyone would recognize him with his new face. Doc really fixed him up in the joint.

Rick made his way to the bathroom, walking gingerly on the cold tile with his bare feet, not wanting to slip and fall, again. He had slipped on the tile floor 3 times this week with his damn sweaty feet. This place needs carpet. Rick thought, and perhaps he needed to buy more socks.

He turned on the light, walked to the toilet and pissed. He squinted his eyes and looked in the mirror at his reflection. He realized the man in the mirror wasn't him. It was his body; and what was left of his brain, and his eyes were the same, but the face was some creation that Doc put together to keep his head from falling apart. Doc had saved Rick's life. He had put him back together, not only his body, but also his soul.

Rick would never forget the first time he saw Doc. He was pulling Rick out of the sewer. God kept Rick's mangled body alive until the day he led Doc his way.

Rick mumbled, "Cuz I should have been dead."

CHAPTER TWO

I don't know how long I'd lain there ... Seemed like months. After those bastards drove me into the Potomac River, I managed to struggle out of my car and float along the river. I was sucked into a drainpipe and managed to crawl; squirm; and drift my way to the end of the line, at the bottom of a sewer. There was a ladder leading up to a manhole at the top, but I couldn't move my arms or legs to climb up. I could hear cars and people right above me, but I couldn't make a sound. I was dying; slowly; painfully. The rats came and nibbled on me from time to time during the days. I guess I didn't taste good enough for the rodents to just eat me up and get the shit over with. If they'd just eat enough of my brain away, that would kill me. Once the brain goes the rest follows.

After what seemed like days, I started thinking maybe if I tried squirming back down the sewer, I could make my way back to the river. I would then drown, because I couldn't use my arms or legs to swim. But at least my sorry life would be over. Why am I still alive?

Rick, just stop breathing! You can do it, just slowly, easily, hold your breath and fade away ... Please – just let me die!

Consciousness faded in and out over the days, and one day I heard faint shuffling noises right above me. Yelling ... more shuffling - two men yelling. I cleaved to consciousness trying to hear what they were saying. Pain shot through the center of my skull reminding me that my ears were full of blood and I was trying to die to end the pain.

A searing noise rang out and I knew this was the moment. God was finally going to let me die. The pressure in my head exploded from the noise, and I felt the remains of my wounded brain spill out of my ears, nose and eyes. I was dead ... I felt dead ... A rat ran across my face and scratched my lip with his claws.

I'm still not fucking dead!

Grating from the sound of the heavy manhole cover being slowly pushed away made me realize I could still hear and the light illuminating through my bloody eyes made my heart race ... Someone was going to find me! I felt a heavy weight press down on top of my body all at once. The remaining bit of my voice left in my lungs rushed out. I let out a loud moan, "Ahhhhhhh."

Then silence. I felt a body – a dead weight body partially sprawled out on top of me. I sucked in as much air as I could through the sewage with my chapped, blistered lips. I felt my blood running down my face and into my mouth ... or was it the body on top of me bleeding on me? The illuminating light was still there. A shadow flickered the light on and off – someone was coming down the ladder. I heard voices ...

"What are you doing?" A man's calm, distant voice from above was asking this shadow coming down, closer to where I lay.

He's going to kill me too.

I heard the shadow's deep rasping voice respond, "There's another body down here ... Go get the car." Footsteps running away ... The shadow was in the sewer ... he was close ...

The dead weight on top of me was relieved. A splash next to me sent droplets of sewage running down my face. I felt pain shoot through my neck as my cracked, bloody head was being cupped in a man's arms. I felt him wrestle the rats off of my wounded body. He took his thumb and pulled my eyelid open ... the light made my head throb and I felt the blood start rushing out of my skull again. I vaguely saw a dark, little man looking at me, holding my head in his lap and shaking his head. His voice wheezed out from low in his chest and I could feel his heart beat through his arms cupping my pounding head. He breathlessly whispered, "My poor boy. Someone has beaten you badly and left you for dead." I heard him sigh. Then silence.

He sat there for a while, holding my head; waiting for the 'car' to come and rescue us. I heard the rats fighting over the dead body next to me ... I guess he tasted better.

I started to drift away. I felt an overwhelming peace, and the pain started to quiet ...

I saw my mother walking on the farm. My sisters were playing barefoot in the mud. I was fishing in the lake ... a fish broke my line and I dove in after it and started to sink because I couldn't swim ... Life was peaceful. I wanted more for my life; I wanted to be a good role model for them. Where did I go wrong?

Pain like fire in my leg brought me back to the sewer. Back to the little man that found me. He was moving me. Shit! I have a bullet in my leg; take it easy!! He was trying to get me up the ladder. I wasn't moving. I was too big and he was too small. He realized this and wheezed as he said, "I'm going to need more help to get you out of here young man."

Quick glimmers of Roland, Smitty and Joe beating me rushed back to my consciousness and I jerked my body trying to get out of his grasp. I hadn't suffered and lived this damn long just to have those three finish me off. "No!" I became frantic; I had to let him know not to call the police.

"Dey ... twied ... to ... kill ... me! Dey ... twied ... to ... kill ... me." I was trying desperately to plead with him not to call the authorities, or a hospital, or anybody! My lips were swollen and rat eaten and I couldn't get them to form the words I wanted to say. "Please ..." I was spitting blood all over him trying to get him to understand that three cops had tried to kill me.

He tried to calm me down, "Shhhhhh, quiet, quiet – you're going to choke on your own blood – look at you!" He tried to examine me while I was trying to get free. "Your skull is cracked ...

by the butt of a gun ... And a large object." He noticed a rat gnawing at my leg and pulled it off. He saw my leg wound, green and infected. The man wheezed out, "Someone wanted you dead ... who did this to you?

I gave it one last effort. I had to let him know what happened. Please lips work one last time! "Cops ... cops ... they ... tried to ... kill me." That was all I had. Everything went black and the pain went away.

CHAPTER THREE

But, pain had become a constant companion; and it came back. The whistle of the train brought me back to the pain. What am I doing on a train? I died in the sewer … didn't I? Men were talking, close. I heard the voices – the same two voices I heard right before I died. The calm voice was right next to me. They didn't know I was conscience …

"I've got it Doc, I won't forget. I have it all written down. I'll do it right for you. I promise."

The rasping voice wasn't as composed. I heard wheezing as he sucked in his breath and grumbled, "Felix, you fail to see the urgency in situations, and I have a hard time depending on you. Can you please make sure you have everything, again?"

I heard papers flipping. Felix started again, a bit more agitated, "I am to contact the infirmary in the morning, and inform them that while in Washington, D.C., you were assigned an unknown soldier "John Doe" and he was taken into custody for treatment. We are transporting him back to Eglin for such treatment and rehabilitation."

Felix hesitated, and then asked, "Doc, if he's an unknown soldier – how are you going to keep him under your supervision once he's healed?"

Doc started wheezing louder and coughing as an asthma attack started to overtake him. I heard him administering an inhaler in between shouting at Felix, "Once he's healed I can make him into anything I want! Look at you!" The whistle from the train drowned out Doc's words. When it stopped, I heard Doc break the silence, "Felix, just do what I tell you, and everything will be fine. Our new family member will be nursed back to health. I'll give him a new face, a new identity, and he'll learn the Method."

I realized; Doc and Felix were plotting my alibi, and planning to give me a new start on life. My health, a new face, and a new identity – it sounded pretty damn good. What was this 'method'? What did Doc want from me?

My mind started racing over the scene in the sewer, trying to remember. The noise, the dead body ... Doc was a killer. He shot a man and threw him in the sewer; but he saved me. Why?

Felix and I were witnesses to his crime. Felix definitely doesn't sound like he'd ever tell on Doc, but you would think he'd want me dead. Why save me and make me new? Guilt? I'd almost believe that one, but Felix seemed too rehearsed in this procedure – like he'd done it before. They were a team: Doc the murderer and mastermind, and Felix the dumbfounded 'Yes" man doing whatever he's told.

I wanted to get a look at them; but the way I was laying, I could only open my right eye. Can I open my eye without them seeing? Hell, can I open my eye? The last time I saw anything out of my right eye, it was rat's teeth ripping out my cornea.

I took a deep breath and tried to open my eye. The pain vibrated through my head and tears welled up in my eye sockets as I suppressed a scream. I felt something wrapped around my head ... a towel? Whatever it was it was working. I didn't feel the blood running down my face anymore, and my skull was still. Why did Doc want to keep me alive?

I gathered my strength, and tried to open my eye again. I was prepared for the pain this time. I seized it in the gut of my stomach, and spread it out throughout my body, like so many times before. My eye inched open slowly, painfully. My eyelashes were stuck together and I felt them rip out of my skin as I pried my eye open. Through the dried blood, tears and skin, I saw two men sitting at a small table across from me, facing each other as they spoke. Doc was pointing his finger at Felix as he spoke,

"Felix, as soon as we get back to Eglin, I want you to …" Doc's words trailed off and out of my bloody eye, I saw him looking at me.

"Felix, he's awake; he may get nervous. Give him a shot, will you please?"

A shot of what? I broke out in a sweat and felt the blood dripping down my face again as I tried to get up and run. I couldn't move. I lay there, paralyzed, watching Felix fumble in a duffle bag. His hands emerged holding a pair of gloves and a syringe. He put the gloves on and turned toward me with syringe in hand.

Oh hell no! What is he giving me? I'll be still … I'll be quiet … I'm not nervous! What are these assholes giving me? I started jerking; the only formed motion I could make. I heard Doc come closer to me. He put is hands gently but firmly on my shoulders and squeezed.

He croaked calmly to me, "Relax son, relax. I ran your fingerprints. I know the Feds pronounced you dead in Fairfax County, Virginia last month. You're one of us now."

I felt his grip ease and he started kneading my broken, sore shoulders into relaxation. He leaned closer to my good ear and said, "I'll be your new doctor now. You can call me Doc; they all do."

I barely felt him grasp my hand with his. Pain shot through my arm and I realized he was shaking my hand. Through my straining eye I saw him smile at me and say, "Glad to meet you, Rick."

He released my hand, stood up, and walked back to the table. When he passed Felix standing in the corner, he barked, "Give him the damn needle and let's get some sleep!"

I started fading in and out of consciousness as I watched Felix gently stick the needle into my arm. It didn't matter anymore anyway, if he was going to kill me there was nothing I could do about it. Hell, it would be welcome after what I've been through. I do recall wanting to die … praying to die … holding my breath waiting for my heart to stop beating so the pain would finally stop.

The pain … where is it? I felt light … easy … this fresh feeling was more than my senses could take. I faintly felt my dick start getting hard it was so pleasing ...

The pain had taken a break from tormenting me, and I was able to drift off to sleep without waiting for my next painful heartbeat pounding my blood through my veins; sending loud, ringing echoes through my throbbing head. It was just calm quiet filling the space between my ears. I vaguely heard voices. Doc and Felix were talking again ...

My eye slowly relaxed back into its socket. I felt blood running down my face like a cool spring making its way down to my chin ... but no pain. I felt my face being wiped, gently. A blanket was lightly engulfing my body as I drifted off into painless sleep.

Whatever Doc gave me ... was just what the doctor ordered.

I was addicted.

CHAPTER FOUR

Yeah, memories of Doc and Felix brought a smile to Rick's old weathered face as he looked into the mirror. Doc and Felix; Rick wondered what they were doing now? Funny how Rick once felt Doc and Felix would be with him forever. It's been six months with no contact from them whatsoever. Once Doc gave Rick his assignment and Deb as a contact, they hadn't spoken. Rick thought about them every now and then … They were his family for 13 years.

Rick shook his head and looked in the mirror. He said, "I don't need family now. That's why I can't contact the family; they have no place in my life now. It's just me, pansy ass Joe, Roland and Smitty. That's it. Once I get rid of those three crooked cops, it'll just be me."

Rick washed his hands and thought, "Perhaps then I'll be able to contact the family and have a reunion. Besides, Deb updated me on what's going on.

She told Rick about Lynn owning a shop - Erica traveling all over the continent, and Pops finally slowing down on the drinking. Strange, Deb didn't have much to update on Sarah.

Sarah isolated herself from the world after Rick was pronounced dead; she couldn't take losing old big brother. Rick always knew Sarah just played tough. Inside, she was the most vulnerable.

Rick knew the family had no need for him anymore. Hell, they never had a need for him; they all somehow seemed to make it through all those tough years without ever needing him. And if they did, Rick wasn't around. He was always trying to find a quick dollar, an easy piece of ass, and a stiff drink. How could he think that now, after 13 years of being dead, he could resurface and announce his years of oppression and expect a Brady Bunch Reunion? No; that's not Rick's story.

For now, he was counting the hours until Deb gets to her office and he could make the phone call at 9:30am. Rick glanced at the clock … 4:45am. Damn, he was anxious! He willed himself to calm down; he didn't want his headache to get worse … just relax and wait for the time. Everything comes in time …

Rick sat up, "Hell, I can't go back to sleep. Might as well make some coffee and go downstairs and get the paper.'

He got out of bed and glanced at his watch again trying to ignore his torment … 4:55am.

He gingerly walked into the kitchen looking over the counter. Where was his medicine? His head was pounding. He couldn't concentrate with the pain so loud in his head. He couldn't remember if he'd taken it out of the suitcase. His hands shook as he reached for his suitcase and tried to open it. He'd been here a week and hadn't unpacked a thing. Guess that's best. Easy in and easy out – after he kills Joe, he'll need to get out of town in a hurry. Hopefully Deb has all three locations set so he can take them out one, two, three, no complications, no mess, no fuss; and get on with my life.

Rick shivered as he heard the wind howl past the windows. With any luck Roland lives in Hawaii, or someplace like that. He could use a vacation.

Rick felt his shorts vibrating … Someone was calling? He reached into his pocket, pulled his cell phone out, vibrating in his hand. Another call? I'm popular tonight. Rick looked at the display. He didn't recognize the number.

Hmmm, it's local. Who knows I'm here, besides Deb?

Rick's head pounded as he stared at his phone. It's got to be the wrong number. He waited for the caller to leave a message …

No message. Guess it was a wrong number.

The wind howled outside the window again and Rick grabbed

his coat off the chair and put it on. He mumbled, "I'm glad I bought this yesterday at the mall! I should have brought more warm clothes! But Rick had to lay low; he took a chance going up to the mall. But if he didn't get a big coat he was going to freeze his ass off! He grumbled as he put the coffee pot on, "My Florida wardrobe is not working up here."

Rick smiled and thought about his journey to the mall ...

It was wild seeing people he hadn't seen in years! He recognized so many people. He wanted to go up to Big Eddy Baker and give him a hug ... but he couldn't. He wanted to trip big ass Bertha Sims as she walked right past him. She managed to look worse than she did 13 years ago; and he didn't think that was possible.

Rick mumbled as he walked to the cold door to open it, "Hopefully, I've changed enough and nobody recognized me."

Rick braced for the cold air waiting outside and opened the door of the apartment. He ran down the stairs and opened the front door. He stepped out quick, grabbed the paper off of the front steps, and ran back in the door and up the steps. He felt his pant pocket vibrating again as it banged against his leg. He ran in the apartment and grabbed the phone out of his pocket before it stopped ringing. Out of breath, he looked at the number. Same fucking local number!

Rick gritted between clinched teeth, "Wrong number again? I doubt it. I can't answer it. The chances I take if it isn't the wrong number, and someone's looking for me ... Who the hell would be looking for me? I'm the one looking for motherfuckers! Let's see if they want to leave a message this time ..."

Rick sat his phone down and started pouring himself a cup of coffee ... He waited for the beep to indicate message ...

No message.

Rick shook his head, "Obviously, someone wants me to answer my phone."

Rick wanted it to ring again; he wanted to answer it this time. Just as he finished the thought, the hum of the phone vibrated on the counter. He slowly walked over and glanced at the number. Same number.

Rick picked the phone up and said, "O.k., I'll bite. What the hell."

"Hello."

He slowed his breathing to quiet the loud painful noise in his brain so he could hear the voice on the other end, but all he heard was a loud 'thump' of the phone being dropped. Fumbling ...

Rick said, "Who the hell is this?"

He barked into the phone again, "Hello!"

Rick heard a squeaky cough, and then, "Hey Ricky; this is Sissy – Sissy Tramble. Remember me?"

Rick squeezed his eyes shut and winced ... Sissy! Of all people ... How did she track him down the first week he's back in town?

Of course he remembered the bitch! She was with him the night he got busted! Hell, she's the one that turned him in! Rick covered his phone and said, "I've been trying to forget you for 13 years!"

Rick put the phone back up to his mouth and said, "Sissy; I think you have the wrong number."

How the hell did she get his number?

Sissy squeaked into the phone again, "Ricky! This is Sissy. Remember? I was with you when you got busted. Remember? You almost ran me over that night those cops got you. I knew you weren't dead baby, I just knew it."

Rick casually responded, "Sissy, oh yeah, yeah – now I remember you. I just got back in town ... How did you get my number?"

Rick clinched his teeth as he tried to figure out who the hell gave this cunt his phone number? Somebody's getting an ass kicking!

Sissy's squeaky voice whined into the phone, "Come on Ricky – you're not happy to hear from me? I promised I wouldn't tell who gave me your number. But, I saw you yesterday at the mall; and I followed you. Look, one thing led to another ... and the next thing you know; I have your cell phone number."

Rick cursed under his breath and covered the phone, "Come on

Rick! You're getting sloppy. If a two-bit whore like Sissy can track you down, you might as well hang a sign around your neck saying, "I'm looking for three cops to kill." How did she find me?

Rick took a deep breath and responded, "I must say you have a keen eye, or you really did love me way back when, because I've changed; everything. How did you recognize me?"

Rick searched his memory, trying to figure out what he did at the mall to give himself away?

Rick heard squeaky giggling on the other end. Sissy said, "Well baby, your not gonna believe this; and hell yes I loved you way back when! How could you have doubted that?"

Rick paced the floor holding his head with his free hand. He thought, "Great, she's getting all emotional on me. Just answer the damn question!"

Sissy squeaked, "Ricky ... you still there?"

He wished like hell he wasn't. He responded, "Yeah, yeah Sissy. How'd you recognize me?"

Squeaky giggling again on the other end, and then, "Well, you have the heaviest walk baby, like you're stepping on something to mash it. But I know baby, that's the way you gotta walk to carry around all that dick you got between your legs. I don't know anybody else that walks like you! Anyway, yesterday you were at the mall walking in front of my girlfriend and me. I noticed your stride and started staring at you. When I saw your face I thought hell no, that ain't him. Then I saw you smile at my girlfriend, and I knew it was you. Nobody ate my pussy like those lips you got, and even though you've changed your face and your hair, you still walk the same and you got those same pussy eat'n lips baby."

Rick almost became nauseas remembering how she had the nastiest pussy he'd ever eaten. He only messed with her for her connection to the dope man. He trusted her and she set him up that night! Rick knew it was her ... who else could it have been? No one else knew what he was doing or where he was going.

Rick's head pounded as he paced the floor. He had to find out who gave her his number! And how could she remember his walk and his lips?? He must have looked right at her yesterday and didn't even notice her.

Rick said, "Wow, you recognized me from my walk and my lips? What, I got a stalker on my hands now or what? I didn't recognize you, have you changed that much?"

Sissy squeaked, "Well, I've put on a few pounds, and haven't been feeling well for a few years now ..."

Rick thought for a moment ... Was she that fat ugly chick I saw with that fine babe at the food court?

He became agitated, "Well, look – thanks for calling to say 'Hi", but it's really early and I'm not fully awake yet. Please thank whomever it was that gave you my number, but please don't call me anymore, and please don't give my number out. I'm here on business – not a personal matter."

Sissy pleaded, "Ricky, come on now. You've been dead to the world for 13 years, and I see you yesterday, alive and back from the dead, and you don't want to see me?"

Rick was silent. He really didn't need her anywhere in his life right now. He would definitely never fuck her again! She'd given him crabs way too many times for him to trust that pussy ever again. Hell, her crabs could crawl up the condom! There was no escape.

He was about to tell her to fuck off, and then he realized he hadn't found out how she got his cell phone number. He responded, "Well, I have a very busy schedule the next few days. What are you doing Saturday? I know you already know where I live; you want to come over for a drink?"

Sissy squeaked into the phone, "Ricky! You gonna make me wait until Saturday to see you? I can't wait! I want to see you now ... won't you let me come over tonight?"

She always did beg. Rick hated a begging woman.

Rick's head pounded with each squeak of her voice. He barked into the phone, "No, Saturday or nothing. Look, I gotta go. You know where I live; so, 7:00pm Saturday, see you then."

Rick slammed his phone shut, ignoring Sissy still pleading on the other end.

He stood still staring out the window. He shook his head ... Sissy Tramble. Wow! He never thought he'd hear from her again. Especially after she set him up! It was Sissy. It had to be her ...

All these years, Rick was so certain it was Sissy who had set him up, but he could never prove it. He could never prove Sissy was the one that narced on him. But who else could it have been?

What if it was someone else?

Doesn't matter now, that was 13 years ago. She was able to get Rick's cell phone number from somebody, and he was going to find out who; and kick their fucking ass!

CHAPTER FIVE

9:30 am. Rick impatiently waited outside the precinct. He checked his watch and decided to give it another 5 minutes, and then he'd call Deb. He couldn't wait in his apartment any longer; he had to get out of there. He'd been waiting in front of the precinct since 8:00am.

Rick checked his watch again and dialed her number. His thumb was shaking so bad, he could barely push the numbers on his phone. He heard her pick up.

"Lt. Shaver, how can I help you?"

Rick wondered why Deb always answered her phone in the same, monotone, 'I could give a shit' voice?

Rick replied, "Hey Deb, it's me – Rick." Rick heard his voice shake with anticipation.

Deb came back, "Hey Rick, right on time. Look I have name, address and place of business for your first eradication. Can't talk now, but meet me after work at …"

Rick cut her off in mid sentence, "Look Deb, I'm right outside. Meet me around the corner at Starbucks. I'm not waiting another minute for this information."

Deb sighed on the other end, "Rick, I do have a job you know. I can't just disappear whenever you want information."

Rick insisted, "Deb, please. Starbucks in 5 minutes?"

She hesitated, then replied, "5 minutes Rick – that's all I got."

Rick hung up and quickly drove around the corner and parked

in the Starbucks parking lot. He anxiously watched the corner waiting to see her walk across the street … Waiting … Damn, it's been 5 minutes already. Where is she?

Rick saw a petite blonde wearing a dark brown trench rounding the corner. There, there she is. She looks worried. Rick wondered what was wrong? He watched Deb as she walked towards him; she kept looking behind her as if she were expecting someone to be following her. Is someone following her?

Rick knew something was wrong; she didn't look good.

He got out of his car and walked into the Starbucks. He stood in line and didn't look at Deb as she joined the line behind Rick. He ordered and took his coffee to a table in the back. Deb ordered, got her coffee and walked to the table next to Rick.

He glanced at her; she wouldn't look at him. She took a few sips of her coffee.

Rick anxiously sipped his coffee … How does she want to do this?

Rick looked at Deb again and said, "Excuse me miss, are you using the vanilla?" He pointed to the vanilla sitting on her table.

Deb smiled and answered, "No, please help yourself."

Rick got up from his table and moved to her table. He whispered, "So, how's it going?"

Deb nervously looked out the window, "Things are getting weird around the office Rick, and IAD has been asking a lot of questions about FEDCURE lately."

Rick sat back in his chair and said, "So what, they'll never find out we have anything to do with the Method. Why are you worried?"

Rick wondered why would Deb be worried about the Method? Maybe she wasn't as connected with Doc as he had thought. Rick knew somehow, Deb and Doc were connected; he just couldn't figure out how and what was the link between them.

She quickly changed the subject, "Look, I've got information on ex-officer Joseph Ramsey."

Rick raised his eyebrows, "Did you say, "Ex-officer?""

Deb pushed a folder towards Rick, "Yeah, Joseph Ramsey is working part-time as a security guard at the U.S. Geological Survey in Reston, VA. He's divorced, no kids, lives alone in Sterling, VA." Deb opened the folder and pointed to a piece of paper. It had an address written on it.

Rick smiled, "He is the perfect target."

Deb continued, "He drives a late model Ford Mustang, red. License #CC2 169. He took early retirement from the force 5 years ago. He couldn't' take the pressure and stress of being a cop."

Rick shook his head in anger and gritted between clinched lips, "Yeah, I guess the joker wore himself out from all of the overtime he did performing police brutality on company time!"

Rick winced as he could still feel that little bastard stomping his little feet into the back of his cracked skull, pushing his face further and further into the mud …

Deb was silent, staring at Rick reminisce. She never commented on his outbursts against the force. She just gave Rick her time, information, efforts, and friendship. Rick wondered why she would agree to help a joker like him.

He knew. She kept helping him 'cause of Doc. He knew it was Doc who put Deb on his assignment. How else would he have a detective at his beck and call? He didn't know how Doc and Deb were connected, and he really didn't give a shit right now. He just wanted information, and then Deb could be on her way.

Rick gathered his composure, people were staring at him raise his voice. He calmly said, "Sorry, Deb. Go on. What's his schedule, when does he go to work, come home?"

Rick salivated thinking about killing him. He wanted to follow the bastard a few days before he took him.

Deb inhaled slowly, and then continued. "Rick, Officer Ramsey was shot in the leg 3 years ago and walks with a cane. He is legally considered handicap and parks his car in the same spot everyday at work."

She handed Rick the folder. Rick slowly opened it. On top of the papers was a map of the parking lot at the Geological Survey. There was one parking space with a red highlight. Deb continued, "That's his spot. He parks there every evening at 6:00pm. You'll have no problem finding him. You can follow him to his apartment in Sterling – he parks in the same spot there also, the handicap spot."

Rick sat back and thought how easy this was going to be. He said, "Deb, is he just waiting around for me to pop him? I mean, he has no family, no career, walks with a bum leg … I almost feel sorry for him."

Before Deb could respond, Rick added, "Key word – almost."

Deb said, "Look Rick, I just get the information for you. I'm not a shrink. He obviously feels some remorse for what he has done in his past. We all do."

Rick looked at Deb for a moment; then added, "Yeah, I guess we do. One thing is for Sam Hill certain … I'll never regret killing these three."

Deb finished her coffee and was gathering her coat and getting ready to get up from the table.

Rick reached out to stop Deb from leaving. He said, "Wait, Deb. How about the other two? You must have something on them. Once I'm done with pansy Joe, I don't want to miss a beat in getting the other two. I could start planning that now."

Rick noticed Deb was ready to go, and impatient. What was eating her?

Deb huffed and responded, "Rick, I have bits and pieces on the other two. Roland is in Seattle, Washington. I have an address, but its eight years old. Not sure if it's current. I have no present employer – he also is no longer with the force, sorry. As for now, there's not much more on Roland. Now, Smitty's the tricky one. I found out that he got married 13 years ago, but never took up residency with a wife. He has always lived alone. He still lives here in Virginia. His address is …"

Rick interrupted Deb, "Wait! Did you say he got married 13 years ago?

"Yes."

Rick grimaced and said, "So, he got married right before or after they killed me. That should be easy to track. Do you have a name on the wife?"

Rick wanted to kill that bitch too!

Deb shook her head, "No Rick, not yet. I'll dig deeper, get a copy of his marriage license. Meanwhile, you've got what you need on Ramsey. How long should this take, so I'll know when to get your flight out to Seattle."

Rick wanted more information, but he could tell Deb was getting tired of him.

He nodded and said, "Well Deb, I'll have to follow him a few days. Decide when and where I want to take him. I'd say give me two weeks – then book my flight."

Rick's mind raced … Would it make more sense to pop ole' Smitty while I'm here?

He asked, "Deb, you think I should just go ahead and pop Smitty while I'm here in Virginia?"

Deb nervously glanced out the window. She said, "No Rick. One dead ex-cop is enough for now. Take care of Ramsey, leave town – take care of Roland, then return and take care of Smitty. A choppy trial is harder to trace. You should know that – stop getting anxious and keep a calm head about yourself, cool?"

Rick was silent as he stared at Deb. He realized Deb did care, about his ass or hers. Either way, she was right.

He exhaled and said, "Ok Deb."

Deb got up from the table and walked past Rick and out of Starbucks. He watched her walk back down the street and around the corner. Rick opened the folder and studied the contents. There was a picture of ole' Joseph Ramsey. Man he looked bad! He looked about 60 years old! He was only 50.

Rick took the picture out and studied it longer. He mumbled, "I guess being a dirty cop takes its toll. Well, you won't have to worry about your past, or future much longer."

CHAPTER SIX

Deb rushed back to her desk and checked her messages. Shit! Captain's looking for her.

She didn't know there was a 9:30 meeting! Deb looked at her watch. Well, she missed it.

She had to think of an excuse to tell Captain why she missed the meeting? Think Deb, think! She quickly searched her pocket for her cell phone, hoping he hadn't called her. Deb pulled her cell phone out of her pocket and checked it. Damn, had it on silent. Yep, Captain had called at 9:45; she was with Rick.

Deb took a deep breath and decided to just go and see what's up.

She put on her game face and left her desk. On her way to Captain's office, she saw three gentlemen standing by the break room. One saw her approaching and nudged the other two. They all three looked her way and stared at her.

Deb looked the other way and thought, who are these clowns? Do they know me? Hmmm, one is rather good looking …

The short one whispered something to the good-looking one. They all smiled at Deb as she approached. She became irritated … What the hell is so funny?

Forget them Deb – you have bigger fish to fry. Just walk past them, no eye contact.

The good-looking one stepped out in front of her. She had to acknowledge him. She stopped and looked him in his eyes. Deb put her hands into her pockets to indicate "I'm not shaking hands."

He smiled. He had perfect teeth. He spoke, "Excuse me, I'm Lt. Hutchison." He was extending his hand and smiling. Deb glanced past Mr. Perfect and saw the other two snickering and waiting for her response.

She wasn't going to make it easy for Mr. Hutchison, "Excuse me, do I know you?" She kept her hands in her pockets and looked him right in his beautiful brown bedroom eyes.

He squared his shoulders, opened his stance and extended his hand closer to her body. "No, you don't know me. I'm trying to introduce myself. I'll give it another shot ... Hi, I'm Lt. Hutchison." His smile had faded and gave way to a stony glare. His hand was still extended. His two cronies had stopped snickering.

Deb slowly took her hand out of her pocket and gripped his firmly, "Hello, I'm Detective Debra Shaver."

He shook her hand. When the handshake was over, he held onto her hand and said, "See, that wasn't so hard Detective Shaver." His smile was back and he turned and pointed to his cronies, "I'd like for you to meet my colleagues, Sgt. Rhodes and Sgt. Landau."

He released her hand and Deb shook hands with Rhodes and Landau. She wasn't sure which was which, but it really didn't matter; they both looked like Null & Void. What was the purpose of this meeting and introduction? It's like they were waiting for her, and now that they've found her ...

Deb interjected, "So, you gentlemen visiting the precinct on business, or are you here to post bail for a friend?" Hutchison's stony glare was back. He didn't think that was funny.

Hutchison calmly replied, "Detective Shaver, we were here to meet with Captain Bloom. We had a 9:30, but all parties for the meeting weren't present, so the meeting got cut short." He paused and his words trailed off.

Deb stared at Hutchison with her mouth open and thought; so, these three are from ...

"Shaver!" Deb heard the Captain's growl from down the hall.

Heavy footsteps echoed through the crowded hallway. Deb didn't turn around; she braced herself.

Get ready Deb! Here it comes.

Rhodes and Landau shrank off into the stream of people walking by. Hutchison remained standing in front of her. Deb glanced up into Hutchison's face, her eyes pleading for him to disappear before Captain reached her. There was a smile forming on Hutchison's face and he hooked his arm around Deb's, spun her around and started walking, pulling her in the direction of the Captain.

Deb hissed, "Excuse me, what are you doing?" Deb was trying to walk in reverse, but Hutchison's pull was too strong. He ignored her question.

Hutchison yelled at Captain over the crowd, "Captain, look who found me!"

Hutchison held onto Deb's arm and continued, "Detective Shaver reminded me I already had my secretary fax over the questionnaire to her this morning asking her to review and complete."

Deb stared at Hutchison, wondering why he was lying to Captain for her?

Captain finally stood right in front of them in the crowded hallway. Hutchison quickly released Deb and reached out his hand for a shake.

Hutchison said, "I apologize Sir for confusing the meeting times. It was completely my fault that Detective Shaver missed our meeting this morning."

Deb stared at Hutchison, and then at Captain - wondering if Captain was going to buy that story?

Captain took Hutchison's hand and gave it a firm shake; "No problem Hutchison, simple miscommunication." Captain made eye contact with Deb as the handshake ended.

Captain rolled his eyes at Deb and looked back at Hutchison, "Well, I'm late for another meeting – Shaver, I'll expect to see a copy of that questionnaire you were completing this morning on my desk this afternoon." Captain turned to walk away, and turned his head to the side, "Hutchison, nice seeing you again."

Captain barreled back down the hall. Deb rolled her eyes up at Hutchison, "Why?"

Hutchison looked down at Deb, and his once beautiful smile turned into a sinister, thin-lipped grin, and he said, "I always try to see how hard it is to get the cop I'm investigating to lie, or go along with a lie to their superior." His words trailed off and he stared at Deb. Hutchison continued, "I guess we see where your threshold is."

He took a step closer to Deb and lowered his voice; "Guess you're relieved that I got you out of that one with Captain. Now you'll never have to tell him where you really were this morning. And if you do, you'll have to admit to him that you lied."

Hutchison turned and started to walk away. He paused, walked back close to Deb and said, "By the way, this is your formal notification that you're under investigation by IAD for suspicion of obstructing justice."

Hutchison turned again and walked away from Deb. She stood there, in the middle of the busy hallway watching the tall, handsome man walking away. Deb couldn't stop trembling, and her shaking made it hard to focus on Hutchison as he disappeared down the hall …

CHAPTER SEVEN

Rick sat waiting in the dark parking lot. He counted his heartbeats with the rhythm of the painful blood flowing through his head. The pain vibrated as he strained to watch the shadows; waiting for a figure to approach the red Ford Mustang parked in the handicap space. The pain made it hard to see through the shadows of the buildings. Where was he? His shift ended at 1:00am. It was 1:25 and no sign of the useless bastard!

Wait …

Just then Rick saw a shadow emerging from the side of the building. There he was … Rick saw a limping figure with a cane approaching the red Mustang. He chuckled and said, "What kind of security guard has a handicap? What a joke. Well, I'm not laughing. Yet …"

Joe hobbled closer to his car, and Rick got a better look at him. He still had those small monkey-ass feet! He looked tired, beaten, and broken. Pain on his face; pain in his walk, he looked like a miserable man. Rick mumbled, "Looks like I'm going to be doing 'Ole Joe a favor anyway by killing him. Looks like he'd kill himself if he wasn't such a pussy."

Rick watched Joe. He could see he was a man that made mistakes; gets sloppy; not aware of life … easy for him to grab him and gag him. Easy target. Rick mumbled again as he watched Joe, "This won't take long. I'll have him in two days, torture him for a day, kill him, and be on my way to Seattle before anyone even notices 'Ole crippled Joe ain't around anymore. I got this."

Joe got in his mustang, and drove out of the parking lot, not noticing the black Ford Explorer following his every turn. Rick kept close to Joe as he drove onto the Toll Road, headed towards Sterling. Rick could still hear Joe's whining voice echoing through the pain reverberating through his brain as he remembered ... Rick mumbled, "I'm going to make that coward suffer. Then he'll thank me for putting him out of his misery."

Joe took the Sterling exit off of the toll road; Rick was right behind him. He followed him through a quite neighborhood into a small townhouse community. He scanned the neighborhood, making note of the surroundings ... A few streetlights were out, large trees surrounding the perimeter. One-way in and out - large sewer drain on the east side.

Rick felt the skin on his back tighten up as a chill ran down his spine. He hated sewers! Every time he saw a sewer, his stomach collected a little bit of vomit to push up his throat. He swallows vomit on a regular basis.

Rick shook his head and thought, "Maybe someone should kill my broken, sick ass self. Might do this joker a favor."

Joe pulled into a parking space in front of a dark brown townhouse. Rick drove passed him and down to the end of the street and parked on the right side of the road. He watched in his rear view mirror as Joe got out of this car and hobbled to his front door. Rick took another look around the neighborhood. None of the town homes had garages. All parking spaces were in front of the house. He'd have to grab him someplace else. Unless he could get inside and play the waiting game and grab him in his house. Or he could wait for him at work when he's walking to his car. Maybe - maybe not. Rick pulled into a visitor parking space, and waited. He wanted to wait awhile, let 'Ole Joe get comfortable; and then Rick was going to peep through some windows, check a few locks.

He watched as lights came on inside of the dark brown

31

townhouse. The sprinkler system came on in a sputter. The porch light came on, and the front door opened. Rick got excited, maybe he could follow the poor bastard tonight and grab him and get this shit over with.

No one appeared in the doorway, but the door was open … Rick's head started to vibrate with pain as he strained to see through the mirror into the darkness behind him. What the hell is he doing?

Just then Rick saw a huge black head emerge from the doorway. A very large black dog was jumping around playfully in the doorway, frolicking in and out of the front door … Rick watched as Joe emerged from the doorway holding a leash; restraining the huge black Rottweiler. Yeah, Rick could see better now … Joe had a huge fucking Rottweiler!

He let out a long, painful sigh … "How am I going to get passed that monster to get to Joe?"

Rick watched as Joe and the big black mass of dog walked down the sidewalk. They walked down the opposite side of the street where Rick was parked. Rick could get a nice good close-up of the two.

Joe was drinking something out of a cup he was holding in one hand; the big black creature was pulling the leash on the other, hurrying to get somewhere. Where are they going?

Rick shivered as he got a better look at the dog. He moaned, "… That is a big fucking dog!"

Rick watched them disappear into a grassy area at the end of the sidewalk.

Rick flopped his aching head back into the seat. Damn! Deb didn't tell him Joe had Bigfoot as a pet! He can't abduct Joe from his house, unless he got rid of the animal. But, that wouldn't work; cause soon as 'Ole Joe comes home and the monster isn't there to greet him; he'll know something's up and get suspicious.

Rick sat up and looked out the window again. He'll have to abduct Joe at his job. He didn't want to do that, but it probably would be easier than facing the beast.

Rick winced as he looked for his prey … He couldn't see through the opening in the buildings until a light outside the last house came on. There was a field with a small pond. Joe was holding the leash and drinking out of his cup. His animal was running to and fro; pissing here and there. Rick watched the mammoth dog play with Joe like he was a puppy. He sat staring at the two as they headed back to the sidewalk.

Rick wasn't in to killing animals; and he didn't think he could take this one out anyway. He'd never seen a dog so big and fierce; yet playful and friendly at the same time. Rick got a closer look at the beast and saw his large, sharp razor teeth playfully nipping at Joe's hand trying to play.

Rick plopped his head back onto the seat. He exhaled long and slow ... He didn't want to tangle with that beast. He'll just drive back down to the Geological Survey and scout out the area. Time to move to Plan B - abduction in the parking lot. That may even work better as a matter of fact.

Yeah; abduct 'Ole Joe in the parking lot; then take him to the place. The survey is closer to the place anyway.

Rick watched as Joe and his creature walked back down the sidewalk, towards the dark brown townhouse. Joe was finished downing whatever he was drinking and the cup dangled in his hand at his side as the creature pulled him towards home. Rick watched as they walked on the other side of the street. When they were directly behind the truck; the dog stopped ... Rick watched through the side view mirror as the creature turned his massive head around and looked directly at Rick. Rick squinted as he focused harder on the creature through the mirror ... He could see the dog's pitch black eyes glaring right into his.

Rick started sweating and whispered, "He's watching me watch them ..."

Rick slid down in the seat and cursed, "There is no fucking way that dog can sense I'm watching them! I can't believe I've been made by the damn dog!"

Rick inched his head up and looked in the mirror again. He saw

Joe walking until the leash jerked his arm. He looked back at his dog, said a command and pulled on the leash. The creature slowly started walking down the sidewalk again, but Rick could still see the dog's big black eyes in the mirror. He was still looking directly into the mirror, still watching Rick's eyes, watching them.

Rick slid down in the seat again, "The damn dog sees me!"

Rick eased back up and looked in the mirror. Joe pulled the leash and the creature followed him down the sidewalk, calmly, up to the dark brown townhouse.

The dog knew I was there; that I was watching him and his master.

As Joe and the creature disappeared into the doorway and the door closed behind them, Rick sat up with his mouth open ... he was astounded by the dog. The ferocious glare in his eye; the power he eluded; the way he knew I was in this truck watching them! Rick visualized the dog's eyes ... the dog knew his master was my prey. That I was planning to kill him.

Rick gripped the steering wheel and said, "Come on Rick! A dog is spooking you! Ok, so he is a big scary dog - he was a good-looking creature though; all big and stocky, black and beautiful ... sort of like me. I bet he's a good pet ... Too bad I gotta kill him."

Once 'Ole Joe is gone, who's going to want to take care of that creature? I'll have to off the dog too, but how?

Rick started the Explorer and backed out of the parking space and started driving back down the street, back towards the highway. When he was passing by the dark brown townhouse, he glanced over. In the top right corner room window facing the street, Rick saw the curtains parted. He winced as his eyes struggled to look closer. He saw the dog's mammoth black head glaring down at him through the curtains in the window. Rick's foot hit the brake and he slowed down for a moment and stared in shock back at the creature. The dog was now preying on Rick!

Rick stared back at the two black eyes glaring at him and gritted, "Alright you cocky son of a bitch! You wanna play? I'll be back for you. Once your pansy ass master is dead; I'll be back for you. Can you read my lips you big bastard?"

A car was approaching behind Rick and he realized he was stopped in the road, staring down the beast. Rick started driving again and realized he was feeling intimidated by the dog! He slowly drove down the road, and back onto the highway; headed towards the Geological Survey.

As Rick drove down the highway, he couldn't get the dog's eyes out of his pounding head. What kind of dog was he ... a Rottweiler? Rick couldn't remember ever encountering a Rottweiler face to face. He wondered what kind of pets they were? Obviously they look like murderers, but he wondered what Rottweiler's were really like?

Rick squinted his eyes trying to quiet the pain in his head and mumbled, "After I kill this one, I'll have to look into getting me a Rottweiler."

CHAPTER EIGHT

Saturday night, 7:00pm. Rick stood in the bathroom brushing his teeth staring into the mirror. His stomach gurgled as he thought about the funky ass houseguest he would be receiving soon. Rick didn't know why he agreed to see her … She's disgusting and annoying. 13 years ago she was annoying; and from the phone conversation earlier this week, the bitch hasn't changed.

Rick rinsed his mouth and looked in the mirror again. He said, "Besides, I need to get some information from her scanky ass. Whoever is giving out my information has to be taught a lesson." Who would be stupid enough to give out my information to any old pussy that asks! That'll get you killed.

Rick heard a knock on his door. Sissy was always on time. She may have been a nasty, raunchy fuck – but she was always on time.

Rick checked himself in the mirror, put his phone on 'vibrate' and walked to the door. He looked out the peephole and saw Sissy standing there. She had gotten ugly in her old age! She was actually not bad to look at back in the day; cute smile, big 'Ole jugs spilling out everywhere, always willing to suck dick …

Rick opened the door, "Hey, how's it going? Come in." He stepped back and opened the apartment door wider so Sissy could make her way in. With a big smile on her face, she walked in and brushed up against Rick as she entered his apartment. She still had the same nasty booty smell, like she had a lifetime-guarantee yeast infection. Rick remembered 13 years ago she always smelled like sick pussy.

He suppressed a smile as he thought; perhaps it's because the Ho always had a sick pussy?

Sissy walked to the middle of the room and turned with open arms towards Rick.

"Ricky; come here Baby! Give your old lover a hug"

Rick closed the door and looked at her, standing there, waiting for him. He inhaled and thought; this was definitely the lowest moment in time since he left the base. She was the most undesirable woman he could think of. Why is it always the ugly ones that want to hug?

How can I get out of this without offending her before I get what I want from her?

"Hey, Sissy … I have your favorite drink." Rick avoided the hug and walked into the kitchen and grabbed the bottle of MD 20/20 out of the fridge. He held it up to Sissy, "I remembered."

She let out her annoying giggle and said, "Oh Ricky, that was ages ago fool! Nobody drinks that stuff anymore." She reached out her hand and took the bottle from Rick, "But is was the shit! Give me that; I think I will have a glass."

Rick gave her the bottle and quickly went to the kitchen to get two glasses. He didn't want to prolong this visit by any means. Get her drunk; make her tell who gave her my phone number, and kick her stank ass out!

Rick walked back into the living room and found Sissy with the bottle turned up, downing the last bit of 20/20. She let out a loud belch, giggled and turned to Rick with big wet lips slurring, "Ricky you know I always had 2 of these 'cause the first one was just a thirst quencher."

Rick knew … that's why he had three more bottles in the fridge. She could down three bottles of Mad Dog 20/20 in less than 20 minutes. They used to call her MD3-PO (<u>M</u>ad <u>D</u>og x <u>3</u> – and <u>P</u>ussy's <u>O</u>n).

Rick smiled and sat the glasses down on the table. He said, "Now come on Sissy; I do remember some things. I may not look the same, but I'm still the same 'Ole Joker from way back when." Rick took the empty bottle from Sissy and turned to get another one, "I have three more for you. I'll get you another one. They even have it in different flavors now!"

Sissy sat down on the couch and giggled again, "Ricky, they've had those flavors for years …" her words trailed off as she suddenly realized … If Rick wasn't dead for 13 years, and not in prison, then where was he?

Rick was walking into the room with the second bottle when Sissy stopped talking. He stared at her … following her thoughts. Rick didn't know if she was going to ask. He cursed under his breath as he realized he didn't have a story for her. Where should he tell her he's been for 13 years? He didn't think anyone would recognize him, so he didn't have his alibi prepared.

Rick regrouped and took a deep breath. He entered the room; determined to get the conversation going his way, so he could get his information. He had to find out who gave her his cell phone number. She was downing the second bottle of 20/20. She stopped to take a breath, and slowly slurred out, "Ricky, if you aren't dead, were you in prison all this time? I mean you had a funeral and everything … what happened baby?"

Rick's agitation made his head start to swell with pressure. He wanted to slap the bitch around and make her tell him what he wanted to know.

Rick walked over to the window, easing his breathing so he wouldn't loose his cool; he could outsmart this dingbat any day. He'll just give her the same story he gave the landlord and get on with this interrogation.

Rick slowly turned around and faced Sissy. He said, "I actually did go to prison. I was sent up north and did my time there. I was released a few months ago, and back in Virginia just a few days to take care of a few things, and then I'm out. I don't want my family

and friends to know that I'm still alive ... 'Cause sort of in a sense ...
I am dead."

Sissy shook her head and poked her lips out, scorning Rick. She
said, "Now Ricky, I got that same story from the landlord and don't
think I believe that for one minute."

The pressure in Rick's head exploded as he thought ... So, the
landlord is the Narc ...

Rick gritted his teeth. He should have known! Who else could
have had that information here in town? That little bastard! Selling
me out! Rick was going to make his miserable little ass pay for this
one. He remembered his ugly face with his hair-lip in a grimace as
spit ran down his lips when he spoke. His hair-lip won't be the only
thing making him spit all over himself while talking after Rick's
through with him. Rick wanted to slice his miserable tongue right
out of his head.

Rick wasn't paying any attention to Sissy as she stood up and
walked towards him. She was taking her shirt off and licking her
lips; looking like an over-the-hill cheap hooker. There was nothing
to justify the landlord telling this slut his personal information.

Rick would deal with him later.

Sissy was standing in the middle of the room, naked from the
waste up. Her once overly large jugs had turned into two deflated,
blemished, spider-veined meat masses that hung down to her waste
line with no sign of a nipple on either. She stood there, waiting for
Rick to answer her question.

Rick began to sweat with agitation. This visit was over; he had
gotten what he wanted. No more pleasantries, no more small talk.
And the bitch definitely ain't getting the last two bottles of MD
20/20! He'd rather give it to the dog.

A vision of Joe's creature flashed through Rick's throbbing head.
The dogs' power and presence was overwhelming. Rick wanted a
dog like that. He remembered the dog's stare burning in his painful
memory. The dog was brilliant ... he could see it in his black eyes.

Not to worry my big, black meat-eating creature ... I'll kill you too. It's a shame. I'd like to know what you're like; what kind of pet you are. Wonder if he had proper training, or if he's a big clumsy, stupid ox. No; he definitely ain't stupid; big and clumsy; but not stupid.

Rick brought his thoughts back to Sissy; she had taken off all of her clothes and was standing in the middle of the room, her arms stretched out waiting for Rick to come to her, "Ricky – didn't you miss me?"

Rick had to hold back the vomit that was collecting in his mouth; his stomach was lurching at the sight of Sissy standing there, naked. There was no way he could fuck her, ever again. She was hideous. There was nothing left of the once attractive body that Rick remembered. She had scars, like someone had cut her up; or maybe it was surgery scars; what the fuck ever!

Rick blurted out, "Look, Sissy; I'm not feeling too good; I've been sick since I got back in this cold weather, and I'm going to have to cut the evening short."

She lunged towards Rick's feet and fell to her knees, "Ricky! Don't make me leave yet! Please, I promise, it'll be worth your while" She was pulling at Rick's zipper on his jeans. She continued, "Besides, if you were in prison all this time, I'm sure you missed having a women's mouth wrapped around this big, black dick."

Rick started feeling better since he wasn't looking at her naked body anymore. He looked down on top of her head. He let her take his dick out … He'd let her suck his dick; but then the bitch has got to go.

She started talking as she fondled Rick's dick, "So, you said you've been sick since coming back to this cold weather. I guess you've been in warm weather since you been away; so that rules out being up north, like you said …"

Rick felt his head surge with blood, and a painful vibration rocked his eye sockets. This bitch is too smart for her contaminated ass! She is not entitled to ask anything!

Rick became paranoid. What if she's here for someone else? She might have opened her big mouth to someone else, and someone might have paid this slut off to find out information.

Rick grabbed Sissy's head and threw her up against the wall. He yelled, "What are you writing a mother-fucking book bitch! Why you asking me all these damn questions! Just suck my dick bitch and put that nasty mouth of yours to good use!"

Sissy was holding her head, with her legs curled up into a ball screaming, "Ricky! Ricky! I'm sorry baby, please! I didn't mean nothing, I didn't mean nothing; I'm just happy to see you and feel you. Don't hit me!"

Rick walked over to her and grabbed her head and made her look up at him, "So, you're so glad to see and feel me; well you gonna feel me bitch; and you gonna tell me everything I want to know!"

Rick threw her up against the wall again and walked into his bedroom. He grabbed the pack of condoms out of his nightstand. If the bitch wants to be nosey; she wants to know so much about where I've been, what I've been doing; I'll give her all the information she needs!

Rick turned his stereo up loud as he was walking back into the living room. He saw her, sitting in a slump against the wall. She started whimpering when she saw Rick walking towards her again.

Rick opened the condom and rolled it onto his dick. He didn't trust fucking her in her pussy; even with a condom on. Her asshole was always cleaner than her pussy anyway; so he'll just get himself some dooty-booty and punish this bitch for following him home and making him see her again!

He grabbed her by her arm and dragged her over to the end of the couch. He bent her over the end of the couch so he didn't have to look at her face and not much of her body. He spread her ass open and rammed his dick deep. She let out a loud scream. Rick grabbed the pillow off of the couch and pushed her face down into it. Her screams were drowned out by the music and the pillow as Rick held her head down. He continued to punish her ass with his dick. She tried to reach her arms behind her and grab him, push him away. But she couldn't reach him; couldn't stop him. Rick held her head into the pillow with one hand, and held her body down on the edge of the couch with the other as he pounded her ass. She was coughing and gasping for air, but Rick didn't care if she suffocated; she asked for it. She calmed down and actually started cumming uncontrollably. Rick let her head off of the pillow, "Who else have you told about me bitch! Who!" Sissy was crying; from the pain or from cumming Rick didn't care; he just kept pounding her, "Who else!"

In between breaths, Sissy managed "No … one … Rick-y … No … one!" He was crushing her body into the side of the couch, but he didn't care; she has to be taught a lesson.

She'll never follow anybody else home again … Rick would Sam Hill bet his dick on that!

CHAPTER NINE

12:30 am, Wednesday morning before Thanksgiving. Rick tried to enjoy the ride to the U.S. Geological Survey, but his thoughts were loud and painful behind his eye-sockets. The car came to a stop in front of the address Rick had given the cabby. Rick reached over the seat and paid the cab diver. He got out of the car and waited for the car to drive off.

Rick watched the car disappear around the corner and started walking up the road. Rick had the cabby drop him off in the apartment complex down the street from the Survey. He had about a half mile to walk to the Geological Survey parking lot.

It was a cold night. Rick winced as the hawk whipped around his head. A pain shot through his ears from side to side, left to right; exploding with a 'bang' through his skull. A tear burned its way down his frozen cheek from the pain. His pace increased, he was on a mission to kill … he was obligated to kill. He justified his assignment; he felt it was right and that he had to complete it. Somewhere in his bruised, broken brain, he was convinced he had to kill all three of them! And he would kill anyone who interfered in any way; or he would die trying. He was approaching the Survey quickly. He slowed his pace. It was 12:50 am; he still had 10 minutes before 'Ole Joe clocked out.

Rick had cased the parking lot and knew where the cameras were situated near Joe's car. He glided through the main gate and through the large empty parking lot like a black panther. He wore a black jacket, black jeans, black gloves and a black wool cap. He was ready to make off with the first of three assailants that took his life and replaced it with a painful memory of a man.

Rick spotted the red Mustang. He walked in between the buildings and slid into the doorway of the locked building outside of the main entrance of the Geological Survey. The red Mustang was parked in one of the handicap spaces directly in front of him.

He had a straight shot at apprehending 'Ole Joe as he left the building.

Waiting … Rick had been stalking Joe for over a week now; it was time. He planned it for tonight because he knew a charity function was scheduled for today; knew lots and lots of people would be attending … holiday weekend with a lot of out-of-towners. Police would have a long, long laundry list to go through once handicap night security officer Joe Ramsey was discovered missing; only to be found dead later. No way to identify Rick as a suspect for murder.

There were 3 other cars parked in the vicinity - probably leftover visitors. However, it was awfully late. Who would be out or at work at 1a.m. Thanksgiving morning? Calm down Rick, it's cool.

He had it all planned. The thing that worried Rick was … no matter how good the plan; something always goes wrong. He just has to be prepared to handle anything.

Rick grimaced as he readjusted his dick while leaning into the doorway in the shadows of the locked building. All of the shadows started blending into one big shadow of darkness. Rick lost his focus as he stood waiting, watching the shadows of the buildings. He started to gently rub his dick to comfort it. Fucking Sissy the other night scraped his dick raw! Damn-it Man! He wanted to punish the whore, but she was enjoying the shit. Rick hoped she didn't give him the crabs. Wouldn't be the first time.

No matter. He found out who gave her his cell phone number … the hair lipped landlord. He should have figured it out, but that's cool. Rick already had plans for the landlord. As soon as he's finished with Joe, the day he checks out of the apartment and is ready to leave town will be the last day the landlord takes a breath from his filthy stool pigeon ass mouth.

Rick saw a shadow emerging from the building ...

His blood pounded loud through his brain as he stopped breathing; thinking the shadows could hear his heartbeat ... watching ... waiting ... to kill. Rick watched the shadow come closer. He visualized seeing the limping figure of Joe Ramsey staggering to his car.

Instead it was a female figure ... walking slowly with a ... a man. Rick heard the mans voice across the parking lot. He was circling the woman as they walked. He was yelling at her. She was tolerating his argument as she slowly unlocked her car door and reached for the door of a dark brown sedan. The man was still yelling at her.

Rick cursed, "Will they just get in the damn car and leave so I can grab pansy ass Joe!! He'll be coming along at any moment!"

The woman started getting into the car, but the man grabbed her arm and pulled her back out. He slammed her against the side of the car.

Rick shook his head as he watched ... "Great, I'm witnessing a domestic dispute!"

A shout echoed through the darkness. The arguing couple both swung around and looked in between the buildings.

Out of the shadows came a figure scuffling towards the couple with a nightstick pulled and pointed right at the angry man. It was Joe. He had walked up on an assault, and was playing "toy-cop." Rick held his breath as he watched Joe interrogate the couple. While Joe was questioning the angry man, another man walked out into the parking lot. He stared at Joe and the couple for a moment, then walked past them and got in a light colored truck, and drove away. Rick was getting impatient; if Joe doesn't let the couple go and let them leave soon; he would have to change the plan. Too many witnesses ... too long in the parking lot ... Timing is all off ...

Rick shifted his weight from foot to foot, rocking back and

forth as he studied the scene. This was supposed to be quick, stop and grab.

He looked back down in between the buildings for an escape route. He was ready to run back to the highway ... Wait. Rick saw the couple getting into the car and driving away. Joe hobbled to his Mustang.

Rick waited for the dark sedan to turn out of the parking lot, and then started walking slowly, quietly up to the Mustang from behind. Rick knew every night when 'Ole Joe got in his car and drove away, he would crack his driver side window. Roll it down just enough for Rick to reach his arm in and tag him flat in the side of his head, and knock his simple ass out. Joe never noticed Rick as he started his ignition ... didn't notice as he lowered his driver's side window that a shadow was standing right beside his car.

Joe put the red Mustang in reverse, and was going to turn his head to look and see if the coast was clear. He never saw the fist that hit him directly in his left temple.

Rick had run up beside the car and punched Joe in his head before he even knew what was going on. Rick laughed to himself as he quickly reached in and pushed Joe's slumped body over so he could unlock the door. You'd think 'Ole Joe would have been a little more alert and pumped up since he got to play 'toy-cop' tonight.

Rick picked Joe up out of the Mustang and put him in the back seat. Rick was so much bigger than Joe, it was easy for Rick to get Joe in the back seat, bound, gag him, and jump in the front seat and drive away, all within 8 minutes.

Rick drove out of the main gate of the survey, and headed east ... Towards Washington, D.C ... towards the Potomac River.

Rick couldn't think of a better way to avenge himself than to torture 'Ole Joe, and drown him in the Potomac River.

He turned and looked at his victim in the back seat and mumbled, "Those bastards thought it was a fitting grave for me 13 years ago; let's see what 'Ole Joe thinks first hand."

Rick drove in deafening pain, waiting to hear any indication that his hostage was awake before he reached his destination. If he wakes up, Rick would have to pull over and bash him in the head again. Rick came to his exit and was at a stoplight. He looked in the back seat at 'Ole Joe again and thought about hitting him. The urge to reach back and hit him overwhelmed Rick's violent emotions. The light turned green and before Rick put his foot on the gas, he lowered his fist down behind the seat, and bashed Joe in his head three times.

The blows to Joe's head made an opening in his skin right above his left eyebrow. Rick was two miles down the road when he turned to check on his hostage and found a pool of blood on the seat, dripping onto the floor. Joe's blood was flowing down his face and onto the floor like a popped tick. Rick got frustrated with himself. His head started to pound loud from anticipation. He was too excited; He couldn't wait to kill him!

Rick squinted as he focused on the road ahead of him. His vision in his left eye started to disappear gradually while pain pounding through his skull made is his hands start to tremble around the steering wheel. He couldn't hold the wheel steady. He drove up to a stoplight. He couldn't see if the stoplight was green or red. He stopped.

He willed himself to control his anxiety and pain. Control … Calm down, you'll get to kill him soon enough.

Rick took two calming breaths to try and ease his excitement pushing the blood painfully through his brain. He slowly lifted one eye towards the stoplight and saw a red glare; it was red. Before he closed his eye again he saw a quick glimpse of green. Rick sat there for another moment.

He glanced in the backseat at Joe. He was bleeding like a dirty pig that he is … Rick wanted to hit him again, but controlled the urge this time. He had to follow the plan; he couldn't start beating him until he's at the place!

Rick eased his foot off the brake and the Mustang took off, through the light, down the deserted road. Rick was relieved there weren't many cars on the road at 2:30 am in the morning, 'cause he ran off the road several times before he and his hostage reached their destination.

The construction site at Jones Point Park was dark and deserted. Perfect for a murder. Rick could barely see his way along the shoreline of the Potomac River as he carried Joe over his shoulder to the trailer. The lighthouse along the shoreline ahead was the only way Rick didn't fall into the river and drown with 'Ole Joe. Rick had drove the Mustang down into the construction site and parked it behind a forklift close to the shoreline. It was the perfect spot to drive Joe and his car into the river.

There was a trailer right beneath the lighthouse that was going to be "left open" with the keys inside, just for Rick's convenience. The workers were off for the holiday weekend, so Rick had four days alone with 'Ole Joe - to do whatever he wanted with him.

That thought made Rick bustle along the shoreline faster; anxious to get inside the trailer and throw Joe against the wall hard and wake him up. He wanted to beat him for a few minutes before he bound and gagged him again. He wanted to feel Joe's flesh cave in around his fists as he pounded his body; watch Joe's face as his teeth fell out of his bloody mouth from being slammed into the floor.

Rick's plan was to leave him tied up, beat, bound and gagged while he went out and picked up the stuff. He actually only had three days to torture 'Ole Joe. Rick had to make his way back to Joe's house and take care of the big black monster that waited for his master ... a master that would never return. He had to take care of the dog.

Rick had it all planned. He finally saw his years of suffering, his constant pain and anguish, his forever handicap of life, being avenged.

For the first time in many, many years, he had a genuine smile on his face as he carried Joe on his shoulder and entered the deserted trailer, closed the door and locked it.

CHAPTER TEN

Deb pushed her way through the crowded grocery store. She almost slipped on the wet floor; the rain was coming down so hard outside the wind was blowing it into the doorway. All she wanted was coffee filters for her coffee in the morning; she didn't stop to think that it was the day before Thanksgiving. The store was a mad house. Someone had dropped a turkey and it was splattered all over Isle 2; an old man had opened a pumpkin pie and was eating it with his fingers. Deb tried to push by without touching him, but he still managed to smear pumpkin pie all over her cashmere scarf ... great.

Deb hated Thanksgiving; it was the most depressing holiday of the year for her. She had no family to share it with, and she was allergic to cranberry sauce ...

She loved cranberry sauce.

Well, she could count her dad as family, if he cared to share any of her life with her. He only called whenever he needed something, or occasionally when he was in the country. She wasn't family to him; she was just a commodity. She realized it a long time ago, and accepted it. It was either accept it, or have no relationship with him at all.

Sometimes she thought the latter would be less painful.

Deb grabbed the coffee filters and pushed her way to the express line. There was a lady in front of her with at least 20 items. The express lane is for 10 items or less. Deb shook her head and thought,

"People never want to follow the rules ... never. I guess if they did, there would be no need for cops".

She finally paid for her pack of coffee filters and made her way back out into the freezing rain. She ran across the parking lot and jumped in her car. She felt guilty about driving to the store, since she only lived 2 blocks away, but if it weren't raining she would have walked, but not tonight. She sat her bag in the seat and started the car, put the heat on and tried to thaw out. The smell of pumpkin pie suddenly caught her attention ... the old man in the store. Deb examined her scarf and tried to wipe off some of the pie; but she smeared it and made it worse. She drove two blocks, and pulled into her parking space in front of her apartment. She grabbed her bag, got out of her car and started sprinting to her front door. She heard a car door open and close behind her as she pushed her front door open. She turned around to close her front door, and was shocked to see Lt. Hutchison standing on the sidewalk in front of her apartment. He was dripping wet and holding up his badge with his slimy grin stretched across his face.

"Mind if a wet IAD Agent comes inside and dries himself a bit, maybe have a good hot cup of coffee before I ask you a few questions." Deb had the urge to slam the door in his face ... but maintained her performance.

Keep it cool Deb. He's a man; you can out-smart this dick. She smiled and said, "Well, I'm not sure how dry you can get in 10 minutes; 'cause I'm on my way right back out the door to a family gathering." Deb stepped back and opened her front door a bit wider. "Come on in Lt. Hutchison."

Hutchison stepped onto her welcome mat and brushed his feet off before stepping past her into her living room. Deb closed the door and walked in front of Hutchison into the living room. She slung her purse on the hutch near the door and held up both her hands at Hutchison as he tried to walk into the room. She said, "You'll have to take a rain check on that coffee Hutchison; I'm in a hurry. What can I do for you?"

Hutchison grabbed Deb's wrist and pulled her arm hard towards him and growled at her, "You listen to me you little hypocrite! I don't care where you're going, you're going to answer a few questions for me right now, and you're going to be pleasant about it, or I'll haul your little ass right down to the station and we can take care of it that way." He threw her arm back at her and it hit her in her side. She turned her head and stepped back, not wanting him to see the fear on her face. She inhaled long and slow to calm herself and got a big, long whiff of old, wet pumpkin pie from her scarf. Heat engulfed her body and she realized she still had her coat on. Sweat broke out all over her body and she felt nauseated. She had to swallow hard to keep the vomit from coming up her throat. Was she going to puke? Deb didn't know what the hell was wrong with her.

She quickly gathered herself and said, "Look, Hutchison; I'll be glad to answer anything you like."

She paused and walked over to her Rolodex on the counter. She grabbed a card and handed it to Hutchison and stared him in the eyes, and said, "…that is, in front of my attorney, whom I will call first thing in the morning and inform you of the time we can meet with you."

Deb turned and walked towards her front door. She winced waiting to feel his grip on her arm again. Her arm throbbed from his grip a few minutes earlier. She opened her front door again, and held it open waiting for Hutchison to leave.

Hutchison's face was beet red. He stood there; glaring down at the card she'd given him … Attorney Ethan Connor. Hutchison looked up at Deb, clinching and un-clinching his fist. He opened his mouth to say something, but shut his tight thin lips hard and shook his head.

Deb readied her hand over her gun in her pocket just in case he got any bright ideas. She stood there, waiting with her door open. Rain was blowing into the doorway but she wasn't going to close it until this arrogant son-of-a-bitch left.

Hutchison's thin lips relaxed, and he shook his head, then broke out into the sinister grin Deb remembered from the first day she met him. She heard a low grumble break out from under his coat ... he was laughing at her.

Just as he started walking towards the wet, open doorway, Deb's cell phone started to ring in her purse. Hutchison stopped walking right in front of the hutch at the doorway; where Deb's purse lay. He looked at her purse, her phone was lying right on top and Deb could see the display light flashing from the doorway. She lunged for her purse and quickly snatched it off of the hutch. She slung her purse over her shoulder, but didn't answer the phone.

She continued to hold her front door open, waiting for Hutchison to get out. "Well, Lt., unless you have a warrant for my arrest, I insist that you leave so I can be about my affairs."

The wind blew Deb's scarf into her face and the wet pumpkin smell engulfed her nose. She felt her stomach lurch and her throat constrict ... she was about to puke. Deb had been feeling sick all week, and it was coming to fruition, right now.

Hutchison opened his mouth to say something, but Deb's cell phone started to ring again. Hutchison acted like he was going to reach for her phone to answer it, and said, "You want me to answer it and tell them you're not home?" He took a step closer to the door, and Deb.

Deb grabbed her phone out of her purse and looked at the caller ID. Shit ... it was Rick. She pushed her phone deep down in her purse, and looked at Hutchison, who was standing close ...

She extended her hand and guided him out into the cold, wet night. She said, "Excuse me, I have to leave." As Hutchison walked out into the rain, he stopped on her welcome mat again. He turned to Deb and extended his hand, as if to shake her hand good-bye. As Deb was about to extend her hand, her cell phone started to ring again. Hutchison broke out into his slimy grin and said, "Go ahead and answer it. You might as well; I'm going to find out who it is anyway when I subpoena your cell phone records."

Deb tried to hide her panic. Subpoena her phone records! She inhaled and the cold rain splashed onto her tongue. She realized it was serious this time.

She stood in the doorway staring at Hutchison as her cell phone beeped loud; indicating the caller left a message this time.

Deb stared at Hutchison; Hutchison stared at Deb. The rain came down in large cold raindrops. Hutchison stood close to Deb, staring at her, daring her to say something or close the door in his face.

She didn't say a word ... She couldn't. If she opened her mouth again, Hutchison would be covered in the vomit she was holding down by swallowing empty gulps of air while breathing through the rain.

They stood there, in the freezing rain staring at each other.

Hutchison finally turned and walked back to his blue sedan parked a few spaces ahead of Deb. Deb watched him as he started his car and drove away. She stood in the doorway drenched in the freezing rain as she watched him drive down the street, turn the corner and disappear.

Deb closed her front door and quickly walked to her car. Her cell phone started ringing again as she jumped in her car; leaned over to the passenger side and projectile puked into the seat.

CHAPTER ELEVEN

Rick walked into the back room of the trailer to check on his hostage. Joe glared at him through the blood running down his face. Rick had beat Joe's head in on one side and it was bleeding atrociously. Rick should have known his pansy ass would be a bleeder.

Rick was going to have to kill him sooner than planned; or the pansy was going to bleed to death. Rick swore under his breath, "Where the hell is Deb!"

He'd called her five times. She wasn't answering her cell phone.

Joe was bound and gagged with duct tape wrapped all around his body. He was lying on his side up against the wall, right where Rick had left him a half hour ago. Rick closed the door and walked back out to the front of the trailer. He dialed Deb's number again. This time, he got an answer.

He heard coughing on the other end … more coughing. Rick yelled into the phone, "Deb! Are you all right? What's going on? Hello."

Rick finally heard Deb's strained voice on the other end, "Rick, Rick. I'm o.k." Her voice trailed off into another round of coughing, then "What is it? Why the hell are you blowing my cell phone up? What's wrong?"

Rick took a calming breath, and said "I've beat him too hard, too quick; he's bleeding all over the trailer and I've got to get him out of here sooner than planned."

Rick heard Deb's hoarse voice on the other end, "How much sooner?"

"I need to get him out of here in about an hour; or he's going to bleed to death before I can kill him."

Rick heard Deb's sigh on the other end of the phone, "I'll have it there in 20 minutes." She was about to hang up, but Rick yelled into the phone, "Deb!"

Deb's strained voice screamed into the phone, "What?"

Rick tried to sound concerned, "What the hell is wrong with you? Are you sick or something?"

Deb screamed, "Yeah Rick! I'm Something!" He heard a click and his cell phone went blank.

Rick looked at his phone and scoffed, "What the fuck is up with her? It's only a day or so before plan; why is she so upset about it?"

He shoved his phone in his pocket and walked over to the small window in front of the trailer. He peeped through the blinds out into the cold rainy night. Nothing. Good. In 20 minutes I'll have all that I need to finish this.

Rick calmed his breathing to quite the noise in his head. He had injured Joe quicker than he had anticipated, but the satisfaction was still there. He had planned to torture Joe all night and tomorrow morning. But after beating him a few hours, it got boring. Rick just wanted to kill him and get it over with. He looked over this shoulder towards the back room and said, "He's not worth my energy."

Rick heard a scuffling noise from the back. He turned and started walking towards the back room. He mumbled, "Don't tell me 'Ole Joe is trying to escape?"

Rick walked to the back room and opened the door. He saw Joe squirming, trying to roll over and break the duct tape. When Joe saw Rick standing there he froze …

Rick walked over to where Joe lay and kicked him in his stomach. His muffled squeals behind the gag in his mouth made it less enjoyable to Rick. He wanted to hear the pain in his voice as he screamed and begged him to stop beating him. Rick reached down and ripped the duct tape off of Joe's face and pulled the rag out of his mouth.

Joe started coughing and spitting blood out of his mouth onto the floor. In a gargled voice he managed, "Who ... who are you? What do you want with me?"

Rick didn't answer him; he just kicked him two more times in his stomach and groin with his steel-toed boots. Rick laughed as he heard Joe squeal like a pig getting his balls cut off. Joe held his head down against the floor and started crying and choking on blood.

Rick was disgusted, "You pansy ass pussy! You can't even take a good ass whipping; but your punk-ass liked giving them out, didn't you!" Rick lifted his foot high above Joe's head and stomped down hard on the side of his head, over and over. Joe's head banged loud against the tile floor.

Rick finally heard something crack ... Done.

Joe's screams faded away into an echo as Rick walked out of the room and left him choking on his own blood. Rick thought he'd heard a car drive up through Joe's screams. He closed the door behind him and walked to the window, peeped through the blinds. *It's here.*

There was a swift knock on the door; Rick took his time in answering. He waited until he heard a car in the distance drive off. Rick walked to the front door of the trailer and opened it. There was a large black sack with thick handles lying right in front of the door. He dragged the bag into the trailer and closed the door. He unzipped the bag and checked the contents. A Beretta Px4 Storm, ammo, heavy-duty duct tape, rope, handcuffs, a large white towel inside a plastic bag, and change of clothes. Rick nodded, "Yep – all here."

Rick loaded the Beretta and put it in his pocket. He walked into the back room of the trailer with duct tape and rope in hand. Joe was still crying into his own blood. Rick walked over and started wrapping the rope around Joe. Joe cried out from his swollen lips, "Please man, why are you doing this to me?"

Rick reached over and grabbed the rag to stuff it back in Joe's mouth. He grabbed Joe's head and squeezed his broken jaw so he would open his bloody mouth to scream. Right before he shoved the rag back in, Rick said, "You never knew me Officer Joseph Ramsey; but I know enough about you to feel justified in doing this to you as payback for all of the innocent victims of police brutality." Rick took the gun out of his pocket. He pointed it at Joe's left kneecap and fired. Joe's kneecap went flying up against the wall and Joe let out a loud squeal and fell limp on the floor.

Rick shoved the gag into his mouth and duct taped it in place. He finished wrapping the rope around Joe and tied it in a knot. He picked up the other end of the rope and dragged Joe's broken, bloody body out into the front room. Rick gave the trailer a once-over to make sure he wasn't leaving anything he needed. He knew in a few hours Deb would send the 'clean-up' crew to wash down the trailer, clean up the blood; get rid of fingerprints; kneecaps …

Rick was impressed with Deb; she was a good cop. However, he knew there were larger counterfeit cops out there making the 'Method" happen. Deb was just a minnow in the ocean. A puppet on a string; she did what they told her to do. And then, there are even smaller tadpoles; like the clean up crew; they do what Deb says. It's a mad, mad, mad world. Rick shook his head as he walked back to the pile of flesh and blood that was once Joe. He picked up the black bag and slung it over his shoulder with one hand, and with the other he opened the door, picked up the end of the rope and started walking out of the trailer; dragging Joe's limp body down the step and onto the wet, muddy ground. Joe's head hit the ground with a "thud!" Rick turned and closed the trailer door behind them. As he walked back in front of Joe's limp body, he kicked him twice in the gut. Joe let out a distressed moan.

Rick smiled to himself through the freezing rain. Good, he wanted Joe awake as he dragged him down the muddy, rocky pathway back to the Mustang.

Rick started dragging Joe down the muddy pathway along the shoreline. Half way to the Mustang, Rick lost his footing. He slipped and fell into the mud face first. He felt his boot kick Joe in the head. Joe's body went rolling into the river and the rope tightened around Rick's hand. The rope was wet and started cutting Rick's hand in two. Rick dropped the black bag and got up. He pulled on the rope with both hands with all of his strength. He didn't see Joe coming up. Rick yelled, "Where the hell did he go?"

Finally he saw Joe's head pop up over the muddy embankment. Joe was coughing through the wet gag in his mouth and crying. Rick's hand was bleeding from the rope. He got angry. He should have just let his pansy ass drown and be done with it.

But that wasn't the plan.

Rick pulled Joe back up onto land. The freezing rain started to fall harder on top of Rick's head and the raindrops felt like sledgehammers. Every drop was followed by a surge of pain through Rick's skull. Rick looked at Joe lying on the ground in front of him. Joe's body was jerking violently as he struggled to regain his breath in between crying through the wet gag in his mouth.

Rick was wet, cold and his hand was bleeding pretty badly now. He started walking down the shoreline again – a bit more careful this time so not to slip and fall again. Joe was considerably heavier now that he was soaking wet. However, Rick's anger and frustration made his adrenaline soar and he felt strong. He was anxious to get this over with and get back to his apartment, clean up, dry off, and get warm!

Rick spotted the Mustang parked near the bridge; the spot where he had left it; where he would push it and Joe into the Potomac. He started walking faster, pulling Joe over boards, glass and rocks. He heard Joe let out an occasional shriek of pain; which made Rick's pain less noticeable.

They reached the Mustang and Rick dropped the rope and the black bag. Rick unzipped the black bag and took out the knife. Joe saw the knife and started squirming and jerking. Rick reached down and cut the rope from around Joe. He grabbed one of Joe's hands from beneath the duct tape. He cut around his hand just enough to pull it through the duct tape. He picked Joe up and threw him in the front seat of the car. Joe was squirming around and wouldn't keep still. Rick was trying to hold him still so he could handcuff his arm to the steering wheel. Joe wasn't cooperating.

Rick took the gun out of his pocket and aimed it at Joe's one remaining kneecap and fired. Joe's kneecap exploded onto the windshield and he immediately went limp. Rick grabbed the handcuffs out of the bag, took Joe's hand and cuffed it to the steering wheel.

Rick stood up and gathered himself for a moment. Thoughts of the dog flashed across his memory ... He's going to have to go back and take care of the dog next. It was a shame cause he's a beautiful dog.

A little voice painfully echoed inside of his sore brain ... *Maybe he could keep the dog.*

Rick chuckled to himself, that won't happen. I'm off to Seattle this weekend to track down 'Ole Roland; what am I going to do with a mammoth dog like that? Keep him in a pound? I could ship him out there to meet me ... Naaaa. I just have to kill him like his master.

Rick looked at Joe; broken, bleeding and slumped over the steering wheel. Rick had waited so long for this moment, and now that it was here - the climax was overwhelming.

Rick reached in the car and gave Joe one last powerful punch to the side of his head. Joe let out a moan. Rick pulled the gag out of his mouth; he wanted Joe to see where he was going to die, and drink in as much Potomac River as he could before his lungs exploded.

Rick picked up the rope and tossed it into the car. He reached in, started the Mustang, put it in neutral and closed the door. He went to the back of the car and started pushing it towards the river. It easily coasted down the bank and made a large splash as it hit the water. The nose of the car went down quick and the taillights slowly disappeared under the smoking, bubbling water. It was done.

Rick let out a long, controlled sigh through the rain beating on his face. He smiled and some rain got in his mouth ...

It tasted sweet.

CHAPTER TWELVE

The warehouse was dark and silent. Clicking from the fax machine echoed throughout the building. He waited anxiously for the fax to finish coming across the machine. He'd get those bastards! How dare they fuck with her! She's not whom they want! They want me.

Doc ripped the last page out of the fax machine and read it. Sure enough – they were investigating his Debra. Doc's hands started shaking and he balled up the paper and threw it against the wall. He started wheezing and his chest constricted as he stared at the ball of paper on the floor. He lunged at the fax machine, picked it up, and raised it high above his head. He grunted loud as he threw it and sent it crashing onto the floor. Pieces of fax machine went flying all over the room. One piece hit the side of Doc's ankle and he winced in pain. He looked down and saw a trail of blood running down his shoe onto the floor.

"Shit."

The back room door jerked open and Felix came running out, "Doc! Doc, what's wrong? What happened?" Felix was naked standing in the doorway; looking at the mound of broken fax machine in a pile at Doc's feet. "Doc, are you alright?"

Doc was fumbling in his shirt pocket for his inhaler. He found it and took two quick puffs. He walked to the chair near the table and slowly lowered his old body down into the seat. He glanced up at Felix still standing naked in the doorway and said, "Felix my boy, it appears that they've finally put two and two together; and are going after my precious Debra."

Felix walked closer to Doc and said very calmly, "Doc, don't worry. We'll take care of everything like we always do, and she'll be just fine." There was a noise from the backroom.

Doc shot out of his chair and glared at Felix, "You idiot! Is the girl still here?" Felix hung his head and started backing away from Doc. Doc gritted, "Felix! How many times do I have to tell you not to let her stay over night! You know my rules, why do you insist on breaking them?" Felix wouldn't look at Doc.

Doc walked into the kitchen and got himself a napkin to clean the blood from his ankle. He threw the bloody napkin at Felix as he made his way toward him. Doc glared at Felix, "So, what have you done to her? Did you treat her like you did last month?" He stood in front of Felix waiting for an answer. Felix kept his head down and was silent. Doc shook his head and walked past Felix.

"Well, come Felix; let's see what you've done to her this time." Doc pushed the door open and looked around the dark room. In the corner he saw the girl. She was hanging from the beams across the ceiling from bungee cords. She was naked and tied up by her wrists with her arms straight above her head, slowly twirling on the bungee cords. Her ankles were taped together, dangling just above the floor.

Doc stared at her and thought; how familiar - Felix had learned that trick from Rick, a long, long time ago.

The girl was twirling towards the door just as Doc came in the room, and when she saw him she started grunting. She had a gag in her mouth and Doc couldn't make out if she was crying or happy to see him. He took a moment to twirl her around and look at her; she wasn't hurt bad.

He smiled at her pleading eyes; she looked inviting hanging there from the ceiling.

Doc turned and looked at Felix still standing outside the room. "Felix my boy, I can understand why you like her … she is pretty." Doc walked out into the hallway and took Felix by the arm and led him back into the room. "Felix, I'll watch one last time and then you'll have to take her down and let her go. She's not supposed to stay overnight. Now I'll have to explain all of her cuts and bruises again."

Doc walked past the girl hanging from the ceiling and took his chair. The girl was squirming around, turning in circles and shaking her head. Her eyes were pleading with Doc, but he refused to acknowledge her appeal.

Felix walked over to the girl and held her still. He leaned close to her and said, "Hey, just once more and you can go. Just once more, I promise." Felix twirled the girl around until her back was towards him. Her face was looking right at Doc sitting in the chair, pouring himself a glass of Hennessy. Her face was wet from her tears; her hair was long and matted to her face. Felix stood behind the girl and gripped her in the back of her thighs. He spread her legs open and lifted her up so there was lax in the bungee cord, giving her arms a rest. Felix braced himself up against the bed, and eased the girl down on top of his big hard dick while he stood and guided her body onto his. She started breathing hard and panting through the gag in her mouth. Felix was lifting her up and down with force as she rode his dick. She was riding him, bouncing uncontrollably against the pull of the bungee and Felix's grip on her thighs pulling her against him hard. Her arms stretched high above her head attached to the bungee cord, her feet never touching the floor. Felix released her thighs and held onto her waist and was gripping her hard. Doc watched Felix and realized where the bruises on her torso came from.

After a while, Doc stopped paying attention … His mind was a thousand miles away. He couldn't stop worrying about her. His Debra was good, not like the others. She had a good heart. He started feeling guilty for ever introducing his Debra to the Method. She didn't deserve it.

Felix was still holding the girl in place as he ground his dick into her dangling body. Doc took his mind off of his worries and decided to enjoy Felix and the girl. He watched as Felix bounced the girl's body up and down onto his dick, springing her up in the air with each thrust.

Felix gripped her body hard and his nails cut into her skin. He grunted as he came and fell onto the bed. Doc watched the girl jerk as she finished climaxing, dangling on the bungee cord. Doc got up and pulled a knife out of his pocket to cut the girl down. He walked up to her, leaned close to her head dangling down between her arm pits and whispered, "You enjoyed that didn't you baby? I saw your cum running down your legs in buckets."

Doc gently wrapped his arm around the girl and cut the cords from around her wrists with the other. She fell into his arms like a rag doll.

He carried her out of the backroom into the front and laid her on the couch. He eased the gag out of her mouth and gently kissed her bruised lips. He whispered to her as he gripped her firm breasts in the palm of his hands, "Now, I'll only be a minute my dear, then you can get dressed and I'll have the car take you home."

Doc eased the girls legs open as he rested his old body in between them. He unzipped his pants and took out his soft penis. She was still wet from Felix, so it was easy for Doc to push his soft dick into the girl and thrust twice before he climaxed inside of her. He collapsed on top of the girl and started wheezing. He lay there for a moment before he fumbled in his shirt pocket for his inhaler. He took two quick puffs and dropped the inhaler on the floor. He raised his aged body off of the girl and his squashy dick eased out of her. He reached down, pulled his pants up and looked at her. She was still and silent. She watched Doc as he went to the table near the couch and pulled out his wallet. He took out three $500 bills and extended his hand to the girl.

As she reached for the money, Doc said, "This is extra; don't tell them that I gave you this extra. This is for you; for allowing Felix and I to enjoy you a little longer than planned." She managed a smile and took the money. Doc took his knife and cut the tape around her ankles and helped her up to her feet. He turned her towards the bathroom and said, "Now get your clothes on. I'll call the car – please be out of here in 10 minutes, or I will take the money back from you and give you to Felix again."

The girl quickly ran into the backroom, grabbed her clothes and bag and ran into the bathroom. She emerged in 5 minutes fully dressed. Doc was standing at the entrance to the warehouse with the door open. He smiled at the girl and said, "Thanks for the evening. You have a nice day." The girl sprinted out of the door and Doc watched as she ran across the empty parking lot and into the car waiting at the end of the street. He closed the door and locked it.

The next day was Thanksgiving, and he had a long list of things to take care of before he and Felix could enjoy their turkey. Doc's stomach grumbled as he thought of eating Felix's dinner. Felix was an excellent cook. His cooking was half the reason why he had kept Felix with him for so long. Felix could make a rabid squirrel taste like steak.

Doc walked back into the bedroom to check on his prodigal son. Felix was still sprawled out on the bed where he had collapsed. Felix was a large man, and Doc couldn't move him if he tried. He covered Felix with a large blanket and left the room. He mumbled as he closed the door, "Poor thing, wore himself out with that girl all last night and this morning."

Doc tripped on a piece of fax machine as he walked into the kitchen to make coffee. As he took the broom to sweep up the mess, he started thinking about his Debra … He dropped the broom and went to his computer and started typing an e-mail. He wheezed and tried to calm his thoughts as he typed the words of his message. His anger got the best of him and he started coughing. He kept typing. He had to teach those assholes a lesson once and for all!

Doc was so engrossed with typing his message; he didn't notice how loud he was wheezing. Felix came rushing out of the room and searched for Doc. He found him banging away at the keyboard and wheezing uncontrollably. Felix ran to the kitchen to find an inhaler for Doc. He searched the left drawer … the right … no inhaler.

Doc started coughing and choking for his next breath. He kept typing. Felix came running out of the kitchen when he couldn't find an inhaler and screamed to Doc, "Where are they?"

Doc didn't answer Felix; he couldn't. He was wheezing so bad he didn't have enough breath to speak. Doc ignored Felix and kept typing his message. Felix ran over and stood in front of Doc at the computer; he was buck naked and trembling with fear at the thought of losing Doc.

Felix started crying like a baby and begging, "Please Doc, where are they?" Doc finished typing his e-mail message, hit 'send' and collapsed out of the chair onto the floor. Felix screamed and reached down to pick him up. Doc's breath was coming in loud, swift intervals. Felix gently lifted Doc off of the floor and laid him on the couch and pleaded, "Doc! Please – point! Where are they? You can't help her if you're dead!"

Felix's words brought consciousness back to Doc long enough for him to point to his pants lying over the edge of the couch. Felix snatched the pants off the couch and searched the pockets frantically. He found the inhaler and shoved it in Doc's mouth. Doc gripped Felix's arm and held on - waiting for Felix to jump-start his lungs. Felix pumped in puff after puff into Doc's wheezing body until he heard a clear, silent breath escape his mouth. Doc released Felix's arm and fell silent onto the wet couch.

Felix stood there, crying … He had urinated all over Doc and the couch in his fear.

He sat down on the edge of the couch and cradled Doc in his arms. He squeezed him close as he realized Doc was getting worse. His attacks were more frequent and longer. The inhalers aren't strong enough. Felix just held Doc and cried. He knew he couldn't live without him. He knew that Doc was his protector; his keeper - and he would kill anyone who tried to harm Doc.

As Felix sat there holding Doc, he realized that if anything ever did happen to Doc, he would just kill himself, and then he would be with Doc again.

The comfort of that thought made Felix feel better. He hugged Doc one last time, checked him to make sure he was breathing; then walked to his room to get dressed.

He had to start cooking the turkey for Thanksgiving dinner.

CHAPTER THIRTEEN

Rick stood inside of the 7-11 and watched the cab drive away. He left the store and started walking down Reston Parkway towards the dark brown townhouse. He was tired; it had been a long night and the pain in his head was excruciating. Each footstep preceded a throbbing jolt through his brain. The pain seared down his spine, which made him limp slightly as he made his way down the sidewalk.

It was a cold Thanksgiving morning and Rick was still wet from the rainy night before. His nose was running but he couldn't wipe it properly because his fingers were numb inside of his black leather gloves. Rick stumbled on a crack in the sidewalk and almost fell. He was weak … He wasn't sure if he could over take the big black beast awaiting him. But he had no choice. He had to kill him. He has to take the dog and dispose of him. Authorities may find out about missing Joe too soon if the dog starts tearing the house apart and is discovered home alone. If Joe and the dog are missing simultaneously, it may seem more like a vacation and nobody is the wiser for at least a week or two. Plenty of time to be long gone, headed to Seattle.

Rick approached the street where Joe used to live. He spotted the dark brown townhouse. He approached it slowly. As he got closer he felt a pair of eyes on him … watching him. He glanced up at the top right window. There, glaring down at him was the beast. Rick kept walking past the dark brown townhouse until he was out of site. He cut around the back of the homes and came up on the house from behind.

He stood at the back door and tried to peer in through a window. He could hear the dog right inside the door growling … waiting for Rick to break in so he could devour him. Rick walked around to the side window. It was hidden behind a large bush. He crawled under the bush and squeezed up in front of the window. He looked down at the latch to see if it was locked. Rick's adrenaline rushed as he saw that the window was not only unlocked … but it was already open about an inch.

He reached down to pull the window up and heard something … He held his breath. Silence … Then he heard it again … A rumbling … he heard a muffled sound and looked down. He noticed a set of fanged, drooling, growling lips right inside of the blinds. The snout of the dog's large head was perched on the windowsill waiting … Waiting for Rick to reach for the window so he could snap his fingers off.

Rick chuckled to himself, 'Bastard, I see you in there." He eased to the side of the window out of the dog's site. Rick dropped the black bag and pulled out the towel filled with chloroform and duct tape. He had to distract the dog long enough to get the window open, and inside without losing an arm or leg. Rick glanced at the arm of his jacket. It was covered with blood … Joe's blood.

He quickly squirmed out of his jacket and propped it against the window with a stick. Rick hid to the side of the window. He held the towel in one hand and the duct tape in the other waiting for the dog's reaction to his master's blood. Nothing. Rick touched the window lightly, and the dog's nose was quickly back up against the window. Growling … then silence. Rick heard a whimper from inside. That was his queue.

Rick snatched the window up so quick and hard it came off the hinges. He dove on top of the dog and grabbed his large head by the mouth. He quickly wrapped the tape round and round his mouth while evading the huge feet flailing under him. Rick took the towel and held it over the dog's face. He had to brace himself against a china cabinet so he could sit on the dog and hold him still until the chloroform took hold.

After what seemed like an eternity to Rick, the beast stopped struggling, and fell limp. The dog had scratched Rick several times on his arm and face and he was bleeding. Shit. More clean up. He released the beast and eased his large head onto the floor. Rick stared at the dog lying there helpless, peaceful, and sleep. He looked a lot less fearful knocked out. He was a handsome dog; black all over with one brown patch of hair in the middle of this chest. His paws were as big as Rick's hands; he stood about 4 feet 9 inches and weighed about 190 pounds, according to Rick's scratches and bruises.

Rick made his way to the window, reached out and pulled his big black bag into the house. He tried to close the window but remembered he had just busted it off the hinges as he cut his finger on the glass. "Shit!"

He reached inside the bag and grabbed the Beretta. He had to kill the dog; it was the only way. Rick walked over clutter and broken glass all over the floor as he made his way towards the big black mass. The television loudly came on and Rick jumped. He looked down and realized he had stepped on the remote control on the floor. The news anchorwoman's voice echoed through the room; "In today's top stories, two bodies were found in the Potomac River this morning. The body of a Caucasian woman, approximately age 45, and an African American male, approximately age 55 was found this morning floating under the Woodrow Wilson Bridge. A car was also found in the river, however police suspect foul play. Cause of death is pending a medical autopsy. Authorities think the two deaths are related. In other news …"

Rick stood frozen for a moment … He picked up the remote and turned the television off. Who the hell was the dead white woman? He killed Joe. Nobody else. Was there a woman's body already in the trunk? Was Joe a killer? Rick's head started pounding loud in his ears, interrupting his thoughts.

Rick, get a grip! You have to kill the dog and get the hell out of town fast! He didn't expect the body to be found so quick. That's fine … a small change in plans; he could manage. Rick walked over to the dog. He had to kill him; but he couldn't kill the dog here.

He'll have to take him with him … kill him and dump him in The Potomac River. Why not breathe your last breath with your master? Rick went looking for a blanket to wrap the dog in and take him from the house. He found a large comforter in a closet and draped it over the dog. Before Rick started rolling the dog up in the comforter, he took the white towel and held it to the dogs nose for a few minutes more. He wanted to make sure the beast was out for the count as he transported him to the truck, and then to his grave. He slowly rolled the comforter around and under the dog's massive body and took one end and started dragging it towards the door.

The front door swung open as Rick bounded out the house pulling the large lumpy bundle to the Explorer parked in front. Rick had left his truck parked there and taken the cab to the survey last night. He knew he would need it now. It was also the perfect story. 'Ole Joe had rented this truck to go hunting with his dog … tragedy strikes and they both end up dead, floating in the Potomac River along with the rented truck. So nostalgic.

Rick put the dog in the back seat of the truck. He jumped in the front seat, started the truck and took off with a screech. He was having an anxiety attack and he couldn't breath. He reached for his phone to call Deb. As soon as his sweaty hand reached his phone it rang in his fingertips. His heart was pounding loud in his chest vibrating through his skull. Rick answered the phone, but he couldn't hear himself say "Hello," so he said it over and over into the receiver.

Rick finally heard a sound, then a voice screaming into his ear as his hearing slowly came back through the pain. The voice was saying, "Rick! Rick! You stupid son-of-a bitch! Listen to me! Get your ass back to your apartment and stay there until you hear from me!" The phone went dead.

Rick pulled his phone back and stared at it ... Was that Deb? It sounded like Deb; who else would be saying those things to him? It was Deb.

Rick swore under this breath, "Dammit man!" She'd seen the news. Rick pounded his fist on the steering wheel and yelled, "I am a stupid son-of-a-bitch! Why did I kill him so fast? It was supposed to last the weekend ... I was too anxious."

He had learned his lesson. He would kill the others quick, like a snake and get it over with. He didn't have the patience to torture.

He regained his bearings and came to an exit. He couldn't remember where he was going. Rick looked around into the back seat and saw the large lumpy carpet moving slowly as the beast slept. It all came back to him. He remembered what Deb had just said ... go straight to his apartment; do not do anything until he hears from her.

He had the black beast in the back seat of his truck.

Rick quickly took the exit towards his apartment. He mumbled and shook his head: "I'll have to take him to my apartment with me ... I'll kill him there."

CHAPTER FOURTEEN

Deb was already on hold, on two different phones making the arrangements. "Yeah, for John Smith, I need a one-way ticket to Seattle, leaving Dulles International first thing in the morning."

She quickly switched back over to her cell phone. "Yeah, make sure the property located at 343 Windward, Sterling VA isn't searched until Wednesday. At that time, I will tell you what you are to find and report to authorities." She quickly switched back over to her home phone. "Thank you, you can fax the flight confirmation to 703-555-2356." Before Deb could hang up the phone, there was a knock at her door.

She stared at the door and slowly hung up her home phone; and held her cell phone to her ear and whispered, "I'll call you back."

Deb sat her cell phone on the table and calmed her thinking. It was Thanksgiving, who the hell was knocking at the door?

She walked over to her front door and looked through the peep hole ... "Fuck ... Hutchison." Deb slowly turned and tiptoed away from the door. She shook her head as she whispered, "Doesn't this guy have any family to spend holidays with?"

Hutchison knocked again, louder.

Deb wasn't going to open the door. She could have a lover over; or what if she was away visiting family; yeah – it was a holiday. She tiptoed further away from the door. She heard a loud voice come booming through the door.

"Shaver, I know you're in there. I've just had your home phone lined traced and I know you're in there on the phone, so open up."

Deb froze in her footsteps. She swung around and gritted, "That bastard is already tracing my phone calls?" She had to get another cell phone.

She slowly walked towards the front door again. Might as well see what the asshole has to say. He isn't going away; and he obviously knows who she was on the phone with.

Deb leaned close to the front door and yelled, "Who is it?" She heard a low grumble of laughter from the other side. She hated his laugh.

She hated his thin little lips and the way they curled up when he was annoying her; which was every time she saw him. She was starting to hate everything about him. She had a quick and sinister thought run across her mind and she caught her breath from the evil of it ... *She could have him killed ...*

Deb! It wouldn't matter. They'd just send another one, and another, and another ...

She unlocked the front door and opened it just enough to stick her face out, "Good morning, happy Thanksgiving." She put on her most appealing smile.

He leaned on the door and pushed it open, running over Deb's foot in the process. "Ouch!" She jumped back holding her toe in her hand.

Hutchison walked into her apartment and closed the door. "Sorry, I didn't see you standing there. Are you alright?" He walked over and grabbed Deb by the arm and helped her to her couch.

He sat down next to her and smiled. "You know, you really should step back when answering the door. One might think they weren't welcome." Deb's fax machine started clicking and spitting ...

Deb broke out in a sweat. The confirmation! Shit!

Hutchison saw Deb start to sweat and turned to watch the fax machine start spitting out a fax. He turned back and looked at Deb, "My, my. Working on the holiday. What a dedicated little cop."

Deb stood up and got his attention as she walked to the other side of the room towards the kitchen. She asked, "Would you like some coffee? I was just about to make me a cup." Hutchison got up and followed her into the kitchen. The fax machine was spitting out paper and as Hutchison walked by he quickly glanced down and looked at the cover sheet. Deb saw him read it, and silently cursed herself.

She quickly got his attention, "So, how do you like it?" She was holding two coffee mugs in her hand. He walked closer to her and grabbed both her wrists in his hands. She was startled and almost dropped the mugs. Deb gripped the mugs tighter and spit out between clinched teeth, "What the hell are you doing?"

Hutchison squeezed Deb's wrists harder, and she dropped the mugs onto the tile floor. They hit the tile with a crash and shattered about their feet. Deb stared up into Hutchison's cold black eyes; the fax machine spitting in the background brought Deb back to grips.

Hutchison grit his teeth and said, "How do I like it? I like it right up front! Everything, right up front!" He yanked on her wrists and she stepped on a piece of glass. He leaned closer and she could smell stale coffee on his breath as he said, "Are you ready to confess and save us both a whole lot of time and energy?"

Deb relaxed in his grip and calmed her breathing … This asshole has nothing solid! He's playing mind games and being a bully!

She let a small grin break through her clinched lips and softly said, "I confess … I think you're an asshole."

Hutchison took Deb's wrists and swung her out of the kitchen onto the carpet on the dining room floor. She bounced off the floor back onto her feet. She bumped up against the wall and took off running down the hallway. Hutchison quickly took off chasing Deb. She ran into her bedroom and locked the door. Hutchison was immediately banging on the bedroom door for a second, then silence. Deb rifled through her drawer and found a gun. She quickly jerked the door open and pointed the gun … Nobody.

She ran down the hall and saw that her front door was open

and Hutchison's car was gone. She spun around and checked the fax machine … Gone! Deb exhaled long and slow. She mumbled, "The fucker took the flight confirmation fax, and left."

She closed her front door and locked it. Deb suddenly felt the pain in her foot and limped over to the couch and sat down. Another long, heavy sigh escaped her lips. She sat the gun on the coffee table and peeled the bloody sock off of her foot. She had stepped on a piece of coffee mug and it was protruding out of the bottom of her heel. As she made her way to the bathroom, visions of Hutchison played across her mind … What kind of tactics was this sick man using on her? One minute she could swear he was coming on to her, the next he was attacking her like she was an escaped criminal.

Deb stopped in her footsteps and thought to herself; "Well Deb, you are a criminal."

She was washing her foot in the tub when her phone started ringing. She didn't want to talk to anyone right now. It was Thanksgiving and she was alone and depressed! She was pulling pieces of coffee mug out of her foot, and the IAD officer investigating her for obstruction of justice at this moment, just got away with a ton of incriminating information. She felt like crying. The phone started ringing again. Deb turned the water off and started rubbing Neosporin on her cuts. The phone kept ringing. She didn't want to talk. If anyone important needed her, they would call on her cell phone.

Deb made her way into the kitchen and started sweeping up the glass. The phone started ringing again. She walked over to the caller ID and looked at the number … Unfamiliar - but local. "No data sent." Deb turned on the answering machine so it would pick up on the next ring. The phone stopped ringing. Deb walked over and started sweeping again. The phone started ringing again. This time, the machine picked up, "Hi, I'm busy, please leave a message. Beep"

Deb heard a man's voice; he was coughing and clearing his throat. Then, a familiar melody croaked out onto the recorder, "Ah, hello Debra. I need to talk to you as soon as possible. Please give me a call at your earliest convenience at 202-987-2345. I'll be awaiting your call … Oh, and by the way – Happy Thanksgiving." The caller hung up, and the recorder beeped finished.

Deb stood there … frozen. She had dropped the broom and was staring at the answering machine … She couldn't believe it … She had to play it back several times.

He wished her Happy Thanksgiving … Her dad had wished her Happy Thanksgiving! She couldn't believe it; he actually said it. He called her himself. Deb remembered the number he called from was local … he was local! He was in the area!

She raced to her bedroom and jumped in the shower. She couldn't call her dad back looking like this!! She had to wash her hair and put on her favorite dress; then she'd be ready to talk to him. She couldn't believe it! He actually said Happy Thanksgiving.

CHAPTER FIFTEEN

Rick pulled the heavy beast up the stairs. He managed to unlock his apartment door and drag the massive dog into his apartment. Rick quickly closed the door and locked it. He stared at the large, bulky bundle in the middle of his living room floor. He quickly realized what he had just done. A cold sweat broke out all over his body and he started hyperventilating as he thought, "Rick, you idiot. You have a drugged, mammoth dog with large teeth locked in your small apartment with you ... When he wakes up, what are you going to do with him?"

Rick quickly picked up the end of the comforter again and started dragging it towards the bedroom. He opened the bedroom door and pulled the dog into the room. He left the dog in the bedroom and closed the door.

Rick felt dizzy and fell against the wall. He slowly made his way back up the hall hoping the beast wouldn't break the door down and eat him while he rested on the couch. He had to decide what the hell he was going to do with the beast. Rick closed his eyes and tried to think through the pain pounding through his head. Why not just kill the dog now?

He couldn't do it. He felt a connection to the big beast that he didn't understand. He didn't want to kill him; he wanted to get to know him. Rick felt nauseated and decided to lie down and try to take a quick nap.

He painfully sought out the remote and turned on the television to look at the news; hoping to find out more about the two bodies found. Nothing. He kept listening and started to slowly doze into a loud, painful sleep. Just as his body was starting to relax, he heard the newsman say, "In recent news, one of the two bodies found early this morning floating under the Woodrow Wilson Bridge has been identified as 45 year old Carmen Balster of Fairfax, Virginia."

Rick jerked his head around to look at the television. There was a picture of the women on the TV. Rick squinted his eyes to get a better look ... She looked familiar, but from where? The newsman continued ... "Balster had attended a local fundraiser on Wednesday and was expected at her sister's house for the holiday. When she didn't arrive her sister called police. Authorities say Balster died from a blow to the head. Police also have an eyewitness linking Balster to the US Geological Survey in Reston, Virginia the night before her death. No word yet on the identity of the man found with Balster. Police suspect foul play. In other news ..."

Rick turned the television off and laid his pounding head on the pillow. Who the hell was the woman, and what eyewitness? An eyewitness linking her to the US Geological Survey ... The survey ... that night ... The woman arguing with the angry man; it was her!

Rick jerked his pounding head off of the pillow and grabbed the TV remote again. He turned the television back on and started flicking through stations, listening to every news broadcast he could find. Finally, the picture of the woman was on the screen again. Rick took a good look ... trying to remember the blurring details from last night. It was dark in the parking lot, and he was quite a distance away from the arguing couple; but he was pretty sure it was her.

Damn. Did the angry man kill her? Did he dump her at the construction site just as Rick had dumped Joe's body?

Did someone see Joe's murder?

Rick pulled his cell phone out of his pocket and dialed Deb. Where the hell is she? She's supposed to be getting me the hell out of here. No answer. I'll just leave her a message. Maybe that's not a good idea. Never know who's checking messages ... Rick tried Deb again; still no answer. Dammit man!

He tried to relax his head back down onto the pillow. He felt his head vibrate on the pillow with each pounding heartbeat. It had started raining again and lightening flickered outside the windows. Rick heard a loud pop, and the electricity went out. Great.

The apartment was pitch black with the occasional flicker of lightening illuminating the room like a broken strobe light. Rick lay there; tired, hungry, and nauseas from the pain pounding between his ears. He eased his breathing down as slow as he could without stopping completely. The blood flowing through his brain slowed down with his breathing, and the pain became more and more quiet.

Rick had to force his eyes closed over his burning eyeballs. He heard voices downstairs; tenants were yelling about the electricity being out. Sirens started filling up the background noise in Rick's mind as he struggled to drift off into a painful sleep. He relaxed his eyes and let the sleep overtake him. He dropped the remote on the floor as he turned to his side on the couch.

Within minutes, Rick's weary body gave in and he started snoring. Visions of the evening filled his dreams. He could see Joe's face as he beat him; feel his blood splatter on his arm as he shot his kneecap off. Rick was reliving the evening in his dreams ... His pain was numb in his dreams as he enjoyed the memories.

He dreamed he heard a yell from downstairs ... then laughter. A woman giggling. It was strange that it sounded familiar. Who is she? A small voice inside of Rick warned him to open his eyes, get up and start packing ... he had to leave town ... so much to do ...

His weary body wasn't moving. Rick was sound asleep.

Last night's events had left him mentally and physically tattered. He slept through the fire alarm in the building next door. He didn't hear a thing. He didn't hear the rustling in the bedroom ... the heavy footsteps on the tile floor, or the scratching on the bedroom door. Rick snored as the heavy footsteps paced the bedroom floor in front of the door. Rick didn't wake up when the loud thud against the bedroom door shook the wall … then another, and another, and another. The bedroom door started to crack.

The thuds continued and turned into a rap song in Rick's dream … a lady was dancing … smiling at Rick. He wanted her …

He tried to dance with the woman, but she became violent. She started hitting Rick in his dream; and each blow was a loud, painful thud on Rick's head. He noticed the woman was holding a large belt with a big metal buckle on the end. She was swinging the belt and hitting Rick in the head with the buckle. Each blow was preceded by a loud thud … over and over again. Finally with one last blow, the buckle cracked Rick's head in two with one final strike!

"Aaaaaah!" Rick jerked his sweaty body off of the couch and tried to stand up. His foot slipped on the tile floor and he fell backwards and hit his head on the corner of the television. His head hit the tile floor and bounced to a stop. His consciousness started diminishing and he felt a cool stream of liquid running down his face. The room was spinning and his tongue was sliding down the back of his throat. A glimpse of lightening flickered through the apartment as Rick gasped for breath. He sucked in enough air to keep his miserable heart pumping slowly.

Rick heard a clicking sound echoing through his brain. Was he dreaming again? He heard it again. Were they footsteps? More clicking … they were footsteps - heavy footsteps. The footsteps were getting louder; coming towards him. The footsteps clicked on the tile floor coming up the hallway like ladies heels … or sharp claws. Rick's eyes strained open as he fought for consciousness. A large dark shadow was blocking the lightening through the window as it flickered the shadow across the wall. The shadow started approaching … Rick's heart started pounding and the blood rushed through this broken skull. The pain sent Rick in and out of consciousness and he fell limp on the tile floor; his head bleeding down the side of this face.

The dark shadow stood directly over Rick's lifeless body … panting, drooling, and annoyed as hell! Wet drool hit Rick's face and he inched one eye open and saw the dog standing above his face looking down at him. The lightening flickered through the apartment and Rick could see the dog was bleeding across his forehead; drizzling drool and blood down on top of Rick. Rick tried to raise his hand to shield his face from the drool. The dog saw movement and leaned close to Rick's face and growled ... The dog's massive head and sharp teeth were inches away from Rick's face. Rick could smell the dog's foul breath as he growled a warning for Rick to stay still. Rick froze; he didn't even breathe.

He thought the dog was going to kill him for killing his master. He was going to die on the floor of this rented apartment. Rick closed his eyes and lay perfectly still. The dog was posed inches away from his face, growling low and gritting his teeth. Rick felt drool and blood dripping on his face from the dog, but he couldn't move. He lay there ... waiting to feel the dog's sharp, jagged teeth enter his neck, puncture his jugular and kill him.

Rick became angry thinking about Roland and Smitty; he had to kill them before his mission was done! Before he could rest his weary soul and die. He couldn't die yet, not yet!

Dog stopped growling at Rick and raised his massive head towards the front door. There was noise in the hallway outside the apartment door. Dog started growling again deep in his chest and stared at the apartment door. Someone was right outside Rick's door. Dog stepped over Rick's body and walked to the front door. Rick tried to turn his head towards the door and look, but as soon as Dog saw movement from Rick, he lunged back towards Rick and threw his head down to growl. In Dog's haste to get to Rick, he slipped on the tile floor and rammed his massive head square into Rick's temple. The collision caused pain in Rick's head that unleashed a series of tremors in his body and he fell limp on the floor again.

Someone was entering the apartment. A key was in the door, and the knob was turning. Dog trotted over to the door and waited behind it. Waiting for the intruder to enter. The apartment door opened slowly and the lightening flickered. Rick inched his eye open and saw a figure standing in the doorway. The big black massive silhouette stood still and silent behind the door, waiting for the intruder to enter. Rick opened his mouth and tried to warn the victim, but his voice wouldn't come out. All that came out was a breathless sigh. The figure in the doorway saw Rick lying on the floor and closed the door. The figure started walking towards Rick. Rick saw the massive black silhouette pounce on the figure and it fell to the floor directly in front of Rick's face.

"AAAAHHHH!" It was a woman's scream. Dog had his mouth wrapped around the woman's arm. She screamed again, "Ricky, Ricky, help meeeee!" It was Sissy.

What the hell was she doing here? And how did she get a key to his apartment?

The landlord.

Sissy was screaming and pulling at the big massive head; trying to get Dog's teeth out of her arm. Dog was pulling her around the corner and down the hallway. Sissy was yelling for Rick to help her while beating the dog with her free arm. Rick couldn't move. His body wouldn't respond to his brain's commands. He heard Sissy's muffled screams as Dog's growling echoed down the hall. Rick heard Sissy coughing and gagging … He knew that sound; she was choking on her own blood. Rick heard clothes ripping and Sissy's grave shrieks and pleadings for Rick to help her continued echoing down the hall. Her last scream ended with a gurgled cough; then silence. Rick heard chewing and crushing bones … Dog was eating her. Rick became nauseas and threw up on himself lying on the cold, hard tile floor. He gagged, choking on his vomit, and passed out.

CHAPTER SIXTEEN

Deb drove home in silence. She had spent Thanksgiving with her Dad for the first time ever. She replayed the day over and over in her head as she drove. Her cell phone was on vibrate and she didn't see or hear it vibrating violently in her purse. Her mindset was to reminisce about the time spent all day with her Dad, for as long as she possibly could before she starts to forget.

It could be another 15 years before she sees him again.

She was so excited after he called! Even Hutchison's thievery couldn't bring her down after that.

Daddy's little girl was finally going to see him again. She was glowing when she saw him standing in the doorway of the warehouse. He looked old and tired. He watched her get out of the car. She was afraid to look at him - to look in his eyes and not see the look ... the way he always looked at her when she was a little girl - like she was his princess.

She had changed. It had been so long. He'd been so distant the last few years. Having other reps call her, having assignments delivered by third parties. He was more clandestine than she could ever remember. What if he didn't love her anymore because of what she'd become?

Deb walked towards her Dad holding her head down. When she was close enough to hear his wheezing breaths, she looked up into his eyes. They were brilliant ... they still lit up for her. His smile was wide and he was holding a tissue as he extended his arms and waited for her to come into his embrace. Deb couldn't wait. She broke out into a run to reach him faster, and grabbed onto him. They held each other.

Felix came to the door and pulled on Doc's arm, "Come, come inside and visit. Dinner is ready to be served."

Doc released Deb and they turned to follow Felix into the warehouse. Felix closed the door behind them and said, "Hello Debra, Happy Thanksgiving."

Deb turned to Felix and smiled, "Thank you Felix, it's good to see you."

Felix served dinner to Deb and Doc at the dining table. He blessed the dinner; then disappeared with his plate into the back room.

Deb felt like the intruder and said, "Dad, he doesn't have to eat in there; why won't he join us?"

Doc took a bite of turkey and said, "Debra dear, Felix knows that I have some business to discuss with you and he is giving us our privacy. Plus dear, don't you want private time? We haven't seen each other in over ten years."

Deb gave up on longing for 'private time' with her Dad a long time ago ... what's he up to?

She smiled at her Dad and said, "Private time Daddy? How long has it been since you used those words?"

Doc put his fork down and searched his pocket for his inhaler. It had been about 20 years since he had 'private time' with Debra. Where did the time go? He looked at her; a successful law enforcement officer, and a beautiful woman he didn't even know. He had turned her life into something he never wanted for his princess. He had used her, and turned her into something she was ashamed of; he saw it in her eyes. He was afraid she would pay the price for his crimes. His chest became tight and he started wheezing, holding back tears.

Deb saw his distress, "Daddy, it's alright. Where is your inhaler?" She got up from the table and tried to help him search his shirt pocket. He pushed her hand away and pointed to the nightstand near the couch. Deb rushed over to the table and searched the drawer. She found the inhaler and handed it to Doc. He puffed the inhaler until his breathing was stable.

Deb slowly walked back to her chair and sat down. She stared at Doc as he put the inhaler in his shirt pocket, and he slowly matched her gaze, "Debra darling, I'm not going to lie to you and tell you that everything's alright. It isn't." Doc took a drink from his glass of wine and continued, "Debra, I'm not proud of what I have subjected you to over the years, and I'm sorry."

Deb cut in and said, "Daddy you don't have to …" Doc put his hand up and said, "Debra, please … let me finish."

Deb anxiously sat back in her chair and struggled to stay silent as her Dad was preparing to make some revelation she wasn't sure she wanted to hear.

Doc looked at his princess and continued, "Debra darling, Daddy's gotten you into a difficult situation and I think your assignment with Rick may be too much for you to deal with right now. I want to take the assignment and give it to someone else until you get through your investigation."

She was crushed. She was humiliated. He didn't think she could handle it! Deb tried to hold back her disappointment and said, "Doc … what have I done wrong? Why are you pulling me off the assignment? Yeah, Hutchison is pressing me hard, but I can handle him."

Doc's tense voice abruptly cut in, "Hutchison? They've already put someone on you?"

Deb hesitated, and said "Yeah, Lt. Hutchison. He's harmless Daddy; a bully."

Doc grit his teeth and said, "Has he put his hands on you?"

She saw the anger welling up in her fathers' eyes. She became fearful for Hutchison's life if she answered the question truthfully. She stuttered, "Well, yes – I mean no; not exactly."

Doc reached over and clutched Deb's hands in his. He gently started rubbing them. His large, warm, hairy hands rubbing hers made memories flash deep in her heart. Doc smiled at his princess and said, "Debra darling, I'm sure this … Hutchison is only trying to do his job the best he knows how. But please understand how important it is for me to know everything that Hutchison does; and says."

Doc's large hairy, hands slowly came to a stop and cupped Deb's hands hard and firm. She winched in pain. Doc pulled her close and angrily seethed out from his wheezing throat, "Now tell me Debra darling, has Hutchison put his hands on you in any inappropriate manner?"

Deb's fingers were turning purple from the pressure of Doc's grip. She started crying and whimpering, "Daddy, Daddy; I'm sorry! I'm sorry! Yes, yes; Hutchison has roughed me up!"

Deb was pulling on her hands, trying to get them out of his vice grip. Doc was silent, and started to slowly wheeze. Deb whimpered, "Daddy please; let me show you."

He finally let Deb pull her hands away. She pulled up her shirtsleeves and showed her father the bruises from Hutchison's grip on her wrists. She took off her shoe and sock and showed her father the slashes in the bottom of her foot from the coffee mugs he made her drop. She raised her pant leg up and showed him the bruise on her leg from hitting the floor when Hutchison threw her out of the kitchen.

Doc was wheezing loud and pointing to the floor. He had dropped his inhaler on the floor and couldn't reach it. Deb ran over to the chair, reached under and grabbed the inhaler. As she helped her father puff and regain his breath, she became angry.

Why should she worry about Hutchison's life … look what crooked cops had done to her father … to her family. Deb knew Hutchison probably beat up all of his culpable suspects, and he probably deserves whatever comes his way. Besides, Deb was secretly relieved now that Doc knew. Deb herself had illicitly wanted Hutchison dead on one or more occasions. Why not just be done with the asshole once and for all?

She slowly walked back to her chair to sit. She added, "Oh, and that's not all Daddy ... Hutchison paid me a visit right before you called this morning. He got away with a confirmation fax from the airline confirming Rick's flight to Seattle. He threw me around and I ran in my bedroom to get my gun. When I came out he was gone and so was my fax." Deb sat down and watched her father take several puffs from the inhaler.

When he had enough breath in his lungs to yell, he yelled, "Felix!!!" Deb heard noise from the back room and then the door swung open.

Felix stood there out of breath and staring at Doc, "Yes, yes, yes Doc. What is the matter?" Felix slowly started walking towards the table.

Doc took another puff and said, "Felix; I'm sorry I startled you, and I'm sorry I have to interrupt your delicious dinner, but could you please go and prepare the car. We're going on an errand."

Felix nodded his head and turned to walk away. He looked at Deb and said, "It was nice seeing you again Ms. Debra, and I hope we see each other again." He turned and left the warehouse.

As Deb drove home and reminisced about the evening, she couldn't stop speculating about whom her father had rushed off to meet; and what was he going to do to Hutchison? Would Hutchison simply disappear or would he suddenly become her best friend and leave her alone?

Deb pulled in front of her apartment and grabbed her purse. Her phone fell out and she picked it up and saw the 'missed call' flashing. She realized her phone was on vibrate the entire day. Damn.

She pushed the button and saw that she had missed 5 calls from Rick. "Shit! Can this day get any more fucked up?" Deb started feeling sick and thought to herself, "Calm down ... you spent the majority of Thanksgiving Day with your Dad. Please, keep enjoying that for a little while longer, please!"

She got out of her car and limped as she walked to her front door. Her bruises were stiff and sore from the drive. Deb entered her apartment and flopped down onto the couch. She reached into her purse and checked her phone again. She didn't want to call Rick yet. She wanted to shower and relax for just a few minutes before she had to climb back into the world of unlawful activity.

She just wanted to replay the day over with her father one more time … just once more.

Deb sat on the couch, her coat still wrapped around her, and she closed her eyes. She started to replay it again.

She was so excited after his call …

CHAPTER SEVENTEEN

The noise was annoying Rick, and it made his headache feel like a freight train going through his skull. He couldn't find it … where was it coming from? It's ringing … it was a cell phone. He tried to answer his phone, but every time he picked it up to speak, it kept ringing. It just kept ringing, and ringing … Rick couldn't stop it, couldn't make the loud ringing stop. His head started pounding louder than the ringing. He couldn't take it. He opened his mouth and heard himself yell out "Stop!"

Rick opened his eyes, and quickly shut them again. The light sent a stab of pain through his bruised skull lying on the cold tile floor … Why was he laying on the tile floor? He prepared himself for the pain, and slowly inched his eyes back open. He was in his living room lying flat on his back on the tile floor. His head pounded profusely at the back of his noggin right where his head lay on the floor. He tried to move his arm. It worked. He reached for the table and pulled himself up. He sat on the floor and felt his head where it was tight. There was a clot of dried blood in his head … he bumped his head? He didn't remember.

He put his face in his hands and exhaled. What happened last night? He didn't remember driving back to his apartment; he didn't remember anything.

Then slowly; the pictures in his brain started coming together. He started to remember …

He remembered … The DOG!

Rick's cell phone started ringing again. He grabbed it out of his pocket and quietly whispered into the phone, "Hello?"

Rick heard Deb's voice yell into the phone, "Where the hell have you been? I've been calling you all morning."

Rick sat perfectly still and peeked in the corner, looking for the big black mass to pounce on him and eat him up. A vivid picture of Dog pulling Sissy down the hall flashed in his memory and it came back to him ... Dog ate Sissy.

He wondered if there's anything left of her? Rick couldn't help but smirk to himself, "I bet even Dog didn't eat that pussy."

Rick checked to see if he could move his legs. He heard Deb yell into the phone again, "Rick, are you there?" Rick whispered back into the phone, "Deb, Deb calm down. I'm in trouble."

Deb let out a long sigh, and said "What kind of trouble Rick?"

Rick crawled over to the couch and pulled himself up. He flattened himself up against the wall in the corner of the living room. He whispered into the phone, "Deb, you know Joe's big ass dog? Well he's in my apartment running loose and I saw him kill someone last night, in my apartment and I think I'm next."

Deb screeched into the phone, "Rick! What the hell is the dog doing alive ... in your apartment?

Rick nervously peered around the room and whispered, "Deb ... you gotta get me out of here. I'm hurt and I'm not sure I can fly."

Deb yelled into the phone, "That's why I've been calling you Rick. I've booked you on a train out of Union Station at 2:00 pm this afternoon. You'll take the train to New York and we'll fly you out from there. When you get to New York someone will be holding a sign reading "Mr. Smith." That's you."

Rick whispered into the phone, "Deb ... I need help with the dog. I don't know where he is, but I don't think he broke the window and jumped two stories. He's in the apartment still, and I think I might need some help getting out alive."

Rick heard the frustration in Deb's voice as she said, "I'll send someone right over, but your ass better be on that train at 2:00, or I'll kill you myself!" The phone went dead.

Rick slowly put his phone in his pocket and looked around the corner into the kitchen. Nothing. He turned around and looked towards the hallway. A bloody handprint was smeared down the wall. Rick tipped across the living room towards the hallway, glancing behind him with each step forward. He saw the truck keys on the floor and reached down to pick them up. When Rick stood back up he had a large rack of sharp teeth growling right in front of him. Dog stared at Rick with his big black eyes; waiting for Rick to make a move. Rick didn't breathe.

Dog took a step towards Rick and opened his large mouth. Rick braced himself for the pain; of feeling large sharp teeth enter into his skin. Dog put his large mouth around Rick's wrist, but instead of breaking his skin, he gently pulled on Rick's arm. He wanted Rick to follow him.

Rick allowed himself to be pulled by Dog. He thought to himself, "As long as he isn't chewing on my ass, I'll do whatever he wants!" Dog pulled him to the front door of the apartment and released his wrist. Dog stood and barked one time, loud.

The loud bark echoed through the apartment and it made Rick wince in pain. Rick stood there, bewildered – looking at the killer blocking the door. Dog wanted Rick to take him out for a walk! You must be kidding …

Dog darted back and forth in front of Rick, playfully raising up on his hind legs and bumping into Rick with his massive head. Rick tried to relax and hide his fear from the killer he saw in the eyes of the Dog even now; in his playful mode.

Rick could still see the killer.

He admired Dog's strong quality of character - a natural killer. He suddenly felt a deep, strange connection to the Dog. And the way he was prancing around, looking like an overgrown mammoth puppy made Rick break out into a smile. Dog saw Rick smile and gave another quick, loud bark.

Rick decided to call him "Dog." He said, "Ok Dog. Calm down."

He glanced down at his attire ... he was a mess. Not to mention he had a large dried blood clot on the side of his head, his clothes were splattered with blood and he smelled like dead body. He couldn't go out like this. Then he looked at Dog – he had a large bloody gash in his forehead, blood splattered down his black mane ... lots and lots of blood ... whose blood?

Rick suddenly remembered Sissy. He turned to walk towards the hallway where he last saw her. Before he could take his second step, Dog had pounced in front of Rick blocking his path. Dog lifted his lips and showed his teeth. He didn't growl at Rick, but he hissed in between clinched teeth as drool fell to the floor. Rick stopped walking and stood still ... He moaned, "This Dog is whack!"

Rick slowly eased around and stepped slowly back towards the door. Dog ran in front of Rick and started prancing again like a little puppy. Rick reached for the doorknob. Dog rammed his mammoth head into Rick's side, pushing him to move faster so they could get outside.

Rick became paranoid ... What if this big black monster just wants me to open the door and let him out? Then kill me once he gets outside! Rick stopped and looked down at the beast. Dog's tongue was hanging out the side of his mouth and he was prancing playfully watching Rick reach for the door. Dog didn't look like he was ready to kill - he had the look Rick remembered seeing on Dog's face when he was with Joe ... when they were playing and going for a walk. Dog stopped prancing and rammed his head into the side of Rick's leg and let out a quick, loud bark again.

When Rick didn't open the door, Dog lifted his lips and showed teeth again and this time, he growled low and close to Rick's leg. Rick could feel Dog's hot breath beating against his leg as he growled and hissed drool all over him.

He had no choice, he had to open the door or fight. And if he lost, Rick knew his fate would be watching Dog eat him alive - a fate that made him tremble.

Rick slowly turned the doorknob. Dog started prancing again, anticipating the door opening. Rick's head was pounding loud in his ears and he didn't hear the door click open. Dog heard the click and rammed his massive head into the crack in the door. The door ripped out of Rick's hand and swung open. Dog ran out the door and bolted down the stairs. His massive head rammed into the apartment building front door at the bottom of the stairs. The door banged open and Dog ran outside.

Rick stood there holding the apartment door open. He didn't know what to do; there was a killer running lose with large teeth. He had just let him loose, and there was nothing he could do about it.

Rick released the door and ran out of the apartment and down the stairs. He pushed the building door open and ran outside. He looked right, left - no Dog. Rick heard a scream on the left side of the building. He ran in the direction of the scream and found an old women standing against a tree holding her heart. Rick ran up to her, "Ma'am, what happened?"

The old women pointed up the hill and said, "Large dog ... not on a leash ... no master ... running wild."

Rick ran up the hill and scanned the courtyard. He spotted Dog taking a large shit in front of the Apartment Leasing office. Rick bent over and put his hands on his knees, gasping as he caught his breath. He raised his head and looked at the beast. He shook his pounding head, "Now what do I do?"

He had to calm his breathing and quiet the pain rushing through his skull; and find a way to get the beast back in the apartment. Rick eased his body up and exhaled, "Do I want him back in the apartment? What am I going to do with him? I should have killed him at the townhouse!"

Dog was finished shitting and spotted Rick watching him. Dog turned and started trotting towards Rick. A loud voice yelling from the building made Dog jump and turn around. Rick saw the landlord's bald pointed head poking out of the office door yelling, "You better fucking pick that pile of shit up and take care of it! That's the law buddy, you have to clean up or pay up!"

Dog started growling and walking slowly towards the Landlord. Rick smiled to himself and thought, "So, the Dog doesn't like him either. Why don't we pay Mr. Landlord loudmouth a visit?"

Rick called to Dog, "Dog! Wait!" Dog stopped walking and stood still. His teeth were clinched and his breath was hissing in and out through his sharp teeth.

Rick yelled to the Landlord, "Sorry Sir, I was just on my way to check out. I'm leaving this afternoon." Rick stood in front of the office door with Dog at his side. The Landlord didn't open the door any wider and yelled back at Rick, "You … you're not supposed to have animals in the units! You'll have to pay extra!"

Rick smiled and said, "Could I come in and take care of my bill and check out?" The Landlord glared at Rick and Dog. He grumbled, "Wait just minute." He disappeared inside of the office.

Rick stood beside Dog and looked down at him. It was amazing! Dog had actually obeyed his command, and waited for him. Rick felt a sordid sense of power that made his chest swell.

His mind was racing to construct a plan to take care of the sniveling, conniving Landlord, and get the hell out of town on the 2:00 train.

And … Get rid of Dog?

Rick put his hand to the door and Dog leaned forward waiting to enter. Rick said, "Stay Dog – I'll be right back after I take care of … something."

Dog looked up at Rick, showed his teeth and hissed stinky breath through his mouth. Dog didn't want to wait outside; he was glaring through the door, staring down the Landlord.

Rick suddenly got an idea … *Let Dog kill the Landlord.*

Rick opened the door and walked in the office with Dog at his side. The Landlord looked up from his desk and screamed, "You can't have that animal in here! He has to wait outside!"

Rick leaned down to Dog's ear and whispered, "Hold him."

Dog pounced on top of the Landlord's desk and tackled him onto the floor. The Landlord started screaming for help. Rick ran to the front door, glanced out the window and pulled the blinds. He locked the door and put the "Closed" sign in the window.

He slowly walked back over to Dog standing on top of the Landlord. The Landlord cried out to Rick, "Please, get him off me – please! I'll let your bill slide and you owe me nothing! Just please, get him off me and leave!"

Rick bent down and calmly said, "Did you give my cell phone number and apartment key to a fat, ugly whore?"

The Landlord whimpered, "What? No, no, I swear! I haven't given anything to anybody!"

Rick looked at Dog and said, "Dog; he's lying to me. Why is he doing that?"

In an instant, Dog's head dropped and bumped Rick out of the way. Dog's mouth was wide with his teeth wrapped around the Landlord's neck. His teeth punctured the Landlord's neck slightly and a small stream of blood started flowing onto the floor. Rick was astonished … the Dog knew exactly what he wanted him to do! How can that be?

Rick leaned down close to the Landlord again and said, "Now, you want to tell me the truth this time?"

The Landlord started crying and gurgled out, "I'm sorry, she said she was a relative and wanted to surprise you! She took me in the back and gave me some head and promised she wouldn't tell you it was me! I'll kill that slut!"

Rick stood back up and said, "Too late; the bitch is already dead … just like you mother-fucker!" The Landlord started yelling again.

Rick walked over to the door and glanced out the window. He calmly said over his shoulder, "Kill him Dog."

Rick heard Dog growling low and teeth clicking; the Landlord's gurgled screams turned into sounds of flesh being torn. Rick turned and dared to take a step towards the desk to watch Dog kill. He saw the Landlord trying to struggle, but that only made Dog angrier. Rick walked back to the window to peek out again, then turned and walked back towards the desk. He could see Dog jerking the Landlord's bloody body back and forth like a rag doll. Dog's teeth were embedded in the back of the Landlord's neck. Dog swung his head from side to side ripping his neck open. Blood was splattering all over the walls and furniture. Rick remembered the bloody picture Joe's kneecap left on the trailer wall … He smiled - bloody revenge was a very pleasing scene.

Dog's massive head was still swinging back and forth, tearing the Landlord apart from head to toe. Finally with one last jerk, Dog ripped the Landlord's head from his body.

Rick couldn't believe his eyes. Dog swung his massive head and tossed the Landlords bloody head into the back wall and it thumped onto the soggy floor. Dog turned his head and looked at Rick. Rick broke out into a sweat, the small office was hot and the smell of flesh and bloody dog breath brought vomit up Rick's throat. He gagged and the pain in his head exploded like a cannon blasting through the top of his skull.

He ran to the door and peered out the window. All clear. He felt heat on the side of his body and he looked down. Dog was standing there; his mouth open, calmly breathing on Rick. Dog pushed his huge head into the side of Rick's leg, prompting him to open the door so they could leave. Rick turned and looked over his shoulder at the bloody mess.

He opened the door and Dog trotted out and turned around with a jump to wait for Rick. Rick locked the door and closed it behind him. Dog started bouncing up and down on his front legs and darting in front of Rick. Rick reached his hand out and Dog trotted over to him. He reached down and for the first time, he petted the beast on top of his head. Rick smiled and said, "Good boy!"

Dog let out a quick loud bark, and took off down the hill. Rick watched Dog turn around and yelp for him to follow. Rick ran after him. They frolicked and played on the way back down the hill and into the apartment building, like they were master and pet.

CHAPTER EIGHTEEN

Deb paced her apartment as she held the line, waiting for the rep to get the information and get back on the phone. Her cell phone was vibrating out of control in her pocket, but she couldn't hang up until she had the information. The monotone female voice finally broke the silence and said, "Shaver?"

Deb tried to keep her voice calm, "Yes, Shaver here."

"Shaver, we sent the package to you last week ... You didn't get it?"

Deb let out a long frustrated sigh and said, "If I had the package would I be sitting here asking you for the fucking information! Time is of the fucking essence here so could you please just give me the name and number of the contact in New York!"

Deb heard shuffling and the phone dropped on the other end. Finally the voice was back, "Yes, I have it here ... I could fax ..."

Deb cut the rep off, "NO! No more faxes; just please read me the name and number and I'll take it from there. Thank you. Thanks for your assistance."

The rep started again, "Ok, the contact is Robert Walden, and his cell phone contact number is ..."

Deb cut the rep off again, "Wait ... Did you say Robert Walden? Is he the little asshole pizza owner from Philly?"

Deb heard silence on the other end, "Hello? Did you hear me?"

The monotone voice hesitantly replied, "...Well ... I'm not sure."

Deb's cell phone was vibrating again and she was becoming irritated, "Listen, never mind; what's the number?"

"The contact's cell phone number is 555-722-3355. He's waiting for your call. His code is Mozzarella."

Deb hung up the phone. Shit! She has to work with that little asshole pizza maker from Philly. She remembered working with him a few years ago on a blackmail to confess case. He was arrogant and hard to work with.

Rick was not going to get along with this guy.

She couldn't let Rick be escorted to Seattle by Robert Walden; Walden can't handle Rick's case. Deb reached in her pocket to find her cell phone. She had to get in touch with ...

Before she reached her cell phone it was vibrating again. She grabbed her cell and looked at the number. It was Rick. She quickly answered, "Hey, what's up? Where are you?"

Rick answered, "Hey Deb, I'm in a cab on my way to Union Station. There's something I need to tell you ... where've you been, I've been calling you for over an hour."

Deb's heart started pounding loud in her chest and she felt lightheaded; "Rick, What do you have to tell me?" Her mind started racing; what the hell has he done now?

Rick purred into the phone, "Well Deb, remember that bimbo I told you about that recognized me? Well, let's just say she won't be recognizing anybody else, ever again ..."

There was a silent pause on the other end, so Rick quickly continued ... "She's splattered all over the apartment. Dog killed her and ate parts of her and puked the rest back up. But the only reason she got ate, is because the stupid ass Landlord gave her a key to my apartment. So; when I went to check out today - Dog killed the Landlord too."

There was still silence on the other end of the phone. Rick inhaled deep, and added, "I think you need to send someone to clean up the apartment and the Leasing office quick, fast and in a hurry cause it's a bloody mess."

Rick exhaled long and slow. He felt so much better now that he had that off his chest. He heard a clank on the other end, and purred into the phone again, "Deb, Sweetie; you there? Did you get all that?"

Deb had dropped the phone and was puking into her kitchen sink. She slowly picked the phone back up and said, "Rick … can you possibly make this assignment any more tragic? You are leaving dead bodies all over the damn city! How do you expect to accomplish your mission if you keep getting sloppy! You're going to get both of us killed or put away for life!"

Deb paused to lurch into her sink again and vomit; then continued, "Rick! You get your ass to Union Station, get your ticket from Will Call and have your black ass on the 2:00 to Penn Station, do you hear me!"

Rick was silent … He knew he had fucked up, but Deb was freaking out. She continued screaming, "There will be a man waiting for you with a sign reading Mr. Smith. You approach him and say, 'Mozzarella'!"

Rick couldn't help it; he busted out laughing into the phone. "Wait, wait, wait, Deb … Mozzarella? People are going to look at me like I'm crazy!" He continued laughing into the phone.

Deb weakly stood there listening to Rick laugh as she admitted she thought the password was silly when she heard it. Her lips curled up slightly and she silently laughed with Rick.

The laughter made Rick's head pound louder, so he eased to a stop.

Deb walked over to her couch and gently relaxed her body down in a slouch. She said, "Rick, you're going to have to start controlling yourself and get back on track, I mean it. This guy you're meeting, Robert Walden; he's a real asshole and you're going to have to work with him on the trip to Seattle; he's your contact. You can't call me while you're there other than extreme emergency."

Rick let out a sigh, and said "I'm sorry Deb, I know I've been a smoking gun the entire time here in Virginia; but it's over and I'm getting the hell out of dodge!"

Anxiety made Rick's breathing labored as he said, "One down, and two to go … any news on Mr. Smitty?"

Deb whispered into the phone, "Yeah Rick, I do. He's here in Virginia … he never left. Which brings us to our next predicament … How to get you back to Virginia quietly after three dead bodies?"

She realized Rick didn't elaborate on the dead victims, and hissed into the phone, "So, what happened? Why did you have to kill the girl and the landlord?"

Rick quickly responded, "Deb, I swear – it wasn't me. It was Dog! He's a killer." Rick quietly added "…like me." He paused, reluctant to tell Deb the whole truth. She would freak out if she knew the whole truth - that he didn't get rid of the Dog.

On the tail-end of Rick's thought, Deb said, "Well, we don't have to worry about that beast anymore! What did you do with the dog's body?"

Pain surged through Rick's eye sockets as he squeezed his eyes shut; trying to gather the lie he was about to tell … "I shot him and threw his body into the Potomac River … with his master."

Deb said, "Well, I guess we can work with that … master and dog robbed, shot and left for dead while on hunting trip."

Rick was relieved by Deb's response. She bought the story. That would buy him some time for now. He didn't want to freak her out anymore at the moment; there were other things he wanted to discuss right now. He said, "So, what's the story on this Walden dude? Is he capable of handling this or what?"

Deb sighed and said, "Well, I was just about to make a phone call on that, but it's way too late to get someone else. And anyway, after all of your fuck-ups, I hesitate to ask for anything more than necessary."

Rick was silent. Deb continued, "So, to answer your question, Walden is competent, but he lacks people skills. He is very hard to get along with."

It was Rick's turn to sigh, "Aw Deb! You mean I have to travel and work with some little asshole the entire time? I can smell disaster, especially with this 'Mozzarella' shit already!"

Deb gritted into the phone, "Look Rick! You've left a horrible mess here for me to clean up, and have back to normal for your return trip. So you better play nice and cooperate while in Seattle! Now this Walden isn't that bad. He owns a pizza joint in Philadelphia, and has been with the Method for over 19 years. He's 5'5, black with dread-locks; four gold teeth in the front of his mouth."

Rick knew he wouldn't like him already; he'd made his mind up.

Deb sighed, "He's a bit paranoid and insists on the password thing, go with it Rick. When you see him with the sign, walk up to him and say the password and greet him as Mr. Smith."

Rick started sighing again, "So Deb, you've hooked me up with a short, ghetto Rastafarian who has a pizza fetish?"

Deb started feeling queasy again and sat up. She said, "Look Rick, if you cooperate and stay cool; this will be over in no time. You can be back here wrapping up this assignment; and you can go and start your new life - or whatever this mission will accomplish for you. We'll never have to have another conversation again. So please, do what you are told with no complications, you got that?"

Rick was quiet. He finally said into the phone, "Thanks Deb. Yeah, I got it. I'll call you when I'm on my way back to Virginia."

Deb abruptly said, "Don't rush; take your time." Rick's phone went dead. She had hung up.

Rick leaned back in the cab and tried to ease the pounding in his head. He figured they'd reach Union Station in about 10 minutes and he had to calm his head so he could deal with phase II of his plan. He was on his way to find and confront Mr. Roland Hoffman; and kill him.

Thoughts of Roland painfully dying brought comfort to Rick, and his head calmed down. The thought of having two down with one to go was even more relaxing to Rick. He calmed his head, and the pain allowed him to play with sleep for the next 8 minutes as the cab approached Union Station.

CHAPTER NINETEEN

Deb's desk phone was ringing off the hook. None of her colleagues dared to answer it … they knew who it was. Captain had been looking for Deb for over 15 minutes. He came yelling down the hall, "Where the hell is Shaver?"

No one answered. Everyone was busy trying to act like they didn't hear the Captain's question. Word had gotten around quick that Lt. Debra Shaver was being investigated by Internal Affairs; they wanted nothing to do with her. The Captain glared at everyone in sight and said, "The first person to see her better send her immediately to me!" He turned and stormed back to his office.

Deb heard it all as she hid behind the door of the ladies' room. She had been throwing up uncontrollably for the last 20 minutes and hadn't been able to make it back to her desk. She took a deep breath and slowly came out of the bathroom and made her way to her desk. No one spoke to her; they just stared at the green complexion on her face. Deb slowly sat at her desk and pulled her desk drawer open and looked at the little white stick once again. Positive. She was pregnant. How could she have let this happen? How! She shook her head in disgust and answered herself … She was stressed out by IAD, Rick and his dead bodies strung out all over Northern Virginia … seeing her Dad … missing her pill three times last month … and fucking Carlito without a condom … that's how.

Deb felt a shadow standing next to her desk. She quickly put the stick back in her desk drawer and looked up. It was Walter from the mailroom - with a message. Deb cautiously glanced around the office, and said, "Yes Walter, good morning."

Walter smiled and looked over his glasses at her. He said, "Excuse me Ms. Shaver, but I have a package for you."

Walter dropped a brown envelope on Deb's desk and handed her the clipboard to sign. Deb reached for the clipboard and noticed the message near her name. It read, "Confirmed; two tickets to New York, with a connection to Seattle. Arriving two days from today."

Deb quickly scribbled her name next to the message and handed it back to Walter.

Walter smiled again at Deb and said, "Thanks Ms. Shaver. You might want to wipe your mouth off before you see Captain." He turned and walked away from Deb's desk and started pushing his mail cart down the hall. Deb took out her compact and looked in the mirror. Ugh! She had dried vomit wiped across her chin. Lovely.

She quickly wiped her face off, put the brown envelope in her desk and locked it. She stood up and started her long journey to Captain's office. She started thinking about the message ... two tickets? Who the hell was traveling with Rick? He said the bimbo was dead; did he pick up another one? Maybe the message meant two tickets after reaching New York. No, it said two tickets to New York ... Deb broke out into a sweat and she felt vomit collecting at the bottom of her throat. Not again!!! She didn't have anything left to throw up!

She darted into the ladies room, ran to the stall and opened her mouth. Projectile vomit was racing up her throat and onto the walls, onto her pants and onto the floor. She missed the toilet. She stood there bent over, trying to catch her breath. Sweat was dripping from her forehead onto the floor. After a long pause, she stood up and opened the stall door. As she slowly made her way to the sink, she heard a loud growl outside, "Where the hell is Shaver?" Deb wanted to cry. And that's just what she did.

She stood there crying into the mirror, wiping her face off and trying to get the vomit off of her pants. The ladies room door swung open and Lt. Marlowe ran in. "Shaver, you better get your ass out here! Captain is threatening everyone looking for you!"

Deb continued crying and wiping her dirty pants, "Marlowe, I can't right now; I'm a mess!"

Marlowe walked closer to Deb and put her arm around her, "Shaver, it's alright. Things are never as bad as you think they are. Now, get yourself together, and I'll go out and tell Captain I found you and that you'll be in his office in 5 minutes."

The sounds of voices yelling in the hallway made Marlowe turn and run out the door. Deb stood there looking at her red swollen eyes, her pasty complexion, and stained, smelly pants.

She blew her nose on a tissue and leaned on the sink. She closed her eyes and tried to convince herself that her entire life was just a dream. That all of her painful childhood was just a movie, and that she was a happy little girl bouncing on her father's lap. She squeezed her eyes shut harder as she imagined herself growing up and marrying a handsome, successful man and having a family. As Deb stood there with her eyes shut, daydreaming about the way she desperately wanted her life to be, she heard the ladies room door open again. No footsteps this time ... no one came in but Deb could hear the noise in the hallway.

She inched one eye open and saw the Captain standing in the doorway, glaring silently at her. He cocked his head sideways and said, "What? Are you in a fucking coma in here? Get your ass to my office NOW!" He turned and walked away as the door slowly swung shut.

Deb stood there a moment longer, then turned and started towards the door. She opened it slowly and walked out. She headed straight towards Captain's office not looking at anyone. She kept her head down and eyes to the ground. If she looked up she feared she would vomit from motion sickness. Deb cursed herself, "What the hell kind of baby is growing inside of me?"

She reached the Captain's office and stopped at the door. She wasn't ready to open the door and enter. Deb heard a voice from inside, "Well don't just stand there, get your ass in here!"

Deb took a deep breath and then regretted it. The smell of burnt popcorn somewhere in the building caused vomit to collect in her stomach again and it gurgled at the bottom of her esophagus. She swallowed mouthfuls of spit trying to keep it down. She opened the door and entered.

Captain stood behind his desk gulping on a cup of coffee. He pointed to the chair in front of his desk. "Sit down. I've been looking for you all morning!"

Deb inched over to the chair and lowered herself slowly down into it. The vomit gurgled louder in her stomach, fighting to be released.

Captain got up and walked around his desk. He slowly started pacing behind Deb's chair. He barked from behind her head, "I got subpoenaed yesterday for a deposition!" He paced to the other side of Deb's head and added, "They want to interrogate me regarding a certain Lieutenant named Shaver!" Captain paced back to the other side of Deb's head and added, "They're particularly interested in activities regarding Fedcure." Captain stopped directly behind Deb and yelled, "What the hell is going on Shaver?"

Deb jumped at his voice and the vomit she was holding at bay at the bottom of her esophagus came rushing up her throat and filled her mouth. She tried to swallow it back down, but when her tongue tasted the hot liquid her body pushed the vomit out of her mouth and onto the Captain's desk.

Captain's mouth flew open. He bent over and yelled down to Deb puking on his desk, "What the hell is wrong with you Shaver?" He ran over to his desk and tried to salvage some of his paperwork that wasn't covered in puke. Deb continued to cough and puke. She turned away from the desk and grabbed the garbage can.

Captain grabbed some papers off his desk and vomit got on his hand and oozed down his shirtsleeve. He tried to wipe it off but it got on his other hand. He felt it slide up his arm and settle in his armpit.

The smell of the vomit started engulfing the office and Captain felt his stomach lurch.

Before Deb could catch her breath she saw Captain rush out of his office. She heard his voice from the hallway, "Get the hell out the way I need to get to the ..."

Deb sat there in the chair holding the garbage can full of puke. She glanced at Captains desk and saw the mess she had made. She shook her head in disgust. How had all of this come about? She stared blankly into space as her stomach settled. She put the garbage can back on the floor and started picking up some of the papers. She noticed her name scrawled across the top of a folder. She opened it.

It was information about her; her bank account; her cell phone records; her doctor's address; Carlito's address! Deb's heart started pumping loud and her blood rushed through her body as she turned the pages of the file. She saw pictures. Pictures of her; at the grocery store; at the post office; at Starbucks ... the morning she met Rick!

Deb closed the file and held it close to her body. She got up and walked to the office door. She slowly opened the door and peeked down the hall. She entered the hallway and walked quickly past her desk, down the stairs and out the front door. She ran to the end of the block. She didn't know where the hell she was going but she had to get out of the building. She had to get away. She stood at the corner waiting for the light to change. She tried to catch her breath and figure out what she was doing.

It doesn't matter that she took the file from Captain. They probably have several copies in all the right hands right now, plotting how to take down a corrupt lady cop. But she wasn't corrupt! She was only trying to correct an already corrupt legal system! Did that include revenge? Fucking A!

The light changed and Deb started crossing the street. When she reached the other side, she reached in her pocket and grabbed her cell phone. She dialed and waited for an answer. A tired, raspy voice answered, "Hello."

Deb was silent for a moment, not knowing what to say. The voice answered again, more annoyed, "Hello, is anyone there?"

Deb felt tears welling up in her eyes and she couldn't see the sidewalk anymore. She stopped walking and leaned against a building. She took a deep breath and whispered into the phone, "Daddy ... I'm in trouble."

Deb started hyperventilating and dropped the phone. She tried to bend down and pick it up, but the sidewalk started moving; and it came crashing into her forehead. The pain took Deb to a peaceful place of relaxation, and she passed out.

CHAPTER TWENTY

Rick arrived at Penn Station an hour late. A snowstorm had delayed all travel on the east coast. It was dark and cold and Rick was hungry as hell. He wanted to stop for something to eat, but didn't want to miss his ride. He walked to baggage claim.

A chill made him shiver and he buttoned his coat up; thankful he had bought a decent coat while in Virginia.

A vision of the pretty girl at the mall ran across Rick's mind. He remembered her smile; she was hot. She was at the mall with Sissy and they were laughing and talking. She was Sissy's friend. She'll probably be at Sissy's funeral. Rick felt sad for Sissy's beautiful girlfriend … but not for Sissy.

He chuckled to himself and said, "That bitch deserved to die. Hell, I did her a favor."

He made his way to baggage claim where a dozen people stood holding up signs. Rick scanned the signs and saw a neatly handwritten sign in red, black and green on a brown piece of poster board. The words read, "Mr. Smith."

Rick walked towards the sign; a short Rastafarian wearing a large yellow and green knitted hat held it. Rick shook his head and walked up to the Rasta man and said, "You Walden?"

The Rasta man huffed, threw the sign down and said, "What de hell man! Dat's not what ya supposed to say!" The Rasta man picked the sign back up and pointed at it. "Are ya Mr. Smith? I'm damn sure dat's not ya name man; so what de hell ya goin sayin my name?"

Rick glanced around realizing they were drawing attention. He raised his hands and said, "Sorry; sorry man. Long day." Rick extended his hand and said, "Hi, I'm Mr. Smith." Walden just stared at Rick.

Rick leaned closer and whispered, "Mozzarella?" Walden let out another loud huff and walked past Rick's extended hand. He grated under his voice as he passed, "Asshole; grab ya bags and let's catch dis damn train to Seattle."

Rick fought the urge to pounce on Walden and beat him in the back of his nappy head. Hot painful blood pulsed through his skull surrounding his anger. His vision blurred and he lost sight of Walden. Rick closed his eyes and rubbed them hard, willing his vision to return. Rick was still rubbing his eyes, when he heard a voice in his ear, "What de hell man; did I make ya cry?"

Rick shot his arm out and grabbed Walden around his neck. He pulled him into a corner and threw him up against the wall. Rick grabbed Walden around the neck again and held him up against the wall. Walden was pulling at Rick's hands, trying to pry them away from his neck. His feet were dangling off the floor as Rick held him against the wall by the neck. Walden kicked Rick in the chin; Rick winched and punched Walden in the stomach. Rick's vision was returning and he could see the pain in Walden's face as he tried to get air back into his lungs.

He released Walden and took a deep breath. He said, "Look Walden, I don't care who fucked you in the ass when you were a kid and made a pussy out of you; but if you keep fucking with me, I'll add your name to the list of mother-fuckers I'm gonna murder." Rick stepped back and motioned for Walden to lead the way, "Now; where do we catch the damn train?"

Walden composed himself, and fixed his shirt. He looked up at Rick and started to walk past him back into the hallway. He stopped right next to Rick and said, "Ya know what man? You ain't de only one know how to murder someone."

Walden walked back into the hallway. Rick followed. He had to put up with this short asshole for now; he needed him. Rick would love to see Dog chew Walden up and hear him pleading for help. A smile appeared on Rick's face as he thought of Dog; where he was right now.

Walden and Rick made their way to the train and found their cabin. Rick fell onto his bunk and closed his eyes. Walden sat on the edge of his bunk and stared at Rick in silence. Rick tried to ignore his presence but couldn't.

He opened his eyes and said, "Look, we don't have to like each other, but we do have to work together. So let's just show respect to each other and get this over with."

Walden huffed out, "Respect man? Would dat be before ya choked me or after ya hit me? Ya can't show respect cause ya don't know what it is."

Walden sat back on his bunk and took out his cell phone. He started punching on it and it sounded like he was playing a game. Rick closed his eyes and tried to rest. He had to figure out a way to explain to Walden that he was carrying a very large package with him. A 190lb package carrying a black, drooling killer that Rick had taken a liking to. Dog was smart; like a human. Hell, he was smarter than many human's Rick knew. And he killed like a wild animal. Rick admitted to himself the beast had scared him at first. But not anymore … Not after the landlord. Dog had played with Rick like a puppy when they were back in the apartment. It was hard for Rick to pull the trigger and kill him; he couldn't do it. So he brought him with him.

Rick heard Walden moving around and his eyes sprung open. He winced in pain as he tried to focus his weary eyes.

Walden was pulling back the covers on his bunk. He saw Rick jerk his eyes open and look at him. Walden smiled and said, "Don't worry man; when I kill ya I want ya wide awake to see de smile on me face."

Walden rested his body down on his bunk and closed his eyes. Rick watched him a few moments longer. He didn't know if the little fucker was joking or not, but Rick already knew this correlation was going to end painful, and bloody.

CHAPTER TWENTY ONE

Deb heard voices. She felt warm and comfortable. The familiar voice was soothing to her ... she smiled in her sleep. She wasn't asleep anymore; she was waking up. She didn't want to wake up yet; she was afraid to wake up. Why?

The voices became louder as Deb woke up, and she could hear the conversation ...

"Felix, if I've told you once, I've told you a million times. You must do exactly as I tell you in order for things to be alright."

The voices were in the room with Deb. She knew who they were ... She knew he would find her and take care of her. She snuggled back under the covers and tried to get more sleep. She wasn't in her bed. Where was she? She didn't care ... She didn't want to wake up yet; she was still dreadfully tired.

The voices were keeping her awake. What was going on? Why was Felix upset? Deb listened closer ...

"Doc, I'm sorry. I just didn't know what to tell him. I know I shouldn't have answered her phone, but it rang non-stop for 3 hours. I started to worry that it was the Method trying to reach her for an emergency in Seattle. I was very vague when I answered ..."

Deb heard Felix's voice pleading forgiveness from Doc for ... answering her phone? Deb's eyes sprung open under the covers. Who was calling? Why were they calling for 3 hours? Deb felt herself start sweating all over. She tried to shift her position to try and find a cool spot and relax again. The voices continued ...

"Felix, please don't try and justify your mistake. Now, tell me exactly what he said to you, and what you said to him."

Felix continued and tried to calm his voice and explain, "Well, I answered her phone and said 'Can I help you?' Then he said, 'I want to speak with Debra Shaver please." Felix paused, and then continued, "I asked who was calling, and that's when he became angry and started cursing and threatening me. I didn't say anything else Doc, I promise. I let him yell into the phone … until he threatened to call the police. That's when I threatened him."

Deb heard Doc wheezing as he let out a long sigh and said, "What did you threaten him with Felix?"

Felix calmly answered Doc and said, "Well, I had to stop him from calling the police, so I told him that if he ever wanted to see Debra alive again, he would stop yelling and threatening me and do as I told him to do."

Doc took two puffs from his inhaler, and asked, "So Felix, what did you tell him to do?"

Felix began again, "I told him that I wanted to know exactly why he was calling this number and what he wanted with Debra Shaver. And he told me he was her boyfriend and they were supposed to meet yesterday, but Debra never showed up and she wasn't at work today and he was concerned."

Deb exhaled under the covers; it was Carlito. He was looking for her. Did they have a date yesterday? She didn't remember planning to meet him.

Doc wheezed a few breaths in between clinched teeth and said, "Felix; did it ever occur to you that this person calling Debra's phone wasn't her boyfriend at all, and they weren't supposed to meet, and he was just feeding you information so you would tell HIM everything HE wanted to know?"

Deb heard Felix let out a long sigh, and Doc continued, "Felix, what did you tell the caller after he told you he was her boyfriend and was concerned?"

Felix started pleading his case once again, "Doc, he caught me off guard … I didn't know she had a boyfriend - and he really did sound concerned about Debra. I thought it was the Method with an emergency."

Deb lay still under the covers listening to Felix give excuse after excuse. Doc finally shouted, "Felix! I give you one thing to do … One thing! And you cause me grief. All you had to do was bring her here, make her comfortable and wait for me to arrive with the doctor! Nowhere in those instructions did I say to answer her cell phone!"

Felix tried to interrupt, "But it kept ringing …"

Doc yelled, "I don't give a shit if it was on fire!! Throw it in the basement and wait for me; but you should not have answered it!"

Deb heard Felix let out a whimper, and he started crying, "Doc, I'm sorry. I'm sorry. I messed up; I'm sorry. It won't happen again, I promise."

Deb pulled the covers back slightly and peeked an eye out. She saw Doc walking across the floor towards Felix sitting in a chair. Doc put his hand on Felix's shoulder and said, "Felix, Felix, calm down." Doc rubbed Felix's shoulders and continued, "Now, Felix; tell me what you told the caller after he told you he was the boyfriend and he was concerned?"

Felix looked up at Doc, and grabbed him around the waist and hugged him. He said in a muffled voice, "I told him not to worry … that Debra was with her father and he was taking care of her. He gave me his name and number and asked me to call him when I have more to tell him."

Doc started wheezing again, and asked, "So, what was his name?"

Felix was still holding Doc and said, "Carlito Dominguez, he said he works at the precinct and he gave me his cell phone number."

Doc took two puffs from his inhaler and said, "So Felix, you told this Carlito that Debra was with her father. You told a complete stranger that I'm Debra's father!" Doc's voice trailed off into a series of struggled breaths.

Doc took another puff, and said "Find him Felix; we have to get rid of him."

Deb threw the covers off of her and jumped out of the bed yelling, "Nooooo!!!"

Doc jerked out of Felix's embrace and spun around. Deb stood in the middle of the floor, hyperventilating. She scanned the room and realized she had no idea where she was. Her glare came back to Doc and Felix. Felix slowly stood up from the chair and said, "Hi Ms. Debra."

Deb tried to catch her breath and said, "Daddy, don't ... Don't hurt him; he's innocent."

Deb felt the room start spinning and she started swaying. She vaguely saw Doc walk towards her and put his arm around her. He wheezed into her ear, "Don't worry darling; Daddy will take care of everything."

Deb tried to pull away from his embrace and reason with him not to harm Carlito, "Daddy, you don't know him ... He's just a cook in the cafeteria."

Doc held Deb close to him and led her back to the bed. He whispered in her ear, "Debra darling, do you really know this Carlito? Has he ever tracked you down before? Did you really have a date with him last night or was it just a sex call? Darling, don't let lust cloud your judgment"

Doc sat Deb down on the edge of the bed. Her mind was swirling and she felt lightheaded. What if Doc was right? Her head was pounding and she was trying to remember if she had plans with Carlito. She couldn't remember making plans with him. And he had never tracked her down before, even when she did stand him up ... Deb started feeling sick. Was she sleeping with the enemy the whole time?

Vomit gathered at the bottom of her throat as she thought; now she's carrying his baby.

As Doc was pulling the covers back on the bed to help Deb in, she leaned forward and threw up all over Doc's pants, and onto the floor.

Doc looked down and said, "Oh, shit!" He turned to Felix and said, "Quick boy, go grab Maria and ask her to come tend to Debra."

Felix disappeared out the door. Deb continued throwing up; Doc continued holding her while she vomited all over him. Felix came running back into the room and said, "She's on her way."

Deb finally finished and fell back onto the bed. Doc looked at Felix and said, "Felix, give her a shot please, it will help her nausea."

Deb heard him and tried to sit up and speak. She gurgled out of her throat, "No, no, no; you can't give me any medicine! I'm pregnant."

Felix paused and looked at Doc. Doc shook his head and said, "Get the needle boy; she's too sick to carry the baby."

Doc took a moment to remember Debra's mother. Her mother was the same way. They had lost two before Debra, and they almost lost Debra. Her anemia is too severe and the baby's not going to be able to live full term.

Felix looked at Deb struggling on the bed to get up. He looked back at Doc and said, "But Doc, shouldn't it be her decision to terminate the pregnancy?"

Deb started coughing and throwing up again on the floor. Doc sighed impatiently and said, "Felix; she can't carry the child full term, the doctor already told me before he left; she will miscarry within a month. Now get the damn needle and give it to her before we are both swimming in vomit!"

Felix proceeded to his little black bag. He turned around and started towards Deb with latex gloves on and syringe in hand. Deb saw him coming towards her and she tried to yell. She only puked more.

Felix reached for Deb. Deb looked at her father with tears in her eyes and gurgled out, "Daddy ... no ... please ... it'll be alright. My baby will be all right ... Don't hurt him ..."

Deb felt a warm sensation flow through her arm, then throughout her body. She became weightless and relaxed on the bed. She saw Felix walking back over to his little black bag, removing the gloves and throwing them in the trash. Deb saw the figure of a woman entering the room and wiping her forehead.

She heard voices but couldn't make out what they were saying. She drifted off into a dream ...

She was pushing a little boy on a swing. He was giggling and kicking his feet. Deb was laughing and pushing him higher and higher. They were having so much fun they didn't notice the trees swaying; the slight breeze that played with the flowers turned into a strong wind. The wind started blowing hard; but Deb kept pushing the little boy – they were enjoying each other's laughter. The little boy turned around in the swing and smiled at Deb. She smiled back; he looked so familiar ... Deb gave one last push right when a gust of wind took the boy out of the swing and he disappeared into the clouds.

CHAPTER TWENTY TWO

Rick paced the hallway waiting for Walden to emerge from the Men's room. He had to find a way to tell Walden he had to go to the cargo baggage claim and pick up a large parcel he had with him.

Rick cursed himself, 'Fuck! What was I thinking to bring Dog with me?'

Walden came out of the bathroom and motioned for Rick to follow him out of the station. Rick quickly ran over to Walden and said, "Hey Walden; I have to pick up something."

Walden stopped and looked at Rick. "What de hell you mean man? What you need?" Walden was staring at Rick waiting for his answer.

Rick ignored his questions and started walking toward cargo baggage claim. Walden yelled at his back, "Where de hell ya going? Da rental car is parked dis way."

Rick kept walking and thought to himself, "The little fucker can't go anywhere without me, so he'll have to follow me until I find cargo baggage claim and pick up my package."

Walden ran up next to Rick and started following him through the station, "Wait man! What de hell is going on?"

Rick saw a sign for cargo baggage claim straight ahead. He went to the large parcel pick-up window. Walden stood next to him and watched as Rick gave the attendant a ticket. She disappeared into the back.

Walden stepped up to the counter and stared at Rick, "Look man, should I know about dis package ya carrying?"

Rick saw the large cage being wheeled to the front counter. Inside the cage, stood Dog.

Dog started yelping with excitement when he saw Rick. Walden opened his mouth and sucked in a loud gulp of air. He turned to Rick and said, "Don't tell me dis dog is ya package man! I ain't havin it!"

Rick ignored Walden and signed the paper the attendant handed him. Rick tried to walk around Walden to the counter door to take Dog out of his cage. Walden grabbed Rick's arm before he got to the door and said, "Look here man, dis is not going to work. Ya can't have a dog taggin along!"

Dog saw Walden grab Rick, and he started showing his teeth. Dog leaned close to the front of the cage and growled low in his chest. Walden, the attendant, and Rick all stopped and looked at Dog.

Rick took Walden's hand off of his arm and said, "I wouldn't do that if I were you. He doesn't like violence."

The attendant nervously said, "Should I call security to help you with your dog?"

Rick walked to the cage and unlocked the door. He took the leash and hooked it on Dog's collar. Dog came bounding out of the cage and stood up on his hind legs and gave Rick a big, sloppy kiss. He then started jumping around and looking for the door to get outside.

Walden stood at the counter watching the large beast. Rick and Dog started walking away from the counter when Walden yelled, "Hey man! Where do ya tink ya goin? I'm not working wit a dog! No body said anyting about a dog!"

Rick continued to the exit. Walden ran up beside Rick and grabbed his arm to stop him and said, "Ya better listen to me man!"

Dog saw Walden grab Rick again, and he let out a loud bark. It startled everyone in earshot. Rick and Walden looked at Dog. He was drooling on the floor as he showed his teeth to Walden. Dog walked closer to Walden and put his nose and his teeth right up against Walden's leg. Walden whispered nervously, "Get ya fucking dog man!"

Rick started sweating and sharp stings of pain vibrated his head. He didn't want Dog taking a piece out of Walden right here in the train station. Rick whispered to Walden, "Just calm down, and stand still."

Walden stood still; his eyes were pleading with Rick

Rick pulled Dog close to him and said, "Look Walden, I'm sorry for the surprise; but I had no other place to keep him until I returned to Virginia. I had to bring him with me and I promise he won't be any trouble."

Rick reached down and started rubbing Dog's head, and said, "Now, just be nice and friendly; and he won't hurt you. He'll stay out of your way and before you know it, Dog and I will be on our way back east."

Walden stepped away from Dog and glared at Rick, "Well, ya better not tink I'm buying a train ticket for dat beast."

Rick guided Dog past Walden and chuckled under his breath, "You already did."

Walden walked quickly past Dog and Rick and said, "Well follow me. If we're traveling wit a dog, I'm going to exchange me rental car for a truck. I'm not sharing a car wit 'em."

Rick saw an exit door and motioned to Walden, "I'm taking Dog outside … go get the truck and come pick us up."

Walden stopped and raised his hands, "Who died and left ya king?"

Dog turned and looked at Walden; he gritted his teeth. Walden turned and said, "Alright, alright. I'll get de truck and pick ya up man."

Walden shook his head and walked to the rental car counter. He couldn't believe it! He was taking orders from a Dog!

Rick guided Dog outside. They walked up the sidewalk until they came to a grassy area. Rick took a moment to inspect his new surroundings as he let Dog do his thing near a parked car. So, this is Seattle. He smiled to himself, Where are you Roland? Wherever you are, you better be making the best of it; cause the day I find you, is the day you die.

A sultry voice pierced it's way into Rick's thoughts, "Bitch, you couldn't find a better place to let your dog take a dump, than right in front of my car?"

Rick swung around and saw a pair of short sexy legs. He followed them up to a plump, juicy little body wearing a jean dress. He finally made it to a cute little face, with big brown eyes surrounded in soft curly locks. Rick stared at her for a moment and said, "Hi." He couldn't take his eyes off of her. He definitely wanted to fuck her!

She put her hand on her hip and pointed at the mound of shit Dog had left in front of her car, "Excuse me, but do you have your plastic bag and scooper to get this shit up?"

Rick gathered himself, "I'm sorry, I just recently got Dog and I'm still in the training stages of our relationship."

Dog trotted over and stared at Rick and the woman. He sat next to Rick and nudged his hand, demanding that he pet him. Rick started stroking Dog's head and said, "I'll go find a bag and um,"

Rick looked around the woman and down. He saw how much shit was piled in front of the lady's car and shook his head. He continued, "I'll find a shovel or something to get that out of your way."

The woman put her hand up impatiently and rolled her eyes at Rick as she said, "I don't have time for you to go searching for shit! Come here." She motioned for Rick to follow her to the trunk of her car as she continued, "Besides bitch, you probably wouldn't come back and leave me here to get this crap up all by myself. I got a bag back here in my trunk." She opened the trunk and pointed to a dumpster, "Go grab some cardboard out of the dumpster and slide that pile in a plastic bag so I can be on my way, thank you!!"

Rick stood there watching her as she fumbled around in her trunk looking for the bag. He slowly walked over to the dumpster. Dog quietly followed him. Rick returned to her car and took the plastic bag she handed him. As he took it, he said, "I'm really sorry. My name is Rick, and it is an extreme pleasure to make your acquaintance." He extended his hand.

She stood up straight and cocked her head to one side. She folded her arms in front of her and said, "Now, is this your way of meeting women? Having your monster dog leave an ICBM in front of her car, so there is no possible way she can escape other than having you rescue her?"

A black Ford F10 truck pulled up next to Rick and the woman and rolled the window down, "Mr. Smith, let's go man, I've been looking all over for ya."

Rick looked over and said, "Damn. Walden." Rick looked at the woman, "Excuse me."

She huffed and slammed her trunk closed, rolled her eyes and crossed her arms in front of her again.

Rick led Dog over to the truck and opened the door. Dog jumped into the back seat. Rick put his bag in the truck and said, "Walden, give me a minute."

Walden huffed and said, "Man what is it wit ya? Ya always aggravate'n situations!"

Rick leaned into the truck and said, "Come on man, give me a minute OK? Look at her. You gotta give me a minute."

Walden put the truck in park and said, "Hurry up man."

Rick walked back over to the sexy, impatient little figure waiting for him. He took the cardboard and pushed the pile into the plastic bag. It was hot and stinky and made Rick's stomach lurch. His head gave a large painful pound and as he stood back up he got a head-rush. He swayed slightly and the woman asked, "Are you alright?"

Rick shook his head and said, "I'm fine, I'm fine. Like I said, I just recently got Dog, and I hadn't had the pleasure of smelling his shit until just now; and it almost knocked me to my knees."

She let out a cute little giggle and covered her nose with her hand and said, "Well take it and throw it away; I don't want to smell it. If it almost knocked you down, it'll kill me."

Rick trotted over to the dumpster and quickly trotted back to the women. She had her car door open and was getting in when he said, "Are you going to tell me your name, or am I gonna have to follow you and have Dog leave another ICBM? You know he has plenty."

She slightly smiled and shook her head. She said, "You seem like a nice enough guy, but I don't need any new friends right now." She nodded towards the truck, and said "And besides, looks like you're just passing through anyway."

Rick licked his lips, smiled and said, "Now you know, sometimes those are the best friends ... the ones just passing through."

She smiled and reached into her purse. She handed Rick a business card and said, "Call me before you leave town. Maybe we can do lunch." She got in her car and closed the door. Rick stood there and watched her drive off. He glanced down at her card. It read: 'Trish Easton, Department Manager – Seattle Mortgage Services'.

Walden honked the horn and Dog growled in his ear. Walden could feel Dog's breath on his neck as drool dripped down his shirt. Rick opened the truck door and got in. He glanced over at Walden with his eyes popped out and his mouth open. Rick looked at Dog growling at Walden and said, "Come on Dog, leave him alone. We need him for now; be a good boy OK." Dog quickly looked at Rick and started licking him and butting heads with him.

Walden exhaled long and slow. He put the truck in drive and started driving out of the parking lot. He looked at Rick and said, "Do ya have control of dis beast man? He seems a bit unstable to me."

Rick turned around in his seat and said, "Don't worry about Dog, he's my problem. All you got to do is tell me all you know about Roland B. Hoffman."

Walden let out a sigh and said, "Dat's what I've been trying to tell the Method man, dere isn't much recent information on da guy;

and all I have to go on is a few old addresses. He's a pretty shady character."

Rick glared into the distance and said, "Yeah, I know. So, we start at the first address you have."

Walden shook his head and said, "First man, we gotta get me someting to eat. We're going to me 'ole friends pizza joint and have us one and a couple of cold ones."

Rick laughed and shook his head. He said, "You know, I thought that was funny; a Rastafarian who owns a pizza joint and loves pizza."

Walden gave Rick a sideways glance, "What man, pizza is an international food. A Rasta man can't like pizza? Dat would be like sayin a black man looks funny eating sushi."

Rick huffed and said, "You know what I mean joker. And no I don't eat raw fish or anything smelling like raw fish! That includes some pussy; unless it's sweet." Rick smiled and said to himself, "I bet Ms. Easton's pussy tastes like hot apple pie!"

Dog let out a loud bark and Walden swerved the truck. "Can ya please keep dat ting quiet while I'm driving man?"

Dog barked again. Rick turned around and rubbed Dog's massive head protruding into the front seat and said, "Ah come on Walden, can't you see he's hungry? He heard me say hot apple pie and wanted to let me know he had a taste for it too." Dog started licking Rick's hand and Rick looked at Dog. He knew Dog was thinking that; he could see it on his face. It was amazing how Rick was connecting with this mammoth beast. What was the fascination? Rick had never wanted a dog before. The only dog he could remember having was 'Bozo' back on the farm, and he was like one of the family. Rick loved that dog. But he was nothing like Dog … Dog was a killer.

Thus … the attraction.

Walden was pulling into the parking lot of an old strip mall. He drove up and parked in front of a hole in the wall pizza joint and said, "Well, ya won't find any apple pie here man, only da best damn pizza in Seattle."

Dog started growling and leaned forward into the front seat. Rick said, "Hey, I'm sure we can find some apple pie somewhere here." Rick glanced around, "Look over there. There's a convenient store, sure to have some apple pie." Dog yelped loud and Walden cursed.

"Get dat fucking maniac out of da truck! Take him and ya get ya apple pie man. I'll be in Johnny's Pizzeria getting me some pizza."

Rick got out of the truck and Dog jumped out behind him. Rick put the leash on Dog, and they walked down the strip mall towards the convenient store. When they reached the store, Rick tied Dog to the pole and leaned close to his massive head. Rick whispered, "Now sit here and don't eat anybody."

Dog sat down, licked his lips and whined to Rick like a small child saying 'hurry back.'

Rick disappeared into the store. Sure enough he found some Little Debbie apple pies. They looked good so Rick bought himself one too. He came out of the store and started opening his pie. He put the pie up to his mouth and was about to take a bite when Dog lunged at him and growled with his teeth pressed up against Rick's leg.

Rick froze and said, "Damn Dog, sorry; sorry. Shit – didn't mean to be rude." Rick eased his hand down with the pie in it and Dog gently took the entire pie into his mouth and slurped it down in two sloppy bites.

Rick untied Dog and they started walking back towards Johnny's. Rick opened the second pie and was about to eat it. Dog stopped walking and showed his teeth again. Rick looked down and said, "Ah come on! This one is mine; you ate yours!"

Dog growled louder and gave Rick a wild look. Rick's appetite for apple pie suddenly faded and he said, "Here, here boy; you take it. I think I want pizza after all." Rick leaned his hand down towards

Dog and Dog slurped the pie out of Rick's hand and devoured it in one swift gulp.

Rick started walking again with Dog trotting happily along side him. Rick shook his head. He wondered if he would be able to control this beast. He watched Dog as he playfully nipped at his hand, wanting attention as they walked.

As Rick petted Dog's head, he whispered, "It's obvious who's in control of this duo ... And it ain't me!"

CHAPTER TWENTY THREE

Hutchison stood waiting in front of Gate 80A, Delta Flight 5712 to Seattle, Washington; leaving Dulles International Airport at 4:40pm non-stop. According to the itinerary Hutchison snagged from Shaver, 'Mr. Smith' should have been boarding this flight. Hutchison stood in the corner watching the airline attendant behind the desk. He had already interrogated the girl and told her exactly what to do when Mr. Smith checks in.

He had been waiting at the gate for six hours. The flight attendant was about to announce last call for the gate, and no Mr. Smith yet.

Hutchison spoke into the microphone in his ear, "Rhodes, Landau; come in."

Rhodes answered, "Yeah boss."

Hutchison replied, "Stand down; doesn't look like Mr. Smith is showing up. We'll give it 10 more minutes then we'll call it a night."

Rhodes answered, "10-4 boss."

Hutchison walked along the window with one eye watching the airport workers on the ground outside, and one eye watching the airline attendant at the counter. He jammed his hands deep in his pockets in frustration as he paced the floor. Hutchison couldn't get a definite make on this 'Mr. Smith, and he hadn't been able to locate Shaver all week. He had nothing solid to bust her ass with yet, and this would have been the perfect lead! Hutchison knew he had to catch this Mr. Smith and close in on Shaver quick. The agency was pressing for a conclusion of the investigation. But Hutchison knew

Shaver was guilty ... he just knew it! He wasn't giving up until he proved it.

He paced the floor trying to put the puzzle together. Why was Shaver playing travel agent for Mr. Smith? And why wasn't she at work all week? Hutchison didn't trust Captain either. He knew Captain was covering for her; giving him the excuse that she was out sick! Hutchison had watched her car every day. It was parked at the station for three days, on the third day a man arrives on foot with keys to her car and drives it to her house; leaves it there and takes a bus back across town. Something was going on with Shaver and he had to find out.

He gripped his fists in his pockets and jammed them against his legs with anger. Something was going on and he felt like an ass for not having a clue!

Two little boys started playing with a ball right next to Hutchison. They were distracting him ... He started thinking about Peggy. She was pregnant with his first child - a boy. Hutchison looked around for the two little boy's parents and saw a couple standing in line. They were smiling at the boys. Behind the parents was a man ... The man was alone. Hutchison's heart started racing and he made his way over to the line.

He whispered into the microphone, "Boys, we might have a catch; be alert."

The airline attendant saw Hutchison walking up to the line and her eyes quickly darted to the man in line behind the parents. She looked frantically back at Hutchison. He slowly shook his head trying to calm her down so she wouldn't loose it and blow the whole scene.

She continued working with the parents until they were done and the parents strolled over to where the two boys were playing. The man walked up to the counter. Hutchison was close behind the man. The airline attendant held back sobs as she squeaked out, "Welcome to Delta Airlines, may I help you?"

The man stepped up to the counter and reached into his overcoat.

He smiled at the attendant and said, "Hi, I'd like to upgrade my ticket."

The attendant nervously glanced around the man into Hutchison's face. Hutchison put his head down and pretended to read the paper in his hand. He cursed to himself and thought, 'if she would just calm down and get the guy's ticket we could get this over with!'

The attendant stuttered out, "S-sure ... um, can I g-get your ticket please?"

The man was still fumbling in his overcoat; he finally pulled out his ticket and handed it to the attendant. She looked at the ticket, and then her eyes flew up and stared at the man. She said, "S-so, Mr. Jackson, you want to upgrade your ticket?"

Hutchison swung around and uttered under his breath, "Damn! I thought I had him."

He said into the microphone, "No catch tonight fellas. I'll see you guys in the morning. Have a good one."

Rhodes and Landau replied, "Got ya boss. See you in the morning."

Landau added, "Hey! Don't forget it's your turn to get the donuts."

Hutchison chuckled and said, "I got it, I got it."

He pulled the microphone out of his ear and shoved it in his jacket. He walked over to an empty area away from the gate, keeping full view of the attendant. He sat down and threw his newspaper in the seat next to him. The attendant announced the gate closing for the flight. There was a small crowd left wandering around the gate. Everyone had checked in and there was no Mr. Smith in sight.

Hutchison knew Shaver would probably make other travel arrangements for Mr. Smith after he stole the fax from her machine. Good thing he phoned ahead to Seattle and gave the heads-up to his buddy Sharkey to be on the look out for 'Mr. Smith' and report back.

The attendant glanced around the terminal and spotted Hutchison across the floor. She slowly walked through the gate door and closed it behind her. Hutchison closed his eyes and rubbed his face long and hard … he was exhausted. When he opened his eyes he saw two men in his peripheral vision. One on his right; and the other on his left. Both were standing in the hallway; wearing dark clothing and sunglasses and watching him.

Hutchison got up and started walking back towards the exit. He casually wandered through the airport, going back to the parking lot. He tried to reach into his jacket and put his microphone back on but he would draw too much attention. He fought the urge to turn around and see if the two men were following him. He got on the escalator and started slowly moving down. He took the opportunity to turn around slightly and glance behind him. Both men were at the top of the escalator stepping on. They were looking right at Hutchison.

Hutchison swore under his breath, "Damn! I was so caught up in stalking someone … that I didn't notice someone was stalking me! Who the hell are they anyway; I'm IAD!" Hutchison got off the escalator and walked quickly through the crowd. As he was entering the main hallway headed to the exit, he spotted two different gentlemen leaning on the wall watching him approaching. They were dressed identical to the men following him. Hutchison turned around to see if they were still there … They were. Hutchison's sweat ran down his face as he bumped into people trying to stay calm. He saw a men's room and darted in.

Hutchison ran to the sink and washed his face. He took three calming breaths and stared at himself in the mirror. "Look at yourself. You'd think you never been in a stalk and chase situation before! Get a hold of yourself!

He tried to relax, but those men looked like something out of a James Bond movie! They're probably not even following him. Dealing with Shaver over the last few months had gotten to him. He knew Deb was mixed up in some pretty shady shit, and it was starting to wear on him. Hutchison relaxed; and convinced himself that he was just tired, and would not give in to his paranoia.

He exited the men's room and quickly scanned the hallway looking for his stalkers … they were gone. He should have felt relaxed, but their disappearance only made him more suspicious. Hutchison started walking towards the exit. He walked to the garage and took the steps up to Level 3 where he had parked.

As he entered Level 3, he started feeling more at ease. He felt silly letting his imagination get the best of him in the terminal. Hutchison thought to himself he should go ahead and take that vacation his boss was always telling him he needed. When Hutchison was a few cars away from his, he reached in his pants pocket to grab his keys. He hit the automatic unlock and the car lights blinked signaling the car was open. As soon as the lights blinked, three men appeared standing next to Hutchison's car. They were lying on the ground next to the car and got up when they heard it unlock. The three men opened the car doors and got into Hutchison's car. Before Hutchison could make a sound or move a muscle, he felt a large bag engulf his entire upper body, his keys were snatched out of his hand and his arms were pinned down beside him.

Hutchison tried to kick and struggle, but he felt at least 5 bodies on him, he felt fists beating him in his face and the back of his head was being pounded by something hard. He yelled and sucked in a mouthful of plastic bag and started gagging for breath. He felt tape being wrapped around him and he was being punched and kicked until he gave way and fell to the ground.

Hutchison didn't try to yell anymore because he needed to keep all of the air in the plastic bag circulating so he could take small breaths. His attackers knew what they were doing. They left just enough air in top of the bag so if he yelled he would suck out the little bit of air he had and he would suffocate.

Hutchison held his breath and braced his body as he lay on the ground and allowed his attackers to beat on him a few minutes more. He felt sets of hands grab him and pick him up and start shoving his body into the trunk of his car. Hutchison felt hands trying to push his legs into the trunk and he tried to kick back and fight one last time. He felt the fists and punches again and Hutchison felt himself drift in and out of consciousness when they finally stopped beating him.

They stuffed the rest of Hutchison in the trunk and slammed it shut. Hutchison heard the attackers get in his car and start driving away.

He laid still in the dark trunk, taking quick, short breaths through his swollen, busted lips. The plastic bag was sticking to the blood; sweat and tears draining down his face. He was suffocating in the trunk of his own car.

He calmed down and tried to gather his thoughts. He had to think of a plan out of this. He winced in pain as he tried to shift his body off of something sharp he was lying on. The car hit a large pothole and Hutchison's bound body went flying into the top of the trunk hard. When he slammed back down; the sharp object he was laying on cut through his pants, and sliced deep into his groin.

Hutchison yelled out in pain. The plastic bag sucked into his mouth and he started gagging and coughing uncontrollably. Each time a cough jarred his body, the sharp object sliced further and further into Hutchison's groin.

He was barely conscious when he heard the car doors slam and realized the car had stopped. He heard voices outside the trunk, then clicking. Hutchison heard an explosion and saw bright lights. He smelled smoke for a brief moment before he realized he was being shot to death from the outside.

Before Hutchison closed his eyes and coughed out his last breath, a vision of his pregnant wife Peggy, flashed across his bloody vision … then she was gone.

CHAPTER TWENTY FOUR

Rick sat in his room at the Hill House Bed & Breakfast on John Street. He stared out over the water; the waves eased the ache in his head. Rick stroked Dog's massive head lying in his lap. He thought to himself, 'how the hell did a joker like me end up with Dog?' Rick realized Dog wasn't just a dog; Dog was like … the master – and Rick was the pet. Rick respected and feared Dog enough that being his pet gave him a sick sense of pride.

A stab of pain shot through Rick's eye sockets. He squeezed his eyes shut and tried to spread the pain throughout his body to ease his suffering. A few moments passed, and Rick inched his eyes back open and stared out over the water again. It was maddening for Rick; sitting in his room waiting for Walden to return with news about Roland. His anxiety made it impossible for him to calm the throbbing in his head.

But he was excited … he was so close to killing Roland.

Rick watched the waves crashing against the rocks below. He smiled … it gave him an idea how he would kill Roland. Dog raised his head and growled at the door.

A knock on the door painfully interrupted Rick's thoughts. Dog was immediately up and stood perched on his feet like he was ready to take off running. Rick got up and laid his hand on Dog's head and said, "Easy boy; it's just Walden. We still need him, so don't eat him up just yet."

Dog relaxed and sat down; he opened his mouth and panted

staring at Rick. He sat there patiently waiting for him to open the door. Knocks on the door again made Rick jump; Dog sat there motionless. Rick observed his new collaborator and was amazed … One minute he was ready to kill, the next he was an obedient pet.

Rick realized that Dog would kill whatever, and whenever he wanted him to. A sense of power overloaded Rick's thoughts and a stabbing jolt shook his head as knocks on the door became louder.

Rick opened the door and Walden stood there … an impatient glare was on his face as he raised his arms and said, "Well, nice to see ya at home man! Ya think ya took long enough to answer da door? I thought ya were waiting for me!"

Rick motioned Walden into the room and said, "Dammit man, I just fell asleep! Get yo big nappy head in the room."

Walden huffed and stormed into the room. He didn't notice Dog standing behind the door in the shadows and he almost stepped on him. Rick was closing the door when a loud bark rang out. Walden jumped and spun around. Dog sat there, staring at Walden. Walden screeched, "What de hell is wrong with dat dog?"

Rick walked over to the sofa and sat down, He said, "Walden, he just wants you to speak to him as well. You entered his home; you need to greet everyone – not just me."

Walden stared wide-eyed at Rick and then back to Dog. He slowly reached his hand out to touch Dog on the head. Dog thinned his lips and showed his teeth. He growled low in his chest and drool dropped onto the floor. Walden froze. He screeched out to Rick, "What de hell man? I'm trying to pet da maniac!"

Rick grinned and watched Dog's killer instinct begging to be released at his command. He rescued Walden and said, "I said he wanted you to greet him Walden … not touch him."

Walden let out a huff and retracted his hand. He stood up straight and said, "Hello Dog, hope ya OK man."

Dog licked his lips and stretched out onto the floor. Walden turned and walked over to Rick sitting on the sofa. Rick was laughing at Walden, and said, "You know Walden, Dog doesn't like you; but you're starting to grow on me."

Walden sneered at Rick and pointed his finger, "Dat's it man! You're on your own!"

Dog jumped up and tackled Walden to the floor. Walden fell hard on his back and his head jarred against the hardwood floor. Dog put his teeth right next to Walden's face and let his drool drop onto Walden's face. Walden lay still and pleaded "Hey man; get ya dog!"

Rick leaned down close to Walden's face. Walden was inhaling quick, short breaths trying not to swallow any of the drool covering his face. Rick whispered, "I wasn't joking. Dog doesn't like you and he's two seconds from eating your nappy ass up; so if I were you, I'd sit down, and with a calm voice continue our business."

Rick sat back on the sofa and said, "Dog – let him up. He needs to tell me something."

Dog pushed off of Walden and Walden let out a loud sigh, "Ouch man! Dat beast weighs 400 lbs man!" Walden rolled over onto his side and curled up in a fetal position as he wiped drool from his face. Dog trotted back into the corner and lay down.

Walden rolled up onto his knees and pulled himself up onto a chair. He glared at Rick wanting to shoot him with his pistol he had tucked in his sock. Rick looked at Walden; he read his thoughts. Rick tilted his head and said, "Are you going to tell me where Roland is, or do you want to go another round with Dog?"

Dog raised his head and looked at the two men. Walden turned and saw Dog's bloody red eyes illuminating from in the shadows and a chill ran down his spine. Walden took a deep breath, turned to Rick and said, "Man, dat's what I've been trying to tell ya. Roland is dead ... he died eight years ago in a ..."

Rick loudly interrupted Walden, "Say what?" Rick winced at the pain shooting through his eardrums.

Dog sat up and watched Rick; waiting for a command to kill Walden.

Walden held up his hands and said, "Calm down man, calm down. Dis Roland died eight years ago in a psychiatric hospital. He went crazy man, eight years ago and killed his parents. Roland was ex-law enforcement, so dey put him in da crazy house under an alias. He killed himself 6 months after he was committed, dat's why we couldn't find him man."

Rick stood up and walked to the window. Dammit Man! He was eight years too late. His anger caused an explosion of blood rushing through his brain that pounded to the top of his skull. Rick felt the top of his head vibrating with agonizing pain. He cupped his head in his hands and spun around. He glared at Walden and said, "I want to see his grave! I need proof that Roland B. Hoffman is dead."

Walden shook his head and said, "Man what you saying? You want me to find his gravesite and take you to it?" Rick stared at Walden and nodded his head slowly. Rick's pain vibrated down his arm and he wasn't able to talk. Rick made his way back to the sofa and collapsed.

Walden shook his head, stood up and said, "No man, I ain't doing it. I did my job; I found Roland for ya and he's dead. I'm on da next train back to New York." Walden started walking towards the door.

Rick managed a painful moan through crooked lips, "Dog ..."

Dog sprang up onto his feet and blocked the door. Walden quickly reached for his pistol in his sock. By the time he had raised it and was going to point it at Dog, Dog's mouth was wrapped around Walden's ankle. Dog's teeth were cutting through Walden's skin and blood started oozing down his ankle. Walden took his pistol and pointed it at Dog's head. Dog tightened his grip on Walden's ankle and Walden let out a shriek and yelled, "I will shoot ya maniac ass! Now let me go man!"

Dog didn't move. Walden stood still; he still had the gun pointed at Dog. Dog let his teeth sink a millimeter deeper into Walden's ankle. Walden yelled again and dropped his pistol, "OK, OK Man! I'll take ya to da cemetery; just call off Dog man!"

Rick couldn't talk or move his arms and legs. The pain shooting from his skull through his left arm paralyzed his body and he was still struggling to regain control of his motor skills. He managed another sound through his slobbered breaths, "Dog … sit."

Dog continued to growl and held onto Walden's ankle. Walden let out a pleaded cry, "Smith man!! He's breaking me bone man!"

Rick could do nothing but watch Dog hold onto Walden's ankle … a pool of blood was collecting on the floor under Walden's foot.

Dog looked over to the sofa and saw Rick struggling, then turned and looked up at Walden. Walden felt his ankle crack as Dog clinched his teeth and gave his ankle one last squeeze before he released it and darted over to Rick.

Walden fell to the floor and held his ankle. He moaned in agony and rocked back and forth. He cursed as he climbed up on one leg and scurried into the bathroom. He spit over his shoulder as he yelled, "Fucking dog! He better have his shots man, 'cause if he give me da rabies I swear I'm going to kill him!" Walden slammed the bathroom door and locked it.

Dog crouched over Rick lying on the sofa. Rick tried to reach out to Dog and say something, but he couldn't. Dog started licking Rick's face; his big sloppy tongue made Rick flinch and he started coughing. The flinching made the feeling in Rick's arm start to come back, and the coughing brought back movement in his lips. Dog continued licking Rick's face until Rick's feeble arm made it's way up to Dog, and he stroked him.

Dog gave Rick's face two more long, wet licks, and then he sat at his feet and yelped loud. Rick managed to raise himself up and sat on the edge of the sofa. He shook his head, trying to comprehend what had just happened. His seizures were getting worse. They were leaving him totally helpless! He couldn't even talk!

There's no way he's going to be able to complete this assignment without help. The only solution for Rick; the only remedy he ever had for holding on to his miserable life for the last 13 years - was Doc. He needed Doc.

The bathroom door sprang open and Walden limped out into the room. Rick watched Walden limp over to the chair and sit down. Rick's vision blurred and he squinted his eyes at him, wondering why Walden was limping. Rick opened his mouth to ask him when his memory came flashing back to him. He remembered Dog biting Walden's ankle, and Walden yelling for help.

The volume of pain in Rick's head escalated. Walden was glaring at Rick. At the same time, they both broke the stare and looked for the dropped pistol on the floor. Rick caught a glimpse of it. It had slid under the magazine rack near the door. Rick looked back to Walden and broke the painful silence, "So, do you need medical attention or are you gonna live?"

Walden huffed and rolled his eyes as he fell back into the chair. He let out a long sigh, looked at Rick and said, "Man, dis is da most fucked up job I have ever had. If I can get rid of ya two assholes, I will be just fine!"

Rick blinked his eyes hard, continuing to regain his self-control. He looked at Walden and said, "Just take me to the gravesite and we're done."

Walden looked at Rick and pleaded, "Ya promise man? Ya promise if I show ya da gravesite, we can get da next train outta here, and I'm done?"

Rick tilted his aching head and said, "Come on Walden, are we that bad?"

Walden's eyes grew large as he said, "Dat bad? Ya traveling with a disturbed maniac who just bit me and probably broke me bone man! Yes; ya really, really dat bad!"

Low grumbling noises started rumbling out of Dog's stomach. Walden and Rick turned and looked at Dog. He was kneeling on his front legs and lowered his head. He opened his large, sloppy mouth and let out a pool of dark red vomit.

Rick and Walden jumped up. A head-rush made Rick dizzy and

he fell back down on the sofa. He raised his arm and said, "Walden, go see what's wrong with him."

Walden shook his head and gritted, "I'm not going anywhere near dat maniac."

Rick tried to stand again and fell to the floor. He crawled over to Dog still kneeling on his front legs. Rick stroked his fallen companion and whispered into his ear, "Hey boy, what's wrong? You sick?"

Walden yelled from across the room, "What de hell man? Of course da dog is sick! He's puking blood all over da place!"

Rick stroked Dog a few minutes more and turned a concerned look to Walden and said, "You don't understand. Dog's been eating people since I met him; he was bound to catch something or get sick." Rick continued stroking Dog's head. Dog started gasping and puked some more. Rick sighed and said, "Walden, I just can't see him like this."

Rick stumbled up to his feet and said to Walden, "You gotta find me a vet we can take him to. I can't travel with him like this."

Walden threw his hands up and huffed. He walked over to Rick and said, "Look man, Dog is puking blood; dat's pretty bad. Dogs aren't supposed to be eating people! He probably won't make it anyway. And besides, he's a bad dog man! He don't listen to ya man, and he just bit me! If he's been eating people and stuff; we should just let him die."

Rick turned and grabbed Walden around his neck with both hands. He gritted his teeth and spit into Walden's face with every syllable as he said, "Get me a fucking Veterinarian for Dog - or YOU will need a Mortician!"

Rick released Walden and walked into the bathroom to get towels. Walden stood there staring at Dog lying on the floor. He saw an opportunity and dropped down quick and started searching the floor; looking for his pistol. Where was it? Walden quickly crawled across the floor and searched under the sofa. His mind was racing; he could shoot Dog in the head and have it over with; quick and easy.

Yeah, Smith would be mad; but once he's dead, he's dead. Walden knew he could take care of Rick a lot easier if the beast was gone. He stood up and looked around the room. He walked over to the magazine stand near the door. He kneeled down to look under the stand and saw a pair of feet standing in the hallway. Walden slowly glanced up and saw Rick standing there, holding Walden's pistol in his hand. The pistol was pointed right at Walden. Rick said, "Looking for this?"

Walden scrambled to his feet and said, "Yeah man, I was looking for dat. It is mine ya know."

Dog started heaving and let out another pile of dark red vomit. Rick ran over to Dog with the handful of towels in one hand, shoving Walden's pistol in his pocket with the other. He kneeled beside Dog and started rubbing his back and wiping up the floor. Rick cooed in Dog's ear, "It's OK boy, it's OK. Daddy Rick's going to take care of you. Just hang in there big boy."

Walden stood there watching Dog and Rick. He realized just how sick the two creatures in front of him really were. Walden stepped back towards the sofa and winced at the pain in his ankle. He fell onto the sofa and moaned. He watched Rick clean the monster up and gently lay the beast on a pile of blankets. Rick cooed to the monster like it was a baby. Walden shook his head and thought; perhaps if he cooperated with them he could get them out of his life, without sustaining any more bodily harm.

He stood up and limped over to the door. He stopped in front of the door and said, "I'll get an appointment with a Vet for ya man. I'll call ya in da morning. We can go to the cemetery after we take care of da mutt."

Rick stood up and stared Walden in the eye. "Asshole, he needs a doctor now! You get me a vet within the hour, or I'll come looking for you and believe me; I'll find you eventually."

Walden threw his hands up and whined, "Man where de hell I'm going to find a vet dis time of da night? It's 2:00 am in da morning man!"

Rick walked over to the door and put his hand on the knob. He stared Walden square in the eye and said, "I really don't give a damn where you find one. But you better find me a vet by 3:00 am, or it's hunting season ... and I'll be tracking Robert mother-fucking Walden!"

Rick opened the door and shoved Walden out into the hallway. He slammed the door and returned to tending to Dog breathing heavily on the floor.

Walden stood in the hallway ... his mind racing. He shook his head as he turned and limped down the hall to his room. He should have quit the Method years ago when things were different ... when he had the chance. Assignments were becoming more and more unconstitutional.

The Method was becoming what they were trying to prevent ... Harmful, menaces to society.

CHAPTER TWENTY FIVE

Deb got out of her car and walked towards the precinct. She had been exhausted over the past few weeks … after her ordeal. She still couldn't allow herself to think about it - not yet. She wasn't finished burying it deep inside of her, where she'd never feel the pain again. The Xanax her doctor prescribed was making her feel much better. She worried she was taking too many. She took 3 before she came to work, but already wanted another one.

She had been on medical leave for the last three weeks, and returning to work was a struggle for Deb. She walked down the hall and to her desk without looking at anyone. She heard a few people saying, "Welcome back Shaver," but Deb didn't respond.

She sat at her desk and started going through the piles of paper stacked on her desk. She wanted to get busy again - burry herself in real investigative work. She couldn't remember the last time she actually participated in a legitimate case and caught a crook doing bad and put him away.

Deb's desk phone rang. She looked at the display and saw it was the mailroom. She answered, "This is Shaver."

Deb heard Walter's voice reply, "Nice to see you back at work Ms. Shaver. I have a delivery down here in the mailroom for you. Would you mind coming down and signing for it? It's too large to bring upstairs."

Deb's heart started racing and she glanced around to see who was watching her. She whispered into the phone, "Sure, Walter ... I'll be right down."

Her chair squeaked loud as she pushed away from her desk and stood up. She started walking down the hallway, towards the stairs. She felt light-headed and had to stop and lean against the wall before she entered the stairwell. She looked down the hall and saw a young pregnant women sitting on the bench outside Captain's office. The women cried into a handkerchief she was holding.

Deb watched as Captain came out of his office and greeted the pregnant women with a gentle handshake. He escorted her into his office and closed the door.

Deb entered the stairwell and started descending to the mailroom. She opened the mailroom door and glanced around. The mailroom was empty. The door closed behind Deb and she turned around to find Carlito standing behind her. His arms were crossed and he was blocking the door.

Deb let out a sigh and ran and embraced Carlito. She cried out, "I'm so glad to see you Papi!"

Her hands gripped the back of his shirt a she held on tight to Carlito and sobbed. Carlito kept his arms crossed at first, but his desire to embrace Deb back was too strong. He circled her body with his arms and matched her embraced. He muttered under his breath, "Well, it's about time you showed me some attention. I've been trying to reach you for over two weeks!"

Carlito held Deb close and he kissed her on the top of her head. He breathed in deep of her and said, "Why didn't you return my phone calls? And what's IAD doing snooping around? I was interrogated three times by the same asshole ..."

Carlito stopped talking when Deb pushed away from him and whispered, "They've been asking you questions? Who? And what are you telling them?" Deb was breathing hard and didn't notice she was hyperventilating.

Carlito reached for her and said, "Hold on babe, I didn't tell them anything. Calm down." He pulled her back close to him and continued, "Now; tell me where you've been, and who are the goons watching your apartment? You changed cell phone numbers, and your home phone is being answered by an answering service ... what's up with that?

Deb pushed away from Carlito again and said, "Wait ... You've been calling me and I have an answering service? And I didn't notice any goons watching my apartment ... and ... and ..."

Deb started hyperventilating again.

Carlito held Deb close and kissed her on the neck. Deb breathlessly continued, "Who has been asking you questions about me?"

His fingers gently massaged Deb's arms, trying to calm her. He answered, "Deb, it was just some asshole agent who liked to play bully with a badge. He tried to push my staff and me around, but he got nowhere. He hung around for a few days and then left us alone."

Deb managed in between breaths, "What ... what was his name?"

Carlito caressed Deb's face as he kissed her lightly from forehead to chin, and said, "Debra, he was an arrogant asshole named Hutchison ... but you don't have to worry about him now; he's dead."

Deb pushed away from Carlito again the stared at him like he was a ghost. She whispered, "Dead? How?"

Carlito paused and looked Deb square in the eye and said, "He was beat, bound and shot to death in the trunk of his own car. His car turned up parked in front of his house a week ago when his wife found his body after following the stench from the bullet riddled trunk."

Deb collapsed in Carlito's arms and he had to brace himself against a cabinet to keep her from falling to the floor. He gripped her close and said, "Deb! Deb babe what's wrong?"

He managed to get Deb onto the postage table and loosened her blouse. Sweat had drenched her clothes and she was shivering. His hands shook as he tapped Deb's cheeks and said, "Deb, babe; wake up. You want me to take you to the hospital, or call your father?"

Deb had fainted. Carlito lifted Deb's legs and laid her out on the table. He finished opening her blouse and started unbuttoning her slacks. He noticed her panties ... they were the red ones he had given her for Valentines Day. He pulled Deb's slacks off and looked at her lying there helpless on the postage table. She was drenched in sweat and her breathing was labored. Carlito started getting aroused.

Deb started mumbling and jerking on the table. He leaned close to Deb's ear and said, "Babe, it's alright ... it's alright ... just breath for Papi and relax ..."

Carlito brushed a light kiss across Deb's open lips. He moved his mouth down her neck. Deb moaned and reached for Carlito's head. She pulled his face close to hers and found his mouth. Carlito grabbed the back of Deb's head and locked her in a deep kiss. He put his hand down her wet red panties and played with her clitoris with his fingers.

Papers fell off of the postage table as Deb started arching her back and pulling Carlito on top of her. She wanted him right there, in the mailroom, on the postage table. Deb moaned and gripped Carlito's arm as his hand brought her to climax. She cried out and Carlito had to cover her mouth with his to muffle the sound.

Carlito released Deb and turned to walk away from her. She moaned, "No!"

He ran to lock the mailroom door, and ran back to Deb's outreached arms. He remembered that Walter and the mailroom crew would be returning in about 15 minutes. Carlito reached Deb on the postage table, and caressed her thighs and moved them apart. He pulled her wet red panties to the side and sucked the remaining cum out of her. Deb let out another wail as she started cumming again. Carlito raised up and tried to quiet her, "Deb, babe; you have to be quiet or I'm not going to put it in. You are making too much noise and we're going to get caught."

Deb reached down and pulled Carlito's head back between her

thighs. She started pumping her hips into his face. She was about to climax again when she felt a sharp stabbing pain in her side. She moaned and turned away from Carlito in pain. He reached for her and pulled her close to him. He hugged her and said, "Babe, I'm sorry. Did I hurt you?"

Deb curled up in Carlito's arms and said, "No Papi, you didn't hurt me. It's just cramping from loosing the baby …" Deb clamped her mouth shut and squeezed her eyes shut to keep the tears back, but they flowed out of her eyes and fell onto Carlito's chest. He felt her tears and pulled her away from him to look in her face.

She raised her eyes and met Carlito's glare. He was staring at her with tears in his eyes. He said, "Babe … you were pregnant with my baby? You lost the baby? Is that where you've been? What … What happened?"

Deb didn't say anything. Her body started jerking and she let out the sobs she had been holding back. Carlito released Deb for a second and reached for her slacks and pulled them back on her legs gently as he continued, "Babe, shhhhhh. Don't cry." He held her head in his hand and pulled her close to him. He whispered in her ear, "It was mine Deb?"

She pulled back and looked into Carlito's eyes and said, "Yes … it was ours."

They embraced each other on the postage table for a long time. Voices in the stairwell made both of them jump. Carlito quickly helped Deb off of the table and they were fixing their clothes. He said, "Babe, how far along were you? How did you loose the baby?"

Deb finished buttoning her blouse and slowly raised her eyes to meet Carlito's. He was looking at her waiting for an answer. She turned around and gave him her back. She couldn't look at him and lie. She quickly said, "I fell getting out of the shower …"

Deb waited for Carlito's reply from behind her, but he was silent. She finished buttoning her blouse and fastening her pants; still no response. Deb had to turn and face him.

Carlito was standing with his arms crossed in front of his chest again. His lips were pursed and his eyebrows were drawn into a scowl Deb had never seen before. A chill ran down her spine. How could she make him understand it wasn't her fault the baby was aborted? She turned away from Carlito and started crying again.

He raised his hands and gripped Deb's shoulders from behind. He leaned down to Deb's ear and said, "Babe, how did you lose the baby?"

Deb didn't answer him; she continued crying. Carlito turned Deb around hard by her shoulders. He pulled her face up and made her look at him. He grumbled under his breath through clinched teeth, "…or did you abort my baby?"

The voices in the stairwell became louder and there was a knock on the door. Carlito walked over to the door and announced, "We're just about done; give us another 5 minutes."

The voices outside the door drifted back up the stairwell. Carlito turned around and started back towards Deb, whose sobs turned to curiosity. She raised her hands to motion Carlito to stop. She asked, "What? Now you run the mailroom? How did you manage to have the mailroom empty for us to meet, and now you send Walter and his crew away to give us 5 more minutes?"

Deb was getting suspicious … her father's words ringing in her memory.

Carlito relaxed and shook his head. He said, "Walter is a friend of mine and I asked him for a favor, that's all. I was tired of trying to call you or reach you at home; so I waited until I saw you come to work and asked Walter for a favor."

Carlito walked closer to Deb and said, "Babe, you don't trust me? Is that why you ran to your father when you were hurt?"

Deb stepped back with her mouth open, staring at Carlito. She blinked and said, "I don't know what you mean … what do you mean my father? I've been home recuperating."

Carlito chuckled and shook his head. He said, "Now babe, I should be the one suspicious of you! When I called you the night you stood me up, some man answered your cell phone and told me that your father was taking care of you and assured me you would be all right. Now, who was that man and was he lying about your father?"

Deb's head started swirling. So much had happened; she couldn't make out what was real and what was a dream. Carlito grasped Deb by her shoulders and gave her a gentle shake. She blinked a few times, shook her head and looked at Carlito with a blank stare. Carlito looked Deb in the eye and said, "You need some rest; I don't think you should have returned to work so soon. Go upstairs, gather your things and meet me out front. I'll take you to my place and I'll nurse you back to health myself."

Deb collapsed into Carlito's arms and started sobbing again.

The voices started again in the stairwell. Carlito led Deb to a desk chair and sat her down. He quickly walked to the mailroom door, opened it and propped it open. She watched as Carlito moved with swift ease around the room, covering all evidence he and her were ever there. He walked over to Deb and eased her out of the chair.

He gently eased her out of the chair and asked, "Are you alright?"

Deb answered, "Yes Carlito, I'm fine." She heard footsteps right outside the room and added, "Now what do we do?"

Carlito walked towards the door and started talking loudly to Deb, "Yes Ms. Shaver, I'll have that order ready for you next week." Carlito winked his eye at Deb and motioned for her to leave the room. Walter and three of his employees were talking in the hallway, pretending not to notice Deb and Carlito in the room. Deb started towards the door, and as she passed by Carlito, he whispered under his breath, "Out front in 15 minutes."

Deb walked past Carlito without speaking. She entered the hallway and saw Walter talking with his guys. As Deb walked past Walter she said, "Thank you for the package Walter."

Walter gave Deb a slight nod and Deb started climbing the stairs back to her office. Walter and his crew walked back into the mailroom and started working. Walter walked up to Carlito and said, "Is everything alright?"

Carlito was watching Deb disappear out of the door at the top of the stairs. He turned to Walter and said, "Everything's coming together nicely." Carlito offered his hand to Walter for a handshake and said, "Thanks for the use of your office. Lunch is on me for you and your crew for the next two months, sound good?"

A wide grin broke out on the faces of the three workers as they overheard Carlito's offer. Walter gave Carlito's hand a hearty shake and said, "Thank you Sir; anytime we can be of service, just let me know."

Carlito left the mailroom and walked out the back entrance to the parking lot. He got in his car and drove around to the front of the building. It hadn't been 15 minutes yet, so he pulled into the visitor parking space to wait for Deb.

Carlito's cell phone started ringing. He pulled it out of his pocket and looked at the number ... no one he knew. He answered, "Yeah."

The voice on the other end started saying something but Carlito couldn't make it out. The voice was deep and muffled. The voice continued, "...do you understand? You are to keep away from Lt. Debra Shaver and have no further contact with her. If you continue contact with Ms. Shaver the Method is not responsible for any damages that might occur to you."

The line went dead and Carlito sat there staring into his phone. Why would they want him away from Deb? What the hell was going on? He had so many unanswered questions for Deb, and what had happened over the last few weeks. His eyes started stinging as he held back tears thinking about his baby ... Did she loose it? Her eyes told Carlito she didn't. He was going to get to the bottom of her story. He looked at his watch; it had been 17 minutes and counting. Where the hell was she?

The hallway was empty as Deb stood watching Captain console the young pregnant woman as they walked out of his office. Captain ushered the woman down the hall towards the front desk. Something about the woman made Deb want to help her. Deb's curiosity got the best of her and she followed slightly behind the two and stood within earshot trying to hear what Captain was saying to the clerk at the front desk.

Captain turned to the young pregnant woman and extended his hand. Deb heard him say, "Thank you Mrs. Hutchison, and Gloria will provide you with all the necessary paperwork to take care of everything. Again, I'm so sorry for your loss; and please don't hesitate to contact me if you have any additional questions."

Deb's heart pounded loud and echoed throughout her body. She froze and stared at the young women. That couldn't be! Mrs. Hutchison? Deb walked over to Captain and the women and said, "Excuse me, did you say your name was Mrs. Hutchison?"

Captain gave Deb an evil glare and ignored her. He turned back to the woman again and said, "You take care."

The woman was turning to walk away, but Deb grabbed her arm and said, "Excuse me; are you Mrs. Hutchison?"

The woman's eyes became wide and she gurgled out, "Ya, ya."

Captain grabbed Deb's arm and made her release the woman. He politely said, "Thank you Mrs. Hutchison, you have a good day."

Captain pulled Deb away from the woman and down the hallway into his office. He slammed the door and said, "What the hell is your problem? Do you need a few more weeks of leave, without pay?"

Deb paced the room and frantically answered, "Was that Mrs. Hutchison? She was married to Lt. Hutchison? She's pregnant! I didn't know …"

Captain slowly walked around his desk to his chair as Deb rambled. He slowly eased down into his chair and said, "That's not the tragedy of it Shaver … She's mentally retarded and is worried sick about taking care of the baby without Hutchison. That's why she was here today; asking for information on the pension benefits for the baby if she gave it up for adoption."

Deb sank into a chair in front of Captains' desk. She stared at Captain with a blank look in her eyes and said, "Sir, I think I'll take you up on that extra vacation …"

Captain silently observed Deb and her emotional state … He calmly said, "Shaver … you take as long as you need."

Deb was silent as she thought about Hutchison's unborn child, and his beautiful retarded wife. Deb continued her blank glare in Captain's direction. Captain continued, "You know, I always thought you were cut out for another life Shaver. You weren't meant to be a hard-ass detective. You have a better heart than that. And if you tell anyone I said that about you, I'll deny it!"

Captain's kind words made Deb's eyes sting with tears, and her chest tightened with emotion. Her breath burned in her chest as she inhaled slowly trying to keep the floodgates from opening. She stood up and said, "I'll submit the paperwork to Gloria and …"

Deb's thoughts trailed off as the timid face of Hutchison's widow flashed across her thoughts. She fell back down into the chair and held her hand over her mouth as she started sobbing uncontrollably.

Captain jumped up from his desk and yelled, "Aw no Shaver! Not again! Don't you dare puke in my office!"

Captain ran around his desk and gently raised Deb up out of the chair. He grabbed a few tissues off his desk and handed them to her as he escorted her to the door.

Captain stopped right before opening the door and looked at Deb. He said, "Shaver, go home; get some rest; get yourself back together. Think about your career; what you want to do. If you want to continue your role here at the precinct we can do that. But I want you to envision your life without the precinct - doing something else with your career path. Either way Shaver, let me know and I'll respect your decision and support you."

Captain opened his office door and said, "I'll have Gloria complete the paperwork for your leave."

Deb brought her sobs to an end and reached for Captains' hand to hold it. She said, "Thank you Captain; for everything."

Deb released his hand and walked out of his office down the hall towards her desk. She sat down at her desk and started gathering her things. She had just returned to work this morning, and two hours later she's leaving to take another leave of absence. Deb paused and shook her head … maybe Captains' right. Maybe her detective days are over and it's time for Debra Shaver to be a normal woman.

She finished restacking the stack of papers on her desk and grabbed her purse. A chill ran down her spine as she thought, "*It's not the force that's destroying your life … It's the Method.*"

Deb's cell phone vibrated in her pocket and as she walked down the hall she pulled it out and looked at the number. Shit! Carlito! Deb glanced at her watch. He'd been waiting for 45 minutes. Wasn't it supposed to be 15?

Deb didn't answer. She let it ring into voicemail. She wasn't sure she should go with Carlito. She wasn't sure of anything anymore, and his actions were getting suspicious. How does he have influence over the mailroom staff? He's a cook in the Café! And the way he swept through the mailroom covering evidence … Deb still couldn't remember why he was tracking her down at Doc's when she collapsed.

She leaned against the wall, threw her head back and let out a long sigh. She shook her head and thought Doc was just making her paranoid about Carlito. He loved her; she could see it in his eyes; feel it in his hands when he made love to her. And; she loved him. She hadn't realized she loved him until she was carrying his child. Now the child is gone; but her love for Carlito is stronger.

Deb's phone started vibrating again. She looked at the number. Carlito.

She answered, "Hello."

She heard Carlito's voice answer, "Meida, where are you? I've been waiting out here almost an hour."

She answered, "I'm sorry baby; ran into Captain and had to take care of something. I'm on my way out. I'll see you in a second,"

Deb hung up the phone and walked to the exit. She left the building and walked down the steps and got into Carlito's car. He looked at her and said, "Everything alright babe?"

Deb leaned over and gave Carlito a wet, sensuous kiss and said, "Please take me to your place and make love to me all day baby."

Carlito put his car in drive and swiftly drove out of the parking lot onto the highway.

Carlito and Deb held hands, and didn't notice the four men in the dark colored sedan following them out of the parking lot, and onto the highway.

CHAPTER TWENTY SIX

Rick sat on the sofa, unable to take his eyes off of Dog sleeping silently on the blanket on the floor. The vet had given him sedatives to put him to sleep after the surgery. Rick still couldn't believe Dog had to have surgery. But when the x-ray of Dog's abdomen showed evidence of parts of a human hand; he knew they had to get it out. Dog never would have been able to pass it, especially with the large ring on … Sissy's finger. The damage to Dog's stomach trying to digest it was leaving scar tissue and making him sick. Rick knew it had to hurt like hell; it had to come out.

What worried Rick was when the vet found another body part lodged inside of Dog. Looked like a big toe stuck in Dog's esophagus. It must have been stuck there since he ate the landlord. Maybe that's why Dog had been so cranky.

The vet started asking questions, and he wasn't going for the excuse of "I don't know how those got there." Rick had to pay the little bastard off to shut him up. He thought he had paid the vet enough money for him to keep his mouth shut … but when Walden drove the truck out of the parking lot, Rick saw the vet writing down their license plate number on a pad of paper.

Rick thought to himself, perhaps Dog and I should pay another visit to the vet when Dog was better …

A knock on the door startled Rick. Dog was out cold and didn't warn Rick of a visitor ahead of time as usual.

Rick got up and walked to the door. He looked out the peephole; it was Walden.

Rick opened the door and let Walden in. As Rick closed the door behind Walden, he said "Morning. Where's my paper?"

Walden walked towards the sofa. As he passed Dog on the floor he looked down in disgust and shook his head. He said, "Ya know what man, dat dog won't be able to travel today. Why don't we just leave him here? He's much better. Ya made me pay a lot of damn money to get dat human hand and big rusty ring out of his belly. Let's leave him at da pound ... somebody will take him."

Rick glared at Walden wanting to punch him in the side of his head as he walked pass. Rick eased down onto the sofa and stretched out his legs horizontally, leaving no room for Walden. Walden huffed at Rick and walked over to sit in the chair near Dog.

Rick ignored Walden's comment. "I said, where is my paper? I asked you to bring me a paper this morning; and you show up without a paper."

Walden plopped in the chair and said, "I didn't get ya paper man! What for? We're leaving on the 3:00 train today back to New York; what ya going needing a paper for?"

Rick slowly shook his head and looked at Walden. He said, "Walden, you idiot. I want to see if our friendly neighborhood Veterinarian reported us to the authorities. You know, he did find two different body parts from two different people inside of Dog. He could have gone to the police even after I paid his pansy ass off. Thus, my reason for asking yo nappy ass to bring me a paper this morning!"

Dog shuffled on the floor at the sound of Rick's raised voice. Walden froze as Dog turned to his side, almost lying on Walden's feet. Walden stopped breathing and said, "OK, OK. I'll get ya da paper. Just be ready to leave in two hours man."

Walden paused, then added, "...And I have some bad news man ... Roland was buried in Virginia. So ya have to look up da cemetery when ya get back"

Rick wasn't paying attention to Walden. He was staring at Dog with a worried look in his eye. He shook his head again and then looked at Walden. He said, "Walden; we won't be traveling today. Dog is too weak. Change our tickets to tomorrow night. He should be able to travel by then."

Walden jerked his whole body around to stare at Rick before he protested. Walden didn't notice his foot stepping on the tip of Dog's ear, as he said, "No way man! I'm not staying here one more night with da two of ya! We're outta here today. Sorry about ya dog man, but he ain't going. I'm leaving on the 3:00 if ya go or not. I'll send someone else from da Method to meet ya out here."

Walden stood up and pinched Dog's skin with his foot. Dog let out a loud yelp and raised his large head. He turned his groggy head towards Walden and stared at him with blood shot eyes. Walden held out his hands and said, "I'm sorry man, I'm sorry. I didn't mean to step on ya, please forgive me."

Dog flopped his big head back around and looked at Rick, then lay back down.

Rick said to Walden, "We aren't traveling today. We are traveling tomorrow. Dog is coming with us, and I don't have time to get another Method."

Rick sat up on the sofa and stared Walden in the eye. He said, "Now, are you sure about Roland being buried in Virginia? You didn't get the name of the cemetery?"

Walden anxiously paced in front of the door. He said, "Look man – I've done all I can do for ya here in Seattle. When ya get back to Virginia, contact your Method for da information ya looking for."

Rick hated to admit it, but Walden was right. There was nothing else he could do in Seattle.

Rick walked over to Dog and kneeled down to pet him. As he stroked Dog's head, he said "You're right Walden. Now, I suggest you find something constructive to do today – and I'll speak with you tomorrow. Oh, book the train tickets for sometime late afternoon tomorrow. OK?"

Walden huffed and turned towards the door. Rick wanted to

harass Walden for his pansy ass comments about Dog, and asked him, "So, what are you going to get into tonight?"

Walden turned to Rick and said, "Hopefully some pussy! I need all da pleasure I can get before ya get us killed man! I'll see ya in da morning."

Walden slammed the door behind him as he left the room. Rick sat there stroking Dog's head. He thought to himself how nice it would be to get some pussy right now. Rick's painful brain showered pictures of Trish across his subconscious. Rick's dick became heavy as he remembered her body; the way she moved. He remembered she had given him her business card.

He got up and walked over to his wallet ... not there. He walked over to the table ... not there either. Where had he put it? Rick's blood started pulsing through his sore head as his anxiety grew to find her card. He remembered the pants he was wearing and went to search the pockets. There it was ... Trish Easton. Rick relaxed and let his bruised mind fantasize about her. She was hot. He fantasized about his large body engulfing her small sexy body under him while he pounded her. He wanted to fuck her ... he wanted to know what she felt like. What she would taste like.

He took his cell phone out of his pocket and punched in the numbers.

Two rings ... no answer. Rick finally heard a sultry voice come on the other end and say, "Hello, this is Trish Easton. May I help you?"

Rick didn't have much time to waste on small talk, so he thought he would get straight to the point, "Hi Trish, this is ... um ... Mr. Smith. We met the other day at the train sta ..."

She cut Rick off in mid-sentence, "I know who this is ... Dude with the big ass constipated dog. How you doing?"

Rick broke out in a wide grin; she was something else. He couldn't believe it; she was making him smile. Rick's dumb-founded reply was, "Yeah, yeah that's me; I mean yeah, that's my dog; I mean my dog is constipated, not me." Rick stopped talking and laughed at himself. He heard a small giggle on the other end and remembered he had to get to the point.

He started again, "Hey, I'm calling because I'm leaving town tomorrow and I've completed my assignment and ... I have nothing to do tonight and would love to see you."

Silence on the other end. Rick was nervous she would say no, and quickly made the offer more attractive, "...If you know where I can get a nice bottle of Dom Perignon to wash down a juicy, tender lobster tail, I'd like to ask you to join me for dinner."

The sultry voice finally reappeared on the other end of the phone and said, "Um that sounds yummy! You say you're leaving town tomorrow?"

Rick quickly replied, "First available tomorrow afternoon."

Trish said, "So, your 'assignment' is over; what type of work do you do Mr. Smith?"

Rick said, "Call me Rick. And I'm a consultant."

Trish replied, "A consultant ... for what? What do you consult on?"

Rick answered, "Personal Investments. I really don't see why it matters what I do for a living; you'll never see me again after tonight."

A brief pause, then Trish said, "So, we'll have a wonderful time tonight, show each other a good time; and then I'll never hear from you again?"

Rick answered, "Well, not unless you want to ..."

Trish quickly cut Rick off in mid-sentence again, "I don't want to."

Rick was silent, not knowing what to say to convince her to fuck him tonight.

Trish broke the silence and said, "I'll be at the Dimitriou's at 7:30 tonight. I'll be wearing a red dress, in case you forgot what I look like. I want you to approach me and introduce yourself. If you turn me on - I'll leave with you and we can fuck all night. If you don't ... well, I hope you enjoyed your visit to Seattle."

Rick's phone went dead. She had hung up. He sat there smiling. He liked her style. He wanted to fuck her brains out; but she had put the pressure on. He only had one chance … one introduction to either get pussy, or jack off his last night in Seattle.

Rick sat his phone on the table and let out a long sigh. He glanced at his watch; it was 12 noon. Rick walked to his bag and started sorting through his clothes. He had nothing to wear to convince a lady to sleep with him. He remembered what he was wearing when he met her. He couldn't wear that; he was wearing it when he met her!

A tap on the door interrupted Rick's search. Dog was still sleeping soundly on the floor as Rick walked to the door. He looked out the peephole and smirked thinking, "Damn, Walden is one ugly dude. He ain't getting no pussy tonight."

Rick opened the door. Walden stood outside the door and shoved a newspaper into Rick's hands and said, "Here ya go man. Enjoy. I'll see ya in da morning. Better yet; I'll send ya a note man telling ya when to check out and meet me in da parking lot."

Walden turned and started walking down the hall. Rick stepped outside his room and said, "Hey Walden, wait man. How do I get to Dimitriou's?"

Walden yelled over his shoulder, "Don't know man, take a cab; I'm sure he can get ya where ya need to go."

Walden reached his room and was reaching for the door to open it. Rick ran down the hall to Walden and said, "Come on Walden, help me out man. I need some new clothes for tonight and I don't know where to go, or how to get to this place I'm supposed to meet her."

Walden shook his head as he looked at Rick and said, "So, ya got ya self a date man. How'd ya get her to say yes? Did ya have Dog growl in da phone at her?"

Walden opened his room door. Rick grit his teeth to control the throbbing in his head. He was getting irritated with Walden and grabbed his arm before he entered his room and said, "Look

Walden, I know you don't like me or Dog; but do me this one last favor; and in return I'll make sure Dog doesn't eat you when we get back to New York."

Walden stood in the doorway staring at Rick. Rick met his stare. They were silent for a moment. A chill ran down Walden's spine as he saw a sinister glimmer in Rick's eyes … Walden believed Rick would sic Dog on him when he was through using him. But that would damage his relationship with the Method and Rick would be on his own; he wouldn't do that. Would he?

Walden tilted his head and tried to decide whether Rick was bullshitting or not. He snatched his arm out of Rick's grasp and said, "Now man, ya telling me ya dog is going to eat me when we get back to New York, and I'm supposed to trust ya?"

Rick stepped back and said, "If you do as I ask and cooperate; I'll control Dog. If you don't … well; let's just say the last few people that didn't cooperate with me turned into Kibbles n' Bits."

Walden imagined what the feeling was like to have a killer monster dog like Dog ripping your body apart. He couldn't imagine what the woman did to deserve to have parts of her surgically removed from the beast. And the big toe! Walden quickly remembered his pact with himself … just do as he asks and get them both the hell out of his life!

Walden shrugged and said, "Alright man, I'll take ya shopping, and I'll give ya directions to Dimitriou's. It's a nice place man; ya should have a good time."

Rick stared at Walden for a moment then nodded his head and said, "Thanks man. I'm glad you changed your mind."

Rick turned to go back to his room. As he walked away from Walden he said over his shoulder, "I'll be ready to leave in 30 minutes, so be ready."

Rick heard Walden pull his keys out of his room door and entered his room. Before he closed the door behind him, Rick stopped in the hallway and yelled back down the hall, "Oh Walden, wait." Rick trotted back down to Walden's room as Walden stood there waiting.

When Rick reached Walden, he said, "You know, I was looking forward to hearing you scream desperate pleas to me to save your sorry ass from Dog's sharp teeth devouring you; but I guess you turned out to be alright after all."

Rick turned and trotted back down the hall to his room and said, "30 minutes out front man, see ya."

Walden stood in his room doorway watching Rick enter his room and close the door. Walden slowly stepped inside and closed his room door. He wanted to leave Rick and Dog and get on the 3:00 out of town and never look back. He still had time …

He paced his room and shook his head. Rick would find him … just like he's hunting down this guy Roland, or the woman. Why did the Method give this damn assignment to him?

Walden could just arrange for Rick and Dog to have an "accident" and he could get rid of them both at the same time. Walden had connections of his own in Seattle; that's why the Method had given him the assignment, and he knew that.

He kicked the small trashcan by the door. The Method shouldn't even take cases like this one! These are two maniacs!

He took out his cell phone and started punching in numbers. He anxiously paced his room as he waited for him to answer. He hissed into the phone when he got an answer, "Dis shit is fucked up! My life is in jeopardy and if I don't complete dis assignment man, I'm going to die! He's crazy and I can't work like dis!"

The voice on the other end started calming Walden down and he sat down on the sofa and started to relax. He nodded his head a few times, then said "Yeah man, he's dead … no man he's buried in Virginia and he's on his way back to Virginia to look at the gravesite, and take out his last target."

Walden nodded a few more times then added frantically, "But ya don't understand man; he's got dis big killer dog as a pet and he's going to tell da dog to kill me if I don't do what he says!"

Walden was silent as he listened to the voice on the other end guarantee him that everything would be all right. Walden nodded some more and thanked the voice and hung up.

Walden stood up and walked to the bathroom. He turned on the water and washed his face. He dried his face on a towel and stared at his reflection in the mirror. He said to himself, "Well get ya ass out and take da freak to da mall and show him where da bar is. Hopefully somebody hears me cries and comes to me rescue."

CHAPTER TWENTY SEVEN

Doc sat at his desk and thought for a moment. He yelled "Felix! Where are you, please come."

Felix came running out of the bathroom wiping shaving cream off of his face with a towel, "Yeah Doc, what's the matter?"

Doc stood up and walked over to Felix, "Felix, did Rick have a dog?"

Felix finished wiping the shaving cream with the towel and shook his head, "No Doc, Rick didn't have a dog."

Doc walked back over to his desk and tapped on the keyboard of his computer. He said, "Well, either Rick has picked up a stray dog somewhere, or our operative with him in Seattle is hallucinating. I just received notice that Rick's assignment is causing bodily harm and threatening the Method operative with a very large, vicious dog."

Felix frowned and asked, "Rick has a large dog with him in Seattle? Whose dog is it? This was not part of the plan."

Doc became frustrated and said, "Felix, if I knew whose fucking dog it was, I wouldn't be asking you! Now, I need to contact Debra and find out what's going on."

Felix cut his eyes at Doc and said, "Are you sure you want to talk to her so soon? She was pretty upset with us after what happened."

Doc sat back at his desk and said, "Felix, she is my daughter. She will always forgive me; and besides, this is her job – it has nothing to do with our personal relationship. Now, get her on the phone for me."

Felix hesitated. Doc started typing on his keyboard. He noticed that Felix was standing behind him, not dialing the phone. Doc sighed and slowly turned around, "What is it Felix?"

Felix hung his head and said, "Doc, when I took Debra back to her apartment; she was crying. She was crying and she was very upset with you and I for aborting her baby."

Doc yelled at Felix from his desk, "Felix! How many times do I have to tell you; she would have lost the baby within a month anyway! She was too sick to carry the baby full term and it was either her or the baby! The same thing happened to her mother; only the last time it happened … I chose Debra."

Felix inhaled long and slow, and quietly asked again, "Doc … she would have lost the baby anyway?"

Doc calmed down, and looked at Felix. He knew Felix loved Debra like a sister, and was just concerned about her. Doc relaxed and spoke to Felix in a soothing voice and said, "Yes my boy, she would have lost the baby anyway. We just made it less painful for her. Now, please get Debra on the phone for me right now."

Felix slowly walked to the phone and picked it up. He punched in several numbers, held the receiver up to his ear and waited for an answer. When Felix heard Deb's voicemail pick up, he turned to Doc and said, "Doc, she's not answering – I got her voicemail,"

A heavy sigh escaped Doc's lips. He said, "Well Felix, leave her a message to call me - and it is of utmost importance." Doc turned to his computer and started typing again.

Felix waited for the 'beep' and spoke into the phone, "Hello, this message is for Debra Shaver. Please call 202-282-5555 at your earliest convenience. Thank you."

Doc continued typing on the computer while Felix put the cordless phone down. He walked over to Doc and said, "Doc, you never told me Debra's mother died giving birth to Debra?"

Doc hesitated for a moment, and continued typing. He ignored Felix standing behind him waiting for a response. Felix was silent for a moment, and then asked "Doc, have you ever told Debra how her mother died? Maybe she wouldn't be so upset with you if she knew she couldn't have children, and …"

Doc cut Felix off and yelled, "Felix! You have no idea what happened with Debra and her mother and me. And for you to sit here and talk about it like it was yesterday's football stat's is demoralizing!"

Doc slammed his fist down on his desk and sent a pile of papers floating all over the floor. He coughed as he started wheezing and searching his pocket for his inhaler. Felix reached for Doc and tried to help him find it. Doc pushed Felix's hand away from him and growled, "Don't touch me!"

Felix froze and stared wide-eyed at Doc with is mouth open. He whispered, "What have I done? Why are you angry with me?" Felix wrapped his arms around himself as he began to cry.

Doc fumbled with his inhaler and took two puffs before saying, "Felix, please; just go away for now. It's taken years for me to get past what happened with Debra and her mother, and for you to bring it up now …"

Felix cut Doc off and yelled in between sobs, "Well … it doesn't look like … you've gotten past anything!"

Doc threw his inhaler at Felix. Felix flinched as the inhaler hit him in the side of his forehead and fell to the floor. Doc stood up from his desk and said, "You little son-of-bitch! I …"

The phone started ringing. Felix was crying and rubbing his head. Doc was wheezing and fell to the floor to find his inhaler. Felix walked over to the table and picked up Doc's inhaler from beneath it. The phone continued ringing.

Doc stood up and Felix handed him his inhaler. When Doc reached for the inhaler, Felix held on to it a second and said, "Doc, I love you. I'm sorry if I said things that hurt you."

Doc took the inhaler and puffed. The phone started ringing again. He looked at Felix and said, "I know my boy … I know. Now answer the damn phone please."

Felix rubbed the tears from his face and answered, "Hello."

Felix heard Deb's voice on the other end, "Hi Felix, this is Deb."
Felix sniffed and said, "I'll get him for you."

Felix walked over to Doc to hand him the phone. Before Doc
took the phone from Felix, he looked at him and said, "I love you too
Felix ... but if you ever talk about Deb's mother again – I'll kill you."

Felix stared at Doc's face and knew that he meant it. Doc took
the phone from Felix and said, "Debra, I need to see you. When
can you come?"

Deb paused. She was laying on Carlito's bed feeling absolutely
wonderful. She smiled and said, "Well ... I'm kind of on leave again
from work and I'm spending time with a friend ..."

Doc hesitated, then said, "I need to have a private conversation
with you ... when can we talk?'

Deb said, "We can talk now; I'm alone at the moment. Carlito
went to the store."

Doc sighed and said, "Debra, no. Please tell me you aren't with
him! He's not to be trusted, and if anything happens to him I don't
want you around."

Deb sat up on the bed and said, "What do you mean if anything
happens to him? Daddy you better not hurt him! Do you hear me?"

Doc could hear the urgency in Deb's voice; and he soothingly
continued, "Now, now Debra. Of course I'm not going to do
anything to him. I'm just concerned about your well-being. Now, I
need to know about this ... dog that Rick has with him in Seattle."

Deb didn't think she heard her father correctly and said, "What
did you say?"

Doc repeated, "What do you know about a dog Rick has with
him in Seattle? The Method operative is threatening a complaint and
I wanted to get the story on this dog. Did Rick buy a dog while in
Virginia or did he get it in Seattle?"

Deb's mouth was hanging open as she realized - Rick didn't kill
Joe's dog! He took Joe's dog with him! He was Rick's pet now? Deb
realized Doc was saying something, "Debra, are you there? Did you
hear me darling? Are you feeling alright?"

Deb swallowed and closed her eyes … This was a disaster. She couldn't tell Doc; she had to lie to her father until she could talk to Rick and find out what the hell he'd done.

Deb mumbled into the phone, "Um, I … don't know. I don't know where Rick got a dog but I'll find out. What's the operative saying?"

Doc clicked through his e-mail and said, "He's being threatened, and Rick is allowing this dog to bite him, etc. It's not a nice story. If you don't know where the dog came from, obviously Rick picked it up in Seattle. I'll contact him myself; it's been a while since I spoke with the boy anyway."

Deb quickly cut in and said, "No daddy, don't bother. I have to call him anyway to discuss arrangements for his return; I'll find out what's going on and report back to you, sound good?"

Doc said, "Alright darling. Call me in the morning. And Debra … please be at your house in the morning."

Deb heard the phone go silent. She held her cell phone in her hand staring at it … She shook her head as she realized … Rick kept the fucking dog! He had lied to her! He told her he had shot it! Why hadn't the dog killed him yet? Deb felt the room tilting around her; and she lay back down on the bed and waited for Carlito to return.

Doc sat the phone down and turned to Felix. Felix was sitting on the couch with a long face; staring right at Doc. Felix sniffed and lowered his head and stared at the floor.

Doc smiled at Felix and said, "I'm not mad at you anymore, let's have a smile shall we?"

Felix didn't smile right away, but he felt so much better after Doc said he wasn't mad. Felix finally looked up and said, "Is she alright?'

Doc nodded his head and said, "She's fine Felix … I'm not sure about Rick though. I need to contact him. But first, I need the update on the Chef … What's his name; Carlito? Where are the guys and when can they get rid of him."

Felix stood up and walked over to Doc. He hugged Doc for a

while, then said, "They're watching him as we speak. They can take him out anytime you say; just say the word."

Doc hesitated for a moment, took a puff on his inhaler then said, "Let's wait a while to see what he's up to. Debra thinks she is in love with him; and we aren't sure who he's working for – so we'll just watch and wait for now."

Doc walked over to the dirty window and stared out, pretending he could see outside. He continued, "We'll give the chef until tomorrow morning; if he's convinced me that he means my Debra no harm; he may live a bit longer. If not, I'll give the word."

Felix picked up his palm pilot and started typing. Doc interrupted him and said, "Now Felix; get Rick on the phone. I need to talk to him immediately."

CHAPTER TWENTY EIGHT

Rick dabbed cologne on his neck and looked in the mirror. He looked good. He will always thank Doc for providing him with a more handsome face than he was born with. Even though his skull was cracked, his face was perfect. He smiled in the mirror and said, "You are getting laid tonight!"

As Rick primped a few more seconds, flashes of his last sexual encounter darted across his bruised memory … it was Sissy. He was fucking her in her ass, trying to punish her for betraying him. She was enjoying it though - the freak. She's dead now.

Rick turned of the light and walked into the front room to check on Dog. He bent down and stroked Dog's massive head and checked his breathing; he was still weak. Rick shook his head and stood up; Dog should have known better than to eat anything on Sissy.

Lessons learned.

Rick was gathering his wallet and cell phone when it started vibrating in his hand. He glanced at the number … Deb?

Rick was excited; then he became nervous. Why was she calling? She had made it perfectly clear there was to be no contact while in Seattle. So, why was she calling? Rick held his cell phone in his hand staring at her number flash on his phone. He didn't answer; he couldn't. He didn't have an explanation for keeping Dog yet, and he didn't want to get cursed out right before his date. Rick decided to let her leave a message and he'd call her back later. No use ruining his hard on.

Rick glanced at his watch and remembered he had to give Dog his medicine before he left. He grabbed the medicine off of the counter and was reaching for Dog's mouth when his cell phone started vibrating again. Rick thought it was Deb and ignored it. He finished giving Dog his medicine and took his phone out to view the missed call ... Doc? Shit! Doc called.

No message. No message from Deb either. Wonder if the two calls are related? Maybe word had reached the Method about Dog. Rick shook his head; no one knows about Dog except ... Walden.

The big-lipped weasel sold him out. Blood surged painfully through Rick's skull as he realized why Walden had been so nice and cooperative all afternoon. Rick slammed his fist down on the table and knocked over the lamp. Dog jerked his massive head up at the sound of the lamp crashing into the floor. Dog looked around. He found Rick and stared at him dumbfounded. Rick quickly cooed to Dog, "I'm sorry boy, I'm sorry."

He walked over to Dog and started rubbing his head. Dog licked Rick's hand, eagerly wanting to jump up and greet him, but he was still weak. Rick's phone started vibrating again and he grabbed it and looked at the number. Deb. Rick walked over to the sofa and sat down. He exhaled long and slow; he had to answer it.

"Hello"

Rick heard a shuffling on the other end, then "Hello, hello; Rick? Is this Rick?"

Rick could hear the anxiety in Deb's voice before they even started talking. He calmly answered, "Yes, Deb; it's me. How you doing?"

There was silence on the other end for a moment, then "Rick ... do you have any idea how much turmoil you are causing in the Method? How much strain and strife you're causing in my life, and what you're doing to the operative there trying to help you?"

Rick opened his mouth to respond, but was cut off by Deb yelling into the phone, "Shut up! Just shut up Rick! What I want you to answer first is ... where is the fucking dog?"

Rick slowly opened his mouth again to speak, and Deb cut him off again yelling, "And don't lie to me dammit!"

Rick opened his mouth to speak again and paused, waiting for Deb to interrupt again. She didn't. He said, "Deb, I'm sorry I didn't tell you; but I didn't even realize what was happening until it had happened. First, I couldn't kill the dog at his house; it wouldn't look like a hunting accident. So, I had to take the dog out of the house, kill him and throw him in the river with his master."

Rick paused, waiting to see if Deb wanted to yell. She was silent, and he continued, "The only thing is; when I was driving with Dog – you called me and told me to go straight to my apartment and wait to hear from you; because of the news and the body being found so fast."

Rick paused again, still silence on the other end; so he continued, "Then Dog killed Sissy ... then the landlord ... it was like we had become partners. Then I couldn't kill him."

Rick paused again, and Deb responded, "Where's the dog Rick?"

Rick glanced down at Dog lying at his feet. Dog sensed Rick's stare and raised his massive head for some attention. Rick stroked his large head and answered into the phone, "He's here with me Deb; right here. He had to have surgery to remove some indigestible body parts, but he's doing fine."

Deb's strained voice came back from the other end of the phone, "Let me get this straight ... you killed Joe Ramsey, and took his dog. The dog kills two people for you; and you lie to me and tell me you've killed the dog, when in reality you've made the dog your pet. While in Seattle, the dog needed surgery to remove ... what Rick?"

Rick didn't want to answer, but it was good to get it all out in the open. He slowly said, "...well, Sissy had a large ring on her finger, which was still attached to her hand in Dog's stomach. And the landlord's big toe was stuck in his esophagus."

Deb cut Rick off again, "What the hell Rick! How do you sleep with that monster in your room? Who the hell did the surgery and what did you tell them? And why are you threatening Walden?"

Rick opened his mouth to try and start answering Deb's questions before she started yelling again, "Deb - Dog is really a smart, loving animal. And I paid off a vet to keep his mouth shut, but he didn't look too convinced when I gave him the excuse of 'I didn't know how the body parts got in Dog'. And I'm sorry for threatening Walden, but he is a pain in the ass! And yes, I was going to let Dog eat him, but I'll make sure he's all right when I leave him at the train station tomorrow. I don't want to cause you or the Method any problems. Both you and the Method have been very good to me and I appreciate everything you do."

Deb yelled into the phone, "And this is how you show your appreciation? Lying; killing people not on the agenda, and threatening the operative? Real genuine appreciation Rick!"

Rick tried to plead his case, "Now Deb, it wasn't supposed to turn out this way …"

Deb cut Rick off again, "Nothing turns out the way it's supposed to with you Rick! Just get your ass back to Virginia as soon as you can. When are you leaving?"

Rick quietly answered, "Tomorrow afternoon. I guess you've heard that Roland killed himself and he's buried in Virginia? You think you can get me information on where so I can see the gravesite?"

Deb replied, "Yeah Rick. And what about the man-eating beast you have with you? Are you bringing him back too?"

Rick paused and stroked Dog's head. He leaned down and kissed the top of Dog's head as he realized how much he cared for the untamed beast. He answered, "Yes Deb; he's my dog now and I'm going to keep him."

Deb sighed into the phone and said, "Rick, Rick; what are you doing? The dog knows you killed his master! He's a killer and he's just waiting for the opportunity to kill you; don't you see? It's crazy karma just waiting to happen to you Rick. You gotta get rid of the dog before you return to Virginia, and stop using the dog against Walden; it doesn't look good for me."

Rick's only response was, "I'm sorry Deb; I don't want to make you look bad. I'll leave Walden alone."

Dog raised his head and growled at the door. A knock interrupted Rick's phone call. Rick said, "Deb, I gotta go now; but I'll call you the minute I'm back in Virginia."

Deb replied, "Rick, when you get back, you have an apartment waiting for you in Tyson's Corner and I'll have a car waiting at Union Station. And Rick ... get rid of the dog." And she hung up.

Rick walked to the door and looked out the peephole ... Walden. Rick was mad at Walden and wanted to punch him in the face for being a little pansy and telling the Method on him; but he promised Deb ...

He opened the door and Walden stepped in the room, "Hey man, ya ready to go?"

Rick was silent and closed the door and stared at Walden. Walden looked around and saw Dog sitting up on the floor, then looked back at Rick. He became nervous when Rick was silent, and added, "Well man, ya ready to meet ya girl or what? I can take ya to Dimitrious but we gotta go if ya don't want to be late."

Rick crossed his arms in front of his chest and said, "You know what Walden, I think I can find Dimitrious on my own; if you write down the directions. I think I want to drive myself." Rick walked over to the counter and took a piece of paper and a pen and handed it to Walden. He said, "Why don't you just write down the directions for me, and I'll take it from there."

Walden nervously took the paper and pen and said, "So, ya don't need me man? Ya sure, 'cause I'm ready to drive ya to da place."

Rick slowly answered, "Well, I do need you Walden as a matter of fact. I need you to stay here with Dog and give him his medicine every 2 hours and make sure he's not running a fever."

Walden huffed loud and said, "No way man! I'm not a babysitter! And even if I was, I wouldn't be watching a beast like dat!"

Rick slowly walked over to Walden and said, "Now Walden ... what would I look like showing up on a date with a knucklehead in tow? I need to get some pussy tonight and I don't need a nappy head tag-a-long. And besides; Dog needs to be pampered tonight so he'll be strong tomorrow and we can travel"

Walden stood in the middle of the floor huffing and flapping his arms up and down; looking at Dog, then back at Rick. He finally gasped out, "And what I'm supposed to do wit da dog man? He's crazy! I'll be eaten before ya get home man!"

Dog growled in his chest and glared at Walden. Rick grinned and put his arm around Walden and said, "Don't worry Walden; I've told Dog nothing's to happen to you; no biting, no eating, no bleeding or broken bones."

Rick paused, looked at Dog and said, "Ain't that right Dog; none of the above."

Dog sat up a bit more and yelped playfully at Rick in agreement.

Walden pointed his finger at Rick and said, "You're crazy man; you and dat dog; I can't take dis anymore!" Walden walked towards the door. Rick barked out, "Dog!"

Dog scratched the floor with his claws as he clumsily got to his feet and stood in front of the door. One of his legs was shaking as he stood on guard with his teeth showing. Walden stopped in his tracks and slowly turned around to face the controller of the beast. Rick had a crooked grin sliding down the side of his face as he asked, "Going somewhere?"

Walden stared into Rick's crazed eyes and felt like he was in the twilight zone of his worst nightmare. Walden closed his eyes and slowly exhaled, praying that when he opened his eyes his two tormentors would be gone. He opened his eyes; he turned around to look at Dog's massive body blocking the doorway; growling and fiercely staring Walden down. Walden looked back at Rick and said, "Now man, I'm supposed to baby-sit dis beast? Look at him! He ready to eat me up already! I can't relax around him; he's already tried to break me ankle man!"

Rick slowly walked toward the door and said, "Dog; sit." Dog stopped growling and sat on the floor in front of the door. Rick turned to Walden and said, "Just sit here, watch him, give him his medicine and make sure he is alright. Watch some TV, call the sex line and have some phone sex; hell I don't care what you do as long as you stay here with Dog and make sure he's all right. I give you my word; Dog won't hurt you unless I tell him to."

Walden walked over to the sofa and plopped down. He reached into his coat pocket and took out the truck keys. He tossed them to Rick and said, "Man, ya better tell de dog not to harm me, and ya better be back here in time to pack and get de hell outta here tomorrow afternoon!"

Rick gathered his wallet from the table and pulled his coat off of the chair. Walden sat on the sofa staring at Dog, stare at him. Walden said, "Man, ya going to tell the dog to behave? I haven't heard ya tell da dog not to eat me man."

Rick walked over to Dog and stroked his head. Dog started licking Rick's hand and bumping his massive head against Rick's leg playfully. Rick said, "Now Dog; I want you to listen to Walden and take your medicine; and no biting. Don't hurt Walden OK?"

Dog yelped loud and licked Rick's hand some more.

Rick turned to Walden and said, "You got my cell phone if anything happens. In case of an emergency, I suggest you call me before he gets to your mouth."

Rick opened the door and walked out into the hallway. He turned around to look at Walden as he closed the door. Walden sat on the sofa looking at Rick like an abandoned child about to be executed. Dog sat on the floor watching Walden as Rick closed the door and walked briskly down the hallway. He was late for his date with Trish.

Rick heard someone come in the lobby door downstairs as he reached the top of the staircase. The wind gusted up the stairs and gave Rick a chill. He paused at the top of the stairs to zip up his coat. Before Rick could start walking down the staircase he heard a mans deep booming voice ask the attendant, "Do you have any guests registered under the name Mr. Smith?"

Rick froze in his tracks. He stopped breathing so the painful pounding of is heartbeat would quiet the noise in his brain so he could hear the conversation. Rick heard the attendant respond, "I'm sorry sir, if you want to visit a guest you must ask for the guest. I'm not allowed to discuss our guest list with you."

Rick was still holding his breath when he heard the booming voice again, "Well then, if you put it that way, can I please speak with your guest, Mr. Smith?"

Rick wanted to run back down the hall and get Dog, but he was afraid the inquisitioner would hear the movement. Rick's heartbeat was painfully ringing through his ears and pounding through his chest as he fought to continue holding his breath. He finally heard the attendants reply, "And what room would your Mr. Smith be staying in sir?"

Rick slowly exhaled and the painful pressure in his head started to pound as the blood started flowing again. He heard the booming voice's irritated response, "I'm sorry, he forgot to give me his room number … can you please ring his room for me? He's expecting my visit."

Rick tried to ease his way back down the hall, but his first footstep backwards brought about a loud squeak in the floorboards, and Rick froze. The attendants voice replied, "Then I suggest you call your Mr. Smith and tell him you're in the lobby and have him ring you up."

The booming voice echoed through the lobby as Rick heard the lobby door open again, "You bitch, you act like this is the Ritz or something! I'll be back with a warrant and I'll search every room and confiscate your records! We'll see how you like that!" Rick heard the front door slam, then silence.

The loud pounding vibrated Rick's head as he held his breath again waiting to hear what the attendant was going to do next. Rick heard her pick up the phone and punch in a number. He heard her voice say, "Hello Mr. Smith this is the front desk. You had a visitor this evening but he failed to leave his name. I didn't give him your room number. I hope you understand our policies for guest privacy. I asked your visitor to call you and confirm his arrival. Sorry for any inconveniences and please call the front desk if you have any questions."

Rick slowly turned to go back down the hall and exit down the back stairs when he heard the attendants voice again, "Hi Dad, it's me. Some big guy was just here asking about one or our guests, Mr. Smith, and when I wouldn't give him any information he threatened to get a warrant and search the building and confiscate our records. He got really nasty."

Rick froze again and stopped breathing. The loud, painful pounding in his ears almost made it impossible to hear the attendant's soft voice. Rick tried to make out her conversation through the loud noise vibrating his skull, "...yeah, he said warrant ... I didn't give him any information ... no, he's the guest with the big dog ... nice guy ... paid for a week in advance ..."

Rick inched his way away from the stairwell and back down the hallway. As Rick passed his room he hesitated; wanting to go in and tell Walden about the incident, but he was already late for his date with Trish. He didn't want to miss out on the opportunity to win that pussy for the night, so he kept walking and quickly descended the back stairs and out the back door.

Rick's mind painfully swirled as he drove the truck out onto the highway and waited at a stoplight. He pulled out his cell phone to make a call. He had to get in touch with Deb and update her on the predator pursuing him. He needed her to intervene and take care of him. The phone rang and rang ... Deb didn't pick up. Rick grew anxious as Deb's voice mail picked up and asked him to leave a message. He gritted into the phone, "Deb, how are you – this is Rick. Look, there's some asshole hanging around the Inn and asking questions about 'Mr. Smith.' I didn't get a look at him, but he sounded like he was a cop on the wrong side of the jail cell. He threatened to get a warrant, gonna search out the Inn for me. We need until tomorrow afternoon; keep him off my ass until then; will you please? Thanks Deb."

Rick snapped his cell phone shut as he entered the parking lot of Dimitrous. He parked the truck and checked his breath one last time and got out. He started perspiring … He walked down the alley to the entrance to the club. He heard smooth jazz playing through the door. He took a deep breath to ease the ringing in his ear, and entered the club. He stood in the entrance for a while willing his brain to stop pounding and for his eye's to adjust to the dim lighting. He scanned the room … he didn't see her.

Think Rick; what she looked like the day you met her … Short, hot jean dress. She's not wearing a jean dress tonight. *She'll be wearing a red dress.* Rick started looking around for anything 'red'. It was dark and he had a hard time focusing. He headed to the bar.

There. He spotted a tight round ass perched atop a bar stool, tightly wrapped in a thi silk red dress. That was her … Rick would spot that ass anywhere. He paused and watched her for a moment.

She was ordering a drink. She stood up and bent over to talk to the bartender and Rick got a birds-eye view of her plump round ass. His dick got heavy as he realized he wanted to fuck her in her ass some kinda bad.

He slowly approached her from behind. How did he want to do this? With all of the events of the evening, he hadn't had time to think of a clever antidote to use on her when he arrived … and she had given him only one shot at making her pussy wet.

Rick watched her as she scooted her ass back on top of the barstool. She started rolling her hips to the music, rubbing her ass around on the stool and snapping her fingers. Rick wanted to stand behind her and watch her all night, but his dick was getting heavier and he needed to move on with this foreplay so he could get to business.

He approached the bar a few seats away from Trish. He motioned for the bartender, and purposely did not look in her direction. Rick could see Trish look at him from the corner of his eye; but he pretended not to notice her. The bartender walked over to Rick and said, "Good Evening; what can I get you?"

Rick leaned towards the bartender and politely responded, "Good Evening my good fellow; you wouldn't happen to know how to make a "Lady in Red" would you? I tasted a little bit of one about a week ago, and now I want the entire thing. So again I ask … Do you know how to make a "Lady in Red?"

Rick saw Trish watching him and made sure she heard what he said to the bartender. She turned her head so Rick couldn't see her rosy-cheeked smile.

The bartender slowly responded, "…Well, I've never heard of one of those, but if you tell me what's in it I'll try to whip one up for you."

Rick tilted his head sideways and said, "I don't know … No one can tell you what's in a Lady in Red. You have to experience it first hand to understand. You see, I think the Lady in Red is made differently for every man."

Rick saw Trish turn her entire body towards him and openly smile at him. She scooted on the barstool and crossed her legs. She was still smiling at Rick as she picked up her drink, tilted her head and watched Rick like he was an entertaining movie.

The bartender was staring at Rick, waiting for him to tell him how to make the drink and said, "Excuse me sir, but I've never had a Lady in Red, so I'm afraid I don't know how to make it. Would you like something else?"

Trish was giggling behind her hand. Rick saw he had her attention and went to work. Rick responded, "Oh absolutely not, I *must* have a Lady in Red." Rick paused and turned his eyes towards Trish. He met her gaze and pointed toward her. He said to the bartender, "There … could you make me that … right there … imagine her as an exotic, intoxicating drink … put it in a glass and allow me to suck it long and slow … until I've consumed it all?"

Rick was smiling at Trish; she was sucking on her straw and started licking it with her tongue. She was flicking her tongue around the straw and smiling at Rick. The bartender looked at the both of them and finally caught on.

The bartender smiled at Rick and said, "Perhaps you would like to ask the Lady in Red what's in the drink?"

Rick looked back at the bartender and said, "You know what, I think that's a good idea. Will you excuse me?"

Rick got up and walked over to Trish and sat next to her. He asked, "Excuse me, what are you made of?"

Trish smiled and said, "Lots and lots of tasty juices, yummy morsels, and delicacies beyond your imagination." She tilted her head back and downed her drink. She stared at Rick, challenging him to entertain her. Rick could see she was getting bored. He cursed to himself 'Damn this bitch is hard!'

Rick turned to the bartender and said, "Excuse me, but it would appear that Dimitrious is not capable of making what I want. So I'd like to pay this ladies tab, and her and I are going to try and find what I'm desiring."

Rick turned to Trish and said, "Would you like to take a walk?"

Trish sat there for a long moment looking at Rick. The bartender came back over and gave Rick her bill. Rick paid with cash and held out his hand to Trish. She sat on the barstool still undecided if she would move.

Trish licked her lips and slowly said, "We're going for a walk; that's it."

Rick nodded and held out his arm for Trish to grab onto. She obliged him and he escorted her out of the club. They entered the alley and started walking. Rick gripped her arm closer to him and said, "You look absolutely delicious tonight."

Trish allowed Rick to hold her arm close and said, "Thank you."

Rick saw a park bench nearby and guided Trish in that direction. He continued, "You know, there really is a drink called Lady in Red."

Trish smiled and said, "There is not; you made that up. Good entrance though, I'll give you that."

Rick and Trish reached the bench and they sat down. Rick

turned and leaned towards Trish and said, "Really, I kid you not; it's real, and it's sweet, and it's warm ..."

Rick leaned closer and tried to kiss her. She turned away and said, "It's getting cold out here. We should be getting back."

Rick was getting impatient with her game. He said, "If I found the drink and tasted it; would you want to know what it tasted like?"

Trish turned to Rick and said, "Well, I guess if you found the drink ..."

Rick quickly jumped down on his knees in front of Trish. He pushed her legs open and grabbed her ass and pulled her torso into his face. He pulled her panties to the side with his fingers and shoved his tongue deep in her pussy.

Trish sucked in a surprised sigh and gripped the park bench. She breathlessly said, "Well ... just help ... yourself." Rick was eagerly licking and sucking Trish's pussy right there on the park bench. Trish tried not to moan aloud, but he was making her legs shake as she tried to sit on the bench and act like there wasn't a man eating her pussy in public. She immediately started cumming. She opened her legs and allowed Rick to suck her cum pouring out of her. Trish let out a long, agonizing moan and a couple walking nearby started looking their way.

Just as quickly as Rick started eating her pussy, he stopped, pulled her dress back down and got back up on the bench and held her close. Trish was still panting and shaking as Rick held her and whispered close to her ear, "The drink is magnificent."

Trish buried her head in Rick's shoulder and said, "Would you ... like some more?"

Rick helped Trish up from the park bench and guided her towards the parking lot. He gritted though clinched teeth, "I thought you'd never ask."

CHAPTER TWENTY NINE

Deb lay in bed watching Carlito sleeping beside her. She smiled; he was beautiful.

He had pampered her the whole day and night. Deb snuggled closer to Carlito and smiled again thinking about the full body massage he gave her after breakfast ... the surprise dozen roses delivered for dinner ... he wouldn't let her sleep all night. He kept his hands and mouth and dick loving her all night long. She watched him sleeping and was getting wet; she wanted him again.

He had made her feel wonderful after her traumatic return to work. He was her rescuer. He wouldn't let her do a thing all day. Deb made the mistake of leaving her phone out after Carlito had caught her talking on it. He took it and hid it so she wouldn't be able to answer it; so she would have to give him her undivided attention. A chill ran down Deb's spine and she shivered and realized what a wonderful father - and husband Carlito would be. And, if her baby were alive, she would have loved to have Carlito as the father of their child, and husband in her life.

Deb's throat became dry and she held her breath fighting back the tears pounding in her eyes. She eased her body away from Carlito and slid out of bed. She wrapped his robe around her and walked into the living room.

Deb paced the floor and calmed her breathing. She spotted her purse on the table and went to search for her Xanax. She opened the fridge to get some water and there, sitting in the butter tray was her cell phone with the display illuminating "(2) new messages."

Deb grabbed a bottled water and her cell phone and walked over to the table and sat down. She reached to push the button on her phone, and then paused. She put her phone down and reached for the Xanax and put it in her mouth. She opened the bottled water and raised it to her mouth and mumbled, "I better take this before I listen to these messages …"

She swallowed the pill, and picked her phone back up. She pushed the button and put the phone to her ear. First message … yesterday … reminder call from the cleaners. Second message … today … Rick!

Deb's heart started pounding hard and Carlito's robe vibrated on her body as she listened to Rick's words … "Deb, how are you – this is Rick. Look, there's some asshole hanging around the Inn and asking questions about 'Mr. Smith.' I didn't get a look at him, but he sounded like he was a cop on the wrong side of the jail cell. He threatened to get a warrant, gonna search out the Inn for me. We need until tomorrow afternoon; keep him off my ass until then; will you please? Thanks Deb."

Deb slung her phone into the couch and hissed, "Damn you Rick!"

She closed her eyes and ran her hands through her hair. She squeezed her temples and rocked back and forth in the chair. Deb slowly sighed out a long shaking breath. She slowly got up to retrieve her phone. When she reached for it between the sofa cushions she saw a shadow in the hallway. Her heart raced as she quickly jerked up at the voice coming from the shadow.

"So, who's Rick?"

Carlito stepped out from the shadows and Deb saw him standing there. His beautiful bronze body totally naked, glistening in the morning sunrays through the window. Deb wanted to run to him and embrace him and tell him everything - all the sordid, gory details of her life. Who Rick really was; what really happened to their baby.

Carlito walked closer to the sofa; closer to Deb and said again, "So, who's Rick?"

Deb opened her mouth to speak when a quick glimmer outside the window caught her eye and she jerked her head towards the window. Carlito became impatient and lunged toward the couch and grabbed Deb's phone out of her hands.

Deb grabbed at her phone and squealed "No Carlito, give it back to me, please!"

Carlito growled at Deb as he stepped back and evaded her, "If you won't tell me who the hell Rick is, I'll call the man back and find out for myself."

Deb ran around the couch and tried to reach Carlito before he punched the buttons on her phone. She wrestled with Carlito and said, "Rick is a business associate dammit, now give me my phone! Why are you acting like this?"

Carlito grabbed Deb and held her close. He whispered in her ear, "Baby, I'm sorry. I love you so much. I just ... I don't want to ... I don't deserve you."

Carlito pulled Deb away from him and looked her in her eyes. He whispered, "I just wanted to be sure before I asked you ... Will you marry me Debra Shaver?"

Deb stood there with her mouth open, staring up at Carlito. She took two long quivering breaths and tried to focus on his eyes to make sure he was serious.

She licked her lips and opened her mouth to speak again. Deb's phone started vibrating in Carlito's hand. They both looked at the phone, then back at each other. Deb reached for Carlito's hand to take her phone; Carlito extended his arm and held it out of her reach. He shook his head and said, "I do not believe you would answer your phone at a time like this! I mean come on Debra, I just asked you to marry me!"

Deb stomped her foot and stood up straight. She pursed her

lips and said, "Carlito you are not being fair! My job requires me to be available via cell phone at all times and you're using that against me." Deb's phone beeped with a message and she tried to grab it out of Carlito's hand again.

Carlito shook his head and walked into the bedroom with Deb's phone. He emerged with a pair of jogging shorts on and headed towards the front door. Deb latched onto his arm and tried to get her phone out of his hands. He was trying to pull Deb off of his arm as he said, "Debra, it's been way too long! Your job has come before me our entire relationship, and today, I demand your attention! You and I are going to talk about everything, and you're going to answer my questions; starting with the last very important question I just asked you!"

Deb was pulling on Carlito's arm, trying to get him to stop. As they approached the front door, Deb saw the flicker of light outside the window again. She released Carlito's arm, paused and looked out the window ... what was it?

Carlito reached for the doorknob and opened his front door. He said over his shoulder, "I'm going to put your cell phone in my car, lock it, and perhaps we can accomplish something." He stepped outside his front door.

Deb's heart started pounding hard in her chest again and she felt a wave of panic engulf her body. She looked at Carlito, then out the window, then back at Carlito again. Her breathless call to Carlito escaped her mouth just as a shot rang out and exploded in Deb's ears. She watched Carlito's beautiful body recoil back into the living room and slam onto the floor. Deb's cell phone went flying against the wall and ricocheted into a twirling circle in the middle of the floor.

Deb heard a car driving off in the distance but couldn't take her eyes off of the lifeless body slumped on the floor. She slowly stepped closer to Carlito and looked down at him. A large whole in his chest was holding a puddle of blood and a small red stream ran down the corner of his mouth. Deb stood there looking down at him in disbelief … *This couldn't be happening … he just asked me to marry him and I didn't get the chance to tell him 'yes'.*

Deb's cell phone started vibrating against the floor. She glanced down at her phone at her feet, then back at her dead lover. Deb felt her head shrinking and became dizzy. A car horn outside startled her and she ran to the front door and closed it. She turned around and saw Carlito's dead body bleeding all over the floor and she felt nauseous. Her phone started vibrating again and she slowly walked over and picked it up out of the puddle of blood. She pushed the button and held it up to her ear and said, "Hello."

A raspy, familiar voice grated into the phone, "Get out of the house now! It's all over; get out of the house immediately!"

Deb loudly cried into the phone, "Why did you kill him daddy? Why? I loved him; he asked me to marry him! I could have had a life!" Deb dropped the phone and collapse down on top of Carlito's body and cried into his bloody chest. Deb's phone started vibrating again, but she didn't care … She had lost Carlito … It was her fault he was dead. She wanted to die with him.

Deb's mind started racing … *where was her gun?* In her purse … she could end it all right now; stop all the pain in one quick moment. Deb looked up to find her purse. Her cell phone started vibrating on the floor again and Deb grabbed it and squeezed it hard, trying to break it. Her body was engulfed in uncontrollable jerks from her deep sobs that escaped her. Deb lowered her head back down onto her lover's dead body and wept.

She continued crying into Carlito's bloody chest until her eyes swelled shut. Her cell phone continued to vibrate intermittently while she clutched it in her hand. Deb was incoherent when a shadow entered the apartment and gathered up her purse and all of her clothes. The shadow picked Deb up off of Carlito's body and carried her out the door and into a waiting car. The shadow then locked and closed the front door to Carlito's house; leaving him lying on the floor in his own blood.

The car drove away and disappeared into the traffic.

CHAPTER THIRTY

Rick smiled to himself as he left Apartment 406. He'd stayed much longer than he had planned, but the pussy was just too good! Rick shivered as he walked to the truck. He smiled again; she can send shivers up his spine just from thinking about her! He knew he would be thinking about Trish for a long time.

He got in the truck, started it and pulled onto the highway. His mind was on Trish ... she was incredible! She definitely won the award for best dick sucking. Rick glanced at his watch and noticed the time. Damn, 2:00 pm. He had to hurry; Walden had booked tickets on the 4:00 pm train.

Rick's fixation on Trish, and rushing to pick up Dog and Walden allowed the black mustang to follow close behind Rick without being noticed. Rick could smell Trish on his body and clothes ... she wore the sexiest perfume. He'd forgotten to ask her what it was she was wearing; he wanted to buy some. He could spray it on his bed sheets and lay there masturbating thinking about her.

A stoplight ahead of Rick turned yellow. He glanced around quickly and pressed the gas pedal. The light turned red just as Rick rolled under it.

The black mustang gunned it and ran the red light behind Rick. The mustang's loud engine made Rick's head pound and he looked in his rear view mirror. Rick sped up and made the next right turn ahead of him into a residential neighborhood. He watched his rear view mirror; he wanted to see where the mustang would go. Rick saw the mustang slowly creep around the corner. Rick gunned the gas pedal and sped around the block, then back onto the highway. Rick looked in the rearview and saw the black mustang fish-tailing around the curves keeping up with him.

Rick yelled, "Fuck! I'm being followed!" He maneuvered the big Ford truck in and out of lanes. Rick could see a cop car waiting for him at the next stop light with the lights flashing. Rick's head started pounding blinding noise throughout his brain and his eyesight became foggy. Rick pleaded, "Please not now! I need to see to get out of this!" Rick cut the wheel and drove onto the median and gunned the Ford F150 across the parallel highway and onto a side road. He looked in his rearview mirror and could see the black mustang slide to a stop; it couldn't follow the truck over the rough terrain. Rick's heart was pounding through his eardrums. The road Rick was driving on started to look like old Babcock Road; 13 years ago. Rick could suddenly smell Roland's nasty cigarette smoke as it burned his eyes. A sharp stabbing pain sliced through Rick's left temple as he recalled the sound of the cinderblock crushing his skull.

Rick swerved and almost hit a mailbox. He jerked the truck back onto the road and turned down the next street, going towards the water. He had to make it back to the Bed and Breakfast, that's all he needed to do! Rick reached for his cell phone in his pocket; punched his speed dial and called Deb.

No answer. Rick slammed his cell phone shut and yelled, "Dammit man!" He threw it in the passenger seat.

Another highway was quickly approaching Rick's path. He slowed down and came to a stop at the Stop sign. He looked left, and then right - no police. He pulled out onto the highway, and as he was turning he looked in his rearview mirror and caught a glimpse of the black mustang quickly approaching the Stop sign behind him. Rick darted in and out of traffic, trying to get lost in the flow. He grabbed his phone and tried to call Deb again ... no answer. Where the hell is she?

Rick hung up and dialed Walden. Walden answered, "Well

man, it's about time ya be calling me! Our train leaves da station in 2 hours, where de hell ya been man?"

Rick yelled into the phone, "Walden, shut up! Listen, there's an unmarked black mustang chasing me, along with a few of the locals. When I was leaving the room yesterday, I heard a man at the front desk asking for a 'Mr. Smith' and threatened to get a warrant. Get your shit and get Dog ready and be in the parking lot ready to go when I get there, 'cause I'm coming in with a heavy load."

Walden replied calmly, "Ok man, Ok. Don't panic Mr. Smith. How far away are ya?"

Rick yelled back into the phone, "I'm about 10 minutes away, I think. I've been taking turns and driving over highways and I don't really know where I am; but I'm heading towards the water and I gotta run into you sooner or later!"

Walden calmly said again, "Ok man, Ok. I got a call from me contact last night telling me someone was trying to get a warrant to search da Inn. We stopped him from getting his warrant, but he was pretty mad man, and I figured he would be finding ya. I've already got another car to take us to da train station, so just get ya ass back here. Dog and I'll be waiting in da front parking lot in a dark red Ford Minivan. Just park da truck, get in da van and we're da fuck outta here."

Rick almost hit a tree as he darted onto a side street while trying to elude the mustang. Rick's head was pounding so hard his vision vibrated with each heartbeat. He was perspiring and yelling into the phone, and didn't notice the stream of blood running out of his ear and dripping onto his shirt. He yelled to Walden, "What? Damn man, you're good! Look, make sure you get all my shit out of the room, and don't forget to get Dog's medicine …"

Walden cut Rick off in mid sentence, "Look man, hey listen. I got all ya stuff packed already and loaded in da van. What I need to know is, how do I get dis maniac dog to listen to me and follow me to da van?"

Rick yelled out "Shit!" as he almost ran over a pedestrian crossing

189

the street. He then said to Walden, "Where's Dog? Put the phone to his ear so he can hear me."

Walden got up and walked over to where Dog was lying, watching his every move. When Walden approached Dog, he raised his head and showed his teeth. Walden heard a low growl escape his chest and said, "Easy boy, easy! Somebody wants to talk to ya."

Walden lowered the phone to Dog, but Dog growled louder. Rick yelled into the phone, "Dog! Dog! Dog, listen to me!"

When Dog heard Rick's voice through the phone he stopped growling and whined like a little puppy. Walden put the phone closer to Dog's ear. Rick was saying, "Dog, Dog – go with Walden to the car and wait for me. Dog, go with Walden to the car, be nice and don't make any noise until I get there. Dog, don't hurt Walden, go with him to the car and wait for me."

Dog jumped up off the floor and walked to the door and looked at Walden. Walden stared at Dog in amazement. Walden put the phone back up to his ear and said, "Man, dis dog is a trip! We'll meet ya in da parking lot. Red Ford minivan!"

Walden hung up and stared at Dog waiting at the door. Dog pounced around gingerly at the door, looking at Walden playfully. Walden slowly walked past Dog and reached for the doorknob. Dog rammed his massive head into the side of Walden's leg and Walden screeched, "Ahhhh!" and froze and held his breath. He looked down at Dog and saw that the beast was just playing; and exhaled slowly.

Walden opened the door and said; "Don't scare me like dat man! Just be cool and follow me to da van and we'll be outta here."

Dog pranced out into the hallway and waited for Walden to lock the door and close it behind him. They made their way to the stairs and went down to the front desk. The clerk greeted them, "Afternoon sir, will you be checking out?"

Walden handed the clerk his room key along with Rick's and said, "Yes ma'am; checking out for me and Mr. Smith." Dog paced in front of the door impatiently waiting to get out. The clerk replied, "Thanks."

She punched keys on her computer and handed Walden the receipt, "Thank you and please come again."

Walden said over his shoulder as he stuffed the receipt in his pocket and walked towards the door, "We will Miss; we will."

Walden opened the front door and Dog bolted out into the parking lot. Walden yelled, "Hey man! Da van is over here."

Dog stopped and trotted over to where Walden was walking and followed him to the red minivan. Walden opened the door and Dog jumped in. Walden closed the door and walked around and got in. He started the van and put it in reverse. Dog and Walden sat there in the red minivan, waiting for Rick …

Rick was parked in an underground parking garage, waiting for the heat to pass before he ventured back out onto the street. He didn't know how many cops he shook, but if he managed to loose the mustang, that would be enough

He started the truck and slowly made his way to the entrance of the parking garage. He entered the highway and made his way towards the water. He was slowly getting his bearings and noticing familiar landmarks. When he realized he was just around the corner from the Bed and Breakfast he got excited and started driving faster. When he turned the corner into the parking lot of the Bed and Breakfast, the black mustang was waiting on the side of the road and quickly cut out in front of Rick. Rick was looking for the red minivan and did not see the mustang dart out in front of the truck. Rick rammed into the side of the mustang and crushed the passenger side flat. The driver of the mustang was trapped in the car; his door wouldn't open and he was yelling out of the window, "You son-of-a bitch! I'm going to get your ass! You can't get away from me you son-of-a-bitch!"

The blinding pain shooting through Rick's skull made his eyesight blurred and he couldn't make out the vehicles in the parking lot. He tried to focus and look for anything red … Rick smiled to himself for a hot second … *he was just looking for something red last night* … Rick took a moment more to remember Trish. He was smiling again when a horn exploded his eardrums and he looked to his left. There was a red minivan with Walden and Dog looking at him. Dog's huge head was sticking out of the passenger window nodding frantically; he was happy to see Rick.

Rick put the truck in park and got out. He left the truck's two front wheels on top of the mustang. The driver was still yelling and cursing at Rick. Rick looked over at the driver and smiled as he walked by. The driver was trying to climb out of the window and get to Rick. Dog was watching from the van and started growling. Walden looked at Dog and said, "Easy boy; we don't' need no more trouble. Just sit here and wait for ya man."

The driver of the mustang started climbing out of the car window, and right when he had his head and one arm out, Rick walked back over to him and punched him square in his temple. The driver let out a loud growl and yelled, "You son-of-a-bitch! That's it! I'm gonna shoot your monkey ass and get this shit over with!"

Rick turned and started running over to the van. Dog jumped out of the van window and sprinted in the direction he was running from … towards the mustang driver.

Rick turned around and saw a gun pointed right at him. The driver had his head and one arm out the window holding a pistol pointed right at Rick. As Rick dropped to the ground, Dog dashed past him. Rick heard a shot and closed his eyes and covered his ears with his hands. When Rick opened his eyes and turned around he saw Dog latched onto the arm of the driver, twisting his large head from left to right, breaking the drivers arm. When the ringing pain subsided in Rick's head he could hear a scream … the driver was screaming and begging Rick to get Dog.

Walden drove the van over to Rick and yelled, "Get ya dog man! We gotta get outta here!"

Rick looked at Walden and then back to Dog. The receptionist came running out of the office and screamed, "Somebody help him!"

Rick watched Dog twist and tear the drivers arm off with a loud crunch. The driver let out one last screech, grabbed his severed arm and slumped in a pile inside the mustang. The receptionist screamed and ran back into the office. Dog finally let go of the arm and it dropped to the ground with a thud. The pistol was lying on the ground at Dog's feet.

Rick put his hand out and Dog came bustling over to him. Dog jumped up on Rick and Rick hugged him and said, "Hey boy; I've missed you too! Good boy!"

Walden blew the horn and yelled out the window, "Can we reunite on da way to da train man? Get de hell in da van!"

Rick started running for the van with Dog at his side. He opened the door and they both jumped in. Walden screeched out of the parking lot and onto the highway; bound for the train station.

Rick slowed his breathing and tried to ease the vibrating pain in his head. He finally said, "So, who was the predator that was chasing me?"

Walden huffed and shook his head. He looked at Rick, then back at the road, then back at Rick and said, "Ya mean da one-armed dude? Well his name was Sharkey - a local bad cop. He got a tip from somebody in Virginia telling him about ya."

Dog let out a loud yelp and Walden turned to look at him, then back at the road. He added, "I guess dey forgot to tell him about ya man-eating beast of a sidekick ya got man."

Rick turned around to pet Dog's head when he noticed blood all around his mouth and on his face. Rick looked at Walden and said, "Do I have blood on me?"

Walden huffed and looked at Rick and said, "Fucking A man! Ya got blood all over ya face! And look at ya shirt man, ya got blood all over it!"

Rick looked down and saw all of the blood on him. Was he injured? He pulled down the visor and looked in the mirror. Rick saw the stream of dried blood running out of his left ear. It had flowed all over his shirt. Rick had Sharkey's blood slopped all over his face from Dog licking him ... he looked a bloody mess.

Rick said, "Walden, I can't go to the train station looking like this!"

Walden huffed and said, "Get in da back man and clean ya self up! I can't stop man, we gotta keep going."

Rick climbed into the back and started rummaging through his bags. He found a clean shirt and a towel. Dog wanted to lick Rick and play, but Rick was stern and said, "Dog! Not now. We're in a shit load of trouble and we gotta get out of town quickly and without creating a lot of attention."

Dog sat still and let Rick change, and then Rick started wiping off Dog's face. They were pulling into the train station when Walden huffed and said, "Are ya done primping man? We got a train to catch."

Rick made his way back up into the front seat and said, "As good as it's gonna get right now. Let me out near the freight entrance so I can put Dog in his cage and I'll meet you at the gate."

Walden pulled up near the entrance and reached into the glove box and pulled out three train tickets. Rick was grabbing his bags as Walden handed him the envelopes. Walden said, "Take deez man, and meet me at da gate in 15 minutes."

Rick took the tickets and said, "Why you giving me yours?"

Walden glanced in the rearview mirror nervously and barked at Rick, "Man get de hell out da van and meet me at da gate, OK? For once in dis fucked up collaboration can ya just do what I tell ya?"

Through the painful noise in Rick's skull he could vaguely make out the sound of sirens in the distance. He grabbed the tickets out of Walden's hand and shoved them in his pocket. He put the leash on Dog and let him jump out of the van. Rick looked at Walden and could see the anguish in his eyes. Rick picked up his bags and said, "See you at the gate in 15 man," and closed the door.

Walden drove off and Rick entered the building and took Dog to the freight check-in. Rick was speaking with the assistant, and Dog sat patiently by his side. Rick was completing a form when the attendant brought out the large cage for Dog and sat it down.

He opened the door and reached for Dog's leash to lead him into the cage. Dog lunged at the attendant and nipped at his hand. The attendant yelped and snatched his hand back. He looked at Rick and said, "Perhaps you should put him in the cage."

Rick jerked on Dog's leash and pulled him back to him. He kneeled down next to Dog and said to him, "Now come on boy; you promised no trouble. We have to get out of here quickly and quietly. Please Dog; get in the cage."

Dog let out a soft whine, licked Rick on his face and trotted into the cage and sat down. The attendant quickly closed the cage door and locked it. Rick watched the attendant roll the cage through two large rubber black doors. Dog was staring at Rick with big droopy eyes, and Rick watched him disappear as the doors closed. Rick wanted to run and give him one last stroke on his big goofy head, but fought back the urge.

He signed the form and left the office. Rick was making his way towards the gate when he noticed a number of police walking briskly ahead of him. As Rick turned the corner, he saw cops - lots of them. They were grabbing and frisking someone.

A painful jolt blurred Rick's vision as he focused in on the man emerging from the swarm of cops around him. They were leading him up the hallway with his hands cuffed behind his back. Rick held his breath as he recognized the red, black and green knitted hat … Walden.

Rick turned around and bent over to drink from a water fountain. As they passed Rick, he heard one of the cops say, "Where are you traveling tonight Sir?"

Walden was dragging his feet, forcing the cops to carry him down the hallway. Walden turned and caught a quick glimpse of Rick turning around from the water fountain. He said, "Man, I done told ya five times, I'm here to pick up a friend! I'm not traveling to no place man!" When Walden started to walk, Rick saw Walden was limping on his sore ankle; the ankle Dog had bit. Rick turned back around to drink from the water fountain again. He couldn't help but wonder why Walden wasn't ratting on him; he had every right to.

The flurry of police dragging Walden down the hall took the attention off of the gate. Rick slowly emerged from the corner and glanced down the hall trying to see Walden. Walden turned just as he was being dragged around the corner and caught Rick's eye. He quickly winked at Rick and yelled, "Ouch man, ya breaking me arm!" Rick watched Walden and the parade of cops disappear around the corner. Rick quickly walked to the attendant, checked in and boarded the train.

He sat on the train and slowed his breathing; trying to calm the painful noise in his head. He closed his eyes and inhaled long and slow. What had happened? Rick shook his head trying to clear his thoughts and remember how things went wrong.

Rick took his jacket off and sat it next to him. Something hanging out of his inside pocket caught his eye. He reached for it and before he held it in his hand, he smiled … Trish. She had given Rick a pair of her panties and he had shoved them in his pocket. Rick raised the panties up to his nose and smelled them. Sweet.

Rick reclined in his chair and reminisced about the last two days. He smiled again and remembered how Trish had moaned his name as she rode his dick … she liked being on top and in control. But she quickly realized just who was in control when Rick brought her to climax over, and over. He had counted at least five times. She was incredible. Dog liked her too. Dog. Rick's head started pounding louder as he worried about Dog and his health. He had to control Dog and keep him from biting and swallowing body parts. Rick laughed to himself and he thought, at least Dog didn't swallow the arm he ripped off of the asshole in the mustang. The asshole in the mustang … who was he? And who had tipped him off from Virginia that he was coming. Damn, the asshole even knew who Rick was fucking. He must have followed him to Dimitrious, then to Trish's house.

Rick sat up and took a deep breath. He thought, 'well – the

asshole won't be driving a stick shift anymore with one arm. A quick picture of Walden being dragged away with his arms cuffed behind his back flashed across Rick's sore brain. Walden - why did he do it? Why did he give his ticket to Rick and be the decoy so he could get away? Why? Rick shook his head and winced at the pain as he tried to make sense of the last few days. His head pounded loud as he became angry and frustrated … he didn't get to kill Roland.

The bastard committed suicide. Rick had a hard time believing that. He needed to see the grave. Rick took out his phone and punched in Deb's number. No answer, Shit! Rick slammed his cell phone shut and threw it to the floor. He pounded his fist down into the seat beside him. A hot piercing pain shot through Rick's eye-sockets and he lost his vision. A wave of nausea engulfed his stomach and he buckled over. Rick got up quickly to run to the bathroom to puke.

He fell to the floor and couldn't see if he had made it to the toilet or not. He felt his stomach constricting as the pain searing through his brain fueled his nausea. His lips parted and were hanging slightly open as warm chunky liquid poured down his chin.

Hot pain continued to shoot through Rick's head. He couldn't see or feel whether or not he was laying on the floor or sprawled over the toilet, but he Sam Hill hoped he'd made it or he was going to drown in his own puke.

CHAPTER THIRTY ONE

Doc took two quick puffs on his inhaler as he leaned his head back on the couch and continued dictating a letter to Felix. Shifting anxiously in his chair, Felix sat at the computer typing. Doc jerked his head up quickly as he barked down to the woman sprawled out on the floor between his legs, "Damn it woman, watch your teeth!"

The woman purred up to Doc, "I'm sorry daddy, I'll make it feel better." She grasped Doc's soft dick in her hands and pushed it into her mouth again. She continued her efforts to get the blood circulating through the mush she had in her mouth. She was eager to get Doc off quickly before he finished dictating his letter. She nervously glanced over at Felix and shivered. She squeezed and pulled on Doc's soft dick more vigorously and sucked harder trying to stimulate it.

Doc took two more puffs on his inhaler and continued, "Felix, the part about the fundraiser in September … did it sound a little harsh when I turned them down?"

Felix stopped typing and turned and looked at the woman sucking Doc's dick. Felix rubbed his huge, rock hard dick and replied, "No Doc, I think you sounded professional and convincing."

With his eyes closed and head leaned back on the couch, Doc started dictating to Felix again, but Felix was watching the woman struggle to keep Doc's soft dick in her mouth. Felix watched a few more moments before he blurted out and interrupted Doc and said,

"Can I have her now Doc? Why don't you watch us; that always gets your dick hard."

Felix had taken his dick out of his pants and was stroking it. Doc slowly raised his head and opened his eyes. He looked at Felix suffering horribly and said, "Alright my boy. You can have her. I'll finish the letter as I watch."

The woman jumped up and held out her arms holding Felix off as she cried, "Please ... nothing rough, OK?" She frantically looked at Doc for help. Doc slowly reached down and pulled up his boxers as he grunted and stood up. He barked at Felix, "Don't hurt her Felix; or leave any bruises. Do you understand?"

Felix had taken off all of his clothes at the computer and was walking towards the woman. His large, hard dick pointed right at her. The woman backed away from Felix with her arms stretched out. She pleaded, "Please ... no bondage this time, OK?" She sucked in a large breath and backed up against the wall and slid down onto the floor. She bent her legs up and wrapped her arms around her knees. She grasped her hands together and held tight making her body a ball on the floor.

Felix approached her, bent down and grabbed her arms. She wouldn't let her arms go from the tight grip she had wrapped around her legs. Felix started pulling and jerking on her arms and her strength gave out. She let out a loud cry, "Doc! Please no! You said only you this time! Only you!"

Felix was wrestling with her and picking her up off of the floor when Doc approached Felix and said, "Felix my boy; be gentle with her this time alright? You make it so she's afraid of you."

Felix ignored Doc and continued wrestling with the woman. Felix couldn't lift the struggling woman up in his excitement, so he let her back down to the floor and gripped the woman's legs and started prying them apart. Felix said through clinched teeth, "...Doc ... I'm not ... going to hurt her. I ... just want ... to ... fuck her!"

Felix fell down to the floor and squirmed on top of the woman, pressing his body to hers. He grabbed the woman's breast and latched on with his mouth. She was pushing Felix off of her, still pleading with Doc, "Please! He's going to hurt me! Don't let him hurt me!"

Doc turned around and walked back to the couch and sat down. He casually said, "Please be quiet. I'm trying to work and write a letter, and your whining is getting annoying. Just relax and let him have his way with you. It will all be over soon."

Felix took his mouth off of the woman's breast for a moment and turned to Doc. He said, "Doc, you mean it? I can have my way with her?"

Doc took out a notepad and glanced over at Felix, naked and straddling the whimpering woman. Doc replied, "Yes Felix; go ahead. Just make sure you gag her ... I can't take her whining anymore."

Felix jumped up off the woman and ran into his room. The woman shakily got up and ran over to Doc and dropped to her knees in front of him. She breathlessly said, "Please; don't let him have me – I'll get your dick hard. Just give me a few more minutes ... please!"

Felix came running back into the room carrying a hand full of neckties. The woman turned around and saw Felix and screeched, "You said no bondage!"

Felix pushed everything off of the old wooden coffee table and dropped the ties. He ran over and grabbed the woman up off the floor. She screamed, "No!"

Doc growled, "Gag the bitch first will you!" Doc took his inhaler out and took two quick puffs. He relaxed back on the couch and started writing on the notepad.

Felix held the woman by her hair as he stuffed a handkerchief in her mouth and tied a tie around her head. He then forced her to lie down on her back on the coffee table. He stretched both her arms above her head and tied her wrists to the legs of the coffee table. He ran his hands down the woman's naked body and took her ankles and jerked her legs apart. She whimpered as Felix grabbed each ankle and tied it tight around the legs of the coffee table.

Felix stood up and looked at her tied spread-eagle on top of the coffee table. He was rubbing his dick as he breathlessly straddled the coffee table above the woman.

Doc stopped writing and stared at Felix in deep thought. Doc said, "Felix ... things are getting complicated in the Method. Too many loose cannons running around ... I have to put a stop to that."

Felix lowered his body down on the woman and placed his dick in between her legs. He guided his dick into her pussy and gripped the edges of the table as he began to thrust in and out of her. The table creaked loud with each powerful thrust Felix drove into the woman.

Doc started writing on the notepad again and continued talking. "You know Felix, I'm afraid our Rick is becoming a problem. I need to talk to him as soon as possible."

Felix was vigorously slamming his body into the woman, gripping the table harder with each thrust. The table was sliding across the tile floor as Felix pounded the woman. She was drooling out the side of her mouth as she gasped for air through the gag. Her legs shook as she came uncontrollably.

Doc watched as Felix gripped the table harder and his body started to jerk. He thrust deep in the woman as he came and his knuckles went white squeezing the edges of the table. Felix let out a loud cry just as the table came apart and crumbled into pieces beneath their bodies. The woman let out a loud moan as their weight came down on her wrists and ankles.

Felix collapsed on top of the woman. She was moaning loud and Doc got up and pushed Felix off of her. He untied her wrists and her ankles; Doc quickly noticed one of her ankles looked like it was broken. He took the gag out of her mouth and she cried, "I told you ... he would hurt me."

Doc picked her up off of the broken table on the floor and laid her on the couch. He pulled her legs apart and she whimpered and reached for her broken ankle. Doc held her down and said, "Not yet; not just yet. You're almost done."

Doc pulled his boxers back down and lay on top of the woman. She moaned loud and said, "Ouch! You're hurting me! He broke my ankle and I think my wrist is sprained. Please, I can't."

Doc covered her mouth with one hand and pushed his soft dick into her wet pussy with the other. He growled close to her face, "I'm paying you enough bitch, to break your leg! Now lay still and let me finish." Doc started wheezing as he felt the blood rush into his dick as it slid into her. He gave two, labored thrusts into the woman and fell limp on top of her as he came. She was crying as she asked, "Am I done now? Can I please leave?"

Doc raised up and rolled off of her onto the floor. He wheezed out, "Thank you for a lovely evening madam. Your package is near the door … please pick it up on your way out."

The woman scampered to her feet and whined loud as she tried to walk on her ankle. Doc sat up and looked at her and said, "I'm sorry about the bruises baby. Please, go to the doctor and send me the bill. Don't worry; Doc will take care of you."

She gingerly stepped over Felix sprawled out snoring on the floor, gathered her things and went to the bathroom. Doc slowly got up off of the floor and pulled his boxers back up. He walked over to the computer and sat down. He stared at the screen a moment and started typing. A few moments later, the woman limped out of the bathroom and stood near the door. She picked up the small bag sitting on the table near the door. Doc stopped typing and looked at her. He smiled and said, "So my darling … same time next month?"

She nodded quickly, opened the door and left. Doc turned back to the computer and started typing again. He opened an unread e-mail and started grumbling under his breath, "Son-of-a bitch! Rick! What are you doing?" Doc started wheezing and couldn't find his inhaler. He let out labored coughs as he tried to catch his breath. Felix started moving on the floor at the sound of Doc's coughing.

Felix turned over on the floor and looked up to find Doc slumped in the chair, wheezing for breath. Felix unsteadily tried to raise himself off of the floor, but his left hand slid across the cum filled tile floor and slid into a 6 inch splinter of wood from the shattered table. The piece of wood pierced Felix clean through his hand and he grabbed his hand screaming, "Fuck!"

Felix doubled over in pain on the floor, squeezing his hand. Doc tried to stand to help Felix as he wheezed heavily. He couldn't, so he tried to sit back down at the computer, but could only manage sliding down onto the floor and leaning against the couch.

Felix stood up again; this time slowing and gingerly stepping across the wet, jagged-edged floor holding his wrist making sure nothing touched the piece of wood protruding from his hand. He made it to Doc and was crying, "Where is it! Where is it dammit?"

Doc looked up to the couch cushions. Felix reached for the couch cushions and ripped them off the couch. He spotted the inhaler, grabbed it and shoved it in Doc's mouth. Felix gave Doc puff, after puff, until Doc reached for the inhaler and took it from Felix.

Felix backed away and raised his injured hand to Doc. His side was covered with blood running out of the whole in his hand around the stick. Felix was crying and holding his hand as he said, "Doc ... what am I going to do? It hurts so bad!"

Doc raised his hand and whispered through labored breaths, "I know my boy, I know. Don't worry, call Marvin Shuester; tell him what happened and he will know. Go ... go call him, right now."

Doc waved his hand for Felix to go, then gave himself two more quick puffs. Felix was crying as he gingerly made his way across the floor again to the other room. Doc pulled his cell phone out of his pocket and punched in numbers. He took two more quick puffs before he said into the phone, "I need you. Come quickly; right now." Doc closed his phone and put it back in his pocket.

He slowly looked around the room and shook his head. He said to himself, "I really need to teach Felix how to control himself." Doc's thoughts raced to the e-mail he had read. He breathed deeply and took a puff. He shook his head again and said, "That is one boy I thought could control himself … Rick my boy, you are disappointing me."

Felix came out of the bathroom holding his wrist. He had a towel wrapped around his hand, crying he said, "Doc, where's the phone?"

Doc reached into his pocket and handed his cell phone to Felix. Felix had put boxers and socks on so he could make his way across the dangerous mess he had made on the floor. He reached for Doc's phone. As Doc handed it to Felix, he said, "You know Felix … sex should be something good. Sex shouldn't be something bad."

Felix shook his head as he took the phone from Doc, and said "But Doc, sex is good and bad … It feels so good when you do bad things."

Doc chuckled weakly and started coughing. He smiled to Felix and said, "I know my boy. I know. Now, call Marvin now before you bleed all over the place and fuck things up even more than you already have!"

Felix limped into the other room and closed the door. Doc eased himself off of the floor and sat on the couch. His mind was racing contemplating what his next steps had to be. How could he make everything turn out the way it should be … The way he wanted it to be.

CHAPTER THIRTY TWO

Deb looked at her watch and hurried to the Café to get a cup of coffee before their meeting. Rick had called last night when he was back in town, anxious to get the information on Smitty so he could finish his bloody rampage ... and Deb would be finished with him. This assignment needed to be over quick so she could lay low for a while and get IAD off her ass. Besides, she was feeling a little overwhelmed lately with things, and she needed a break from it all.

Deb was rounding the doors of the Café when she heard a man's voice saying, "...I'd like to introduce you to the new Chef, Ronald Swift ..."

Deb's throat constricted and she stopped walking in her tracks. She heard another man's voice, "...so, where did Carlito Dominguez go?"

Deb inhaled and fell back against the wall ... *he said Carlito's name.* Deb noticed passerby's looking at her, and one woman stopped and asked, "Are you alright Shaver?"

Deb nodded and said, "Just a bit of indigestion; I'll be alright. Nothing a cup of coffee won't fix."

As Deb continued into the Café, she noticed a few people shaking hands with a man wearing the white chef's coat that Carlito would always wear. She quickly took her eyes off of the new chef and hurried over to the coffee stand. Her hands were shaking as she poured the cream in her cup, then she frantically dashed out of the Café before she could hear anymore about the 'new chef'. Deb bumped into Walter as she rounded the corner and almost dropped her coffee.

"Oh! I'm sorry Walter, I didn't see you coming."

Walter smiled and said, "That's alright Ms. Shaver; I was standing here waiting for you."

Deb's heart raced quickly and she inhaled sharply; remembering the last time Walter came looking for her. Deb's eyes looked up at Walter and her voice was a strained whisper as she said, "You have a package for me?" Deb willed for Walter to lead her to the mailroom … for her to find her Carlito smiling, standing there waiting for her. In some way – some how, have it all just be a really bad dream.

Deb's eyes started to water and Walter hung his head and said, "I'm sorry about Mr. Dominguez Ms. Shaver. He was a real fine man; and he loved you."

Deb looked away and said, "Why were you waiting for me Walter? I have a meeting to go to and I'm late."

Walter cleared his throat and said, "Your meeting place is no longer safe. It is suggested that you change your meeting to another location."

Deb looked back at Walter. He nodded and politely said; "Now if you'll excuse me Ms. Shaver, I also have work to do."

Walter turned and started walking back down the hallway. Deb stared at him until he disappeared. She slowly started walking down the hall back to her desk. Her mind raced, "Someone knows about me and Rick. Then they know about the Method … Do they know about Doc?"

She quickly made her way back to her desk and sat down. She took out her phone and text a message, "Meeting place is changed. New place – Food court at Galleria Tyson's II." She nervously looked at her watch as she reached for her coffee. She heard Captain screaming at someone in the hall and turned around to see who it was. Hmmm, Walter. Why was Captain yelling at Walter? Interesting …

Deb closed her phone and put it in her purse. She let out a long sigh, reached in her brief case and pulled out the manila folder of information on John C. Smith, a/k/a 'Smitty'. She added a few more pieces of information she was holding in her desk and put the folder back in her brief case. As she closed the clasp, the worn, barely readable inscription on the handle caught her eye ... "To my Darling Debra, the most beautiful, and smartest investigator of them all." Deb squeezed her eyes shut and cursed, "It's not fair! Why am I always the one alone? Everyone I've ever loved, I could never be with. And now ... my baby and my Carlito are gone ..."

She squeezed her eyes harder holding back the hot tears burning her ears. When she finally found the courage to open her eyes again, she looked up and spotted a familiar face in the crowd standing at the Help Desk ... Hutchison's widow. Deb sat up straight and moved her chair so she could get a better look at her. Deb's heart leapt out of her chest as she watched the woman hold and stroke her swollen belly, protecting her unborn child from the crowd of people shuffling around her.

Deb reached down and stroked her empty stomach. Her fingers felt like knives against her skin as she imagined the life that died inside of her. Deb jumped up from her desk and ran to the bathroom. She held her stomach and paced the floor, looking at herself in the mirror trying to shake the pain in her stomach.

She looked at herself in the mirror and cursed, "Damn! It's just not fair! Everyone deserves a little companionship; love; and happiness in life! Everyone has something or someone but me! Doc has Felix; Captain has his wife; hell ... now, even Rick has his homicidal maniac Dog!"

Deb hung her head and leaned against the sink and said, "I want my Carlito back ..."

She ran into a stall and closed the door. She plopped down on the stool and put her head in her hands. She cried into her hands as she mumbled, "I need someone to take care of me ... and I want to take care of someone who needs me ..."

Deb jerked her head up as an idea flashed across her sullen thoughts … "I could adopt Hutchison's baby!

She quickly grabbed some tissue and wiped her face off. She came out of the stall and checked herself in the mirror … She looked horrible.'

She shook her head and headed back to her desk. She looked for the widow in the crowd, but she was gone. "Dammit!"

Deb sat down and heard her phone buzzing in her purse. She took it out and looked at the display, "New Text Message".

Deb opened her phone and read the display "New Message from Rick." The message read, "What! Why? Cool, I'll be there. Pls don't be late."

Deb closed her phone and looked at her watch, "Hell, I'm already late."

She was putting her phone back in her purse when it started vibrating in her hand. She looked at the display … Rick calling. Deb quickly gathered her briefcase, coffee and her coat and headed for the door. She was making her way past the Help Desk, and couldn't stop the urge. She made her way to the clerk and said, "Hey Judy, I saw Hutchison's widow here a few minutes ago. What did she need?"

The clerk walked over to Deb, "Hey Shaver … you look bad; are you feeling alright?"

Deb gave Judy a shrug and said, "I've been sick … now what's up on the widow?"

Judy reached for a large envelope from the desk behind her and said, "She was here to drop off this package for Captain. Apparently, he is working closely with her; helping her with all the pension and adoption stuff."

Deb leaned closer to Judy and said, "Adoption … is it definite. She's giving her baby up for adoption?"

Judy answered, "Yeah; got all the information right here."

Deb smiled at Judy and said, "Can you hook me up with a copy of what's in the package girlfriend?"

Judy nodded and replied, "I'll have it on your desk in the morning."

Deb reached out and touched Judy on the arm and said, "You're the best! See you later."

Deb made her way to the exit and walked to her car. She was smiling as she reached for her keys. Her cell phone started vibrating in her purse again and she pulled it out ... Rick calling. Damn this man is impatient, "Yes Rick, I'm late alright! I'm getting in my car as we speak and I'll be on my way."

Rick replied, "Damn! Ah, yeah Deb, good morning to you too. Ah, I thought it only natural when you make an appointment with someone it's customary to call and cancel if you aren't going to show up."

Deb drove out of the parking lot and smiled as she said, "Sorry Rick; busy morning you know. Some of us have to work for a living. I'm on my way. I'll be there in 15." Deb hung up and put her phone away. She smiled as she drove to the Galleria - thinking about the possibilities of her adopting Hutchison's baby.

Rick closed his phone and put it back in his pocket. He was sitting in the food court watching the business people shuffling about. He watched a young couple window-shopping. They were holding hands and stealing quick kisses. Rick sipped his coffee and reminisced about the last pair of lips he'd tasted and felt around his dick.

He took out his phone again and searched his phonebook ... There it is. Tricia Easton. Just seeing her name and number made him smile. He'd been fighting the urge to call her and talk to her ever since that last day they saw each other. He remembered Tricia standing in her bedroom door, naked and smiling at him. She was rubbing her pussy trying to tease him into staying another night with her.

Rick slammed his phone shut and mumbled, "Dammit man! She was good."

He wanted to call and talk to her. But what would he say? What could he say?

Rick put his phone back in his pocket. He watched the couple walk past him, and he shook his head and mumbled again, "It's better like this. I'm no good for anyone to be around. I can't bring anyone into my life. Hell, nobody wants to be in my life anyway … besides Dog."

Rick smiled to himself as he thought about the big, goofy, fearless friend he had waiting for him back at the townhouse. Dog was amazing! The way he could be playful as a puppy, and a heartless, cold-blooded killer all at the same time. Rick had much respect for Dog, and he had to finally admit it … He loved him.

Rick's thoughts were interrupted by a familiar voice, "Hey stranger, is this seat taken?"

Rick looked up and saw the figure of a woman who favored Deb. He stood up to get a better look and replied, "Ah, no. Deb … is that you?"

Deb gave Rick an evil glare as she pulled out the chair and sat down, "Yes Rick; it's me. How have you been?"

Rick eased himself back down into the chair and stared at Deb. He said, "Well, I've been alright. Deb, what's going on? You don't look so good."

Deb pulled out the manila folder from her brief case and laid it on the table. She raised her eyes to Rick's and said, "I've been through a lot since we last met. I guess it shows."

He looked down and saw the label on the folder. He got excited and said, "Is this it? Is this the info on Smitty?"

Deb pushed the folder over to Rick and said, "Yeah, here it is. The long and short is: Smitty got married 13 years ago. No record of a divorce, but he lives alone in a studio apartment in Arlington, Virginia. He's a contract undercover agent now for a branch of the government that we can't tap into, and all I can give you is an address."

Rick's temples started vibrating as a sharp pain shot from eye socket to eye socket. He took a deep breath before he said, "...And there's no fucking record of a Mrs. John C. Smith?"

Deb shook her head and replied, "Oh come on Rick! How many Mrs. John Smith's do you think there is in Virginia, huh? A whole fucking lot! Besides, you aren't looking for the wife; you're looking for him. Why are you asking about her?

Rick clinched his jaw to calm the pain as he replied, "Because Deb ... If you ever want to find a motherfucker; all you gotta do is find out where his pussy is. He's bound to show up sooner or later."

A vision of Carlito's bloody body banging against the floor flashed across Deb's mind. She sucked in hard and closed her eyes. She thought about what Rick just said ... wherever his pussy is; he'll be there. Carlito was with his pussy when they found him ... whoever killed her Carlito.

Rick grabbed Deb's shoulder and shook her, "Deb ... Deb, you alright?"

She opened her eyes and looked at Rick with tears running down her face and said, "They killed him Rick ... They killed my Carlito."

Rick's mouth fell open. He slowly said, "Who ... killed him?"

Deb was wiping her eyes with a tissue, and quietly replied, "Well, I'm not sure, but I think it was the Method."

Rick shook his head and asked, "But ... why?"

Deb quickly calmed herself as she realized she was giving way to much information to Rick. She inhaled, looked at Rick and said, "That has nothing to do with your case. I'm fine, and ... thanks for listening."

Deb pointed back to the folder and said, "There's pictures inside along with his address. Oh, I do know that the woman Smitty married was black."

Rick's mouth fell open again and he blinked his eyes and leaned closer to Deb to make sure he heard correctly, "Wait a minute. You mean to tell me 'Ole Smitty married a black woman?"

Deb nodded, "Yep."

Rick chuckled and said, "That's probably why the bastard doesn't live with her ... He likes fucking her but can't bring her home to momma! But why marry her? They got kids?"

Deb shook her head, "No record of any children." A sharp pain jabbed Deb in the stomach as she finished her sentence. *No children.*

Deb stood up, picked up her brief case and held out her hand, "It was good to see you. Call me when this is complete."

Rick grabbed the folder and stood up. He said, "Can I at least walk you to your car?"

Deb shrugged and said, "You can walk me to the exit. I can't be seen walking to my car with you."

Rick caught up with Deb who had already started walking to the elevator. He said, "So, what's all been going on in your life since my last visit?"

Deb stopped and turned to Rick. She angrily replied, "Look Rick, I have to work with you. That doesn't mean you get to ask personal questions about me! What you should be worried about is keeping that maniac dog of yours under control. I got you a townhouse with a fenced backyard to contain the beast."

Rick replied, "Yeah, I never got to thank you for the nice rental you got us staying in. So, thank you Deb for looking out."

Rick reached out and gently grabbed Deb's arm so she would stop walking. Deb turned and stared at Rick. He said, "I mean it ... you've been very good to me and I'm sorry for ... well, all the trouble that seems to follow me."

Deb was silent, and Rick continued, "...And by the way; what happened to Walden? Is he alright?"

She tilted her head sideways and said, "Now you're concerned about Walden? You torment the man for two weeks, threaten his life with your beast-dog, and now you're concerned about him ..."

Deb yanked her arm out of Rick's grasp and said, "Don't thank me Rick; it's my job. Just keep that bloodthirsty dog from killing anymore people ... that will be thanks enough."

She got on the elevator and pushed the close door button. She stared at Rick as the doors were closing and said, "Walden's fine. We'll have him out and home in about a week."

Rick quickly stuck his arm in the elevator and the doors opened again. He stepped closer to Deb and said, "So, he's fine … that's good. Look Deb, you think you can arrange for me to see Roland's gravesite?"

Deb shook her head and said, "There is no gravesite for Roland … He was cremated."

Rick was silent as he stared at Deb, willing her to be lying. Deb pushed the button and said, "He was cremated and Smitty has his urn of ashes." Rick backed away from the elevator and watched as the doors closed and Deb disappeared.

Rick stood there for a moment and said to himself, "This makes no sense. Roland kills his parents, and then kills himself. Then, Smitty ends up with his ashes."

Rick turned around and started walking to the exit on the other end of the Galleria where he had parked. He held on tight to the manila folder clutched under his arm. He was anxious to pour over the contents and start making his plan of attack.

Rick knew Smitty would be the hardest to take out; that's why he saved him for last. The bastard works undercover for a branch of the government no one knows … married to an anonymous black woman … lives alone in Arlington, Virginia. Rick walked faster. His anxiety to read the information and start stalking the residence was pushing painful blood flow through his veins and making it hard to keep his vision from blurring. He slowed down and took two calming breaths to slow down his heartbeat.

Rick left the Galleria and walked across the parking lot to his rented minivan. He got in and locked the doors. He glanced around the parking lot. Clear.

He opened the folder and poured out the contents on the seat. There, amidst the papers and pictures was a close up of the face Rick remembered. The face taunting him … holding him … beating him … kicking him … and finally … bashing him in the head with a cinderblock. Rick picked up the picture of John C. Smith and held it close to his face so he could get a good look.

Smitty was smiling in the picture, but Rick could see the hatred shining through his eyes. Rick put the pictures and the papers back in the envelope and started the van.

He was headed to 7347 Lee Highway, Arlington, Virginia. Smitty's address on the file.

CHAPTER THIRTY THREE

Dog stood up on his hind legs and rested his two front paws on the table. The table shook under his weight and slid slowly across the floor. Rick yelled, "Dog! Get off the table will you; I'm trying to pack the bag!"

Dog jumped down and barked. He wanted to play.

Rick fumbled with the duffle bag; trying to stuff it full of necessities he and Dog would need for the stakeout at Smitty's house. Dog jumped back up on the table and grabbed a towel out of Rick's hand. Rick started grabbing for the towel trying to get it back.

Dog pranced around on the floor, left to right avoiding Rick. Rick grabbed for the towel and said, "Dog, give me the towel. We don't have time to play right now."

A searing pain shot through Rick's temple and he jerked his body down and grabbed his head with both hands. He groaned in pain, "Ahhh shit!"

Dog saw Rick bent over in distress and dropped the towel. He walked over to Rick and whined as he licked Rick's sweaty face. The pain tightened and Rick felt his skull collapsing inside his head. His ear's rang and Rick's eye's fluttered as he screamed, "Help me!" He fell to the floor and curled up in a ball.

Dog yelped and started licking Rick vigorously across his face. Rick started coughing and jerking his body. Dog kept licking. Rick was coughing so hard he sat up and pushed Dog away. He caught his breath and took two long slow breaths. The pain quieted in his head and he opened his eyes. Dog was standing in front of him, panting and drooling on the floor. Rick smiled and wiped drool off of his mouth and said, "How many times you gonna save my life? Why don't you just let my sorry ass die?"

Rick heard a growl grumbling deep in Dog's chest. Rick looked up and saw Dog growling and showing his teeth as he stared at Rick. Rick saw the look in Dog's eyes … the look right before he devours his victim. Rick stopped breathing and said, "Dog … you alright boy? You scaring me … what'd I say?"

Rick sat up straight and said, "Dog … I'm not going to die, all right? I was just kidding. I'm not going to die. That is; unless you decide to kill me."

Rick chuckled nervously. Dog's demeanor quickly changed and he started prancing around Rick again, bumping the side of Rick's shoulder playfully. Rick slowly got up off of the floor and leaned on the table. He saw the open, partially packed duffle bag and remembered Smitty's house … he had to get back.

Rick slowly started packing items in the bag again. Dog yelped and bumped his head against Rick again. Rick walked over to the back door and opened it. Dog sprinted out the door and into the fenced back yard. He turned and looked at Rick as if to say, "Come on! Let's play."

Rick slowly shook his sore head, and as he closed the sliding door he said, "I can't play now Dog. Give me 20 minutes and we're out of here."

Rick walked back over to the table and finished packing the bag. He calmed his mind and started concentrating on his plan. He had to get some kind of lead on how to find Smitty or his estranged wife. Smitty's house seemed deserted. Rick had watched it all day and night with no activity; not even the mailman. He finally had to leave to get Dog and some clothes, snacks, and drinks. However; he was on his way back with reinforcements. Someone had to show up at that house sooner or later … and when they did – Dog and Rick would be waiting for them.

Loud thuds against the back door startled Rick. He turned around and saw Dog banging his head against the window, yelping. Rick grabbed the bag and slung it over his shoulder. He walked over to the door and opened it. Dog ran in and pranced around Rick.

Rick said, "Come on boy – we're on our way to a party. They're serving your favorite dish … human flesh,"

Dog barked excitedly and ran to the front door, back to Rick, then to the front door again. Rick said, "Ok boy, Ok, here I come."

Rick walked to the door, opened it and he and Dog ventured out. He locked the door and smiled. He mumbled under his breath as he walked to the van, "Smitty; I'm coming to get you … I know you feel me coming … you can run but you can't hide motherfucker. I'm coming to get you …"

CHAPTER THIRTY FOUR

Deb hurried down the hallway and checked her watch ... late again. She started to sweat, mad at herself for not being able to make it on time for the most important meeting of her life ... to sign the adoption papers.

Deb saw Captain coming down the hall towards her, and she couldn't hold back the big, giddy smile as she said, "Good morning Captain. You done already?"

Captain stopped in front of Deb and said, "Now calm down. All the hard stuff is over with; all you got to do now is sign the paperwork, and you're going to have a baby."

Captain rubbed Deb's shoulder and pushed her along down the hallway towards the conference room as he continued walking past her.

Deb took a long, deep breath and continued towards the conference room. She broke out in another giddy grin. She shook her head and quietly said to herself, "What would I ever do without Captain?"

Deb didn't know how he made it all happen so quickly, but once Deb told Captain she wanted to adopt Hutchison's baby, he worked hard to make it all happen. And now, two weeks later, it's coming true. Deb was adopting a baby. She couldn't believe for once in her life, she was getting what she wanted.

As Deb turned the corner and was about to enter the conference room, she saw a large shadow approaching the doorway and a man appeared. He looked at Deb and said, "Excuse me, I was just leaving."

Deb was about to introduce herself when she looked down and saw he only had one arm. She looked back up to the man's dark face and said, "I'm sorry, I didn't get your name. This is a private meeting."

The man smiled at Deb and said, "Oh, I'm just like part of the family. Just stopped by to say hello to an old friend,"

The man turned and walked down the hall towards the exit. Deb watched him for a moment, and then slowly entered the conference room. She saw a nurse sitting at the table with Mrs. Hutchison. Mrs. Hutchison was sobbing silently into a tissue as the nurse rubbed her back. Deb quietly said, "Good morning. Is everything alright?"

Mrs. Hutchison looked at Deb and started crying harder. The nurse stood up and walked towards Deb and said, "Perhaps you should just leave and let her calm down,"

Deb shook her head and said, "No, no – it's alright. I should be here for her. If she's having mixed feelings about her baby, I want to know."

The nurse looked at Deb sternly and said, "She's not having second thoughts about the baby; she's distraught over you!"

Deb's eyes grew wide and she said, "What? Me? What's the matter? What did I do?" Deb tried to walk past the nurse and sit with Mrs. Hutchison, but the nurse grabbed Deb's arm and said, "How could you?"

Deb yanked her arm away from the nurse and opened her mouth to yell, when she looked over at Mrs. Hutchison's wide teary eyes staring at her. Deb calmed herself and said, "Please … please. Just tell me what you're talking about, and we can discuss this calmly."

The nurse looked at Deb, then to Mrs. Hutchison. Mrs. Hutchison nodded her head in agreement and they all sat down at the conference table.

The nurse held Mrs. Hutchison's hand on the table and said,

"We were just informed that … well … you were the one that ordered the hit on Mr. Hutchison and had him killed."

Mrs. Hutchison broke out in loud, screeching sobs and the nurse held her close and continued, "…So, you see why we have to consider other parents for the baby!"

Deb sat there for a moment and stared at the two women, trying to register what she had just heard. The nurse was rubbing Mrs. Hutchison's hand and trying to calm her. Deb shook her head and slowly said, "I … had nothing … to do … with Hutchison's death. Who informed you of this?"

The nurse and Mrs. Hutchison looked at Deb. Deb sat there, waiting for an answer. They were silent. Deb finally slammed her fist down on the table and yelled, "Who told you that!"

The nurse and Mrs. Hutchison jumped, and Mrs. Hutchison started silently sobbing into the tissue again. The nurse stuttered out, "…The … the gentlemen that was just here. Mr. Sharkey."

Deb yelled, "Who? That – that creepy guy I passed on the way in?"

The nurse nodded, and said, "Apparently he was a good friend of Lt. Hutchison, and Lt. Hutchison told Mr. Sharkey you were trying to kill him."

Deb shook her head and said, "I didn't do it! I don't know this Mr. Sharkey, and I didn't have Hutchison killed!"

The nurse lowered her head and said, "He also said that you would deny it …"

Deb threw her arms up and started pacing the floor. She turned and looked Mrs. Hutchison right in the eyes and said, "Do you think I'd kill your husband, and then desperately try to adopt his baby and love it as my own? Do you?"

Mrs. Hutchison continued to sob into a tissue she held to her mouth. The nurse walked over to Deb and said, "You should leave now, you're upsetting her."

Deb turned to the nurse and yelled, "I'm not going anywhere until I've signed the papers and the baby is mine!"

The nurse went running out of the room. Deb sat next to Mrs. Hutchison and grabbed her arm to keep her in her chair. Deb leaned close to her and said, "People lie everyday, and there are times when you want to believe something so bad; even though you know it's a lie."

Deb searched the young woman's face looking for some sign of understanding.

Deb continued, "I did not kill your husband. I love your baby inside of you; and I want to be its mommy ..."

The nurse came running back into the room with two policemen. She pointed at Deb and said, "There she is officer! Arrest her, she is assaulting my patient!"

The two policemen looked at each other, then back at Deb. One finally spoke up and said, "Ah ... Shaver; you want to tell us what's going on?"

Deb looked at the policemen, then back at Mrs. Hutchison. Deb whispered, "I'm ... becoming a parent ..."

The nurse ran over to Mrs. Hutchison and said, "No she isn't! My patient does not want to give her baby to this woman now, she's changed her mind."

Deb lunged for the nurse and grabbed her around her neck. The nurse started kicking and screaming as Deb wrestled her to the floor. The two policemen ran into the room and were pulling Deb off of the nurse. As they separated Deb and the nurse, Deb said through gritted teeth, "How dare you try and take away my happiness! I love that baby! You hear me? I love that baby!"

The policemen pulled Deb's hands off the nurse's neck, and were pulling her out of the room. The nurse was crying and yelling from the floor, "Arrest her! She's a killer! She's a killer!"

Through the yelling and screaming, came a loud, high-pitched screech, "Wait!"

The policemen stopped dragging Deb, and the nurse stopped yelling. They all looked over to the conference room table to see Mrs.

Hutchison standing there. Her eyes were bulging and red, and tears still streamed down her face. She was looking at Deb.

Mrs. Hutchison opened her mouth to speak, but only a squeak came out. The nurse got up off of the floor and was reaching for Mrs. Hutchison. The frail pregnant woman saw the nurse and held up her hand to the nurse, stopping her.

Mrs. Hutchison looked back at Deb and opened her mouth again, and said, "You ... you love ... my baby?"

Deb's eyes filled with tears and the room became a blur. Deb nodded her head and said, "Yes ... yes I do."

The nurse hissed to Mrs. Hutchison, "This woman killed your husband! You're not going to let your baby be raised by her are you?"

Mrs. Hutchison, still staring at Deb said, "Did ... you ... kill ..."

Deb interrupted, "No! No, I did not."

The nurse looked at Mrs. Hutchison and said, "You're not going to believe her are you?"

The policemen released Deb and backed away. Mrs. Hutchison stared into Deb's pleading eyes with tears streaming down her face. Mrs. Hutchison whispered through quivering lips "I ... believe you."

Deb broke out into a sprint and ran around the conference table and embraced Mrs. Hutchison. The two women stood there crying into each other's shoulder. The nurse sat down in a chair and said, "I don't believe this." The nurse shoved her hands in her pocket and felt a piece of paper. She took it out to see what it was. As she stared down at the business card, she remembered ... "Raymond D. Shark, Private Investigator." The nurse smiled and put the card back in her pocket. She flinched and rubbed her bruised neck. She looked at the two policemen and pointed at Deb. She said, "I want to press charges against her for choking me."

The two policemen stepped outside the conference room and one said, "Well, I suggest you find some witnesses who saw her do it."

They turned and started walking back down the hall. Captain was approaching the conference room and said, "Hey! Walker,

Stone – what's going on in there? I got a call there was a disturbance in the building here."

The two policemen shook their heads and one said, "No disturbance here Captain; just the normal noise and fuss that goes along with bringing a baby into the world."

CHAPTER THIRTY FIVE

A loud fart blasted out of Dog's ass and Rick yelled, "Come on Dog! You got to shit again? Stop eating those chicken nuggets!" Rick grabbed the empty McDonald's box off the seat in front of Dog and threw it in the back of the van. Rick sat up and looked at the house again to see if anything had changed. Nothing.

Rick cursed under his breath, "Dammit man! We've been staking out this house for two weeks! I can't take this any more!"

Rick took out his phone and punched in numbers. He heard Deb's voice answer, "Yeah, what's up?"

Rick anxiously responded, "What's up is, you've been neglecting my assignment and not providing me with any fucking information other than sitting in front of a fucking abandoned house!"

Deb's relaxed voice came back and said, "Oh Rick, I'm sorry – I've been busy. Look, I forgot to give you this address I got yesterday …"

Rick yelled and interrupted Deb, "You mean to tell me, you've had another address since yesterday and you forgot to tell me? Deb, what the fuck is up? I could have been there all day instead of sitting here in dead water smelling Dog's rancid farts all day!"

Deb cooed into the phone, "Now Rick, Rick, calm down. I'm sorry … I'm adopting a baby and it's taking up a lot of my time alright?"

Rick was silent for a moment. He didn't know what to say. He thought to himself, "Why would anyone bring a baby into this cruel world?"

He finally said, "...Well, congratulations. What's the other address?"

Deb replied, "65 Stagestone Way, Manassas, VA. Rick, I'll have a map waiting for you at the townhouse ..."

Rick cut Deb off, "I know where it is ... I used to live in Manassas Deb, remember? Who lives at this address?"

Deb replied, "We found an old address that was still receiving mail for Mr. Smith. Look, I'm going to be out-of-pocket for about a week, so you're on your own until next Friday. Can you think of anything you might need before then?"

Rick sighed long and slow; he needed Deb to be more focused on his case! He closed his eyes, trying to calm the painful noise in his head as he swore under his breath, "She's fluttering around trying to convince herself she could be a good mother, while she leaves me sitting in front of this house for two weeks!"

Dog started growling. He jumped in the back seat and pressed his nose against the window and growled louder. Rick turned his head towards the house and saw a large man walking towards the front door. Rick quickly slouched down in the seat and hid. Dog's growl became louder and Rick hissed, "Dog! Quiet!"

Rick heard Deb's voice, "Rick! Rick, are you still there?"

Rick raised his head and peeked out the window. The man was standing at the door ringing the doorbell. Rick couldn't see his face, but one arm looked considerably larger than the one he had shoved in his coat pocket. Rick eased back down in the seat and whispered into the phone, "...Deb, there's a man knocking on the door of the house ... I'll call you back."

Deb replied, "Rick! Wait! Who's the man? What does he look like? Maybe we can run him."

Rick eased back up and peeked out the window again. The man was walking in front of the house, peeking in the windows. Rick whispered into the phone, "Deb ... he's about 6'5, 280 lbs ... Looks like he's got one arm."

Dog growled in the back seat and a knot tightened in Rick's skull as he realized ... "That dude looks like dude from the Mustang ... Washington State ... Dude with his arm chewed off ... Seattle ..."

Deb's yelling voice was echoing out of Rick's phone, "Rick! Did you say he had one arm? Rick wait ... I know this guy ..."

Rick wasn't listening. He was watching the one armed man case the house. Rick cursed under his breath, "How the hell did he find me? Walden must have squealed!"

Rick hissed into the phone, "Deb, I'll call you back." Rick closed his phone and put it in his pocket. Dog was growling low in his chest watching his previous victim walk back towards the street.

Rick turned around and looked at Dog. With a sinister grin on his face he snickered under his breath saying, "How'd you like to get the rest of that shoulder blade steak over there, huh boy? We had to leave before you could finish your meal the last time." Rick hesitated and peeped out the window again. He saw the man walking towards the van. Rick snickered again saying, "Looks like the coast is clear this time; and your steak is being hand delivered right to you."

Dog flexed his massive muscles in his legs as he gripped the seat with his claws. Deep, heavy growling escaped his chest as he watched the one-armed man walking closer, and closer, approaching the stop sign ... right in front of the rented mini van. Rick whispered to Dog, "Easy boy; easy. We gotta wait until he's closer ... don't let him hear us first or he'll know we're here."

Rick eased onto the floor and reached for the rear door handle. Dog was low; his claws ripping wholes in the seat cushion as he gripped into the seat; anxiously awaiting to pounce on his victim.

Rick put his hand on the door handle and whispered to Dog, "Get ready boy. I want you to rip his nuts off this time Dog; and then kill him."

Dog growled low in chest; and gripped the seat harder. His teeth were out and he was drooling ... watching the man approach. Rick looked up at Dog and saw that wild, killer look he had in his eyes. Rick shuttered as he remembered seeing Dog look at him that way.

Rick was about to pull down on the handle when he heard a car pull up and voices. Car doors opening … more than one door … more than two voices.

Rick let go of the door handle and froze. He whispered to Dog, "Quite boy! Quiet!"

Rick tried to hear what the men were saying, but he couldn't make it out. He heard one loud outburst, "…Nothing!" More door's closing. The car drove away and there was silence.

Rick let out his breath and started breathing again. Dog whined and looked in the direction the car had disappeared. He yelped like a puppy that didn't get his snack. Rick sat up and said, "Yeah yeah, I know boy. I'm disappointed too!"

Rick climbed back in the front seat and continued, "We've been sitting at the fucking house for two weeks; and I finally see some action and it's the asshole from Seattle! Then, at the perfect time to whack this joker, his cronies show up! They probably dropped him off and cruised the neighborhood while he checked out the house. We didn't see him drive up."

Rick exhaled; exhausted and put the key in the ignition to start the van. Dog put his big, wet nose right in Rick's ear and growled low and deep. Rick froze again and stopped breathing. He whispered, "What Dog? What's the …"

Rick stopped talking as his eye caught movement from in front of the house. Dog stopped growling and sat down. Rick leaned back and watched … it was a woman. She was checking the mailbox. She turned and walked toward the house. Rick winced as he squinted to get a better look at the woman. He couldn't tell if she was black or white. She walked up to the front door of the house … put a key in … and walked in the front door. Rick saw lights come on in the left downstairs room.

He turned to Dog and said, "Well what do you know! Somebody finally fucking came home!"

Rick shook his head in disbelief. What should he do? His plan had totally gone out the window after the first week. A woman … Rick thought.

His head was sore from the pain and he needed some rest. One-arm dude and his cronies could still be lurking around the neighborhood. If she leaves he could follow her. But for now, Rick decided to lay the seat back and stretch out for while … watch the house for the night. He was satisfied; his first major lead to killing Smitty just walked right into his lap.

Rick winced as he slowly forced his eyelids shut. He said to Dog, "Wake me up immediately if anyone goes in or out of that house! And wake me up in two hours regardless."

Dog yelped and licked Rick on the side of his head.

CHAPTER THIRTY SIX

Deb held up a pair of blue baby booties against a denim infant jumpsuit. She smiled and said, "Perfect match!" The sales clerk approached Deb and said, "Buying a gift from a registry?"

Deb looked at the girl and smiled, "Nope. This is for my son. I'm adopting a baby boy ... I'm going to be a mommy."

The sales clerk smiled and said, "Congratulations! That's a nice outfit; it has a matching hat and coat over here."

Deb followed the girl; in amazement at how much she loved shopping for baby clothes. They were so cute!! Deb was ready to buy the whole store. She envisioned her son in every outfit she picked up. She wanted to dress him up everyday. Deb never knew how much she loved the color blue, especially now that everything was final. Mrs. Hutchison's son is due any day; and he'll belong to her.

Deb's phone started vibrating in her pocket and she took it out and looked at the display. The sales clerk started talking about the matching outfit and Deb interrupted, "I'm sorry; I have to take this call. Thanks for your help, but I think I got everything I need."

Deb waited for the sales clerk to walk away and answered her phone, "Rick; didn't I tell you I'd be out-of-pocket? This better be good."

Rick's agitated voice grated back at Deb, "Oh yeah ... this is fucking good!"

Deb walked into a corner and said, "Well what is it? I don't have all day."

Rick's voice quivered as he tried to control his anger. He said, "Smitty's bitch left the house around 7:00 am this morning; so Dog and I followed her. She led us straight to the other address you gave me. We parked, and I watched her get out of her car and walk to her front door. The neighbor was outside and they started talking … Smitty's bitch turned around and looked in our direction and I got a good look at her face …"

Deb quickly interrupted, "Rick, Rick; let me explain …"

Rick yelled into the phone back at Deb, "What the fuck do you mean explain? When were ya'll mother fuckers going to tell me that Smitty's bitch ass wife … is my sister Sarah!"

Deb hissed as she whispered into the phone, "Rick I didn't know! I didn't find out until yesterday."

Rick screamed back, "What do you mean yesterday? You mean yesterday when we talked yesterday; 'cause yesterday you forgot to tell me!"

Deb said, "Look Rick, what was I supposed to do? My assignment is to assist you with disposing of your targets; it said nothing about taking care of your family affairs."

Rick hissed into the phone, "Oh, what? Now you big and bad 'cause you do everything daddy tells you to do Debra! Isn't that what he calls you, Debra?"

Deb stopped breathing and was silent. Rick continued, "Oh yeah, you think a joker like me couldn't figure that shit out? You and Doc daddy sit back and decide what people should and shouldn't be told! She's my sister Deb!"

Deb forced herself to breath, and responded, "I … I don't know who or what … you're … talking about. I don't know anyone named … Doc … and my father's … dead."

Rick squeezed his eyes shut to prepare for pain as he yelled into the phone, "Stop with the lies dammit! The fucker is your father, and Felix is probably your retarded ass brother; I don't give a shit! Smitty's married to my sister!"

Deb was quiet, then said, "Rick; I didn't know until yesterday.

When I was told; I was instructed not to tell you … it was thought that it might sway your sense of logic."

Rick replied through gritted teeth, "…My sense of logic … Deb! I'm on a mission to kill my brother-in-law, who tried to kill me! There is no sense of logic! How long have they been married? Don't tell me they've been married for 13 years! That Sarah married the mother fucker right after he tried to kill me!"

Deb replied, "Rick; apparently she married him right after your disappearance … 13 years ago."

Rick felt sick. He slammed his phone shut, hanging up on Deb. He looked at Dog, then back at the house where his younger sister had just entered. Rick shook his sore head and said, "I'm getting to the bottom of this shit right now!"

He opened the van door and started getting out. Dog let out one loud bark. Rick looked at him and said, "No, you can't come! I'm afraid I might command you to kill her!"

Rick slammed the door and locked it. He crossed the road and started walking towards the house. His mind was racing with questions, and his vision blurred. He didn't see the dark blue sedan approaching the street. Dog was barking frantically from within the minivan, but Rick couldn't hear him.

As Rick approached the door, he heard a car slowly passing by. His attention sharpened and he realized his surroundings. He could hear Dog barking from the van. Rick cursed under his breath, "Fuck! Now who's following me?"

The car had stopped in front of the house next door. Rick couldn't turn around and leave without ringing the doorbell; he'd draw too much attention from the onlookers in the car. So, he rang the doorbell. Rick's bruised mind raced with something to say when she answered. He heard footsteps approaching the door and he braced himself …

The door opened, "Yes, can I help you?"

Rick stood there … Staring at his younger sister, Sarah. His strong, confident sister Sarah was standing in the doorway …

married to the man that cracked his skull and tried to kill him 13 years ago. Rick quickly cleared his throat and said, "Ah, yes Ma'am. We're conducting a survey of the types of cable television you currently use?"

Sarah smirked and said, "You've gotta be kidding, right? I don't have cable, I don't even live here, so sorry – I can't help your survey." Sarah closed the door without giving Rick a second glance. Of course she didn't recognize him; but Rick knew Sarah. She had the same bitter, distant glare in her eyes; she was never happy as a child – and apparently she's still fucked up.

Rick paused and slowly turned around to walk away. He noticed the dark blue sedan still sitting down the street watching Rick. Rick had to continue his facade of surveying the neighborhood, so he walked to the house next door. The dark blue sedan crept up closer to Sarah's house and parked in front. Rick continued to the next house and rang the doorbell. He waited and prayed for no one to be home. Good … no answer.

Rick turned to walk to the next house and caught a glimpse of someone getting out of the dark blue sedan. Rick continued walking towards the last house on the block. Dog was watching Rick from the van … waiting for a signal. Rick glanced slightly over at Dog and shook his head slowly as to tell him "Stand down …"

Rick approached the last house and rang the doorbell. He glanced over at Sarah's house and saw a tall man in a brown suite approaching the house. The tall man rang the doorbell, and the door was opened. Rick was watching Sarah's house so closely he didn't notice the door in front of him had opened and an old man wearing overalls was standing there looking at Rick. The old man said, "Yep, what can I do for you?"

Rick stood there for a moment staring at the man, then replied, "I'm sorry – I have the wrong address."

The old man smiled at Rick, and said; "Well, tell me what address you're looking for and maybe I can help you."

Rick smiled and said, "65 Stagestone Way …"

The man smiled again and stepped out onto his porch. He pointed to Sarah's house and said, "Well you ain't too far off – there's 65 Stagestone Way there ... but don't know who you going to see. That house has been vacant for 2 years. The owners were going through a divorce; don't think either one of them lives there now."

Rick turned and looked at the house. The tall man had disappeared inside and the porch was empty. Rick looked back at the old man and tilted his head and said, "Well, the couple I'm looking for had children ..."

The old man stepped back in his doorway and shook his head, "Those two didn't have any kids, they were never together! He was gone for weeks at a time, then she would leave for weeks at a time ... was the strangest thing I've ever seen. No wonder they split up."

Rick tilted his head towards the old man and said, "Thank you sir for all of your help. You have a good day."

Rick turned and started walking back towards the street. The dark blue sedan was gone. He looked up at the house ... Nothing. Dog was barking frantically from inside the van. Rick made his way back to the van, glancing around slightly to view his surroundings; opened the van door and got in.

Dog stopped barking and looked at Rick like "Well, What did you find out?"

Rick grabbed Dog behind his ears and rubbed him hard, and said, "Hey boy, you miss me? I didn't find out shit! Well, I know that my sister's married to shit eating' Smitty. They had no children and obviously lived in two separate houses. She married him right after the accident. Right after those fuckers tried to kill me Dog! She married him."

Rick sat back in his seat and gently laid his pounding head back on the headrest. He squeezed his eyes shut and then flung them back open. He looked at Dog and said, "Dog, what's even more crazy is ... Smitty knows who she is. He knows that Sarah McNeal is my sister. Why would he marry her? I mean, yeah Sarah's cute, but I don't see that good 'ole boy marrying a black women and taking her home to Momma 'an Nem."

Rick started the van and eased out onto the road. Dog started whining and Rick shook his head and said, "Damn Dog, again? I need to take you to the doctor and get your bladder checked out 'cause you be pissing every hour."

Dog leaned his nose close to Rick's neck and growled deep; Rick felt drool spraying on his neck. He stiffened up and said, "Hey, hey, hey! No more doctors all right? I was just kidding, I was kidding ..."

Dog stopped growling and licked Rick on his neck, leaving more drool. Rick was getting used to the drool now. He didn't mind it anymore. Dog let out another whimper and rocked on the seat.

Rick said, "Alright, alright; there's a parking lot up here. I'm stopping, I'm stopping."

He pulled into a restaurant parking lot and parked in the back. He opened the van door and let Dog out and he ran in between two cars to a grassy area. Rick put the van in park and stared into the rearview mirror. His mind was aching from the turmoil. Why did Smitty and Sarah get married? She knew something ... Sarah found out something about my 'death' and confronted Smitty to ... blackmail him?

Rick shook his head and mumbled, "That's not Sarah's style. She wouldn't do that. I have to talk to Deb. Deb knows more and she's not telling me."

Rick pulled out his phone to call Deb, and then hesitated. He looked at Dog trotting back to the van and said, "I just hung up on Deb; what can I say?"

Dog let out a loud bark and stood up on his hind legs and leaned on the van window, poking his head in licking on his face. Rick smiled and said, "Yeah, you're right. Who can stay mad at me?"

He turned around in the seat and closed the door; leaving Dog sniffing around outside. He called Deb. She answered on the first ring, "What Rick! You want to yell at me some more?"

Rick took a deep breath and said, "I'm ... I'm sorry for hanging up on you earlier. But Deb; you gotta admit … this is some deep shit for me to absorb."

Deb replied, "Yeah Rick, I know – but we all got our problems, alright. Deal with it! Now, what are you going to do?"

Rick hesitated, then said, "…Deb … what's the story on Smitty and my sister? And don't go into the 'I can't tell you everything' shit! I need to know Deb … I have a right to know."

Deb was silent. Rick waited.

A loud thud against the minivan startled Rick, "What the …"

Rick looked out the window and saw Dog prancing, banging his head against the rear door. Rick told Deb, "Hold on a second."

He reached back and opened the door. Dog jumped in and Rick said, "Are you done? 'Cause if you have to go again before an hour has passed, I'm going to …"

Rick let his sentence trail off as Dog leaned closer and looked at Rick; waiting for him to say 'doctor'. Rick heard Deb's voice through the phone, "Rick, what's going on?"

Rick started up the van and pulled back out onto the highway. He replied, "Nothing Deb, nothing. Dog was just taking a shit, that's all. Look – don't change the subject! Tell me what the hell is going on!"

Deb sighed and said, "All right, all right! Look … After you were pronounced 'dead' 13 years ago, your sister Sarah didn't let it go. Sarah and your sister Erica were pretty involved in trying to re-open your case. Eventually, Erica started traveling a lot with her job and fell out of the picture. But Sarah continued, and about 6 months after you disappeared, Smitty and Sarah got married. Now … rumor has it – she found something and presented it to Smitty. They struck a deal; he'd marry her, she could quit her job and collect disability; some stress-related illness. She'd get all the benefits and pension, and not put up with being a real wife to a real husband."

Rick was slowly shaking his throbbing head as he listened to Deb tell him this nightmare. He slowly replied, "Is the rumor true

Deb … did she find something on Smitty and his two cronies and sell me out?"

Deb was silent. Rick waited.

Deb finally said, "Rick … the night you were busted; when you were caught right in the middle of your drug deal … and Smitty, Roland and Joe chased you down Babcock Road, beat you and left you for dead … it was your sister Sarah who tipped off police. She knew the true story the entire time … Only after Erica started traveling and wasn't around anymore, and everyone else had given up on your case, did Sarah approach Smitty with the deal."

Rick's brain was about to explode from the painful rush of emotions. He slowly replied, "…My sister Sarah … was the one that had … the cops waiting for me behind Jorge's that night? She tipped the cops off … got me beat to death; left paralyzed living in the sewer with rats for weeks … and married the mother fucker who tried to kill me?"

Deb whispered, "…Yes."

Rick's vision blurred and he couldn't see the road. He slowed down and tried to focus on the street signs. He was close to the townhouse. Rick squeezed his eyes shut and cursed, "Shit! I'm almost there …"

Deb said, "Rick … Are you alright?"

Rick responded, "…Yeah Deb; I'm fine. Look, I need some time to register all of this … I'll call you in the morning."

Deb quickly responded, "Rick, wait – I need to talk to you about …"

Rick closed his phone and hung up on Deb again. He drove slow as he crept closer to the townhouse. Dog was scooting and whining on the back seats, and let out a quick, loud bark.

Rick winced as pain shot through his eye sockets. He turned to Dog and said, "…Dog, please … We're almost home … You can shit in a minute."

Rick blindly drove the van up to the townhouse and parked. He turned the van off and opened the door. Dog jumped over Rick, out of the van and ran into the front yard. He sniffed around a bit then ran around the side of the house. Rick sat in the van for a moment and breathed long and slow. The pain settled, and his vision slowly returned. He slowly got out of the van and walk unsteadily to the front door.

Dog came prancing around the corner to meet Rick at the door. Rick was trying to find the keyhole and didn't notice Dog's teeth showing. Rick put the key in the door and opened it. He walked in the house and Dog slowly followed behind him. Rick closed the door and was slowly making his way to the bathroom.

As soon as Rick reached the bathroom and flicked the light on he heard a loud scream. "Ahhhhhhhhh!"

Rick turned around and saw Dog's mouth latched onto a large dark shadow. Rick staggered back out into the front room and saw Dog's massive head twisting and his legs pulling a man out of the shadows. Rick grabbed his throbbing head and said, "Oh … Shit!!"

The man was screaming and punching Dog's head with his fist … his one fist. Rick winched as he focused to see … It was the one-armed man! Dog's teeth were latched onto his groin; twisting his head from left to right. Rick stared at Dog slinging the man's torso back and forth and finally the one-armed man dropped to the floor, screaming in agony trying to get away. Dog continued to pull and twist his head as his sharp teeth sunk into the man's groin. The man was sliding across the floor as Dog pulled and tugged at his nuts. Rick squeezed his eyes shut at the site of the man's jeans finally giving away, and Dog's bloody mouth jerking away with bloody flesh drizzling down his neck. Rick became dizzy and his words came rushing back to him … *"I want you to rip his nuts off this time Dog; and then kill him."*

The screaming stopped and Rick slowly opened his eyes.

Dog was standing over the one-armed man. Blood was gushing out of the man's abdomen … and Dog was chewing on something. Rick stumbled closer to Dog and the bloody mass on the floor. He saw a stream of blood coming from under the man's head and followed it to a whole in the left side of the man's neck. Dog bent down and sunk his teeth into the other side of the man's neck and ripped out another chunk of meat.

Dog looked up at Rick as he finished chewing the flesh and swallowed. Rick took a deep breath and said, "…Good boy …" right before his knees buckled and he fell backwards collapsing onto the floor.

CHAPTER THIRTY SEVEN

Deb got out of her car and took a deep breath. Her palms were sweaty and she dropped her keys as she tried to put them in her purse. She knew he was watching her.

Why was she so nervous? He had called emergency meetings before. But Deb was afraid this time. What if he had found out about her baby and didn't approve? What if he wanted to take her Little Carlito away from her?

Deb smiled as she thought about her *Little Carlito*. She already had his name embroidered on his crib blanket. Carlito Dominguez Shaver. Every time Deb thought about the baby she felt a rush come to her face, and her cheeks became warm. She was happy.

Deb approached the door and it was opened before she could knock. Felix greeted Deb, "Hello Ms. Debra, it's very nice to see you again."

Deb smiled and before she opened her mouth to greet Felix back she remembered Rick's words, *"Felix is your retarded brother."*

Deb looked at Felix closer and her eyes played tricks on her. Her and Felix had the same color eyes, same color hair - she's known Felix all her life. She never realized it before, but her and Felix looked alike. Deb blinked her eyes and said, "Hi Felix, it's good to see you too! Where's Doc, he sounded anxious to see me."

Felix guided Deb into the house and closed the door. He said, "Oh Ms. Debra, he's always anxious to see you. He's in his office. Please, follow me."

As Deb followed Felix down the hall she noticed the cast on Felix's left hand. She asked, "Goodness Felix, what did you do to your hand?"

Felix glanced down at his hand and said, "Oh, I hurt it doing some wood working."

Doc was standing at the window as Felix and Deb entered his office. He turned and said, "Clumsy boy; always trying to do more than he should. Debra my darling, how are you? Come and sit with your father and let's talk."

Doc motioned for Deb to sit at the table set with tea and sandwiches. He asked Deb, "Would you like a glass of wine?"

Deb didn't want to drink, but a glass of wine might ease her anxiety. She smiled and said, "Yes, that would nice. Merlot please."

Doc looked at Felix and said, "Two glasses please. Thank you Felix."

Deb was still standing, looking at the attractive place settings at the table. She knew Maria's handy work anywhere; she was the best maid anyone could have. Deb remembered the last time she saw Maria; and a chill ran down her spine. She was taking care of Deb while her baby was being aborted ...

Deb sucked in hard and said, "Well, I know you didn't call me all the way out here to have tea and sandwiches with me daddy; so why don't we just get right to it, because I can't stand the anxiety."

Felix entered the room holding two glasses of red wine. He said, "Here you go. Let me know if you need anything else."

Felix handed the glasses to Doc and Deb and left the room.

Doc held up his glass to Deb and said, "To new beginnings."

Deb raised her glass and took a sip. She responded, "So, are you leaving town again? Off to another adventure far away; a new beginning?"

Doc smiled and said, "Well my Debra, it means a lot of things."

Doc made his way to the table and pulled out a chair. He said, "Please; sit."

Deb walked over to the table and sat down. Doc sat down and

said, "Debra my dear, I know you are adopting the dead cop's baby. Why didn't you tell me I'm going to be a grandfather?"

Deb raised her glass and took a big gulp of her wine and sat the glass down. She looked her father square in the eye and slowly said, "...I was afraid you would take my baby away from me again ..."

Doc leaned forward and gently grasped Deb's hand in his and said, "My darling Debra; I only want you to be healthy and happy. I only do what I do to protect you always. If you want to adopt a child; then I support you 100%. Please understand ... the situation before was different. You can not carry a child to childbirth; but if you want to adopt a child – well, that's no harm to you my darling."

Deb felt her cheeks stinging as they became warm and her heart fluttered. She smiled at Doc and said, "Then ... you're not upset about the baby?"

Doc let Deb's hand go and sat back in his chair. He took a sip of his wine and said, "Well, I didn't say I wasn't upset about whose baby you are adopting; but if you want a child my dear – adoption is the safest way for you. Why you have to adopt the dead cop's baby is very strange and kind of ironic; but I think I can accept your decision my dear."

Deb broke out into a huge grin and stood up and hugged Doc. She said, "Thank you daddy ... thank you."

She sat back down and said, "Well, if you are alright with my adoption; then why the meeting?"

Doc sighed and took another sip of wine. He looked at Deb and said, "It's about Rick. He's a lose cannon and it's causing some undue attention to the Method. I think we may have to abort his assignment ..."

Deb shook her head and said, "No; we can't. He just found out his sister is married to the last target ... We can't abort. We've identified the target – if we abort and he completes the assignment; he could identify the Method."

Doc nodded his head and said, "That's why we may have to make Rick a target as well ..."

Deb stood up from the table and said, "What do you mean? Rick was your pet project. He was like a son to you! How can you just write him off just like that?"

Doc slowly shook his head and said, "Debra, Debra my darling; you know he is causing problems. He's killed several innocents and he jeopardized several Method informants. He has sorely disappointed me."

Deb breathed deep as she paced the floor, trying to think of a reason to spare Rick's miserable life. She turned to Doc and said, "Well, he's not going to be so easy to get rid of ... He knows you're my father."

Doc slammed his hand down on the table and said, "How the hell does he know that Debra? Did you tell him?"

Deb squealed, "Of course not! He's not stupid daddy – he figured it out."

Doc sat back in his chair and said, "You're right Debra ... Rick's not stupid, but he's reckless and he's costing the Method more money than they are willing to spend on him."

Doc took another sip of wine and continued, "Now, Debra – if Rick doesn't get into anymore trouble or kills another innocent; then perhaps the Method could forgive his past actions and we can finish this assignment and Felix and I can be off to our new winter home in Brazil."

Deb flopped down in her chair and whispered, "What do you mean Brazil? You're moving to Brazil?"

Doc reached for Deb's hand and said, "Now, now my darling; it'll only be for a year or two. You know every now and then I have to live outside the country. And don't worry ... I'll be back before your son realizes his grandfather was ever gone."

Deb lowered her head and tried to hide her tears. Doc reached for her chin and made her look at him. He said, "You are going to be a wonderful mother my darling ... absolutely wonderful."

Deb lost her control and fell into her father's arms crying like a child. He stroked her hair and cooed into her ear, "It's alright. It's all right. Daddy will never let anything happen to you."

Deb's phone started vibrating in her pocket and she slowly reached down and took it out. She looked at the display ... Rick.

Deb's eyes met her fathers and he nodded and said, "Well, answer it. I wonder what trouble he's gotten himself into now. Go ahead Debra; answer it."

Deb slowly opened her phone and put it to her ear. She answered, "Hello."

Rick's groggy voice replied, "Deb, it's me. Look; I'm in some deep shit here and I need you."

Deb closed her eyes and took a deep breath. She replied, "What is it Rick? What happened?"

Rick coughed and continued, "Well, you remember I told you about the one-armed man? Well, he was here in the townhouse waiting for me when I got home. He was hiding in the hallway, and Dog got a hold of him and ... let's just say the rest of his body is with his left arm now OK."

Deb grimaced and whispered into her phone, "Dog killed the one-armed man?"

Rick coughed again and his hoarse voice replied, "Hell yeah; ripped him to shreds. There's blood all over the house here, not to mention a half eaten human body; so I really need some help over here. Dog and I are going to have to get out of here. This guy travels with a bunch of goons and I'm sure they're looking for him by now. Oh and Deb; one more thing ... Do you know how to get in touch with Doc? My seizures are getting worse, and sometimes I black out from the pain and I can't see ... I don't think I can drive."

Rick started coughing again into the phone. He squeezed his eyes shut, trying to calm the painful vibrations in his skull. He whispered into the phone, "Deb ... I don't know how much longer I'm going to be around, you know. So, I really need to finish this assignment as soon as possible."

Doc sat quietly in his chair; watching Deb. She slowly looked at Doc and started shaking her head. She replied to Rick, "Look, Rick – get out of the house ... they'll be a car waiting for you at the corner 7-11. Be there in 30."

Deb closed her phone and stared at Doc. She said, "He's in trouble ... Dog killed the one-armed man."

Doc replied, "You mean the one-armed private investigator from Seattle? Debra, another innocent?"

Deb shook her head and said, "No, no daddy; this guy was bad. He tried to kill Rick! He lied on me ... he was friends with Hutchison and some how tracked Rick back here."

Deb opened her phone again and punched in numbers. She spoke into her phone, "Be at the 7-11 down the street from #4 and take them to the safe house. And make sure there's accommodations for a large dog."

Deb closed her phone and looked at Doc, searching his face for some type of compassion ...

Doc was shaking his head and said, "Debra my darling; admit it. Rick is more trouble than he's worth. Because of him, you are now the subject of an IAD investigation."

Deb shook her head again and said, "That's not true. IAD hooked on to me after the Collin's case. Rick had nothing to do with it."

Doc replied, "But he hasn't helped you clear your name either. If anything, he's leading IAD straight to you. Now he's killed a decorated retired cop."

Deb said, "No, not Rick – Dog. His Dog killed the one-armed man. He was a dirty cop daddy! He'd been lurking around here the last few weeks after he lost his arm to ... Dog. He even showed up at the precinct telling Hutchison's widow that I had Hutchison killed."

Doc slightly nodded and said, "As dirty as he may have been, Lt. Sharkey was a retired cop with honors. Now he not only lost an arm to this beast; but I take it most of the rest of his body has met the same fate? How can we give Sharkey's mangled body back without some type of explanation! This isn't going to go away easily Debra. Rick has really fucked this one up."

Deb exhaled long and said, "Daddy, he was only defending himself. This 'Sharkey' was waiting for Rick in his house. What was he doing there? He was breaking and entering and Dog was protecting his master."

Doc chuckled and took a sip of his wine. He looked at Deb and said, "His master? Rick killed his master and abducted the dog! Why this beast hasn't killed Rick yet is beyond me; but come to think of it, they are very much alike ..."

Deb said, "Daddy, just give Rick this one last target and he'll be gone. He can go off and live the rest of his life in peace."

Doc sat his glass down and stared at Debra. He solemnly said, "Now Debra ... do you really think someone like Rick, will get to live happily ever after?"

Deb slowly replied, "...I didn't know Rick was dying daddy ... why didn't you tell me?"

Doc shook his head and waved his hand at Deb and said, "Oh Debra, he was dead when I found him! I brought him back to life as much as I could, but I couldn't give him a new brain. I knew it would only be a matter of time before the seizures would kill him."

Deb stared her father square in the eyes. Her heart was racing inside her chest as she asked, "...And Felix ... where did you find him?"

Doc took his eyes off Deb, and slowly glanced towards the door to the other room. He turned back to Deb and said, "Oh I found Felix long before Rick ... a long time ago."

Deb's voice quivered as she slowly replied, "...Where did you find Felix daddy?"

Doc's face turned to stone and his eyes burned fire at Deb as he gritted out in between clinched teeth, "Why the sudden interest in Felix, Debra my darling? Has someone been talking to you?"

Deb shrank back in her chair and broke out into a sweat as her father stared her down with vicious eyes piercing her soul. He

waited for an answer ... Deb swallowed and slowly responded, "...
No reason ... just curious."

Doc sat silent staring at Deb. He slowly smiled and leaned back
in his chair. He picked up his glass of wine and said, "Debra ... you
know; I'm the only one who can protect you and take care of you.
And I need you to trust me, obey me, and most importantly; listen
to everything I tell you. I will never steer you wrong my dear."

Deb relaxed and started breathing again. She didn't realize she
was holding her breath; but the look in her father's eyes scared her.
He looked wild and out of control; ready to kill. Deb shivered, as she
comprehended for the first time, her father was a killer ...

He had killed her unborn child ...

He had killed her Carlito ...

Deb's breath caught in her chest and she stopped breathing
again. She felt sick; the room started shrinking. Her throat burned
and she wanted to run and hide from her thoughts ...

She didn't want her son anywhere near her father.

Deb sat up and looked at her watch. She said, "Daddy, is
there anything else you wanted to discuss? I have to prepare some
paperwork for tomorrow and should really be going."

Doc slowly finished his wine and sat the glass on the table. He
looked at Deb and smiled. He said, "Rushing off? I can remember
when you would throw everything to the wind when I called for you.
Now I only warrant an hour of your time?"

Deb sat silent as Doc shook his head and stood up. He continued,
"Debra my darling, remember what I just told you ... I am the only
one you can trust."

Deb stood up and kissed her father quickly on the cheek. She
turned and started walking down the hall to the front door. Doc
yelled, "Felix! Come see our guest out please."

Deb reached the door as Felix came rushing to open it for her.
Felix paused with his hand on the doorknob. He smiled and said, "I
hope you've enjoyed your visit Ms. Debra."

Deb looked at Felix and noticed a smudge below his right earlobe that looked just like her birthmark in the same spot ...

Before Deb could stop her urge, she had reached up and touched Felix on the shoulder. She slowly nudged his earlobe with her index finger and realized the 'smudge' was actually a birthmark ... identical to hers.

Felix stood still, staring at Deb as she fondled his earlobe. For an instant, Felix thought Deb was flirting with him and he became aroused. Felix cleared his throat and said, "Ah, Ms. Debra; is everything alright?"

Deb pulled her hand away and pointed to his ear. She said, "What's that?"

Felix smiled and stood up straight. He leaned closer to Deb and his eyes roamed her breasts. Felix said, "You like my birthmark? I have another one."

Felix rubbed his growing dick and said, "It's on the side of my thigh."

Deb shook her head quickly and said, "Oh no Felix, I'm sorry – I just thought you had a smudge or something on your neck and I was just going to tell you to clean it off, that's all."

Felix leaned closer to Deb's ear and whispered, "I thought you knew what it was, since you have one just like it."

Deb jerked away from Felix with her mouth open. She took a deep breath and said, "When were you looking behind my earlobe?"

Doc's raspy voice came echoing down the hallway as he walked towards the door, "What's going on out here? Felix! What's the matter?"

Felix backed up into the wall and bumped his sore hand. He wince in pain and stuttered as he nervously replied, "I ... I was answering Ms. Debra ... she asked about my birthmark, and ..."

Doc jerked his head and looked at Deb. She shrank back against the other wall as Doc yelled, "What about his birthmark Debra! You've never noticed it before, why now?"

Doc walked towards Deb. Felix slid down the hall and ran into the other room. Doc got close to Deb's face and gritted through tight lips, "Whom have you been talking to my darling Debra? Why are you asking questions about Felix as if you didn't know him?"

Deb stared into vicious eyes full of malice, searching her face for an answer. Deb was silent as her breath quivered through her open lips. Doc leaned close to Deb's ear and whispered, "Tell me who told you Felix was your brother …"

Deb sucked in and held her breath. She slowly slid sideways down the wall and stared at Doc. She breathlessly whispered, "… Felix is my brother?"

Doc walked over to Deb and slammed his fist into the wall right next to her head. She screamed and covered her face. Doc yelled, "Tell me who told you Felix was your brother!"

From behind trembling hands covering her face, Deb cried out, "Rick! Rick! It was Rick!"

Doc grimaced and said, "What? Rick!"

Deb pulled her hands down and cried, "Well, he didn't really say he was my brother; he was upset about something and was telling me he knew you were my father, and that Felix was probably my retarded brother."

"He called me retarded?"

Deb and Doc turned around and saw Felix standing in the hallway. He had his arms wrapped around his torso, slowly twisting from side to side. Hugging himself with tears welling up in his eyes. He asked again, "Rick called me retarded?"

Deb was silent. She turned to Doc. Doc smiled and said, "There, there my boy. Rick has been under a lot of pressure, and …"

Felix burst into tears and yelled as he turned around and slammed the door, "He called me retarded!"

Doc slowly turned to Deb. He walked over to the door and opened it. He looked at Deb and said, "Well, I guess you'd better be running along if you are to complete all of that paperwork for tomorrow."

Deb took a long, quivering breath and marched out the door.

She got in her car and drove onto the dirt road. She had to get as far away from there as she could. She never looked back, didn't turn to waive; didn't honk the horn. She drove solemnly onto the highway. Her eyes burned as she stared at the road without blinking; she was in an emotional comma. Little by little, her shoulders began to shake as she silently cried.

Deb felt her phone vibrating in her coat pocket. She slowly pulled it out and looked at the display … Rick.

Deb reached over and shoved her phone deep inside of her purse. She started crying again as her feelings overwhelmed her.

Deb never, ever wanted to see her father again.

CHAPTER THIRTY EIGHT

Rick slammed his phone shut. "Shit!"

Dog and Rick were standing at the end of the street. Rick looked left, and saw a 7-11 a block away. He slowly turned and looked to the right and saw another 7-11 a block away. Rick rammed his phone back into his pocket and hissed to Dog, "There's two fucking 7-11's at this intersection! Which one Deb! Answer your fucking phone once in a while!"

Rick pulled on Dog's leash and started to walk. He said, "We'll just head south first and wait there for a while ... if nothing happens; we'll just head north."

As Rick pulled Dog along the sidewalk, he mumbled, "Why the hell don't Deb ever answer her phone Dog? She's supposed to be my partner in crime."

Dog looked up at Rick and barked. Rick smiled at Dog and said, "You're right ... you're my partner in crime boy!"

Dog started pulling Rick on the leash as he darted forward. Rick looked up and said, "Hey boy, what's the hurry?"

Rick saw in the distance, two women walking on the sidewalk headed north. Rick smiled and said to Dog, "Good boy ... you sniff'n out pussy for daddy."

Dog let out a quick, loud bark. The women slowed down and grabbed on to each other as they saw Dog and Rick approaching them. Rick yanked on Dog's leash and said, "Quiet boy! You're scaring them … let 'em get closer so I can get a good look at 'em first."

As Dog pulled Rick closer to the women, Rick winced as he squinted his eyes to focus on the two figures approaching. Rick could see a playfully smiling white redhead … clinging to the arm of a sexy Spanish chic. Rick smiled and said, "Oh yeah … this could be fun Dog …"

Dog whined and pulled Rick closer to the women walking towards them, the two women were slowly walking and holding each other. Rick saw the Spanish chick rub on the redhead's ass and whisper in her ear. They both started giggling and the redhead reached up and squeezed the Spanish chick's tit. Rick smiled and pulled on Dog's leash. He whispered as he grinned at the approaching women, "Great … lesbians. This is better than I thought Dog"

Rick pulled Dog close to him and the women stopped right in front of them. Rick smiled and said, "I'm sorry if Dog scared you two beautiful ladies, but he's quite harmless." Rick pulled Dog off of the sidewalk so the ladies could pass. He continued, "Please, go ahead – he won't hurt you."

The redhead giggled and said, "He's a big dog! What kind of dog is he?"

Rick smiled and said, "He's a Rottweiler; his name is Dog."

The Spanish chic stepped towards Rick and curled her lips as she said, "Dog? How 'Tarzan'!"

She left the redhead on the sidewalk and walked around Rick as she circled him and Dog. She said behind Rick's back, "And what's your name, Dick?"

Dog growled low in his chest and Rick jerked on the leash. Rick waited for her to get back on the sidewalk with the redhead and replied, "Ah no, my name is Rick. What's yours?"

The Spanish chick snaked her arm back around the redhead's waist and smiled. She said, "My name's Rita, and this is Perri."

Perri giggled and extended her hand. She said "Nice to meet you Rick and Dog."

Dog yelped and whined, trying to get to Perri for a lick but Rick clinched tight to the leash holding him close to his side.

Rita pulled on Perri's waist and said, "Well, we must be on our way; our car broke down over there and we're on our way back home."

Rick said, "Well, I'm sorry I don't have my car with me to give you a lift; but Dog and I would be happy to walk you home to make sure you get there safely."

Rita quickly replied, "No thank you Rick, we live right around the corner. We've already called a tow truck to get the car; and we even ordered pizza for dinner. So you see … we don't need a man."

Dog growled low in his chest. Rita looked down at Dog and said, "…And we don't need his broke dick Dog either."

Dog barked and showed his teeth to Rita. Rick kneeled down and held Dog. He petted him and held him close, willing him not pounce on the hot, sexy meat standing in front of him. Rick cooed in Dog's ear, "Now, now. Let's not be rude Dog. The ladies just don't know us, and I can see how they would be cautious; us being strangers and all."

Perri was clinging tight to Rita's arm. She managed a quick giggle before saying, "I like your dog Rick." She turned to Rita and said, "I'd like for them to walk us home Rita; it'll be fun."

Rita pulled Perri close as she glared at Rick. She looked at his clothes bag hanging over his shoulder, and the duffle bag dangling from his hand. She looked back at Rick's face and said, "And where are you on your way to? Looks like you're ready to catch a bus out of town; how do you have time to walk us home? Are you homeless and trying to prey on two unsuspecting females?"

Rick glared back at Rita and said, "No. We're visiting friends and we were on our way to catch a ride from one friends' house to the others. I saw you two walking down the sidewalk and my dick got hard and I deviated from my plan. Now, can Dog and I walk you ladies home or should we continue to the 7-11 where we're supposed to catch our ride?"

Perri was smiling and looked at Rita. Rita's stare didn't leave Rick's. Rita finally let a small smirk come to the side of her lips. She said, "Well, I guess it wouldn't hurt to have a little company on the way home. You guys like pizza?"

Dog barked loud and started pulling on the leash trying to reach the women. Rick smiled and thought of Walden ... He said, "Well, that just happens to be our favorite dish."

Rita smiled and pulled Perri along. She said over her shoulder, "Well, you boys are in for a treat tonight."

Rick and Dog started following the women back down the sidewalk. Dog was trotting next to Rick. Dog looked up at Rick and let out a quick bark. Rick looked down at Dog and said, "I know, I know ... we're supposed to be catching a ride out of here. But these girls are just too hot!"

Dog started pulling Rick on the leash; Rick's pace was slowing down and he almost stumbled. Burning pain shot through Rick's brain and he could barely make out the two women walking in front of him. Rita and Perri were fondling each other and giggling as they walked ahead of Dog and Rick. Rick shook his head as he struggled to maintain the searing pain in his head. He whispered to Dog, "... Besides, I ain't gonna be around much longer; I might as well enjoy all I can right now. I'll call Deb and let her know I got side-tracked and have her send the car tomorrow."

Dog barked and bumped his big head into Rick's side as they followed the women. Rick managed a crooked grin and said, "Yep ... going to be some pounding tonight!"

CHAPTER THIRTY NINE

Deb paced her living room floor as she yelled into the phone, "What do you mean he didn't show up? Are you at the right location?"

The voice on the other end replied, "Yes ... well – there are two 7-11's in this location; so we had one car waiting at the north location, and we're at the south. There's no sign of the subject and his dog. We've been on location for 3 hours. We must leave and check in."

Deb sighed long and loud and slammed her phone shut. She put her fingers to her temples and closed her eyes. She mumbled, "Rick, Rick, Rick ... why are you making it so easy for daddy to have a reason to kill you?"

She opened her eyes and walked over to the window and looked out. She thought to herself, "...he's dying anyway; he has nothing to lose."

Deb's phone started vibrating in her hand and she slowly looked at the display ... the Method.

Deb answered, "Hello."

The voice on the other end replied, "We have a location on your latest target."

Deb walked to her desk and said, "Great, where is it?"

The voice responded, "For the past month, the target has been working at the Fairfax County Police Department ... Precinct 144. He's in the Shipping and Receiving department under the name of William Smith."

Deb's breath was caught in her throat and she wasn't breathing. The voice on the other end continued, "He's staying at a location different from the two communicated to you earlier. He's at ..."

Deb interrupted, "Excuse me! Did you say he's working at Precinct 144?"

The voice responded, "Yes, Precinct 144. He has a new temporary address of 343 Windward Avenue, Sterling, Virginia."

Deb almost dropped the phone. She felt faint as she stared into space ... *Smitty has been living in Joe's old townhouse ... and he's working in her mailroom!*

Deb started gulping in air and the room started swaying. The voice on the other end continued giving Deb information on the target; but she couldn't hear him. Her mind was in a whirlwind. She tried to gather her thoughts on what to do next. She finally heard the voice on the other end saying, "...is that all you require from me at this time?"

Deb whispered into the phone, "...Yes, yes; I'm sorry. Thank you for the information and I'll call if I have any questions."

The phone went dead and Deb closed her phone. Her heart was pounding out of her chest, vibrating down her arm. Her hand was shaking as she flipped her phone back open. She had to call Doc and tell him ...

Deb paused and froze as she was dialing his number. She couldn't call him ... she couldn't talk to him. If she called him, he would kill Rick. But even worse ... Doc would have a reason to be back in her life. He would rescue her once again from her fate. Deb shook her head and closed her phone.

She had to break the bond she had to him. She didn't want him in her life. She didn't want him in her son's life.

Deb eased herself down onto the couch and said out loud, "I'm going to have to change my life. I'm going to resign from the force, and quit the Method. I'm going to move far away where he can never find me. I'll get a regular career and raise my son as normal as I possibly can in this crazy world."

She took a deep breath and exhaled. She stared at her cell phone in her hand and mumbled, "So, who's going to rescue me from my fate this time?"

Deb's phone started vibrating in her hand and it startled her. She fumbled her phone and dropped it on the floor. She scrambled to her knees, grabbed it and looked at the display ... Rick!

Deb answered, "Rick! Where the hell are you?"

Deb heard Rick chuckling into the phone and she heard music and a woman giggling in the background. Rick's voice was slurred as he replied, "Hey Deb! What's going on? I wanted to call you and say Hi."

Deb stood still for a moment, holding the phone to her ear with her mouth open; not sure what she wanted to start yelling about first.

Rick continued on the other end, "Hey Deb, you there? Look - about that ride I was supposed to catch at the 7-11; there were two 7-11's at the end of the Parkway. And in between the 7-11's ... Dog and I met 2-10's!"

Deb heard Rick laughing and more giggling. Deb stomped her foot and said, "Now you listen to me you worthless vagrant! We have some serious shit going on here, and you're out getting drunk and eating pussy!"

Rick responded, "Hey, hey, Deb; no need to get nasty. I just got a little side-tracked."

Deb heard Rick cover the phone and say, "Hey ladies, I have to take this call. Excuse me for a moment ..."

Rick walked into the bedroom and continued, "Deb ... I'm sorry I fucked up; but we ran into these ladies, and ..."

Deb cut Rick off, "Rick! Don't you get it! You made a choice; you don't get to meet people and have a good time! You're on assignment with deadlines and meetings to keep! You blew off two cars waiting to pick you up! I knew there were two 7-11's at the intersection, I had a car waiting at each; and you still didn't show up! You keep fucking around and you're going to end up on the hit list!"

Rick covered his mouth with his hand so the women wouldn't

hear him yelling, "Deb! It really doesn't matter what list I end up on! I'm dying!"

Deb was silent and Rick continued, "Those three mother-fuckers succeeded 13 years ago! They killed me then Deb! It's just taken me 13 years to die!"

Deb said, "Now Rick; don't say that – you're not dying …"

Rick hissed into the phone, "Deb! I'm dying OK! I feel my brain deteriorating more everyday. My so-called 'seizures' are getting worse; and soon … one of 'em is going to take me away from this cruel world Deb … and it'll all be over."

Deb replied, "Rick … maybe Doc can …"

Rick yelled, "Doc can't help me anymore Deb! I'm dead!"

Rick paused to guzzle down his beer. He continued, "So … I decided to enjoy some pussy one last time before I take care of Smitty and check out of here."

Deb remembered Smitty and said, "Rick! I need to tell you … we've found Smitty."

Rick's voice came back over the phone deep and sinister … he said, "Where?"

Deb stood up and started pacing her apartment floor. She took a deep breath and said, "Rick … you're not going to believe this; but Smitty's been living in Joe's old townhouse for the last month; and he's working at the precinct in the mailroom."

There was silence on the other end, and Deb waited for Rick to digest what she had just said.

Deb waited … Finally Rick responded, "…You mean to tell me … Smitty moved into Joe's old crib; and now he's working at your job? Deb … he's on to you."

Deb sucked in a gulp of air and said, "I know Rick! What am I going to do? I don't have time to deal with this right now; I'm bringing home my new baby boy next week! I'm going to be a mommy and I have a crooked cop stalking me in my office!"

Rick said, "Now, now Deb … calm down. I'll be done here by morning … you send the car to the SOUTH 7-11 on the Parkway.

Get me another rental car and I'll stake out your job all day. When Ole' Smitty leaves for the day, I'll follow him and finish this job tomorrow. You can be home with your baby; I can be on the next bus out of here; and we're done with it. Are you with me?"

Deb's heart ached; wanting to believe what Rick was saying. She squeezed her eyes shut, praying it would all work out the way he said.

Rick's voice rang out, "Deb! Are you with me?"

Deb took her time and calmly replied, "...You have your raunchy ass at the South 7-11 at 7:00am tomorrow morning, or I swear I'll walk away from you and this assignment and you'll never see or speak to me again; do you understand me?"

Rick was silent. Deb yelled into the phone, "Do you understand me Rick?"

Rick quickly responded, "Yeah, yeah Deb ... I understand."

Deb added, "...And if that fucked up mutt of yours kills or maims anybody else ... he dies."

She slammed her phone shut.

Rick closed his phone and put it in his pocket. He walked back out into the living room and saw Perri and Rita kissing on the futon couch bed. Perri reached into Rita's blouse and pulled her large tits out. She started fondling Rita's nipple until it was rock hard. Rick rubbed his dick and slowly walked over to the table and sat down. He licked his lips and thought, "I'm fucking one of these bitches ... I don't care which one; but I'm fucking one of 'em!"

Dog was sitting on the floor and scooted closer to Rick and nudged him with his head, wanting attention.

Rick ignored Dog and licked his lips again, watching the two women play with each other's body. Perri saw Rick sitting there and pulled away from Rita. She said, "Hey big boy ... Rita was saying how hot she thought you were ..."

Perri bent down and licked Rita's nipple and sucked on it. Perri's lips pulled away from Rita's nipple with a loud smack. Perri looked at Rick and said, "...Don't you want a taste?"

Rick stood up and quickly walked over to the futon to join the women. Rita shot Perri a glaring look as she got up off of the futon. As she passed Rick, Perri said, "Now, just a taste ..."

Perri sat down at the table as Rick lunged to the floor in front of Rita and latched onto her exposed breasts. He grabbed her and held her in place as he suckled her two large nipples, one by one. Rita glared at Perri sitting at the table. Perri looked at Rita and smiled as she rubbed her own breasts ... watching Rick devour Rita's.

Perri wanted to watch Rita and Rick first ... then she wanted her Rita's sweet pussy deep in her mouth.

Perri stopped smiling as she watched Rick's hand wander down to Rita's pants. He was done with her breasts and was pulling off her tight jeans. Perri jumped out of her seat and stood up. She yelled out to Rick, "Wait ... she doesn't want to ..."

Rita cut Perri off in mid sentence, "Yes! Yes I do ..."

Rita glared at Rick and growled, "Well, are you going to fuck me big boy or are you just gonna stare at it?"

Rick finished pulling Rita's jeans off and picked her up and turned her around. He propped her up on her knees and pushed her head down onto the futon. Rick quickly undid his pants and pushed them down to his ankles. He stood on the floor and pulled Rita's naked ass close to the edge of the futon. He was entering her from behind, doggy style. Perri plopped back down in the chair at the table, watching from behind. She saw Rick's big dick slide into Rita's pussy with force.

Rita let out a loud cry and buried her face in the futon pillow. Perri saw Rick's naked ass muscles tighten and his leg's shake as he thrust his dick in and out of her Rita's sweet pussy. She closed her eyes as she saw Rita's cum flowing down Rick's dick. Rita raised her face off the futon and screamed, "I'm cumming!"

Perri shifted in her chair and scowled at Rick as he slid his dick in and out of Rita. Dog sat at Perri's feet, staring at her, playfully licking her ankle, and trying to get her attention. Perri ignored Dog and stared at Rita. Why was she doing this to her? She wanted to tell Rita to stop – but it was her own fault.

Perri would beg Rita to do it; because Rita never wanted to. But it made Perri so hot to watch Rita flirt with men and play with them. Then, make the man watch as she made her Rita cum.

But it didn't always work out that way.

"Dammit!" Perri swore under her breath. She didn't want Rita to get mad at her!

Now she had to sit and watch Rick ram his big, nasty dick in and out of Rita's sweet pussy! Perri slammed her fist on the table and started silently crying. Dog whined and licked Perri's ankle again.

Rick turned around and saw Perri crying at the table. He eased his thrusting to a slow rhythm and said over his shoulder, "…Hey; why don't you come over here and let me watch you lick on this bitch!"

Dog got up off the floor and started trotting over to Rick. Rick looked at Dog and said, "What the … Hell no! Not you Dog!"

Dog stopped trotting and paused. He growled and showed his teeth to Rick.

Rita lifted her face out of the pillow again and screamed, "No! Let the bitch watch me cum all over your big dick! You better sit right there Perri and watch! Now, fuck me harder!"

Rick turned back around and started pounding Rita's pussy again. Dog started growling again. Rick turned back around and breathlessly said, "Not now boy … please!"

Perri jumped up crying and said, "Fuck you both! I'm taking Dog for a walk!"

She grabbed Dog's leash and ran to the door. Rick turned to catch a glimpse of Perri and Dog leaving the house and closing the door behind them. Rick stopped thrusting and was about to pull out and run after them. Rita quickly hopped off of Rick's dick, turned around and shoved it in her mouth. She started sucking and licking it. He grabbed her head and pushed his dick deeper down her throat. Rick leaned his throbbing head back and winced … he moaned deep in his throat. He forgot about Perri. Rick gripped Rita's hair in his fists and rammed her head deep onto his dick as he ejaculated deep in her throat. Rick's head exploded with pain as his body shook uncontrollably. He forgot that an innocent woman had just walked out on the street with a physically powerful, untamed, cold-blooded killer.

CHAPTER FOURTY

Rick couldn't breath ... the man's foot was pressing on his chest, holding him down. He saw the man raise something over his head ... it was a cinderblock.

Rick tried to move his arms to shield his face ... he couldn't. He tried to get up, but the man was wearing large boots and he pressed his foot down harder on Rick's chest. Rick could feel the pain in his back as his ribs started to crack under the pressure ... he tried to yell but he didn't have air in his lungs.

He squirmed frantically as he lay there helplessly watching as the man brought the block down fast and smashed it into his skull.

Rick jumped up and yelled "AAHHH!!!" Rita went flying off Rick's chest and off the futon, onto the floor. She yelled, "What the hell is wrong with you?"

Rita stood up and groggily ran her hand through her hair. She looked at Rick and said, "You had a bad dream, or was the pussy that bad last night?"

She slowly walked around the futon and into the bathroom and closed the door.

Rick sat on the edge of the futon and gently placed his pounding head in his hands. He whispered, "Damn, these dreams are getting too real!"

Rick raised his head and looked around ... It was quiet; too quiet. Where was Dog?

Rick's heart started to race as he remembered the last time he saw Dog ... leaving the house with Perri last night.

He eased his body up and pulled on his pants. He slowly tiptoed into the kitchen and looked out the window ... almost morning. Rick's heart started racing again as he remembered ... *"You have your raunchy ass at the South 7-11 at 7:00am tomorrow morning, or I swear I'll walk away from you and this assignment and you'll never see or speak to me again; do you understand me?"*

Rick turned around and looked for a clock; he spotted one on the microwave ... "Fuck! 6:00am."

He quickly started gathering his things and tiptoeing around the house ... looking for signs of ... Rick shook his head as he realized he was looking for signs that Dog had ate Perri; or left her wounded somewhere. But Rick didn't see anything ... not even a drop of blood anywhere. They were still gone.

Rick heard Rita coming out of the bathroom and he met her in the kitchen.

She swung around and said, "Good morning. Coffee?"

Rick paused to take in the beautiful women standing in front of him; her long dark silky hair flowing down the long nightgown she'd put on. He remembered the night before and smiled. His head exploded and his throat constricted; he coughed deep and hard.

Rick had to take a deep breath to calm the painful ringing in his ears. He said, "No ... thank you. Where's your friend with my dog?"

Rita turned to Rick and smirked. She said, "You wanted to fuck her instead of me, didn't you?"

Rick impatiently exhaled and said, "I didn't give a shit which one I fucked as long as I fucked! Now where is she?"

Rita swung back around and continued making coffee. She said over her shoulder, "She's probably at Barbara's house. She always spends a night there when we fight."

Rick smiled and said, "Oh, I see. She didn't want you to fuck me but you couldn't resist this dick."

Rita laughed and swung back around and said, "Please! Perri wanted to see me flirt with you and get you hard. That turns her on."

Rita smiled and continued, "Then her and I would fuck in front of you and make you watch."

Rick stared at Rita. She smiled again and said, "…Perri likes that kind of foreplay. But I told her I didn't like you and I didn't want you touching me, but she persisted. So I fucked you in front of her to punish her."

Rita turned back around and finished making her cup of coffee. She said over her shoulder, "I still don't like you and you can't fuck."

Rick yelled, "And that's why you came all over my dick bitch! Now where is Dog? I need to get the fuck up out of here!"

Rita turned to Rick and said, "Calm down dammit! She should be home any min …"

The front door swung open and interrupted Rita. Dog came bounding into the room and Rick yelled, "Dog! Where you been boy?"

Dog ran into Rick's arms and licked him. Rick rubbed his big head and checked his face to see if there were any traces of blood.

Perri came walking in behind Dog and closed the door. She stood at the door with her head down. She slowly looked up at Rita and said, "Good morning."

Rita walked over to Perri and slowly snaked her arms around her waist. Perri looked at Rita with tears in her eyes and said, "I'm sorry."

Rita nudged her nose down Perri's neck and said, "Don't worry baby … I forgive you."

Rick stood up and said, "Well, now that everybody's accounted for – Dog and I have to be leaving now. It was certainly a pleasure meeting you both."

Rick turned and finished putting his clothes on. Perri looked down at Dog and said, "Well, couldn't you two stay for breakfast?"

Rita and Rick said at the same time, "NO!"

Rick looked at Rita, then to Perri and said, "I mean, Dog and

I have to catch a ride at 7:00 at the 7-11 up the street. We gotta be going."

Perri threw her hands up and said, "I don't see why they can't stay for breakfast!"

Rita pointed her finger at Perri and said, "You don't even like dogs!"

Dog growled and lunged at Rita. Rick grabbed Dog and quickly clutched his leash in his fists. He said, "Now, now boy; let's leave like gentlemen."

Perri started crying and said, "Well ... I hope you enjoyed your night!"

Rita yelled at Perri and pointed down the hallway, "Go to your room! I will deal with you later!"

Dog pulled on the leash and barked at Rita, showing his teeth. Perri walked past Rick and Dog. She sniffed through tears as she did as she was told, saying, "Good bye. It was nice meeting you."

Dog yelped and licked Perri's leg as she walked by. Rita yelled, "Watch that mangy mutt! He looks like he bites!"

Rick winced at the leash being drawn tight around his hand as Dog lunged to get at Rita. Rick said through clinched teeth, "Please ... stop calling him names. He's very sensitive."

Rita walked over to the front door and swung it open. She said, "Get out!"

Rick nodded and pulled Dog close to him as they walked towards the open door. Rick held tight to Dog's leash ... he knew Dog wanted to rip Rita to shreds and he shook as he prepared to pass Rita standing at the doorway. The leash started vibrating in Rick's hand. Rick gripped tighter as he realized Dog was growling deep in his chest.

When they were right at the doorway, Dog lunged at Rita's legs and sunk his teeth into her gown. Rita saw Dog coming at her and she quickly jumped back. Rick pulled on the leash and tried to pull Dog out of the doorway, but not quick enough. Dog had a mouth full of Rita's gown in his mouth. She was screaming and pulling at her gown, trying to get it out of Dog's mouth. Rick was pulling on Dog, "Let go boy! Let go!"

Rick gasped out as he struggled to keep Dog's mouth away from the woman, "Can you close the door? Please, just close the door."

Rita kept screaming and pulling at her gown. Rick huffed, "He doesn't have your leg, does he?"

Rita shrieked, "No, no – please!"

Rick said, "Just close the door; close the door. I can't hold him much longer. Close the door so he can't get you!"

Perri came running out of the bathroom and started screaming as she saw Dog pulling on Rita's gown, trying to get to her. Perri ran to the door helping Rita inch the door closed. Rick heard the women crying and screaming on the other side of the door. Rick still gripped the leash as Dog stood growling; Rita's gown closed in the door. Dog's mouth was still gripping and pulling the gown in his mouth. Rick bent down and said, "Let go boy – she's gone. She's behind the door and you can't get her … either one of 'em! Now, let go … or I'll just cut the gown and we can leave with a wad of fabric in your mouth."

Rick stood up and said, "Ok, suite yourself." He reached in his pocket and pulled out a switchblade. He reached down to cut the gown and Dog jerked his head hard into Rick's hand and growled. Rick pulled his hand back and hissed, "Come on boy! You gotta let it go! What you gonna do, hold onto it until the cops get here? Come on Dog … if I miss this appointment, it's over for me!"

Dog growled and held onto the gown a minute longer, then slowly released the fabric he was holding in his mouth. He paced the doorstep, smelling and licking it. He whimpered …

Rick gently pulled on the leash and said, "I know boy … I know. It's hard to walk away from something good when you find it."

Rick slowly shook his head thinking about Tricia as he led Dog away from the house.

Dog finally allowed Rick to lead him back down the Parkway towards the 7-11.

CHAPTER FOURTY ONE

Deb sat at her desk pretending to read the newspaper. She picked up her coffee, took a sip and set it back on her desk. She flipped the paper over and pretended to read the next page.

She nervously peeked over the paper, scanning the precinct. She set the paper down and checked her e-mail ... nothing. She checked her phone to see if she missed a message ... nothing. Why isn't he responding to her?

Deb had sent Walter an urgent message for him to contact her. She had to talk to him about his new employee, but he wasn't responding.

Deb started doubting everyone ... What if Walter was the enemy all along?

She slammed the paper shut and threw it on the floor next to her chair. She checked her e-mail again ... Walter!

Deb opened his e-mail and read it, "Package will be delivered at the Cafeteria loading dock at 9:30am."

Deb looked at her watch ... 9:15am ... great.

She closed down her computer and gathered her coat and briefcase. She was headed to the exit when she ran into Captain. Deb smiled and said, "Good morning sir."

Captain stopped in front of her and said, "Good morning? What in the hell you mean, 'good morning.' You're going the wrong way, I need to talk to you."

Deb stopped and opened her mouth, waiting for a good excuse

to pop into her head. She finally blinked and said, "Can it wait Captain? I just got a lead on the Murphy case and I was going to check it out."

Captain put his hands on his hips and squinted his eyes at Deb. He nodded and said, "Alright Shaver ... alright. It can wait. I'll be anxious to hear what your lead has to say about the case when you get back."

Deb smiled and walked past Captain. As she passed, she whispered "Anything you say, sir."

She would forever be grateful for everything Captain had done for her. Over the 5 years she'd worked for him, she had never seen the soft, caring man she now knew him to be. Deb had a rush as she let her heart speak out, *"...I wish I had a father like Captain ..."*

Deb quickly shook the thought and continued making her way out of the building. She walked past the Information Desk and out the door. She didn't notice the man in the delivery suit following her every move with his eyes. He delivered a package to the Information Desk as he watched Deb leave the building and get into her car.

She pulled around the building and slowly approached the loading dock. She pulled next to the dumpster and stopped, hiding her car from the building. She made sure her doors were locked and put the car in park. She waited ... watching the dock. Deb's phone started vibrating in her pocket and she grabbed it and looked at the display ... Rick.

"Hello."

Deb heard Rick's sarcastic voice on the other end, "And just who the hell are you stalking in the parking lot behind the dumpster?"

Deb quickly jerked her head from left to right and said, "Where are you?"

Rick replied, "I'm following Smitty ... waiting for his ass to leave work so I can kill him; and I see you creeping around the building and parking behind the dumpster."

Deb nervously replied, "...You followed him here this morning?"

Deb heard Rick yell in the background, "Dog! Get out of the

chicken nuggets!" Then he said to Deb, "Yeah; he's wearing a delivery suit. He went to the other two precincts in Fairfax, and then he came here. He delivers packages to the other offices I guess. He just made his last delivery, 'cause when he leaves work today, he's going on long term disability."

Deb said, "I'm waiting to talk to Walter; the Mailroom Manager; and see what he has to say about him … if he's been asking questions about me."

Deb looked around again and said, "Where are you Rick … I don't see you."

Rick chuckled into the phone and said, "That's the whole idea of stalking Deb … you're not supposed to see me."

Deb saw Walter coming out onto the dock. She said, "Here he comes, I gotta go. I'll call you later."

Rick quickly added, "Deb, why you worried about what Smitty is doing? He's going to be dead by tonight – so you won't have to worry about it."

Deb quickly replied, "You don't have to worry about who else is coming after you Rick! I'm adopting a baby tomorrow and I don't want my motherhood to start out with someone trying to kill me! Who knows whom Smitty has working for him or with him! Now, I gotta go!"

Deb closed her phone and put it in her pocket.

She watched Walter as he made his way around to the passenger side of her car, opened the door and got in. He looked at Deb and said, "Good Morning Ms. Shaver … you know – you can come to the mailroom to meet with me. We don't have to sneak around like we're stalkers or something."

Deb looked away and said, "…I can't come back down to the mailroom just yet Walter … not since the last time …"

Deb's words trailed off and she sat staring out the window. Walter interrupted Deb's reverie and said, "So … what's on your mind?"

Deb turned back to Walter and said, "Walter; you have a new employee?"

Walter smiled and said, "Nothing sneaks by you Ms. Shaver. Yes, I do. I guess you know he's been placed here undercover by another branch of the agency to watch … well, to investigate."

Deb banged her hands on the steering wheel and said, "To investigate what? Walter, please … I'm adopting a baby boy tomorrow, and if your new employee was sent here to watch me, I'd really appreciate it if you told me. And … any other information you think would help me."

Walter looked down at his hands and said, "…Help you what, Ms. Shaver?"

Deb touched Walter on his wrist and said, "…Help me stay alive long enough to move far away from here and raise my son to be a wise, strong, young man."

Walter raised his eyes to meet Deb's. He opened his mouth slowly and said, "…He's placed here alone, he drives in between offices delivering mail and packages. He reports to some guy named Sgt. Blount. He's been asking questions, but not specifically about you. He starts conversations about things around the precinct that somehow seem to always lead to you. He's been here two weeks; hasn't missed a day of work."

Deb started her car and put it in gear. She looked at Walter and said, "Thank you Walter. I think your new employee is going to be on long term disability after today; so you can throw that 'employee of the month' certificate away."

Walter smiled and opened the door to get out. He said over his shoulder, "You be careful Ms. Shaver; and I wish you the best of luck with your new life."

He closed the door, and Deb watched as Walter made his way back into the building. She stopped to think about Walter's words again, "…best of luck with your new life."

She smiled as she drove her car out of the parking lot onto the highway. She said to herself, "What a perfect thing to say. I'm adopting a baby; a new life - to be a part of my new life; away from crime, lies, death, secrets ... Doc ..."

Deb smiled as she drove down the highway, headed for 'Babies R Us' to pick up some last minute things for little Carlito. She pushed in her CD and turned it up loud as she sang "Isn't she lovely" at the top of her lungs.

Deb bounced in her seat and sang out loud, reveling in her happiness.

She was unaware of the delivery truck following her down the highway.

CHAPTER FOURTY TWO

Rick threw his phone down into the passenger seat and yelled, "Dammit man! Why doesn't she ever answer her phone when I call?"

Rick darted in and out of traffic, trying to keep up with the delivery truck, following Deb.

Rick squinted his eyes, trying to keep the searing pain at bay inside of his head. He couldn't black out now ... not now! Dog barked at Rick, noticing he was drifting off ...

Rick shook his head and said, "I'm alright boy ... I promise, I won't kill you in a car crash."

Dog growled at Rick and showed his teeth. Rick looked at Dog and said, "Hey, hey, hey. What's the matter? I was just kidding! I'm not going to kill you in a car crash ... or any other way. Jeez, you need to relax Dog."

Rick watched as the delivery truck followed Deb from the Babies R Us, headed towards her house. He picked up his phone and tried again to reach Deb ... no answer. Rick threw his phone in the seat again and said, "Fuck it! I'll just wait until the bastard makes his move on Deb ... and I'll get him."

Rick glanced over at Dog and said, "Now Dog ... when I give the word; I want you to rip this guy's head off ... you understand?"

Dog barked and growled at the windshield, his eyes burning a path to the delivery truck in front of them. Dog gripped the seat with his claws, his legs ready to pounce at Rick's command.

Rick smiled and watched the truck in front of them. He mumbled, "Your minutes are numbered Shit-head ..."

As Deb entered her neighborhood, the delivery truck slowed down and followed far behind Deb. Rick had to quickly dart into a parking space on the side of the road to keep from getting too close. The guy in the car behind Rick blew his horn at him and yelled out his window. Dog started barking in Rick's ear, trying to get at the driver. Rick let go of the steering wheel and cupped his hands over his ears as his head exploded with pain and his brain vibrated with painful spasms. Rick tried to open his mouth and tell Dog to stop barking; but he couldn't move his lips. His eyes fluttered as Dog continued to bark; Rick couldn't see the delivery truck anymore ... he couldn't see at all.

He felt his body lose control and his head fell against the window with a thud. His convulsions took him into darkness.

CHAPTER FOURTY THREE

Deb finished hanging the Mickey Mouse mobile over the crib. She twisted the knob and watched it slowly circle as it played "Twinkle, Twinkle Little Star." She smiled and said, "There … the finishing touch."

She watched the mobile twirl above the crib as she daydreamed about Carlito … He loved Mickey Mouse. It was weird how she remembered things about him now that she never noticed when he was alive. She looked down into the empty, plush, clean, crisp crib that would be holding her new son tomorrow. She reached down and touched the blanket. She imagined the little body under her hand … how soft it would be … how it would feel when she held it.

Deb turned around and looked at the room that was once her office. It was totally transformed into a baby nursery, decorated in vintage Walt Disney. She smiled and walked to the closet to put away the baby outfits she had bought. She picked up the garbage from the floor from the mobile and put it in the bag. She walked to the bedroom door and paused. She turned back around for one more look, imagining little Carlito playing and laughing with all the toys she had waiting for him. Deb slowly closed the door and turned to walk down the hall to the kitchen.

As she entered the living room she sensed a presence … then she heard a voice come from the sofa, "I hope you have lots of insurance 'cause your new baby's gonna need it."

Deb swung around and saw a man sitting on her couch pointing a gun right at her. She froze and stared at him. She slowly said, "How … did you get in here? What do you want?"

The man stood up holding the gun pointed at Deb and said, "First of all, I can get in any place I want. Don't you know the government has a master key to every lock in this country?"

The man took a few steps towards Deb. Deb took a few steps backwards and the man continued, "Second, I don't want your body babe; you're not my type. What I do want is information … where is that black bastard with the dog?"

Deb squinted her eyes and said, "…Smitty?"

The man smirked and Deb's heart painfully skipped a beat as it started racing in her chest. She quickly glanced around the room looking for her purse. Smitty raised his hand, Deb's purse dangling from his wrist. He said, "This what you're looking for? Too late kitten; I've got your gun and your phone. Now, tell me where they are."

Deb slowly stepped backwards, trying to make her way to the kitchen. She said, "I don't know who you're talking about. I don't know anyone with a dog."

Smitty laughed and said, "Well kitten; I'm going to kill you whether you tell me where they are or not; so … you can tell me, and die quickly. Or you can not tell me, and die slowly, with me torturing you all afternoon. So, take your pick."

Deb smiled and said, "What about option #3?"

Smitty cocked his gun and said, "There isn't an option #3"

Deb gritted her teeth and said in between clinched lips, "Oh yes there is!"

She dove into the kitchen just as Smitty got off a shot. She rolled onto the kitchen floor and yanked the knife drawer open. She grabbed a steak knife out of the drawer but before she could do anything with it, Smitty was on top of her. He pistol whipped her head a few times and put his hand around her throat. He gritted, "I don't like games bitch! Now, tell me what I want to know and I won't make you suffer!"

Deb was coughing and grabbing at Smitty's hand around her throat. She was blinking hard, trying to keep the blood out of her eyes. She gasped, "Please, please … I'll tell you … Just don't hit me anymore."

Smitty rose up off of Deb and picked her up by her throat. Deb screamed and pulled at Smitty's hand, but he wouldn't let go. He stood Deb up on her feet and pushed her back against the fridge. Deb pulled at his hand with one hand, but kept the other hand behind her back … the one holding the steak knife.

Smitty leaned up against Deb's face and said, "Where are they?"

Deb took a deep breath and said, "…Right here!" She took the knife and sunk it deep into Smitty's stomach. He yelled and threw Deb out of the kitchen onto the floor in the dining room. She rolled against the wall and got up and ran down the hallway into her bedroom and closed the door and locked it. She heard Smitty yelling and shots firing as she ran.

Deb screamed for help, and slouched down onto the floor next to the door. She shook her head and thought … "Isn't this dejavu?"

She heard more shots fired and the door was exploding with each shot.

Smitty yelled through the door, "Bitch! I'm gonna rip you to shreds!"

More shots into the door. Deb covered her ears with her hands and squeezed her eyes shut. She started to cry softly as she sat on the floor thinking about little Carlito; waiting for her killer to seal her fate. Smitty punched his fist through the door and yelled into the hole, "Where are they!"

Deb heard a loud crash; then a booming voice shouted, "Here we are you son-of-a-bitch!"

Deb opened her eyes at the sound of the familiar voice, and a dog barking. She yelled, "Rick!!!"

Smitty swung around and fired his gun, but the bullet went up into the ceiling as Dog plunged into Smitty's arm and sunk his teeth into his triceps. Dog stood on his hind legs and pushed Smitty into the door. The door cracked in two and Dog pinned Smitty down on the broken door with his body hanging halfway into the room. Deb jumped across the room and slid under the bed. She looked up at the door and saw Dog sink his teeth into Smitty's neck and jerk his massive head from left to right. Dog held Smitty's body in place on the broken door as he tugged and pulled on Smitty's neck.

Deb screamed and fainted at the gruesome sight of Dog's head jerking up with Smitty's head dangling from his mouth.

Dog swung around, splattering blood across the wall. He trotted up the hallway towards Rick.

Rick was leaning against the front door, holding onto the doorknob to keep from falling down. Dog walked to Rick's feet and dropped Smitty's bloody head at his feet.

Dog looked up at Rick with his face dripping with blood and whimpered. Rick dropped his hand onto Dog's head and said, "… Good boy …"

CHAPTER FOURTY FOUR

Deb felt tugging … someone was pulling her shoulders.

She jerked up and bumped her head on the bed, "Ouch!"

Rick whispered, "Easy, now; easy. Let me pull you out from under there."

Deb allowed Rick to help her up from under the bed. Rick held Deb up by her shoulders and looked her in her face. He saw the bruises on her face and said, "Are you alright? Did he hurt you Deb?"

Deb focused on Rick and slowly remembered what had happened. She swung her head around to the broken remains of the bloody bedroom door … She screamed, "Where is he?"

Rick grabbed Deb and held her close. He said, "Don't worry, don't worry … it's all over. He's gone. Me and Dog took his body and put it in a few garbage bags and took 'em out back to the dumpster."

Deb turned back to Rick with her mouth open. Rick smiled and continued, "…I didn't think you'd want me to wake you up with dude's body and severed head laying all over your bedroom; so we cleaned up a little first."

Deb frantically looked at Rick and said, "Dog! Where's Dog?"

Rick said, "Don't worry … he's alright. He's out in the living room waiting to meet you."

Rick started to lead Deb out of the bedroom. She gripped onto Rick's arms and gasped, "Rick! He's a killer! I saw him … he … he … ripped his head off!"

Rick held Deb still and said, "Deb; he saved your life. I've been through a lot with him; he's my friend and I love him. Now, I've told him all about you and he's waiting to meet you."

Deb shook her head and said, "I'm scared of him Rick! He's ... he's ... he's your executioner!"

Rick smiled at Deb and said, "He only kills when I tell him ... or; when necessary ... Whatever; come on; let's go meet Dog so we can get the hell outta here. You need to call somebody to come clean this mess up."

Rick led Deb out of the bedroom and down the bloody hallway. They entered the living room and Deb froze when she saw the massive beast lounging on the floor licking a wound on his giant paw.

Dog raised his head when they entered the room and looked at Deb. He barked once and got up off of the floor.

Deb grabbed onto Rick and squealed, "Rick! I don't want to meet him. Please!"

Dog stopped and stared Deb down. Rick said, "You had better introduce yourself ... he's very sensitive."

Deb stuttered, "Hi ... I'm ... I'm Deb. It's nice ... to meet you."

Dog barked again and walked over to Deb and sat at her feet. He looked up at her and whimpered for attention.

Deb smiled and said, "...He's kind of ... cute." She reached down and pet Dog on his head. He bumped his head against her leg, demanding her to continue petting him.

Rick smiled and said, "See! I told you he was a sweetheart."

Deb looked at Rick and said, "Well Rick ... it's over. You've done it. Your assignment is complete."

Rick stopped smiling and said, "Not quite yet Deb. I still haven't seen proof that 'ole Roland is dead. I want to go back to Smitty's house and look at that urn he's supposed to have containing his ashes."

Deb threw her hands up and said, "Come on Rick! He's dead; it's over!"

Rick gritted his lips and said, "I won't be finished until I see the urn. Now, I don't expect anything else from you Deb besides those bus tickets outta town. You got my ID for being legally blind so I can take Dog on the bus?"

Deb slowly nodded and pointed towards the door, "Everything's in the duffle bag over there near the door."

Rick walked over to the door and grabbed the bag. He looked at Deb and said, "Deb, don't worry. You go and get your new son tomorrow and take him far away from here. Leave all this behind - you deserve a better life."

Deb rushed over to Rick and wrapped her arms around him. She said into his chest, "Rick ... I'm going to miss you."

She pushed away and looked him in his eyes. She said, "Take care of yourself Rick."

Dog barked and Deb jumped and said, "Oh! And ... and you take care of yourself too Dog."

Rick slung the duffle bag over his shoulder. He snapped his fingers and said, "Come on boy! We got one more stop before we're outta this town."

Dog jumped up and pranced around the door waiting for Rick to open it. Rick cracked the door and Dog ran out.

Rick turned to look at Deb before he stepped out the door and said, "Thanks for everything Deb. I'm gonna miss you too."

CHAPTER FOURTY FIVE

Sarah checked her watch; he was late. He was never late. She took out her phone and called him again. No answer. She got up and paced the floor

Something was wrong; she could feel it. Ever since Joe was murdered, Smitty's been on edge; worried about everything. And now this ... Smitty was always on time; from the day she met him 13 years ago. Sarah took out her phone and dialed him again ... no answer.

She got her purse and keys and decided to drive over to the house to check on her husband.

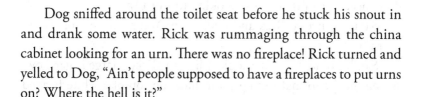

Dog sniffed around the toilet seat before he stuck his snout in and drank some water. Rick was rummaging through the china cabinet looking for an urn. There was no fireplace! Rick turned and yelled to Dog, "Ain't people supposed to have a fireplaces to put urns on? Where the hell is it?"

Rick walked back into the living room and looked around. He whispered to himself, "...unless there aren't any ashes of Mr. Roland, and the fucker is still alive ..."

Rick heard a key in the front door and froze. He hissed, "Dog!"

Dog came bounding out of the bathroom and stood next to Rick. They both stood there motionless looking at the front door; waiting for it to open.

The door opened and Sarah walked in. She turned and closed the door before she turned around. She switched on the light on the table and looked up. "Ahhhh!"

Sarah had her hand on her heart and her mouth open. Rick nodded and said, "How do you do?"

Sarah stuttered, "Are ... you friends ... of Smitty's?"

Dog barked and Rick petted his head. Rick replied, "Ah, yeah; Smitty asked us to wait here for him. Things got a little wild at work today ..."

Sarah exhaled and said, "Well, you two gave me a scare. I was wondering where he was. What happened? He didn't get the chance to kill that bitch cop he was following?"

Rick gritted his teeth as he watched what was once his sister. He replied, "Ah, no. There was a problem with that, and he had to take care of it. He sent me and Dog over here to retrieve something for him."

Sarah walked into the kitchen and said, "What do you need? His stash is in the bedroom."

Rick thought for a moment; a 'stash' of what? Dog bumped Rick's leg with his head and Rick focused again. He said, "No, we don't need any of that. We're looking for the urn."

Sarah turned to Rick and said, "Urn? You mean that old thing over there?"

Sarah pointed to what looked like to Rick, a large sugar bowl sitting on the formal dining room table on top of a white beaded cloth.

Rick slowly walked over to it. Sarah said, "It's just got the ashes of that dead cop in it from Seattle. What would you need with that?"

Rick picked up the urn and held it close so he could read the inscription. It read, "Here lies my only one true friend, Roland B. Hoffman. I will forever miss you."

Rick mumbled under his breath, "I guess Joe was everybody's bitch!"

Sarah said, "Excuse me? Did you say something? Hey, what did you say your name was?"

Rick slowly turned around and faced Sarah. He said, "I'm sorry, I didn't introduce myself."

Rick extended his right hand and held the urn in his left. He walked towards Sarah and said, "My name is Rick and this is Dog."

Dog barked at Sarah and waited for attention. Sarah paused and slowly acknowledged Dog with a slight pet on his head. She kept her eyes on Rick and slowly said, "…Rick …"

Rick kept his hand extended, waiting for Sarah to shake his hand. She didn't. He brought his hand back to his side and said, "Nice to meet you too Mrs. John C. Smith."

Sarah squinted her eyes and whispered under her breath, "… Rick?"

Rick gave Sarah a cold dead stare before he finally responded, "…Good to see ya Sis."

Sarah backed up into the china cabinet and knocked over a plate and sent crashing into pieces behind her. She shook her head and said, "You're dead … it's not you … it's not you!"

Rick rubbed his face long and slow and said, "The face is different Sis, but it's me. How's the family?"

Sarah yelled, "Shut up! Just shut up! You're not my brother and I don't know how you got in my house and I'm calling the police right now!"

Sarah made a move for the phone and Rick snapped, "Dog!"

In an instant, Dog leapt to his feet and lunged toward Sarah. He growled low in his chest and showed his teeth.

Sarah snatched her arm back close to her body and froze. She turned to Rick and said, "So it was you … You killed Joe and took his dog. You probably went looking for Roland and couldn't find him 'cause he was already dead. Now you're here, looking for Smitty …"

Sarah's words trailed off ... She stared at Rick searching his face. She screamed, "You killed him! You killed my husband?"

Rick shook his head and said, "Sarah; you fail to see the issue here. You married the man that killed me! What the fuck is wrong with you?"

Sarah started shaking and she grabbed herself to control her words as she screamed again, "Did you kill my husband Rick?"

Dog leaned his body closer to Sarah and barked. Rick said, "Easy boy! Easy."

Rick walked closer to Sarah and said, "Just tell me why Sarah ... just tell me why?"

Sarah looked at Rick with hatred in her eyes and said, "You wanna know! All right! I'll tell you Rick. John and Roland came by the house way back when we lived in the old red house. You were selling drugs and they were asking questions about you. John was really nice and we started seeing each other."

Rick held up his hands and said, "Wait! You started dating Smitty in high school? Sarah I knew you were hard up, but Damn!"

Sarah shook her head and said, "Yes Rick, somebody loved me! Somebody cared! He was the only one! And he promised to marry me if I ..."

Rick's head exploded and a trickle of blood started streaming out of his ear. He squinted his eyes at Sarah and said, "He promised to marry you if you ... if you turned your 'old brother Rick in to the cops. Is that it Sarah? Is that it? You gave me up to the cops for a piece of white dick? They tried to kill me Sarah! They didn't want to arrest me; they wanted to kill me! And you gave me up!"

Sarah yelled, "So what Rick! One less black menace to society! You served no purpose whatsoever! No one missed you or cared that you were dead Rick! So what was the big deal?"

Rick closed his eyes and took a deep breath to try and silence the pain throbbing between his ears. He opened his eyes and said; "I cared Sarah ... I cared if I lived or died. Oh, and Dog cares right now."

Rick turned and looked at Dog and growled, "…Kill her …"

Dog jumped on top of Sarah as she screamed and fell down on the floor in between the china cabinet and the formal dining room table.

She was pinned down under Dog and Rick heard her muffled screams. Her leg kicked over a chair and it bounced off of Dog's massive body jerking as he covered her with his claws and teeth. Rick fell up against the wall and almost dropped the urn. He clutched it tight against him and stumbled into the bathroom.

He opened the toilet and held the urn above it. He opened the lid and dumped the ashes into the toilet. Rick pushed the lever down and flushed the toilet. He watched the ashes twirl around as he said, "Now; you're where you belong you son-of-a-bitch."

Rick stood up and looked in the mirror. He saw the blood streaming down his face from his ear and took a towel and wiped it. It was silent in the front room now, and Rick slowly made his way back out to the dining room. He saw Dog licking his front paws. When Dog saw Rick he barked and stood up, wanting his attention. Rick slowly walked over to the place where his sister was once standing. He looked down and saw her mangled body - her chest and stomach totally eaten away. One of her eyes was gone and a pocket of blood was in its place. Her other eye stared blankly into space …

Rick turned away and closed his eyes. He wanted to cry for his family … but he figured he did them a favor getting rid of wicked ass Sarah. Rick shook his head and said to Dog, "She was never happy; Dog. Never."

Rick turned and grabbed the duffle bag. He looked at Dog; who was covered with blood. Rick sat the bag down and said, "Dammit man! Come in here; I can't take you outside looking like that! We gotta find a cheap motel next to the bus terminal, so we can catch the first bus outta here in the morning."

Dog barked and looked at Rick. Rick said, "Oh! I forgot … Good boy!"

Dog barked and playfully bumped Rick in his side as he followed him into the bathroom.

CHAPTER FOURTY SIX

"Felix, why do I always have to repeat myself to you? If you just do as I ask everything would be so much easier."

Doc shook his head as he walked back into the building, leaving Felix to re-pack the van with their luggage. Felix said, "I'm sorry Doc, I was never good at packing and traveling, you know that. I'm sorry; I'll do it again."

Doc walked back over to his computer to check his e-mail one last time before shutting it down and putting it in the box.

He sat at the desk and slowly grabbed the mouse. He clicked "New Mail" and up popped 5 unread mails. Doc took out his inhaler and took two quick puffs and held the inhaler in his hand. He clicked 'open'.

Doc read the first e-mail and chuckled. He said to himself, "Good, good; for a change I have some good news. The deal on the condo closed. Doc shouted, "Felix my boy! The condo in Brazil is ready and waiting for our arrival!"

Felix yelled from the van, "That's great Doc! I can't wait."

Doc clicked on the second e-mail. He sucked in a gulp of air and coughed. He took two quick puffs and said, "Shit! Felix, I'm going to kill that asshole!" Doc shook his head and said under his breath, "…You drove my baby away from me you son-of-a-bitch, and now you have to pay."

Felix came running into the room. He ran over to Doc and said,

"What is it? Doc don't get yourself all worked up right before a trip. You know how the altitude makes you wheeze."

Doc shook his head and looked at Felix with tears in his eyes. He said, "Felix I'm sorry ... I'm really sorry. But I have to kill Rick. He has ruined my Debra's life, and has driven her away from me. He's a loose cannon; I thought his seizures would have killed him by now, but they haven't. I didn't want to do it; but I have to."

Doc started crying and Felix walked over to him and hugged his head against his body. Tears streamed down Felix' cheeks and he said, "Do we have to? He's going to die soon anyway Doc; why can't we just leave him to die?"

Doc pushed away from Felix and got up from his computer. He logged off of his computer and shut it down. He told Felix, "Load it into the box and meet me in the van. We have several things to take care of before we leave in the morning."

Felix watched Doc walk outside. He turned to the computer and started taking it down. He started crying again, thinking of all the things he and Rick had done together. All the things Rick had taught him. Felix loved Rick like a brother; but Doc had always told Felix not to get too attached to Rick, because he was going to die soon. Year after year when Rick was still alive, Felix forgot about him dying and thought Doc was just telling him that because he was jealous of their friendship.

But then, Deb said Rick called him retarded ... Felix slammed the keyboard in the box, as his feelings started hurting all over again. That had hurt really bad; he couldn't believe Rick would say that about him. Felix wished he could talk to Rick one last time so Rick could tell him that he didn't say it ... But it's too late.

Rick is going to die; either from his seizures; or Doc's going to kill him. Felix cried harder. He was going to miss Rick. He grabbed the computer off of the table and shoved it in the box. He stood up and closed his eyes. He wanted to say a quick prayer for Rick ... "Lord, please forgive Rick; he didn't mean to hurt anyone. He never got a good chance to start his life out right. It was bad for him the moment he was born. Don't make him suffer too much when he dies. Let it be quick. Amen."

Felix picked the box up and headed for the front door. Doc passed Felix on the way out. Doc walked around the room and gave it a once over.

He slowly turned around and walked out the door, closing it behind him and locking it.

CHAPTER FOURTY SEVEN

Deb sat at the terminal staring at little Carlito sleeping in the carrier. She smiled ... he was beautiful. She knew that her baby didn't have any of Carlito's genes ... but she could swear he looked like him. Olive skin, dark hair, full lips ... he was her 'lil Carlito.

Deb's cell phone started vibrating in her pocket and she opened it to look at the display. She said, "Good."

She pushed the button and said, "Morning Walden, how's it going?"

Walden replied, "Top 'O da morning to ya Ms. Debra. I wanted to call ya and let ya know dat me uncle is ready and waiting for ya at his hotel. Ok? So ya get to da Divi Divi Hotel on da east side of da island. Ask for Mr. Papio; he's expecting ya."

Deb smiled and said, "We're at the airport waiting for the flight to board to Aruba now. Thank you Walden."

Deb paused to fight back tears as gratitude engulfed her heart. Walden had come through for her. After everything, he came through for her. Deb took a deep breath and said, "Walden, you take care of yourself, OK?"

Walden purred into the phone, "Ms. Debra, ya know me ... I always land on me feet man!"

Deb smiled and closed her phone. She put it back in her pocket and stared at little Carlito some more. The flight attendant came over the microphone, "We will be boarding flight 6128 non-stop to

Aruba at Gate 47 in 5 minutes. First to board will be senior citizens and passengers with small children."

Deb gathered her carryon bag and stood up, waiting for the attendant to call for boarding. Deb's phone started vibrating in her pocket again. She grabbed it out of her pocket and looked at the display ... Rick.

Deb's heart stopped and she froze. She stared at the display as it blinked, "Rick calling ... Rick calling ..."

She didn't want to answer it, but her finger pushed the button before she could stop it.

"Hello."

Rick's voice came booming into the phone, "Deb! Good Morning. Hey, I wanted to call and make sure you were alright, you know. That you got your kid and everything's OK ..."

Deb smiled and said, "Yeah Rick, I got him. He's mine and I have a family now."

Rick said, "Good, good. Look, I know we'll probably never talk again after this, but I want you to know that, you are one hell of a woman. I'll never forget you Deb."

Deb stopped smiling and said, "Look Rick ... I'm retiring. You're right. We won't talk after this. I wish you well, and take care."

Rick quickly yelled, "Wait! Deb ... I wanted to thank you ... thank you for making my assignment a success; I couldn't have done it without you."

Deb said, "Good-bye Rick."

She closed her phone. The attendant was calling senior citizens and passengers with children and Deb picked up the carrier and started walking. There was a water fountain in the atrium next to the gate and Deb stopped to look at it.

She slowly walked over to the fountain and tossed her cell phone in the water. She turned around and walked to the gate. She gave her tickets to the attendant and said, "Morning, how long is the flight?"

The attendant smiled and said, "12 hours, but not to worry – in first class you will have a variety of movies, books and cuisine to choose from. And we even have a fold out travel bed for your baby."

Deb looked down at little Carlito sleeping and smiled. She said, "Thank you. I'm sure we'll enjoy the flight."

CHAPTER FOURTY EIGHT

Dog and Rick sat at the bus terminal. Rick had on his dark sunglasses with the special leash around Dog. Rick looked around behind his dark glasses, looking for anyone suspicious.

He switched positions on the hard terminal bench and thought, "Deb really sounded happy … really happy." He pulled Dog closer to him and said, "You know boy, it's nice to see someone in this crazy life gets to experience happiness. Deb deserves it."

Dog barked and Rick said, "Shhhh, quiet boy! We don't want any unnecessary attention on us right now."

Dog lay at Rick's feet and was quiet. Rick looked at his watch … bus will be here in 10 minutes. Rick leaned down to Dog and said, "You know boy; I'm not sure where we're going right now. What do you think? You wanna go to Florida? It's nice there this time of year. I can get a job and we can camp out in a small bungalow on the beach. What do you say?"

Dog stood up and looked Rick in his face. He started growling low in his chest and showing his teeth. The bus drove up and the passengers were getting in line to board.

Rick looked at Dog and said, "What's the matter boy? You don't like Florida? We can go wherever you want."

Rick stood up and tried to look blind as he tried to lead Dog to the bus. Dog wasn't budging. Rick bent down and said, "Come on boy … we can't stay here."

Dog pulled and tugged on the leash, backing away from the

bus. A few passengers came over to help Rick, but Rick held up his hands and said, "It's alright, it's alright. He's afraid of traveling; we go through this all the time. He'll be fine."

The bus driver stepped down into the doorway after all the passengers were on the bus. He yelled to Rick, "Do you want me to wait? I can call an officer over to help?"

Rick walked away from the bus to calm Dog. He yelled back, "No, no sir; it's alright. We'll just catch the next bus. When does the next bus arrive?"

The bus driver looked at his schedule and said, "In an hour and a half."

Rick swore under his breath, "Fuck!" Then he smiled and waived to the bus driver, "Thank you sir, thank you. We'll wait for the next bus."

The driver walked back up onto the bus, closed the doors and drove off. Rick turned to Dog and said, "What the hell is wrong with you? We were supposed to be on that bus! What freaked you?"

Dog stopped growling and stood there, staring at Rick. Rick shook his head and looked around. Every body was gone. There were a few people at a stop down the way, and Rick gritted his teeth and shook his head again. He said, "Now we gotta wait here for a fucking hour and a half until the next bus!"

Rick started walking back to the bench and pulled the leash. He said, "You better get over your bus phobia 'cause with or without you I'm getting on the next ..."

Rick's words trailed off as his body jerked; something had tugged on his leg and he couldn't move it. He looked down to see a chunk of his thigh missing and his pant leg ripped with blood stains forming down his leg. Rick looked at Dog and saw him chewing and swallowing. He had blood running down his jaws. Rick shook his head and said, "What the ... Dog, you hungry?"

Dog lunged for Rick and knocked him down behind the bench. He stood on top of Rick's chest and lowered his head down close to Rick's face. Dog growled and stared Rick in his eyes.

Rick saw the look in Dog's eyes … he was going to kill him. Dog was going to kill him. Rick said, "No boy! No!"

Dog's teeth sinking deep into Rick's face puncturing his tongue, interrupted his words. Rick started coughing as Dog released his face and watched him choking on his own blood.

Rick looked at Dog's hatred in his eyes and couldn't believe it. It was Dog all along … Dog was the one setting Rick up for the kill - since the beginning. It was always Dog.

Rick tried to raise his arms and push Dog away, but Dog sunk his teeth into Rick's arm and twisted his massive head. Rick moaned through a swollen, bloody face and turned his head; searching for anyone to help him.

Rick saw a dark van sitting at the bus stop … Dog barked at the van and growled. Rick squinted his eyes and could see two men in the van looking at him. One of the men got out of the van and yelled, "Rick!"

Rick tried to speak when he noticed the man standing by the van was Felix, but Dog sunk his teeth deep into Rick's stomach. Rick curled up in a ball of pain, gripping Dog's head with his body. Dog ripped his head away, pulling Rick's intestines out with him.

Felix screamed and pressed his hands against his mouth. He screamed louder and ran around the van, but Doc grabbed Felix by his arm and held him still. He said, "No my boy … it has to happen. Let him finish."

Felix closed his eyes and cried. Rick saw Doc sitting in the van watching him. Rick turned back to Dog and watched him as he violently ripped his body in two at the torso. Rick was numb … he couldn't feel the massive beasts teeth anymore. There was a cool blast of air on Rick's hot; rotten brain and his head didn't hurt anymore. He lost consciousness as he saw Dog's teeth coming at his face again.

With his last breath, Rick whispered, "…Good boy."

CHAPTER FOURTY NINE

Felix stood and watched as the airport attendant loaded the luggage onto the private jet. The attendant threw the bags on the conveyor belt and they glided up the ramp and fell into a pile with a 'thud'.

Felix laughed and said, "Look! I wonder if I could ride it up!"

The attendant looked at Felix and said, "Ah, no sir. You have to take the steps up to the door of the plane to board."

Felix looked past the attendant into the distance at the figure approaching and smiled. He said, "She made it!"

Felix slowly started walking pass the attendant and headed towards the figure approaching him. Felix stopped and said, "I wasn't sure you would come … I'm glad you did."

He reached out his arms and embraced her tightly against him.

Doc pulled up to the plane in the dark van. He parked and got out; he slowly walked up to the attendant and pointed to Felix. He said, "Well, well, well … will you look at that!"

Felix came walking back to the plane, holding the hand of the woman. Doc met them at the steps of the plane; he looked down at her cast on her foot. He said, "I trust you are healing fine my dear …"

The woman gripped Felix's hand and held her head down. She said, "Yes sir … I get it off in a week."

Doc nodded and said, "You're a brave young lady …"

The woman still wouldn't look at Doc; she held Felix's hand and blushed. Doc said, "Well go ahead, get on the plane! Brazil awaits!"

The woman finally looked up at Felix and giggled and ran up the steps onto the plane. Felix watched her enter the plane and quickly turned to Doc and said, "Doc! You really mean I can keep her?

Doc chuckled and looked at Felix. He said, "Well, unless you've kidnapped her family and have them at gun point Felix, it looks like she wants to keep you too."

Felix let out a loud laugh and gripped Doc in a bear hug. Dog patted Felix on the back and pulled away. Doc turned around and started walking back towards the van. He said over his shoulder, "You know Felix; you're not the only one that's found a friend to bring to Brazil ..."

Doc opened the back door of the van and Felix saw a large dark shadow emerge. It turned and looked at Felix and Felix gasped, "That's the dog ... The dog that killed Rick ..."

Doc petted Dog on his head and said, "Come."

Dog pranced around Doc as they walked back towards Felix and the plane. Felix was still standing with his mouth open pointing at Dog.

Felix looked at Doc and said, "What ... what are you doing?"

Doc walked up to Felix and rubbed his shoulder. He said, "Felix my boy; this is my new pet. He's one of us now. Accept him Felix; and love him as any of my others."

Felix stared at Dog; and Dog stared at Felix. Doc broke the silence and said, "Come; let's board the plane Felix; it's getting late. You'll have to give Dog a shot for the flight, so hurry,"

Doc turned and started walking up the steps. Felix and Dog stood at the bottom of the steps, still staring at each other.

Doc got to the top, turned around and yelled, "Felix, why do I always have to repeat myself? Please ... it's time to go."

Felix raised his arm and said to Dog, "After you ..."

Dog slowly stepped up onto the steps to the plane. Felix followed behind Dog and said, "I'll never trust my back to you."

Dog stopped and turned his massive head around to look at Felix. He growled low in his chest and showed his teeth.

Felix smiled and leaned closer to Dog. He said, "Everything dies … You are no exception."

They entered the plane and the attendant closed the door. They taxied onto the runway and took off … slowly ascending up into the sky.

THE END.

Printed in the United States
By Bookmasters

Printed in the United States
By Bookmasters